"The author's writing mixes fascinating deep dives into the gadgetry and tactics of aerial combat with gripping action scenes conveyed in brutally evocative prose. Chadwick is an appealing hero—stoic and resourceful, but quietly marked by the horrors unfolding around him. A captivating war novel that immerses readers in the craft of killing and its somber results."

- Kirkus Reviews

"Exciting WWII aviation action, with a firm sense of tech and history. Forsyth, as always, captures the thrill of flight and the terror of battle with a nuts-and-bolts accuracy that, crucially, doesn't slow down the suspenseful storytelling during scenes of action."

- Publishers Weekly
BookLife Review

"Eric's third novel essentially tells the sum of Britain's RAF challenges and successes during the Second World War. The story is accurate, authentic and realistic. It is an exciting read and a fitting tribute to the intrepid young men of Britain and the Commonwealth who braved the deadly skies. The average age of a bomber crew was 22; 44% (55,573) were killed in action—the highest casualty rate of any Allied command during the war."

- Jack Doyle,
U.S. Naval Flight Officer who flew
F-4 Phantoms and F-14 Tomcats

WINGS OVER GERMANY

Other Works by Eric B. Forsyth

An Inexplicable Attraction: My Fifty Years of Ocean Cruising (2018)

Memoir in which Captain Forsyth recounts his many years sailing the oceans and exploring remote corners of the world on his Westsail 42, *Fiona,* including two circumnavigations of the globe, cruises through the Northwest Passage, the Panama Canal, and to the Baltic, and several excursions to both the Artic and Antarctic. Included on Kirkus Review's list of the 100 Best Memoirs of 2018.

Wings Over Iraq (2020)

Historical novel set in Iraq in the turbulent 1920s between the wars. Introduces the main character featured in the "Wings" series, Allan Chadwick, a newly qualified RAF pilot posted to a bomber squadron near Baghdad. His story plays out against the background of Middle Eastern conflict, the rise of fascism in Europe and the slow build-up to another world war.

Wings Over the Channel (2022)

It is the mid-1930s and Britain is threatened by Nazi Germany. Allan Chadwick is posted to RAF aviation research in southern England and is involved in their frantic effort to build an effective radar screen, while British intelligence feeds false reports about it to the Germans. The success of the deception—and Chadwick's life—are threatened when an accurate report of radar performance is stolen by a German spy. Kirkus Reviews called it "A rousing, detailed RAF thriller that delivers an effective climax."

WINGS OVER GERMANY

A NOVEL

ERIC B. FORSYTH

This novel is a work of historic fiction. It is loosely based on actual events which occurred in the 1930s and 1940s during the period when Britain entered into war with Germany. Although several well-known historic figures are mentioned to give the story some credibility—e.g. Winston Churchill, Hermann Göring, Hitler—all incidents and characters are products of the author's imagination. Dialogues concerning those persons are entirely fictional and not intended to portray actual events. Any resemblance to any other actual person, living or dead, is entirely coincidental.

Copyright ©2023
Eric B. Forsyth

Published by:
Yacht Fiona Books
www.YachtFiona.com

Edited by:
Margaret Daisley
Blue Horizon Books
www.bluehorizonbooks.com

Cover and design by:
Jay R. Pizer
Imax Productions
www.imaxproductions.com

Publisher's Cataloging-in-Publication data:
Forsyth, Eric
Wings Over Germany
ISBN 979-8-9853220-7-1

Table of Contents

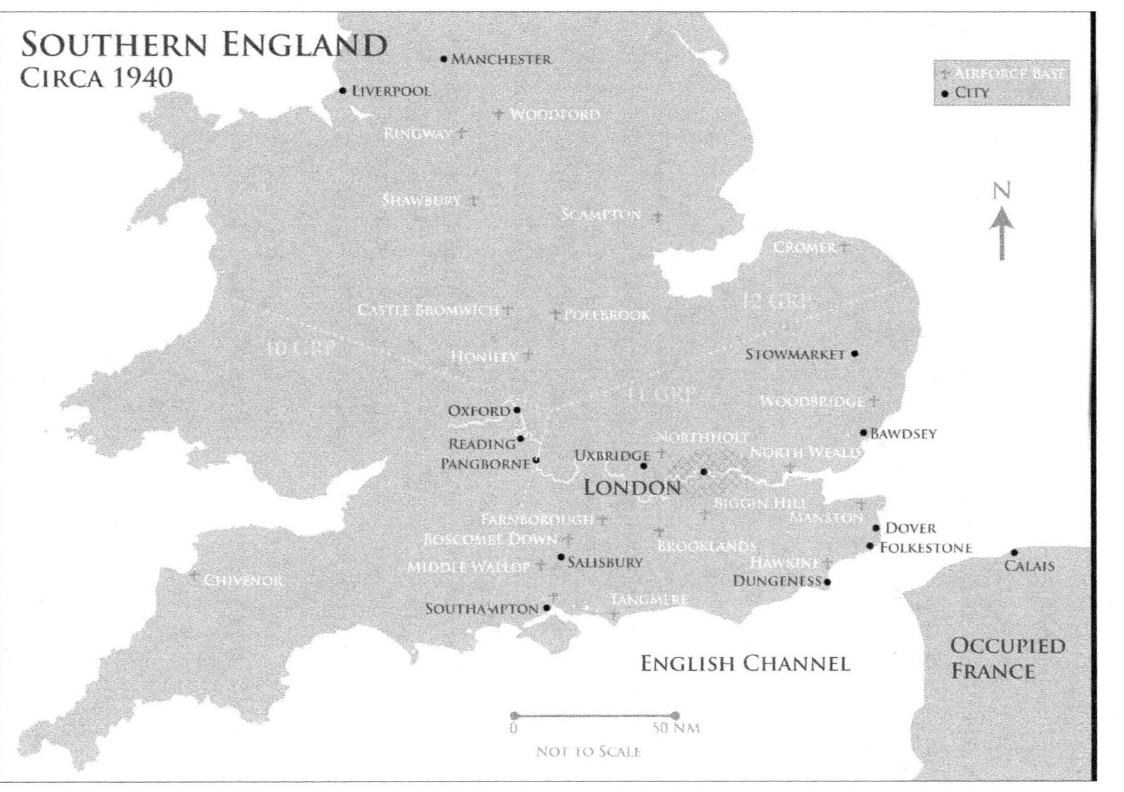

SOUTHERN ENGLAND
CIRCA 1940
AIRFORCE BASE
CITY
MANCHESTER
LIVERPOOL
WOODFORD
RINGWAY
SHAWBURY
SCAMPTON
CROMER
N
CASTLE BROMWICH
POLEBROOK
12 GRP
10 GRP
HONILEY
STOWMARKET
11 GRP
WOODBRIDGE
OXFORD
NORTHHOLT
BAWDSEY
READING
NORTH WEALD
PANGBORNE
UXBRIDGE
LONDON
BIGGIN HILL
FARNBOROUGH
MANSTON
BOSCOMBE DOWN
DOVER
BROOKLANDS
FOLKESTONE
MIDDLE WALLOP
SALISBURY
HAWKINE
CALAIS
CHIVENOR
DUNGENESS
SOUTHAMPTON
TANGMERE
OCCUPIED
FRANCE
ENGLISH CHANNEL
0
50 NM
NOT TO SCALE

Preface

The novel covers one of the most dramatic periods in recent history, the first part of World War Two. The Germans suddenly invaded Poland, and after a pause, they invaded Denmark, Norway, and their Panzers and Stuka bombers rolled through Belgium, the Low Countries, and France. The speed of the advance was a shock to the British and, I think, even a surprise to the German General Staff. By the summer of 1940, Britain faced alone the seemingly unstoppable might of the German military machine. After the fall of France, Churchill declared that the Battle of Britain was about to begin.

When we meet Allan Chadwick in my first novel, *Wings Over Iraq*, he is a young Royal Air Force pilot posted to Iraq, flying obsolete Vimy bombers. On his return to Britain four years later, he travels overland and is imprisoned in Berlin after an unwarranted arrest by the Gestapo who accuse him of spying. Back home, he assists with the development of radar and becomes involved with an influential appeasement clique called the Isbell's Insiders, based on the real-life Cliveden Set. Working in conjunction with British military intelligence, Chadwick leaks misleading reports on the performance of radar to the Germans. His race to stop a spy who has stolen accurate assessments of radar is an exciting conclusion to *Wings Over the Channel*, the second book in this series.

Much of the story in *Wings Over Germany* is based on real events with some distortion of the time frame. For example, Chadwick serves as commanding officer of a squadron of Spitfires at the height of the Battle of Britain, and is forced to send barely qualified pilots against the battle-hardened Luftwaffe. Fortunately, radar-directed interception gives the Royal Air Force an advantage, preventing the Luftwaffe from gaining control of the skies over the English Channel. Had it not been for this development, it is almost certain that Germany would have attempted to invade the British Isles.

After relinquishing command of the Spitfire squadron, Chadwick is involved in methods to improve the accuracy of strategic bombing by the rapidly growing fleet of four-engined heavy bombers. In a raid over Germany, Chadwick flies with a bomber crew to evaluate equipment performance. The plane is damaged and eventually crashes. Chadwick bails out over France and evades the Germans with help from the French résistance.

When I served on 613 fighter squadron in the 1950s, I flew with several pilots that had fought in WWII. Two had been shot down and became POWs, but one got as far as the Spanish border before he was caught. His stories inspired me to write of Chadwick's adventures as he is spirited into Paris by the French. The way Chadwick eventually returns to England, however, owes a lot to my imagination.

The story continues with a fictionalized version of real developments involving the newly introduced fighter bomber, the Mosquito. It was called "The Wooden Wonder" because much of it was fabricated from impregnated plywood, which was not a strategic material like aluminum. The aircraft was used to precisely bomb targets from a low level. A raid which interrupted Reichsmarschall Göring's nationwide speech on Berlin radio actually occurred. The Reichsmarschall had loudly claimed that Berlin would never be bombed, so the raid was a terrific propaganda coup.

The use of a Mosquito to spirit a spy out of neutral Switzerland is also based on reality. The RAF really did have a squadron of Mosquitos fitted out to smuggle VIPs out of European countries. The most famous was Professor Niels Bohr, who was flown from Sweden to join the Manhattan Project in the middle of the war.

The entry of the USA into the war brings the 8th Air Force to Britain; their hard-fought learning experience includes a setback as German fighters inflicted unsustainable losses, countered eventually by providing American fighter cover for the bomber fleets as they attempted to disrupt German industrial production.

British Intelligence detected worrisome German developments at the Peenemunde research center on the Baltic coast. A raid by hundreds of British heavy bombers delayed the introduction of V-2 rockets into the conflict, but the onslaught on Britain by hundreds of pilotless missiles, the V-1, starts shortly after the raid, signaling the beginning of a new era of the war in the air. The success of German engineers and scientists to bring the V-1 and V-2 to fruition in a country wracked by almost continuous bombing, and shortage of materials and fuel is astonishing, and yet a few hundred miles away the same engineering genius was devoted to designing extermination camps for those the Germans considered to be sub-human.

The public revelation in the closing months of the war that the Nazi Party was committing genocide on an industrial scale changed the perception of the fight. It wasn't just another of the interminable European conflicts over territory—it was literally a fight of good versus evil.

Eric B. Forsyth
Brookhaven, New York
May 2023

WINGS OVER GERMANY

Chapter One

Squadron Leader Allan Chadwick entered the officers' mess at RAF Farnborough, hung up his coat, and was just in time to hear the grave voice on the wireless announce, "This is the BBC home service. Here is the Prime Minister, the Right Honorable Mister Neville Chamberlain." After a pause, a higher pitched, slightly nervous voice continued.

"I am speaking to you from the Cabinet Room at Ten Downing Street. This morning, the British ambassador in Berlin handed the German government a final note stating that unless we heard from them by eleven o'clock, they were prepared to withdraw their troops from Poland at once, a state of war would exist between us. I have to tell you now that no such undertaking has been received, and that consequently this country is at war with Germany." He went on to express his personal disappointment at the development and squarely laid the blame on the shoulders of Adolph Hitler.

When he finished, a babble of talk erupted in the room. It was quelled when a voice shouted, "Attention!" and the station commanding officer, Group Captain Delaney-Jones, addressed the assembly.

"We have received the following from the Air Ministry— 'the Royal Air Force is now on a war footing; all leave is canceled. No one may leave the station without permission.' To which I can only add my heartfelt concern for our country and wish us Godspeed in defeating the enemy. Stand easy."

Chadwick relaxed. He was a little taller than average and presented the calm, self-confident demeanor of a man forced to save his life by split-second decisions. Scars on his face showed he had not always escaped scot-free. He found he was relieved at the news. The baffling foreign policy moves in Europe and by Britain were past. The situation was simple. The British Empire was at war with Germany—again.

After lunch, Chadwick stopped by the office of Wing Commander Codrington. "Good afternoon, Sir. This is certainly a date we won't forget in a hurry."

"Come in, Allan, I was going to contact you, as you may remember it, for two reasons. We just received your new posting."

"Oh, and where am I going, Sir?"

"You're posted to the Armaments Research Establishment at Boscombe Down."

"That's mostly bomber development there, right?"

"Yes, and to some extent you can blame yourself. You worked with the bombsight people under Dr. Thorpe, and an analysis of bombing results has convinced the Air Ministry that to achieve strategic success with heavy bombers, they should be capable of carrying at least twenty thousand pounds, for a range of at least two thousand miles."

Chadwick expressively lifted his shoulders and said, "My God! That will be a huge plane. Four engines. They'll take years to build."

"You're probably right, but there's some sentiment that the process can be speeded up by modifying some medium bombers now in limited production. This is where you come in. Dr. Thorpe was impressed with your experience of bombing both in the field and during trials of the new bombsight. He recommended you to Boscombe as an intermediary between the RAF and the manufacturer of a potentially desirable machine. I spoke to a friend at Boscombe to express how sorry we will be at Farnborough to lose you. However, there's a bright side. The plane selected is the Avro Manchester, so you'll be spending some time in Lancashire."

"Well, that'll make a nice change, Sir. I'd like to thank you for all your help while I've been stationed at Farnborough."

They shook hands and Chadwick went to the administrative wing to pick up travel documents and say goodbye to Group Captain Delaney-Jones.

At the officers' mess he packed his uniforms and flying gear in his issue tin trunk. The Air Force would get it to RAF Boscombe Down. His civilian clothes and personal effects went into two suitcases, which he placed on the back seat of his old Bentley. Chadwick took a quick walk to the crew room to make his farewells with the fellows who were there. They exchanged strained jokes about the rate of promotion now that there was a war.

Back at the mess he found the public phone booth in the lobby unoccupied and he was able to make a brief call to his mistress, Lady Melanie Fitzgibbon, to talk about the serious news of the war. He knew she would be concerned, as her son was in his twenties and almost certainly would join the Army. He tried to cheer her up and promised to visit her home in Pangbourne at the first chance he got.

Chadwick fired up the car and left for the one-hour trip to Boscombe. The roads were fairly quiet, apart from a traffic jam in Basingstoke. Once clear, he was able to tool along nicely in fourth gear. As he headed for Andover, his mind wandered to the same trip he had made a few years before when he took a German student to Stonehenge. *What was her name? Julia— that was it.* He wondered what had become of her. Presumably, she was back in Germany.

As his thoughts meandered, the great car drove sedately at about thirty miles per hour and he remembered that after Stonehenge they drove to Melanie's house at Pangbourne, his first visit. Suddenly he realized that while his thoughts were far away, he had driven through Andover and he had better start looking for signs to Amesbury and RAF Boscombe Down.

At the station he signed into the officers' mess and was just in time for afternoon tea. He glanced round the room but none of the faces were familiar. Then he unpacked his things, had dinner and went to bed. In the morning he signed in at the orderly office and the adjutant introduced him to the officer he would be working under, Wing Commander Rowley.

Chadwick looked at him carefully. This was the man who was commanding him in war. Rowley was in his late forties, sported a mustache, and had greying hair.

"Very pleased to meet you, Squadron Leader Chadwick. You come highly recommended from Farnborough. Even before war was declared we were under considerable pressure to produce heavy bombers that met the strategic bombing goals of carrying at least twenty thousand pounds for a range of at least two thousand miles. Now they've lowered the boom," he laughed. "No pun intended—the urgency will get worse."

Chadwick cracked a wintry smile and said, "They told me before I left Farnborough that there was a plan to modify the Manchester medium bomber to meet the new specifications."

"Yes. If it works, that will be much quicker than designing a bomber from scratch, although that approach is also being followed. I'd like you to act as liaison between Boscombe and the A.V. Roe people in Manchester. The managing director is Reginald Dennison and the chief designer is Fred Entwhistle, both top-notch men. A prototype Manchester was flown here and we've prepared a report on the changes needed."

He handed Chadwick a thick folder. "When you've digested that, I suggest a talk with some of the test pilots and engineers, and then take a trip to Manchester to talk it over with the Avro people. Your task, in a nutshell, is to get a prototype Manchester Mark II down here as soon as possible. Please see the orderly sergeant and get yourself some office space."

Chadwick spent the rest of the day reading the report and another day talking to people who had flown the Manchester and evaluated its performance. The next day, an RAF blue car dropped him at the Salisbury railway station and he converted his travel warrant for a first-class return ticket to Manchester, London Road, via Euston station.

On the platform he put a penny in a slot machine and extracted a bar of chocolate from a sliding drawer. *I wonder how long I'll be able to keep doing that?* he thought. *Rationing is surely coming if this war lasts any length of time.*

He arrived in Manchester as night was falling. A taxi dropped him at the Midland Hotel. Wing Commander Rowley had given him Reginald Dennison's private telephone number. Chadwick called to make an appointment, and Dennison suggested a meeting at the Chadderton factory in the morning, saying he would send a car. As he tucked into an evening meal at the hotel, Chadwick greatly enjoyed the northern accents of his fellow diners.

In the morning, the Avro car picked him up at eight-thirty and made its way past the dreary, shabby houses and nondescript factories of northern Manchester. He was soon sitting in a conference room with Reginald Dennison and the chief designer, Fred Entwhistle. Chadwick explained his responsibility to get a modified Manchester to Boscombe as soon as possible, and produced the folder with the suggested changes.

"We've got one of those of our own, too," Entwhistle said. "I'll get you a copy."

"In your own words, Mr. Entwhistle, what was the problem with the first prototype?"

"It was a fair number of small things and one large one," Entwhistle replied. "We deliberately made the fuselage and main spar robust so that future improvements would not be a problem. These things increased the weight. The cruising angle of attack increased at the cost of increased drag. To compound the problem, the Rolls Royce Vulture engines didn't produce the thrust at altitude that was planned. Also they proved to be unreliable, although that could be dealt with, I imagine."

"What are your major recommendations to reach the twenty-thousand-pound load specification?'

"Wing span increased to one hundred and five feet, and the two Vulture engines replaced by four Merlin engines."

Chadwick, Entwhistle, and Dennison got involved in a long technical discussion which was interrupted by a knock on the door. An elderly woman poked her head in.

"Come in, Mrs. Battersby," Dennison said.

The woman entered pushing a trolley. "All that talking must have made you dry. 'Ave a nice cuppa tea." She poured tea from a large teapot.

The men continued their discussion over tea, and finally Dennison said, "I think it's time for a tour of the factory, Squadron Leader." He led the way down some metal stairs to the factory and opened a heavy door. The incessant noise of riveteers and machines swept over them.

"Here at Chadderton we manufacture the major aircraft parts. They're transported by road to Woodford for final assembly and flight test." He pointed to many components for the Anson, an aircraft that was in strong demand by the RAF. Chadwick was interested to see the assembly jigs and asked a number of questions about the necessary accuracy.

"We're making duplicate jigs and assembly fixtures for a shadow factory," Dennison told him, "in case Chadderton is bombed. We're still producing about three Manchesters a month. Here's the production area for that. After lunch I suggest we drive to Woodford to see the activity there."

They ate lunch in a small dining room for senior staff only. Afterwards, a car met them at the main door, and Chadwick, Dennison, and Entwhistle climbed in for the drive across the East Manchester suburbs to Woodford. It took about an hour before they drove through the charming village of Bramhall and up to wrought iron gates set between two brick columns. A man came out from a small hut and opened the gate, giving them a mock military salute as they swept through.

They were met at the main door by a small knot of men. Dennison introduced the works manager, Mr. Bob Wattis, and the chief test pilot, Phil Donovan. After walking past several offices, they passed through a small door into a cavernous building which echoed with the sound of riveters. A dozen Ansons stood on the concrete floor in various stages of completion.

Dennison marched past the Ansons to the far wall, where a Manchester was coming together. A corner of the building was hidden behind a high canvas screen, but Dennison opened a small door and they entered a darkened area.

"This is what I particularly wanted you to see, Squadron Leader," Dennison said as he pointed upwards. As Chadwick's eyes adjusted to the gloom, he found he was staring at a huge bomber looming above him.

"There's the Manchester, the Mark II. A private venture, hasn't cost the government a penny— at least not yet."

Someone laughed.

"When we discovered the shortcomings of the prototype, Fred went into a flurry of calculations and we decided to modify a Manchester already in production to the new design. So, what do you think of that?"

Chadwick was silent for a moment, and then said, "It's amazing. It does seem to be short of a few things, like four engines."

"Yes, that's something we want to talk about."

"Why don't we take a look inside, Squadron Leader?" Donovan said, as he led Chadwick to the entrance hatch.

Chadwick scrambled aboard and walked up the steep floor to the cockpit. The pilot's seat and control column had been installed, but most of the flight instruments were missing.

After walking the full length of the fuselage, he climbed back to the ground and Dennison suggested they retire to an office for a discussion of what they had just seen.

"We built the Mark II that you've just examined to get a head start on the changes that will be needed," Dennison told Chadwick. "But there's a problem. Six months ago, the Cabinet directed the Air Ministry to prepare for the defense of the British Islands in the event of war by equipping seventy fighter squadrons with new, monoplane aircraft. To that end, Rolls Royce was ordered to increase production of Merlin engines, to be used entirely for new fighters. We've tried but we can't get any Merlin engines diverted here to power the Mark II."

Chadwick thought about the situation for a few moments. "Have you been to the Air Ministry to plead your case, Mr. Dennison? A.V. Roe has been supplying the RAF for many years. You must have some good contacts?"

"I traipsed down to London and talked to a very high civil service mandarin, who pointed out that policy originated at the Cabinet level. Only they can change it."

"The Air Force uses hundreds of Merlins. There must be a few reconditioned engines we can use."

"The older models would be no good. The new Merlins put out twenty percent more power. They employ two-stage superchargers, high octane fuel, and numerous component design changes to deal with the increased power. They're designated the Merlin XX. In order to prove the performance of the Mark II, those are the engines we must have to provide greater thrust."

After a lengthy silence Dennison continued, "It doesn't help our case that the plane you saw was built privately. We have no purchase requisition from the government. And even if we did, it wouldn't enable us to jump the queue for Merlins, I suspect."

Chadwick was surprised. "But surely the bigwigs can see we need fighters *and* bombers."

"I tried that tack," Dennison said. "The high and mighty mandarin told me I didn't have the strategic knowledge available to the Cabinet. Defense must come first. When the Air Force and Navy have stood firm, then it will be time to plan an offensive war."

Chadwick groaned. "Can the Vulture engine be saved? Can you tell me a little about it? In Iraq, I became very familiar with the Rolls Royce Eagle engine."

Fred Entwhistle answered him, "On paper, the Vulture looks like a winner. Two Kestrel engines, one on top of another. Four pistons sharing a common crankshaft throw, six banks of four in an X-pattern, twenty-four cylinders. On paper, two thousand horses with a relatively small cross-sectional area. It bogged down in the details, mostly bearing problems. RR doesn't want to waste any more time. They just want to concentrate on the Merlin XX."

"Our engineers have spent many hours looking at this, and their conclusion is go for the Merlin. Besides, the Mark II wings are built to accept the Merlin XX," Dennison said.

After more discussion, Chadwick said, "I have a friend in Intelligence who's very much into making people believe what he wants, even if it's wrong. Let me think what he would do in this situation."

"I think this is a good time to stop for today," Dennison said, "Let's reconvene here tomorrow morning and see if a night's sleep helps Squadron Leader Chadwick come up with anything."

As they walked to the waiting car, Donovan said to Chadwick, "Are you doing anything tonight, Allan? How about some Lancashire food and a show? I can meet you at the Midland."

The two pilots met at the hotel at six-thirty and Donovan suggested a restaurant he knew of, off Deansgate, that served genuine local food. Chadwick enjoyed a Lancashire hotpot followed by winberry pie with thick, fresh cream. They walked to the Palace Theatre, an ornate Victorian edifice that showed signs of neglect. The gilt was peeling off the façade and the seats were worn.

Nevertheless, they enjoyed the show. Arthur Askey was the star, and he came on stage between turns and sang comic ditties accompanied by a talented pianist. Chadwick really enjoyed the jokes about Liverpool, which was both Askey's and his hometown. However, he missed having Melanie sitting next to him, and being able to share the jokes with her.

Back in his room at the hotel, Chadwick was horrified to see how dirty the collar and cuffs of his shirt had become. He had forgotten how polluted and sooty the air was in the north of England. He put his shirt in a bag, and placed it outside his room with his shoes. In the morning, his clothes were returned cleaned and pressed, and his shoes polished.

Chadwick continued to enjoy Lancashire gourmet cooking by ordering black puddings, smeared with Colman's mustard for breakfast. The orange marmalade for his Hovis toast was homemade, with thick slices of rind. The Avro car was prompt and he rejoined the team at Woodford before nine.

Chapter Two

"Squadron Leader Chadwick, have you given any thought to the engine procurement dilemma?"

"Yes, as I hinted yesterday, I think we must resort to a little subterfuge, all in a good cause, of course. How many Spitfires and Hurricanes are being manufactured at the moment? For example, do you know how many Spits are being made by Vickers Supermarine at Southampton, Mr. Dennison?"

"I'm on good terms with the Chairman of Vickers, Sir Walter Embry. We often discuss allocation of resources. At present, they're turning out a machine every two days—fifteen Spitfires a month."

"Do you know him well enough to arrange an unofficial loan of four engines? You could plead a short blockage in the pipeline and promise to return them as soon as possible."

"I can only try. Perhaps if I give him six strokes next time we have a round of golf he may be amenable."

"Next question—how does the Air Ministry keep track of engine allocation?"

The works manager, Bob Wattis, was able to answer that. "It's one of the resident inspector's responsibilities. When an engine is certified complete and functional at Rolls, it's assigned to a factory producing aircraft, which has a valid purchase order—for example, Vickers. The paperwork carries the aircraft order requisition number and the engine purchase order details. When it's dispatched by road, the inspector at the receiving end logs it into the factory."

Chadwick digested this information. "So, once it's in the factory it sits until there's a finished aircraft for it? Sounds like we could steal a few for a short time if there was a stockpile of engines." He was quiet for a short time. Everybody waited for his next question. "Mr. Entwhistle, you probably know the answer to this. What is the weight of a Merlin XX?"

"It weighs approximately three quarters of a ton."

"Good. It could be carried in the bomb bay of a Vickers Wellington. My suggestion is to 'borrow' four engines from Vickers and fly them one at a time in a Wellington to Woodford, thus avoiding any paperwork for road transport. As soon as feasible, they would be returned the same way."

There was some heated discussion when Chadwick unveiled his plan. It was suggested that it was possibly criminal.

"Good point," Chadwick conceded. "We must keep this little stratagem between ourselves and regard today's discussion as very confidential. It would help a great deal in terms of the legal ramifications if Avro had a purchase requisition for the Mark II. That's something I must get onto as soon as I return to Boscombe. In the meanwhile, Mr. Dennison, we need Vickers to be our partners in crime. Would it be possible for you to speak to Sir Walter today?"

"I'll take care of that this afternoon. We can meet tomorrow morning to see how far the scheme has progressed."

Dennison turned to Phil Donovan, "Phil, I suggest you give Squadron Leader Chadwick a tour of the area in an Anson this afternoon. At some time in the future, he'll probably be doing some flying from Woodford."

After lunch in the factory cafeteria, Chadwick and Donovan walked to the dispersal area. They stopped at a small flight-crew room and Donovan donned a pair of white overalls. He tossed a spare leather flying helmet to Chadwick. They walked to an Anson standing on the tarmac.

Donovan explained, "This aircraft has been flown twice since it was completed. Several minor problems have been corrected and I have to certify ready for delivery to the Air Force. If you'd care to make the flight with me, I can show you some of the local countryside."

They carefully examined the exterior of the plane, and waggled the control surfaces. Donovan climbed aboard first and settled into the left-hand pilot's seat. He gestured for Chadwick to sit on the right, and then ran through the cockpit checks and signaled to the waiting ground crew that he was ready to start the engines. All seemed well, and after checking the engine instruments and brake pressure, he waved away the chocks, called the tower, and taxied to the runway. After a magneto test, he slowly increased the engine rpm and climbed into the air. It was a typical early autumn day, with cloud cover at 5,000 feet and a visibility of three miles.

At fifteen hundred feet, Donovan throttled back to cruising condition, about one hundred knots indicated, and turned left. After a minute, he tilted the right wing. Chadwick could see four shiny railway lines. "Main line, Crewe to Manchester, useful navigational landmark. Look left. You can just see Ringway airfield, under construction. Doesn't do to get it mistaken for Woodford, but it's happened."

They flew northwest. "We're flying over Sale." Ahead was an extensive conurbation of factories and oil refineries. "Trafford Park—some park! Here's the ship canal. The small grass field is Barton."

Donovan set the plane on a westerly course and asked Chadwick if he would like to fly. Chadwick nodded, saying, "I have control."

Soon the River Mersey came into view. Ships of all sizes and description lined the river banks. Donovan pointed north and

Chadwick gently banked the plane in a rate one turn as they flew over the great port of Liverpool.

"I was born here," he commented to Donovan, who joked, "It looks like a good place to be *from*!"

"Turn east and let's climb to twenty-five-hundred feet," Donovan said. "Winter Hill is poking up and it's getting murky."

The visibility had indeed deteriorated. Dirty yellow and black smoke poured from countless tall chimneys. "Wigan and Bolton," Donovan said. "You can just see Kearsley over on the right."

Chadwick glanced through the windscreen. The cooling towers stood out like stepping stones in a swamp.

"Swing right, Allan," Donovan ordered. "You can let down over Manchester and make a straight approach to Woodford."

He made a brief transmission on the H.F. wireless they carried and Chadwick adjusted the rate of descent to make a landing on the main wheels first as they crossed the airfield boundary. He taxied to the dispersal area and shut down.

"I think this kite is good enough for the Air Force," Donovan joked. "I'll sign it off."

Chadwick thanked him for the flight and Donovan called for a car to take him back to the Midland. Chadwick spent the evening writing down his recollections of the plan they had hatched to get the Mark II flying.

In the morning meeting, Dennison said he had spoken to Sir Walter, who had given his general approval to their scheme. He insisted the details were up to the works manager, Claude Palmer, at Supermarine in Southampton. Donovan suggested that he and Chadwick fly to Southampton that very day and acquaint Mr. Palmer with their plan.

As it turned out, Mr. Palmer was not overly enthusiastic about it, but said it had Sir Walter Embry's approval and he would do his best to accommodate Avro. He suggested they fly down in a Wellington so that an adapter could be made to carry a Merlin engine in the bomb bay.

Chadwick called Stew Piggot, the chief test pilot at Vickers, Brooklands, from Palmer's office to discuss flying a Wellington to Southampton. Piggot said a Wellington could be made available for a short trip to Southampton in two days, Chadwick asked him to reserve the time on the test schedule.

When they returned to Woodford, Dennison was pleased they could get things moving so quickly. He said it would be "cleaner" if Piggot and Chadwick flew the engine to Woodford. If Donovan flew with them it would implicate Avro a little deeper in the scheme than he wanted, should an official inquiry ever materialize.

Chadwick left for Boscombe the next day on an early train, and was able to catch Wing Commander Rowley before he left for the day. Rowley was very pleased at the spirit shown by Avro to make a start on the Mark II prototype. He was dubious about the plan to smuggle four Merlin engines from Vickers but told Chadwick to go ahead, saying, "All is fair in love and war."

Chapter Three

Two days later Chadwick made the drive from Amesbury to Brooklands in the Bentley. He parked at the usual spot near the flight office. Stew Piggot reminded him that each engine successfully delivered to Woodford would cost him a lap in the Bentley on the banked track. Chadwick was only too happy to agree.

It was a short flight to Southampton. Chadwick and Piggot were drinking tea with Claude Palmer before eleven o'clock. Chadwick outlined the problem faced by Avro in powering the new prototype but emphasized the urgent need felt by the Air Force to get it flying. Their admittedly dubious scheme could potentially save months.

Palmer shook his head and wagged a finger at Chadwick. "It's your career you're gambling with, Squadron Leader, and I'm just following orders." When he understood the details, he called for the works foreman. "Bring a tape measure," he ordered.

The foreman, Edward Lockwood, listened with interest as Chadwick described the plan. They all went down some stairs to the factory floor and Lockwood led the way to a spot where workmen were stripping the packing cases to expose Merlin engines. Chadwick noticed the engines were bolted firmly to heavy timbers using the engine mounting points. The outside planks were simply protection against the weather. Lockwood jotted down numerous measurements and then asked to see the Wellington.

At the plane he asked Piggot to open the bomb bay doors, and then he ducked underneath to take more measurements, mumbling to himself. When he re-emerged they went back to Palmer's office.

"Well, Ed, what do you think?" Palmer asked.

"The engine is too high to go in vertically. It might just fit sideways, mounted on a special frame. The weight could be taken by a strong point in the top of the bay."

"What would it take to make the frame?"

"It could be put together from inch and a half steel pipe. A 'U' pattern would encircle the engine with a lifting ring welded above the center of gravity. Pads could be welded in the right places to fit the engine mounts."

"How long would it take?"

"Find me a machinist and a welder. I could have it ready in a day."

Palmer glanced at Chadwick. "Are you game to give it a try?"

"Absolutely. Do you have a Merlin we could fly out tomorrow afternoon?"

Palmer hesitated, then said slowly and with obvious reluctance in his voice, "Yes, I suppose so, though I think we're all going to go to prison." Turning to Lockwood he said, "Please get onto it as soon as you can, Mr. Lockwood."

Piggot said, "That's it then. We'll fly back to Brooklands and return about lunchtime tomorrow."

When Chadwick was about to climb into his Bentley at Brooklands, he turned to Piggot. "What time should I be here tomorrow?"

"Would ten o'clock be satisfactory? Gives us time to call Avro if things go well for a delivery in the afternoon."

Chadwick glanced at the sky, which was clouding over and darkening. He pondered the trip to Amesbury and a return early in the morning with distaste, as it was looking like rain. Then he had a happy thought. Pangbourne was much closer. He would surprise Melanie.

About an hour later Chadwick pulled up in front of Clair Court Hall, climbed the steps, and pulled the old-fashioned knob. After a few moments, the door opened.

"Mr. Chadwick, this is a surprise."

"Who is it, Myrtle?" Melanie Fitzgibbon walked up behind her housekeeper.

"My Goodness! Allan."

"Yes, it's me. Good evening, Myrtle and Melanie. I happened to be in the neighborhood and thought I'd stop by."

Melanie led the way into the living room, where a cozy fire burned in the grate. She pointed to the sideboard. "Help yourself to a drink."

Chadwick poured a Scotch and added a splash of soda water, and raised a glass to his old paramour. "Cheers!"

Music from a BBC light program pulsated at high volume from the radiogram. Chadwick walked up to it and twisted the volume knob. "May I?"

Melanie was a trim, fortyish widow from an aristocratic background. She used make-up sparingly and was always dressed well. She had been steered towards Chadwick by the leaders of the Isbell's Insiders before the war. Surprisingly, a genuine affection for Allan had developed and the love-making was a pleasant diversion, but it was not an all-consuming passion. She was more concerned than she cared to admit about the impending intention of her son to join the army.

It had been over two months since she last met Chadwick. He looked at her keenly. Her face was drawn and her eyes were red. He realized she'd been crying.

"I was involved in something at Brooklands. In fact, I have to be back there in the morning. I wasn't looking forward to all that driving, so I thought I might cadge a bed for the night."

"Of course, you're welcome anytime, Allan." She pushed a switch, and when Myrtle appeared she said, "Squadron Leader Chadwick is going to stay the night. Please make up the bed in the spare guest room."

Before Myrtle left, Chadwick quickly added, "Some pajamas would be welcome, if you have a spare."

Allan settled in his chair and said nothing. The fire made a comforting noise.

"It's wonderful to see you again, dear Melanie. I've been so busy since the balloon went up. How do you feel?"

"What do you think? I'm terribly depressed by this ridiculous war. This situation is exactly what the Isbell's crowd was trying to avoid. John is home—you'll meet him at dinner. I know he's keen to join his father's old regiment. I know he'll look so handsome in his uniform, but then he's off to war and comes back injured...or worse, disfigured." Tears ran down her cheeks.

"Oh, God, I'm awfully sorry, dear. It's terrible to be a mother at this time." He stopped and then cocked an ear. "I can hear rain on the windows. Excuse me for a minute, Melanie. I must put the car away."

He quickly walked to the front door and let himself out. He fired up the Bentley and drove past the front of the house to the stable, and parked next to the old Rolls Royce limousine. As he stepped down he heard a car approaching and a Vauxhall swept into the stable and stopped. A tall, fair young man stepped out.

Chadwick extended his hand. "Good evening! You must be John. My name is Allan Chadwick."

John Fitzgibbon knew exactly who Allan Chadwick was and how he fit in. He had been exchanging secrets with Myrtle since he was a small boy.

They both walked back to the front door, which was ajar. "Your mother is in the living room, John."

The young man poked his head round the door. "I'm back, mater," he said, and then he ran lightly up the stairs.

Chadwick picked up his half-finished drink. "Maybe it will be over by Christmas, Melanie. I'm sure the government is bringing a lot of diplomatic pressure to bear."

Melanie said nothing, and Chadwick desperately racked his brain for a safe topic to talk about. "Have they canceled lectures at the university? Perhaps John will be going back shortly."

Melanie was silent, and then abruptly rose to her feet. "Excuse me, Allan."

Just as she got to the door, Myrtle opened it. "Dinner in five minutes," she announced.

Chadwick followed Melanie up the stairs. In his room he found a clean pair of pajamas on the bed, and on the dresser Myrtle had left a razor, a stick of shaving soap, and a mug. He washed his face and went downstairs. Melanie was already seated in the dining room. After John joined them, Myrtle brought a tureen of soup. "Help yourself," she announced.

"Thank you for the stuff you left for me, Myrtle," Chadwick said.

"Myrtle's used to my friends suddenly staying over," John explained.

"Will you be returning to college?"

"I don't think it's functioning, under the circs, Allan. I want to talk to the colonel of my father's old regiment, the Ox and Bucks—sorry, the Oxfordshire and Buckinghamshire Light Infantry."

Melanie looked distraught at that announcement. Chadwick said nothing.

Myrtle cleared away the soup dishes and brought in a plate of sliced meat which she placed in the center of the table. She returned with potatoes, sprouts, and gravy. "I didn't make a sweet, but there's fruit in a dish on the side, if you want."

They ate in an awkward silence. "I must be away fairly early in the morning," Chadwick said. "I'm driving back to Brooklands." A thought crossed his mind, "I may be finished there tomorrow afternoon, probably late. Perhaps I could come back for the night?"

Melanie seemed to awaken with a start. "Oh, yes, Allan. Come back tomorrow. Feel free to use Clair Court whenever you like."

John disappeared after the meal and Melanie and Allan went to sit by the dying embers of the fire in the living room. The wireless was still playing music, softly.

"Melanie, dear, I can't think of a damned thing to say that would cheer you up. Of course, wiser heads have anticipated the war, but I don't blame the people at Isbell's for trying to avoid it."

Melanie spoke slowly. "Chamberlain tried. I'm afraid our little affair is going to be snuffed out, Allan."

"Please don't say that, dear. I'll try hard to see you whenever I can."

"Well, we'll see what Herr Hitler has to say about that."

Chadwick poured himself another drink. "Can I get you anything, Melanie?'

"No, thank you. I'm off to be bed. I'll see you in the morning if I'm up early enough." Melanie crossed over and gave Allan a light kiss on his cheek, "Good night, dear Allan."

Chapter Four

In the morning Chadwick ate breakfast by himself. When he went to the stable he found John Fitzgibbon standing by the Vauxhall.

"Good morning, John. Are you off somewhere?"

"I'm off to Aldershot to see if I can fix up an interview with the colonel."

"You're going to join the Army, then?"

"Yes, looking forward to a good scrap."

"Your mother is very worried and anxious."

"I know. I'm terribly sorry, but what am I to do? Our family is important locally. I have to set an example."

Chadwick sighed. "At your age I was just like you. But I can tell you from first hand, war is awful. Death, particularly of your friends is so…permanent."

"But you fly. Don't you run that risk all the time?"

"I suppose so, John, but you always think it won't happen to you, just the other fellows."

Chadwick drove to Brooklands. The weather was overcast, but seemed to be flyable. Stew Piggot was waiting for him at the crew room. "I've telephoned Southampton. They have an engine ready."

They climbed aboard a Wellington. Piggot took the controls and made the flight to the Vickers airfield. As he entered the circuit and completed the downwind vital actions, he made a brief transmission on H.F. He turned to Chadwick, who was seated at the navigator's table. "They've set aside a screened area for the trial hoisting of the engine."

When they were parked and the engines shut down, Piggot and Chadwick descended to the tarmac and Palmer and Lockwood came out to meet them.

Palmer greeted them. "Good morning! Ed here has put in a big effort to get things moving. Just inside the hangar we have a Merlin engine with the lifting mount already attached. Are we ready to give it a try?"

"Let's see what we've got," Chadwick said, as Palmer led the way into the hangar door.

The engine lay on its side on a scissor platform. It was encircled by a frame of steel pipe with a ring welded in the center.

"We've tested lifting it using a block and tackling attached to the ring. It's nicely balanced. Once inside the bomb bay we can use rope to tether it after it's lifted."

With a command from Ed Lockwood, two ground crew moved the platform to the nose of the Wellington. Lockwood handed Chadwick a large steel shackle. "You can do the honors, Squadron Leader. Please open the hatch in the floor over the bomb bay. When you've opened the doors we can maneuver the engine so that that you can slip this shackle between the ring and strong point in the bay."

Chadwick climbed back into the plane and opened the bomb bay doors. He had a little difficulty locating the observation hatch into the bay, and called to Lockwood for a torch. The men moved the engine into the bay. Chadwick called directions as he peered down and eventually had the two rings almost touching. He placed the shackle between the rings and inserted the clevis pin. Lockwood had given him a tommy bar to tighten it. When the pin was well tightened he called for the crew to lower the platform. As the weight came on the shackle, the engine rotated lazily.

Piggot called to Chadwick, "Let's see how the doors close, Allan. Please crank them shut slowly."

Chadwick began to close the bomb bay doors, but after a few seconds there was a cry from outside. "Stop! The door is catching a corner of the engine."

Eager hands moved the engine from underneath.

"Keep cranking, Allan," Piggot called.

The doors closed satisfactorily this time.

"Congratulations, Mr. Lockwood," Chadwick said. "You got the measurements perfect."

Palmer stood with them by the plane. "Well, that went better than I expected. I think you have time for a spot of lunch while the crew rig the ropes."

The works manager led the two pilots to a dining room for senior staff, but Ed Lockwood didn't join them. Chadwick was sorry that Lockwood had been excluded, as he had a question about the strength of the single strong point in the Wellington.

Just as he finished his main course, a man entered and excitedly made an announcement. "Listen, everybody! I just heard on the BBC News that the USSR has invaded the eastern frontier of Poland! I think this is going to bring the war to a stop. The Germans are far outnumbered by the Soviets."

Piggot looked at Chadwick. "Tough luck, Allan. No quick wartime promotion now."

"I'm not so sure, Stew. I can't make sense of it. The Germans and the USSR signed a treaty only weeks ago."

Chadwick called Phil Donovan at Avro to let him know they were on their way and to get a reliable forecast.

"Let's get the engine to Woodford as soon as possible, the forecast is for a lowering cloud base."

The pilots scrambled aboard the plane, Piggot started the engines, ran through the checks, and took off with a 2,000 foot ceiling. He elected to fly a little west of north, which took them over Oxford and Birmingham. Then they picked up the main railway line to the north and followed it to Crewe. The ominous clouds pressed them close to the terrain, and Chadwick was grateful for the navigation tips that Donovan had given him earlier. When they spotted the airfield, Piggot gave the tower a call and was cleared to make a direct approach to Runway 24. Ground crew waved them to the screened area of the assembly building.

Donovan, the works manager Bill Wattis, and a knot of men were waiting for them with a scissors platform. The men quickly got the platform under the nose of the plane. Chadwick handed the tommy bar to Piggot. "Here you are, Stew. You can get the rig under the engine."

Piggot climbed in, opened the bomb bay doors, and directed the ground crew to position the platform under the engine. When the engine was safely resting inside the building, Piggot said, "We're off, before the clouds get any lower. We'll get Avro to send the mounting support back to Southampton in a couple of days."

As Chadwick climbed into the plane, he said to Wattis, "What's happening with the war?"

"Soviets have invaded Poland. Seems to be a real free-for-all."

Chadwick turned the news over in his mind as they busied themselves getting ready for the flight. Was it good or bad? He had the feeling the world was rushing to a conflagration, but he shook his head and concentrated on the task at hand. The pilots flew back on a reciprocal of the route they had followed north and landed at Brooklands an hour or so later.

When they stopped by the crew room, Piggot said, "That's another Bentley lap you owe me, Allan."

Chadwick happily agreed. "It went very smoothly, Stew. I'm really grateful to those chaps at Southampton. Let's hope the next three engines go as well."

"I'll give you a call when the next is ready, Allan. I assume you'd like to fly that one to Woodford too."

Chadwick started off for Pangbourne, and at a convenient petrol station he stopped to fill up. The attendant looked at the gauge when the tank was full. "You're going to have trouble with this monster when rationing starts," he said lugubriously.

"What do you hear?" Chadwick asked.

"Talk is rationing by the end of the year, as little as two hundred miles a month, less for your car."

Chadwick paid the attendant and drove away thinking about what to do with his beloved "Green Machine." It was yet another problem to solve. The traffic was thicker in the late afternoon and it was well past cocktail time when he parked at Clair Court.

Melanie was delighted to see him, and if anything looked slightly more cheerful.

"How about a drink together and then I suggest a cozy dinner at the Blue Bell."

"That sounds all right to me, dear."

"We'll have to drive in your horseless carriage. John has taken the Vauxhall. He's gone to Aldershot and probably won't be back for a few days while he tries to charm the colonel."

They settled down in the living room, each with a drink. Myrtle came in to adjust the curtains, saying, "Cedric says there was a chink of light showing past the black-out curtains."

Chadwick laughed, as a pilot he knew how difficult it was to make sense of lights at night, especially dim ones.

When they were seated at the pub, Chadwick wondered whether he ought to mention the war. Melanie was clearly on edge, but the Soviet invasion was possibly good news.

"I heard from someone this afternoon that the Russians had invaded Poland. He assumed it was to stop the Germans. It might be good news, something that could bring the war to an early end. Have you heard anything, Melanie?"

"I only listen to music on the wireless. When the news comes on I turn it off."

Chadwick ordered a steak, which he ravenously tucked into when it was served. Melanie pecked at an omelet and left half of it on her plate. When she put her fork down and refused a sweet he suggested a liqueur.

"Lovely, a Drambuie."

He ordered one for each of them.

As they sat quietly at their table, contemplating the liqueur, an elderly couple rose to leave the restaurant. The man suddenly stopped in front of Chadwick's table.

"Excuse me, Squadron Leader. I don't want to interrupt you and your good lady, but I noticed your uniform, and I just had to say, 'Thank God for the Royal Air Force and the Royal Navy now that we're fighting the Germans and the Russians'."

"The Russians?"

"Yes, just caught it on the wireless as we were leaving the house. When Russian and German forces met in Poland they embraced at an agreed demarcation line. It must have been part of the damned treaty they just signed. A very good night to you, Sir and madam."

Allan looked at Melanie, who was now quietly weeping.

"Oh God, Allan, what terrible news. We're doomed."

"All is not lost, Melanie. We're still fighting with France on our side, and the British Empire is behind us."

"I don't trust the French, and the empire is thousands of miles away."

They finished their drinks in silence and drove back to Clair Court. At the foot of the stairs Melanie said, "I'm going to bed. I'm sorry, Allan. I'm not the most cheerful company." She gave him a kiss on his cheek.

Chadwick returned to the living room, poured a drink, and stirred the cinders in the fireplace. A flame flickered into life. He turned on the wireless and waited for the music to finish.

"Here is the nine o'clock news with Alvar Lidell reading it. The Foreign Office just issued the following communiqué—'We have received a notification from the Foreign Service of the Soviet Union that the actions in Poland are part of the mutual defense treaty with Germany and do not constitute an act of war against Great Britain or France'."

Ah, Chadwick thought, *that simplifies things. The Russians are protecting their flank.* He finished his drink and went to his room. In the morning he made an early start and left for Boscombe without seeing Melanie.

Chapter Five

At Boscombe Down, Chadwick told Wing Commander Rowley that the first Merlin engine had been successfully delivered to Avro. They had a long discussion about other work that was needed in order to get the Mark II in the air. In particular, Chadwick felt that a suitable propeller was not available. Rowley encouraged him to pay a visit to De Havilland with Fred Entwhistle, and told Chadwick that a requisition for the prototype Mark II was at the Air Ministry and should be approved within days. However, that would not immediately solve the engine problem and the surreptitious plot would have to be played out.

Two days later, Phil Donovan called. The engine they had flown up from Southampton had been fitted to the prototype without difficulty. But he really called, he said, to offer Chadwick a flight in a new Manchester, which had just been flight tested. He suggested Chadwick stay a few days at the Midland the next time they had an engine to pick up from Vickers. Chadwick thought this was an excellent idea, as he could combine it with a discussion with the engineers at Chadderton about propellers for the prototype.

The opportunity came later in the week when he made the tedious train journey to Manchester and left the first day of his visit free for the flight in the new Manchester bomber. The day after, he would fly with Piggot to collect another Merlin.

He read the *Manchester Guardian* carefully as he ate dinner at the Midland Hotel. Military maneuvers in Poland had almost ceased, and the country was completely occupied by German and Soviet forces. He was particularly interested in an article by the correspondent of an American paper who had witnessed the invasion. The reporter described the bombing attacks by massed Ju 87s in support of the Army. He reported that the dive bombing formed a kind of flying artillery and it made Chadwick realize once again that the tactics of the new war would be completely different than the Great War.

Avro sent a car in the morning, and he met Phil Donovan in the crew room as he was donning his flying overalls. The Manchester had been inspected by the ground crew, but nevertheless, Donovan walked around it to make sure the control surfaces were not locked. They climbed aboard, along with a flight engineer and wireless operator. As the plane was so new, Donovan performed the cockpit checks carefully, including lowering and raising the flaps. They took off with clear weather up to 7,000 feet, wind southwest, fifteen knots. They settled on a course to the south at 5,000 feet, and Donovan invited Chadwick to take the controls.

Chadwick acknowledged and put his hands and feet on the column and pedals. He tried a few experimental maneuvers, and thought the plane felt sluggish after the many hours he had spent flying Sally, his Spitfire. Then he realized the Manchester was the heaviest plane he had ever flown; there was much greater inertia.

As they flew over Crewe, Donovan asked Chadwick to fly on 250, magnetic, at 150 knots. To maintain the indicated air speed Chadwick was using near full boost on the Rolls Royce Vulture engines.

"Try single-engine performance, Allan," Donovan said over the intercom. "Throttle back on one engine."

Chadwick pulled back the throttle lever of the left engine and increased the boost on the right. He was flying with nearly full rudder trim to keep the course on 250. He noticed the vertical speed indicator was showing a slight descent of a hundred feet per minute, and so he pushed the right throttle. But the engine was putting out all it could. Try as he might, Chadwick could not maintain height.

He spoke to Donovan. "Seems very reluctant to hold the height at these settings, Phil."

"You're so right, and we're not carrying any bomb load. Try slowing down a little. That should give you less drag."

Chadwick spent twenty minutes trying to find a comfortable cruising condition under one engine, but the plane had lost over 1,000 feet when finally Donovan said, "Enough. Climb back to five thousand, Allan."

Chadwick opened the throttle of the left engine and began to regain altitude. Suddenly there was a loud backfire and the fire warning light for the right engine came on.

"I've got it," the engineer shouted and pushed the fire extinguisher button.

Donovan said, "I have control. Shut down the right engine, flight."

"I think the time we spent at full power buggered the right engine, Phil," the flight engineer reported over the intercom.

"We don't want to bugger the other one too," Donovan said. He pulled back to 2200 rpm, and the plane settled down to 125 knots, with a 250 feet-a-minute rate of descent. "I don't think Shawbury is too far away," Donovan said. "Ops, see if you can get a radio bearing on Shawbury."

The operator fiddled with the Bendix DF radio. "Naught six four degrees, Phil," he called after a couple of minutes.

Donovan told him to declare an emergency on H.F. wireless and tell Shawbury that they planned a single-engined landing in about ten minutes. "Also contact Woodford on telegraphy and let them know we're experiencing engine failure and landing at Shawbury in about ten minutes."

Chadwick peered intently ahead through the windshield. Soon he had the airfield in sight.

"I'll make the touchdown, Allan. I'll be crossing the fence at a hundred knots. Keep singing out the airspeed and handle the flaps and gear as I say."

Donovan kept plenty of height in hand and made a masterly landing. They had to wait on the runway for a tow. When they reported to the tower, they were informed that Avro had dispatched a car, expected to arrive in about two hours.

Night was falling when they got back to Woodford. Donovan told the driver to take Chadwick to the Midland Hotel after he had dropped off the Avro people. As he was leaving them, Allan called out, "I can see your job has its moments, Phil."

At the hotel Chadwick had a hot bath, changed into a clean shirt, put on his civilian suit, and wandered down to the bar for a drink. He recalled that Phil Donovan had mentioned sometime earlier that single ladies were not allowed in the bar at the Midland. All the stools at the bar were occupied and when he had a drink in hand he sat at a small table against the wall. In a while, a short man with Brylcreemed hair asked if he could sit on the empty chair.

Chadwick waved at the chair. "By all means."

"Crowded tonight."

"Is it? I'm just visiting. I don't get to Manchester often."

"Still, you're from this part of the world. Let me guess—Liverpool?"

"Good guess. I grew up there."

"See. Shaw was right in *Pygmalion*. A person's accent always gives him away. I can pin a Mancunian down to within a few streets of where they live. Of course you need a good ear."

"Really, the difference is that distinctive? What about foreigners, can you do the same with different countries?"

"Usually. I can tell the country they're from. Some countries have a wide range of accents—Germany f'instance. I have a theory about accents. It's a bit of a hobby of mine. I think accents are an evolutionary thing, so that early people can recognize strangers, who were usually dangerous."

The talkative man put down his glass, which was empty. "Let me get you another drink," Chadwick said.

"Thanks, pint o'bitter."

Chadwick managed to get the attention of a waiter and ordered a drink.

"Are you a teacher?"

"Crikey, no, I left school at fourteen, knocked about a bit. I was just old enough to 'ave a couple of years in the Army at the end of the war. I was a bricky after I left school, but now I work in an office."

"Were you in the trenches?"

"I was lucky. Managed to avoid France. Woulda been a death sentence for Tommies like me. Wound up in Egypt."

"How did you like Egypt? The way things are going, you might find yourself in the Army again."

"Hot, but otherwise very interesting. Do you think this war's going to last? I'm in my forties now—middle-aged, as they say."

"Don't ask me," Chadwick said. "I have no idea. But as you said, humans have been fighting strangers for a long, long time."

"True enough. You sound like you've had an education. I would respect your opinion. Do you think we can beat Germany?"

"I don't know, but we have to fight. People who don't wind up dead or enslaved."

"You're probably right. Depressing though. To change the subject, did you come into the bar looking for a little companionship?"

"Oh, no. Just killing an hour before dinner."

"You're staying at the hotel. Then you must be rich. This is Manchester's finest."

Chadwick laughed. "I'm not rich. Let's say my employer is paying."

"Right. Regarding my earlier question, there's a nice class of ladies usually at the Wellington, and there's some rough trade at the Gaumont."

Chadwick suddenly got suspicious of the little man and wondered if he was procuring. He rose and left some money on the table. "Very interesting talking to you. Please excuse me. Good night."

When Chadwick later picked up his key at reception he found a message from Avro—a car would pick him up at eight-thirty and take him to Chadderton.

The meetings at Chadderton lasted two full days. Chadwick met primarily with Fred Entwhistle and experts from the design department. Many questions asked by the Avro people required answers from Air Force operations planners and Chadwick spent hours on the phone to Boscombe Down. They were able to nail down specifics of the maximum rate of climb with full load, cruising duration, range, and other factors that enabled the propellers for the four Merlin engines to be designed. Chadwick was exhausted at the end and caught an express to London with relief. At Boscombe Down, he wrote a long summary of the decisions made in Manchester.

Three days after he returned, Chadwick got a call from Stew Piggot. Another Merlin was ready for delivery to Woodford. Chadwick felt it was important for the Air Force to have a part in the smuggling plan and made arrangements to drive to Brooklands. At the back of his mind was also the thought that he could stay at Clair Court Hall for a night, with the hope that Melanie was recovering from her depression.

The flight from Brooklands to Southampton was routine and the Vickers crew had the engine ready to load as soon as they taxied to the assembly building. Chadwick was concerned that the full weight of a Merlin on a single eye strap in the bomb bay might lead to a structural failure, should the plane experience turbulence and the G-forces become high.

While Stew Piggot supervised the mounting of the engine, Chadwick mentioned his concern to a Vickers design engineer, who suggested a quick examination of the strap. The effective cross-section of the eye was a little under half a square inch, and after a minute pushing his slide rule, the engineer was of the opinion that a force less than three "Gs" would be well below the yield strength.

As they cleared for a flight to Woodford, the tower operator told them that Fighter Command had reports of German fighters operating singly over Britain. "So keep a look out for a lone wolf," the tower operator advised.

"What shall we do if we spot one?" Piggot asked Chadwick. "We have no gunners or guns mounted."

"Drop a Merlin engine on him," Chadwick joked.

After they landed at Woodford, the Avro crew unloaded the new engine and then left it on a scissors platform at the entrance to the assembly hangar. Donovan dragged Piggot off to look at the Mark II. Chadwick was left by himself when he became aware that a man in a rumpled suit and a bowler hat had quietly materialized by his side.

"What's this then?" the man asked.

Chadwick was startled. "I don't know. Something Avro is up to, perhaps repowering Ansons."

"Oh, aye. That thing would pull the wings right off a bloody Anson. I'm a ministry inspector, Squadron Leader, so I'm not a fool. Everyone in t'factory knows what's going on in there," he said, jerking his head toward the interior. "If it helps to win the war, we're all for it." He favored Chadwick with wink.

On the flight back to Brooklands, Chadwick recounted the conversation to Piggot, who was not at all surprised.

When the short flight was over, Chadwick suggested there was time for the two laps in the Bentley he owed for the successful deliveries. The two of them climbed in, Piggot on the right, and when two laps at over a hundred mph were accomplished, Chadwick suggested two more.

When Piggot climbed down at the dispersal area Chadwick slid into the right seat and said, "That's two more engine deliveries you owe me, Stew." They both laughed.

Chapter Six

Before Chadwick left Brooklands, he managed to make a quick call to Clair Court and alert Myrtle that he planned to spend the night there. Melanie was waiting when he arrived and gave him a warm hug. Chadwick decided her depression was lifting. She told him her son had joined his father's old regiment and was off somewhere training.

"Well, I'm sorry to see him go, but at least I have my car back."

Chadwick mentioned the conversation with the attendant at the petrol station, that rationing was on the way.

Melanie said, "Everything is changing, my dear. I have something to tell you over dinner. I suggest our old favorite, the Blue Bell."

It was still fairly early, and so Chadwick begged to be excused so that he could go to his room for a hot bath and a change into civilian clothes.

Chadwick drove them both to the Blue Bell in Melanie's Vauxhall.

At the restaurant Melanie suggested a stiff drink to prepare him for her announcement.

"A man was round at the house a few days ago. He was measuring the rooms and asking how many people lived at Clair Court."

"Really, what was that all about?"

"He said it was very likely the house would be requisitioned by the Army."

"My God, Melanie! Where does that leave you?"

"He suggested renting something in the village, but I told him I could 'do up' the apartment over the stable."

"What about Myrtle and Cedric?"

"Ah, that's the ironical bit. They can stay in the servant's quarters because Cedric is needed to keep the boiler running. The thing is, my dearest love, it makes me think about us. It was in this very place, a few short years ago, that we agreed to a romantic adventure. I think that circumstances are forcing us apart. The war changes everything. You're an airman. You could be sent anywhere at any time. From what I've read, the lull in fighting at the moment is the calm before the storm. When the weather improves in a few months the pundits predict all hell will break loose."

"Melanie, my love, nobody knows what's going to happen."

"Allan, I have thought very hard about it. To face what's coming we're both better off without entanglements. I have decided I was indulging myself, and sacrifices have to be made in times like this."

Chadwick could not resist saying, "From what you told me that was not your attitude in 1917."

"That was different. John wanted an heir, and he knew he ran a high risk of becoming a casualty. When I lost him I was heartbroken. They say time is the great healer, but it takes years. I'm not going through that again."

Chadwick was silent for a few minutes. "Sometimes you amaze me. We have such affection for each other. We've enjoyed each other so much, in so many ways."

"I know, I have come to enjoy the physical side of love much more as I get older. You've been very good for me. I don't want to quarrel, dear. I honestly think it's for the best." A tear trickled down her cheek.

They were interrupted by the waiter bringing the meal they had ordered.

Chadwick began to eat, but the food tasted like ashes in his mouth.

They were both quiet and when they returned to Clair Court, Allan stopped by the front door. "Melanie, my love, at least for the moment, I think it's time to say goodbye. I'm going upstairs to get my things, and then I'll put your car away and drive to Boscombe in the Bentley. Adieu, my love."

Melanie gave him an anguished look, and then turned and fled into the house.

In the morning Chadwick threw himself wholeheartedly into the task of getting the Mark II in the air as soon as possible. He told Wing Commander Rowley that numerous trips to Manchester would be needed, but he also had to maintain a presence at Boscombe, and taking the train lost two days in travel. He mentioned the Spitfire he had at Farnborough for liaison. Rowley laughed, "I'm afraid we don't have a plane like that lying around." The thought crossed Chadwick's mind that he was losing two mistresses when he really needed them both.

Later, Rowley approached Chadwick with a suggestion, "We have a De Havilland Rapide that's not too busy. I can assign a junior pilot to fly you and other senior ranks on liaison trips. Most days you should be able to make a visit and return to Boscombe without significant lost time."

Chadwick agreed it was worth a try. When Stew Piggot called to let him know a Merlin engine was ready for pick-up, he flew to Brooklands in the Rapide, accompanied Piggot to Southampton and Woodford in a Wellington, and returned to Boscombe the same day in the Rapide. He realized that some days the weather may delay the Rapide and leave him stranded for a night, so carrying a few personal items on each trip seemed like good insurance.

Even though the problem of engines had been solved, that was only the tip of the iceberg. Numerous issues had to be resolved between the design staff at Chadderton and the operations planners at Boscombe.

One decision which generated a lot of debate was the idea of equipping the Mark II with only one left-hand seat for the pilot. The plane would not carry a second pilot. After some debate, the policy was adopted of giving the flight engineer some piloting experience. Assuming the pilot was injured during operations over enemy territory, it was hoped the flight engineer could fly the plane home and land it. But there was no intention of sending flight engineers to flying training schools, as these were overloaded anyway. The training would be done informally by crews once assigned to an aircraft. The arrangement produced a great deal of skepticism.

A decision by Fred Entwhistle to keep the main spar high enough to leave the bomb bay unobstructed meant that movement in the fuselage for the crew was difficult. And finding spaces for the navigator, flight engineer, and wireless operator all required compromises. In addition, three turrets for machine guns and the bomb aimer's position had to be squeezed in. A dome for astro navigation was needed. Often during bitter discussions, Fred Entwhistle would say, "This plane is a bomber, so the bomb bay is the most important space. Everything else is secondary." He usually got his way.

Like the nerve and circulation systems of a human being, a bomber required an enormously complicated network of wires, piping, fuel lines, hydraulic hose, and trays for machine gun ammunition. The operations planners often insisted that vital services be duplicated so that battle damage would be minimized.

All these components were installed in the prototype Mark II as soon as the designers had finally agreed on routing. Each crew station required communications, oxygen, and electrical power. During installation technicians often encountered interference between components occupying the same space. All these problems had to be sorted out in consultations between designers and builders. Chadwick was pleased that all services, hydraulics, air pressure, vacuum, and electrical generations were provided by at least two engines.

But the great plane slowly came together. Four engines had been installed with all the umbilical connections that they needed. The massive undercarriage wheels were installed under the two inner engine nacelles. Squadron Leader Chadwick was so busy that almost before he knew it, they were celebrating the New Year in the mess bar one night.

Petrol rationing was announced. Chadwick realized he had to put the old Bentley away for the duration of the war.

He called his father, who found a shed behind one of his butcher's shops in Liverpool. Chadwick got permission to leave the base for forty-eight hours and drove the old car non-stop to his parents' house. His father promised to get a mechanic to properly prepare the car for long-term storage. His parents complained they rarely saw him anymore. "There's a war on, Mother," he reminded her gently.

She wiped a tear away. Allan put his arm round her and pressed her face against his chest, "I'm doing my best to stay alive."

For the first time in years, Chadwick spent the night at his old home, but so much had happened to him it seemed like it was someone else who had once lived there. In the morning, he took a train back to Salisbury, which took all day. The trains were packed with men in uniform. Chadwick traveled in civvies and bought a third-class ticket.

The day after Chadwick returned he got a message from Phil Donovan. They were ready to for taxi trials, and it was anticipated a first flight may be possible within a month. Chadwick flew to Woodford as a passenger in the Rapide and sought out Phil. As might be expected, the taxi trial was delayed by some small problems but would be accomplished fairly soon. To eliminate the tedious ride into central Manchester, Avro had found Chadwick a room in Cheadle, nearby.

He climbed aboard the Mark II to look at the progress made since he last inspected it. It was beginning to look like an airworthy plane. The cockpit was fairly complete with a full range of flight instruments. He felt a glow of pride, this marvelous creation owed a little bit to his efforts.

That night after dinner in the small inn where he was staying, he caught the BBC News. The Luftwaffe was attacking British shipping in the Channel. RAF Bomber Command was making raids over German military targets such as naval dockyards and railway marshaling yards. Both sides had agreed not to bomb civilian areas. In confidential discussions at Boscombe, he had learned that RAF losses in daylight raids had been higher than expected and the daylight raids had been suspended. To the disgust of the air crews, the night raiders only dropped propaganda leaflets. Following the invasion of Poland there had been no further battles on land. An American newspaper correspondent called it a "phony" war.

The next day Dennison approved some taxi trials. All four engines were run up to full power, throttled back, and the plane steered along the runway and perimeter at speeds of fifteen knots. All the functions were tested and hoses and lines were examined for leaks. The first flight was set for the next day.

Donovan was at the controls, Chadwick represented the Air Force, and the crew consisted of a flight engineer, a wireless operator, and three technicians. Dennison, Entwhistle, and several senior engineers from Chadderton came to Woodford to witness the take-off. The flight went smoothly—so much so, Donovan had to throttle back carefully, as it had been agreed not exceed an air speed of 175 knots until chart recorders installed for the test had been examined after the flight.

Two days later, a longer test was scheduled. Donovan invited Chadwick to slide into the pilot's seat for half an hour. For a plane of that size and weight, Chadwick found it light on the controls, which could be trimmed so the pilot could fly the plane "hands off."

And then, a few minutes after Chadwick relinquished the controls to Donovan, they were startled by explosive impacts. A German fighter flashed in front of the windshield.

"My God, Phil," Chadwick cried over the intercom, "it must be one of those lone wolves we were warned about earlier."

The cloud base was about 2,000 feet, with four-mile visibility. They were flying just below the clouds over the foothills of the Pennines, east of Woodford. It was countryside that Donovan knew intimately.

"Well, we have no guns on board but I can give the bastard a fright, I think. Allan, please go aft to see if anyone was hurt or if there is obvious damage." Donovan eased the plane up slightly, turned left and entered cloud.

"There are some fairly high hills on this heading. Let's hope he hits Kinder Scout, just over two thousand feet."

"I got a glimpse of him, Phil," Chadwick said. "Think it was an Me 110."

"Still," Donovan said, "time to head for home. Ops, get me a bearing for Woodford."

They stayed in cloud for another ten minutes, slowly edging left, which would bring them over Stockport. Then they let down, and they could see the ground through ragged breaks in the cloud and landed safely. They never saw the German fighter again.

On the ground they counted three bullet holes in the fuselage. Donovan was of the opinion the fighter had used twenty-millimeter cannon.

Back at Boscombe Down, Wing Commander Rowley was delighted that the Mark II was flying. He told Chadwick to get it down to Boscombe as soon as possible so that flying trials could begin to assess its operational capability.

This put Chadwick in a dilemma. Fred Entwhistle wanted to make some engineering changes before the plane was delivered to the RAF. Even Chadwick had a minor issue to investigate in an area in which he had specialized knowledge—the autopilot was not functioning correctly; changes in heading and height resulted in an overshoot before the plane settled on the desired value. He knew this could be corrected by adjustment of a factor called "damping."

Eventually, he was able to make a compromise. Avro technicians and engineers would make the changes at Boscombe as RAF trials were underway.

The Air Ministry was persuaded to give A.V. Roe an order for a hundred production aircraft; the new plane was to be called the Lancaster, to honor its birth in Lancashire. When a couple of minor faults were corrected and the bullet holes patched up, Chadwick felt it was a great privilege to fly the prototype as captain to Boscombe Down. He had never officially flown a four-engine plane as first pilot before.

He carried a full crew of Avro personnel and when the weather turned foul, he was glad the wireless operator was able to give him compass courses obtained from the new Bendix direction-finding radio. Once he had the airfield in sight he could not resist making a low-level pass over the control tower. On the final approach he was able to see a crowd of men watching the landing. He carefully taxied the plane to the dispersal, obeying signals from a ground crew with wands, and when he shut down the noisy Merlin engines, there was a cheer from the spectators.

Wing Commander Rowley grasped his hand as he climbed onto the tarmac. "Congratulations, Squadron Leader Chadwick. This is indeed a very significant moment for Bomber Command."

Specialized experts took over the trials of the Lancaster. They determined bomb loads, fuel usage and range, and wrote the "Pilots Notes," guidance for all pilots who would fly it in service. The plane was fitted with guns and a bombsight, and operational flights were simulated. Many changes to the interior resulted and Chadwick spent days back at Woodford and Chadderton correcting the detailed specification for the new aircraft now in production.

He had an idea that he broached to Wing Commander Rowley. As the specifications for the production planes were being refined, he suggested letting some crew that had actually been on bombing missions over Germany fly in the Lancaster for their assessment. Rowley thought it was an excellent idea, and so Chadwick called the commanding officer of a bomber wing he had worked closely with a couple of years before when he was staging RDR trials—Wing Commander Harris at RAF Church Fenton.

As Chadwick suspected, the Wellington bombers of Harris's wing had flown daylight bombing raids over Germany in the opening months of the war. When Chadwick explained his role in the production of the Lancaster bomber and how he believed that this was the time to incorporate lessons learned in actual combat, Harris expressed interest but also caution.

Rowley asked Chadwick how much time would be needed for the flight to Church Fenton and agreed to block out three days in the flying schedule. Rowley also cleared the experiment with Bomber Command, as it was necessary for the period of the Lancaster assessment at Church Fenton to avoid overlap with operational missions.

Eventually, Chadwick piloted the great plane to Church Fenton with an air crew of RAF specialists. They were received with enthusiasm and spent several hours at first just giving bomber crews a tour on board.

The next day Chadwick sat down with Harris and crews of two planes that had participated in a daylight raid over the naval dockyards at Kiel. Harris started the session by describing the raid in general terms. "Twenty-two Wellingtons had left three bases in England, rendezvoused over the North Sea, and arrived over the target as a single wing of three squadrons. The weather was a typical autumn day, with high cloud and eight-mile visibility over the target. We flew at fifteen thousand feet and encountered anti-aircraft flak as soon as we crossed the German coast. Navigation was entirely visual and we could clearly see the Kiel Canal on the approach to the target area. The wind at altitude was twenty-five knots from the northwest. The flak stopped when we were ten miles from the dockyard and swarms of Me 109 fighters appeared. The fighters were extremely well-organized and attacked in coordinated moves. Later on we were told was because they had communication by wireless between planes.

"After each squadron made a bombing run, the wing re-formed as tightly as possible and we were harried by fighters on the way home until the coast was crossed. Six Wellingtons went down over Kiel and two more were lost on the way home. This corresponds to a thirty-six percent loss rate and is completely unacceptable. In addition, several planes were damaged, of which a further two were scrapped. Six crew members in planes that returned were wounded, two quite badly. Photos taken the day after showed almost negligible damage to the dockyard."

Harris stopped at this point and his face appeared white. Clearly the re-telling was highly emotional for him.

Chadwick was shocked. The bare numbers were far worse than the vague rumors that had circulated. "I'm sorry, Sir, I didn't... didn't..." He stammered to silence, not quite sure what to say.

"The men have been through a lot, Squadron Leader, but I'm sure they'll be happy to give you the benefit of their experience in developing this new bomber."

"Well, then," Chadwick said, "I'll start with a few questions, and then make note of any suggestions any of you may have. I think tomorrow, if the weather cooperates, I'll be able to take a cross-section of crew specialists for trip in the Lancaster."

His first question was based on his own experience of bombing trials when he was stationed at Farnborough. For the bomb aimers, he posed a question, "Due to enemy action, how far from the nominal aiming point were the cross-hairs when the bombs were released, on average?"

"Ye must be joking, Sirr." A sergeant with a heavy Scottish accent volunteered his thoughts. "We were so busy dodging fighters we were lucky to see Kiel on the screen."

"I'll note that as a mile or two," Chadwick said. "Considering the ferocity of the German fighters, how do you rate the defensive armament?"

"I can make a comment of that," Harris said. "The fighters coordinated their attacks when possible so that we were approached from both sides at once. The Wimpy has poor lateral defense."

Another man chimed in; his tunic brevet showed that he was an air gunner. "The turrets 'ave almost no coverage to the side. The field of view is chopped up by the wing for the front gunner and the tail for the rear gunner."

The flight engineer spoke up, "Both the turrets have cams that interrupt firing when the barrels are pointing at the wings and tails. Stops these lads sawing off part of their own plane."

There was some restrained laughter and Chadwick was pleased to detect a slight improvement in the heavy atmosphere.

"How about the future," Chadwick asked. "How can we attack Germany and keep the loss rate sustainable?"

"The bigwigs in Bomber Command will have to answer that," Harris said, "but for my own part I think we are limited to night raids for the present." There was some clapping and foot stamping at that. "I'll post a list of those selected to fly in the Lancaster with Squadron Leader Chadwick tomorrow in the crew room shortly."

Chadwick dropped into the bar in the officers' mess before dinner. He tried to gauge the mood of the fliers in the mess, but it seemed no different than a score of other bars, and he decided that the appalling loss over Kiel was sufficiently long enough ago that it had been largely forgotten.

The next day he took off in the morning with the selected specialists taking the place of the crew that had flown up with him. Leaving Wing Commander Harris in the pilot's seat, Chadwick wandered around and talked to the specialists scattered throughout the plane. Most seemed happy with the design. A gunner pointed to the trays for the machine gun ammunition. "How many rounds will it carry, per gun?"

"I think it'll be between six hundred and a thousand rounds."

"You can double or triple that. When we were flying back from Kiel, the Jerries were onto us for about twenty minutes. Most of the gunners had already used up their ammo. The mid-upper gunner can only cover one side at a time. There's no belly defense."

"Thank you, Sergeant. I'll bring that to the attention of the right people."

Chadwick went to the cockpit and stood next to Harris. "What do you think of the plane, Sir?"

"I think we'd better get a thousand of them double quick."

Chadwick turned to the flight engineer. "What do you think, Flight?"

"She's a beauty, all right."

"How can she be improved?"

"There is very little armor plate. She needs some behind the flight engineer's instrument panel, the pilot's seat, and the navigator's seat. I'm not sure about the fuel tanks but I hope they're self-sealing."

"Good observations. Let's ask Wing Commander Harris to open up and see what she'll do, unloaded."

Chadwick turned back to the pilot, and glanced at the instruments. They were flying at 5,000 feet, heading east, and that seemed like a safe condition. "Give her a bit more boost, Sir, and see what she'll do."

Harris advanced the throttles, pushing all four at once, and powered the plane to 250 knots indicated air speed.

"Hooray," the engineer cried. "That's as fast as I have ever flown." Searching his instruments carefully he added, "And nothing is getting too hot."

After another thirty minutes, Chadwick suggested they head for home.

After landing, he swapped the visitors for the original Boscombe crew. He thanked Harris sincerely for the useful information he had gathered and left for the short flight back to Boscombe Down.

He wrote up the suggestions for consideration by the evaluating team at Boscombe, but the major impact of the visit to Church Fenton had been on himself. He realized after meeting the bomber crews— who were in the trenches, so to speak— that if the war heated up, he would have to wangle a posting to an operational squadron. Although he knew that development of the best weapons was very important, he also felt that he had a responsibility to the Air Force and his country to fight. *My God*, he thought to himself, *I'm no different than John Fitzgibbon, and I thought he was just a young fool!*

Armed with a list of modifications, Chadwick flew back to Woodford to discuss the operational considerations with engineers at Chadderton. Dennison was pleased that these changes were being handled so early in the production program, as late changes were much more difficult to incorporate.

When he was sitting in Dennison's office one afternoon, alone with the Avro manager, Chadwick asked for his honest opinion of when the first production Lancasters would enter RAF service.

Dennison grimaced. "I know there's a war on. We're doing our very best, but I can't see the forming of the first squadrons for a little over a year. When production hits its stride we're aiming at fifty planes a week. There are plans to have Lancasters built in Canada at a new factory, too."

When Chadwick returned to Boscombe, Wing Commander Rowley told him the Air Ministry was considering buying an American-made heavy bomber, because they were already in production and on the market. The designation by the United States Army Air Corps was the B-17. At a public unveiling in the States, a newspaper reporter noticed it had so many guns that he described it as a "Flying Fortress," and the name stuck, so that was what Boeing was calling it. The company was flying a model to Britain and France to attract sales. Chadwick was told he would be on the assessment team when it was at Boscombe.

Chapter Seven

Military activity continued to be fairly quiet. The Soviet Union was in a war with Finland and German planes continued to attack British shipping. A British Expeditionary Force was built up in northeastern France, in anticipation of a possible German thrust through Belgium. A handful of RAF squadrons occupied French airfields to work with the Army.

Wing Commander Rowley called a meeting of the people who would assess the American heavy bomber. Nobody knew exactly what role the U.S. Army had in mind for the plane, but a friend with connections to Washington said that "precision, high altitude, daylight bombing" was a phrase that was constantly repeated there. When Rowley repeated it, Chadwick was immediately skeptical—"high altitude" and "precision" were opposing factors, which he knew from his own experiences at Farnborough when he was assisting in the design of a bombsight.

When the B-17 with civilian registration marks landed at Boscombe Down, the team charged with determining its capability consisted of the chief test pilot, two engineers, and Chadwick, who was specifically asked to compare it with the Lancaster. They were introduced to the visitors by Wing Commander Rowley in a briefing room near the dispersal area. The head of the Boeing team stood on the platform at one end of the room. He was a broad-shouldered man in a leather jacket and scruffy khaki pants. "Good morning," he said. "My name is Paul Kowalsky. I've been flying for Boeing for four years and before that I flew for Uncle Sam."

Kowalsky showed a slide of important characteristics. Speaking with a broad American accent he explained, "Range and ceiling depend entirely on the fuel and bomb loads. With no bomb

51

load, the range can exceed three thousand, five hundred miles at twenty-five thousand feet. The ceiling can reach thirty-five thousand feet, unloaded. However, the load can vary from four thousand to eight thousand pounds, depending on the mission. The plane carries a crew of ten, which includes five gunners, and the co-pilot also doubles for the flight engineer. Economical cruising speed is about one-seventy knots. Maximum speed is two-fifty knots. The B-17 has almost three-sixty degree horizontal machine gun coverage. Later models will have a tail gun, giving better vertical coverage, and will possess an upper turret and a belly turret. Most of the guns are twin fifty-caliber. Any questions, so far?"

The Boscombe test pilot stood up, "Mister Kowalsky, you have admirably described the best features of the B-17. With so much armament, no wonder it's termed a Flying Fortress. My feeling is that the bomb load is a trifle meager and has been sacrificed to provide lift for the gunners, the guns, and the ammunition. What do you say?"

"Now you're treading on mission description. Boeing only makes planes to the specifications of the users. In this case the Army Air Corps. They believe precision daylight bombing is only possible with heavily-armed bomber formations. Small formations or single sorties are too vulnerable to fighters. I guess it's a trade-off of the total number of bombs you can carry to the target and the split between bomb load and armament weight for individual planes. Someone must have done the arithmetic."

Chadwick raised his hand and Rowley gestured for him to rise. "You mention precision bombing, but at the same time you say the planes will be in formation. In that case, only one plane can get the target position in his bomb sight. If all bombs are dropped following action of the leader, surely the rest will be off target?"

"Depends on your definition of 'precision,' sir. I believe the acceptable range of hits on a precision target is within five hundred yards." Kowalsky paused for a moment. "I guess that margin of error is okay for a factory or marshaling yard. For a target such as a bridge, the mission planners may briefly change the shape of the formation or make multiple passes. Good point, though.

"While we're on the subject of bombing," Kowalsky continued, "the model we're flying today doesn't carry a bombsight. That's a top secret device. I don't think I'm giving away any secrets when I tell you the bombardier can actually take control of the autopilot during the final run to the target. This greatly improves accuracy."

After several more questions and some discussion, Rowley suggested a break for lunch and said the team would fly with Mr. Kowalsky in the afternoon.

The British team climbed into the B-17 and found several Boeing people already on board. Kowalsky took the left-hand seat and the chief test pilot climbed into the right-hand seat. Take-off went smoothly and the plane climbed at well over a thousand feet per minute. Chadwick wandered around the fuselage and noted that the plane was not carrying guns. He found that when the waist gun ports were open, the cold was numbing. A Boeing representative showed him a heated flying suit which crew members needed. At the radioman's position, he asked the Boeing man what a large panel containing numerous calibrated dials was for.

"That's the Command Radio set-up, Sir," he was told. "Each dial is a self-contained radio covering a piece of the shortwave band; preselected frequencies are set up before a mission. Should the area catch a bullet it might take out one or two channels, but the rest will continue to work."

"What is it used for?" Chadwick asked, rather naively.

"Why, the command radios provide inter-ship voice communication, up to about fifty miles. For long-range Morse transmission we have the main radio here." He touched a beautifully built receiver and transmitter above a desk with a Morse code key.

Chadwick was impressed by the workmanship and finish of the plane. It made the Lancaster look slightly old-fashioned, even though the B-17 had been designed and built several years earlier. He moved into the cockpit. The British co-pilot stood up and told Chadwick to take the right-hand seat. He talked to Kowalsky over the intercom. "Take the control column, Sir," the American ordered.

Chadwick placed his hands on the half-wheel, saying, "I have control." He glanced at the instruments and then through the cockpit windows. Horizontal visibility was good.

"Try a few maneuvers, Sir," Kowalsky suggested.

The plane seemed stable but reasonably light on the controls. Chadwick added an inch of boost to all four engines and started a gentle climb. He asked the American where the autopilot control was, and Kowalsky touched a square panel forward of the throttle quadrant. Chadwick set a heading twenty degrees to port of the plane's direction and selected "Engage." The Fortress flew smoothly onto the new heading without overshoot or hesitation. Chadwick pointed to the column and said, "You have control." Kowalsky nodded.

When they returned to Boscombe Down, the plane was examined by a large number of RAF people while Paul Kowalsky stayed in the plane and answered dozens of questions. The assessment team gathered in Wing Commander Rowley's office.

The test pilot spoke first. "It's a first-class aeroplane, Wing Commander, but it has too many tits and whistles and guns. Eliminate a few and carry more bombs and you might have something." That was the general consensus, but Chadwick added that the quality of the workmanship was impressive.

Chapter Eight

Chadwick was working at A.V. Roe Company in Manchester when he heard on the wireless that British forces and naval ships were engaged in fighting in Norway. "Why the devil are they fighting there?" he asked.

Several men were listening and one of them said, "You don't know your geography. That's the way Germany gets their iron ore and coal."

A week or so later, Chadwick was cleaning up some paper work at Boscombe when the gossip in the bar at lunchtime was that the Germans were invading Denmark and Holland, and the British were pulling out of Norway, apparently defeated by the Germans. Somehow it seemed to him that British war leaders just couldn't get things right. Obviously, other politicians thought the same way because a vote in Parliament to support Chamberlain's leadership only narrowly passed and clearly his time as Prime Minister was over. To the surprise of many people, Winston Churchill was asked to form a government and the King appointed him Prime Minister.

Chadwick was reminded of the days before the war when he attended meetings of an appeasement group, the "Isbell's Insiders," as an observer for British Intelligence MI5. The group had worked hard to get Chamberlain appointed Prime Minister after Baldwin resigned. It seemed a long time ago and now Chamberlain was gone. He wondered how long Churchill would last.

That same day, the Germans launched the long-expected strike against Belgium and France. Within two weeks their Panzer tanks swept through the Ardennes and outflanked the British Expeditionary Force in the northeast. There was a good deal of talk at Boscombe of the failure of one of Britain's most advanced fighters, the Defiant, when faced with the German Messerschmitt or the Focke-Wulf fighters. The consensus was that the Defiant was just too slow and too heavy to maneuver as well as the Luftwaffe planes. However, the reports of the Spitfire and Hurricane performance against the Germans were encouraging.

Somehow the Royal Navy and a motley fleet of peacetime pleasure boats managed to lift a substantial number of British and French troops off the beach at Dunkirk. The RAF also played an important role by flying from bases in England and intercepting German attacking planes on the French coast. However, without doubt, the defeat of the British Expeditionary Force was a disaster. The Army had abandoned virtually all its heavy weapons and the defense of the country fell to the Royal Navy and the Royal Air Force.

To Chadwick's surprise, most of the French troops rescued from Dunkirk were quickly transshipped to the Normandy coast in northwest France. They were joined by a British Army Division. This last show of resistance was quickly defeated by the German Wehrmacht and France asked for an armistice.

As the French tottered on the brink of defeat, the Italian government, like a vulture sniffing a corpse, declared war on Britain and France. France was divided into two parts, the north and west under German control and the south under a puppet government led by Marshal Petain. Britain stood alone against the seemingly invincible enemy. The Battle of Britain was about to begin, and Chadwick was determined to be part of it.

The speed of the French collapse not only took the British by surprise but apparently the German High Command as well. Their Army and Air Force had to regroup and establish bases on the north and west French coasts in preparation for continuing the war against Britain. This took time and gave the British, under Churchill's urging, chance to prepare for an invasion by fortifying the south coast. Civilians were evacuated, and children from London were taken to northerly regions, much to their dismay. Squadrons which had been part of the

British Expeditionary Force escaped by the skin of their teeth, due to the speed of the German advance. Their planes were often flown to RAF airfields in the south of England with no prior planning and left there, as pilots and ground crews were exhausted.

Pilots and technicians from units which had not been involved in the fighting were rushed to RAF bases in the south such as Tangmere, Biggin Hill, Manston and many more, to gather the planes scattered higgledy piggledy. Once serviceable, they were flown to fields further north out of reach of the Luftwaffe.

Chadwick was delighted to find himself flying a Spitfire again and, over a period of ten days, delivered a dozen planes to squadrons that were reforming after the chaos of the evacuation. He flew a Spitfire to RAF Ringway; 613 Squadron, Royal Auxiliary Air Force was based there. The commanding office, Squadron Leader Roger Danfield, told him that the squadron had decamped from a field in France with minutes to spare before German Panzers roared through. Some of the ground crew were captured and some drove to French ports in heavy lorries, but managed to get to England.

Chadwick introduced himself and said, "You sound Australian."

"Too right. I joined this mob in peacetime and now look, there's a bloody war on."

Chadwick laughed, and looked at the sky. "I have to organize myself back to Boscombe Down."

Danfield took Chadwick to his office and he telephoned Boscombe. He was told a Rapide would pick him up in the morning. And then Danfield took Chadwick to the officers' mess, a sturdy building built in the peacetime expansion of the Air Force.

"Once you're settled in, join me for a drink in the bar."

Chadwick soon had his elbow on the bar, drinking a pint of bitter. "So what's the state of your squadron, Roger?"

"I reckon the squadron can only muster fifteen qualified pilots at the moment. It was a weekend warriors unit, best flying club in the world. Now Hitler's gone and spoiled it. There are about six former weekend chaps still flying, but conditions in France over Dunkirk took a few. Here, I'll introduce you. Hi, Pete. Come over and meet a guest."

A fair-haired young man wandered over. Danfield gestured, "Pete Sillitoe, this is Squadron Leader Chadwick. He just returned the kite that Harry Bradshaw carelessly left at Manston."

"Jolly decent of you, Sir."

"Pete was with the squadron a few months before the balloon went up. You were a teacher, weren't you, Pete?"

"Yes, that's right."

Chadwick sensed the young man was very tense, and changed the subject. "I've done some flying around here, flew heavy stuff out of Woodford."

Sillitoe suddenly said, "You sound like you were born in Lancashire, Sir."

"Yes, you can take a lad out of Liverpool, but you can't take Liverpool out of the lad."

"So you've been flying a long time. Pardon me for asking but what is the campaign ribbon?"

"Iraq, four years staring at the desert." Chadwick found that the ice seemed to have been broken and Sillitoe relaxed and chattered away about the mysterious East.

Danfield gave him a wink. "Time for some dinner, I think?"

The German High Command knew that air superiority over the English Channel was essential if a successful invasion was to be launched. To begin with, they attempted to lure Fighter Command into air battles as shipping was attacked, but the chief, Air Marshal Dowding, was not to be drawn into committing precious resources to duels of attrition. But in this he had to fight Churchill, who had not fully grasped the enormity of the air battle that lay ahead once the Luftwaffe was fully ensconced in former French airfields near the coast. The Germans captured the British Channel Islands without a shot being fired. They were too far from the British Isles to be easily defended and the loss was not serious in a military sense but it was very bad for British morale.

At this stage, the American Ambassador, Joe Kennedy, became convinced the British would be overrun or simply negotiate an armistice with Hitler, who admired the British and hoped they would realize their position was hopeless. Kennedy's gloomy forecast upset the American president, Franklin Roosevelt, who dispatched a diplomat familiar with Britain and military matters for an independent assessment. The diplomat was more optimistic, and in his report, stated that Churchill, who was not a particularly good tactician but an excellent strategist, was convinced that if Hitler failed to occupy the British Isles, Germany would lose the war.

The president was further persuaded to help the British because of the problem posed by the French naval fleet in the Mediterranean. If the admiral in charge declared allegiance to the Nazi-controlled government under Petain, it would seriously jeopardize British naval power in the region. When the Admiral dithered, Churchill ordered the Royal Navy to sink the French warships, which, until a couple of weeks before, had been allies. Churchill's determined leadership in a tricky situation convinced Roosevelt to do all in his power to help the British.

Chadwick followed all these staggering developments with passionate interest, but for a brief period the air war over England was fairly quiet. Then German bombing raids began in earnest. The bombers were escorted by fighters which stayed a thousand or two feet above the slower bombers. The German Messerschmitt 109 and British Spitfire were evenly matched. The slightly slower Hurricanes went for the bombers. Thanks to the early warning generated by the Chain Home radar stations, the Spitfires were usually at a height which gave them an advantage in diving down on the escorting German fighters, much to the surprise of the enemy pilots.

However, losses on both sides were high. After two weeks of fierce fighting, Fighter Command was pressed to get all its fighters in the air when the radar operators sounded the alarm. Units not engaged in combat, such as research and development establishments, were scoured for qualified pilots.

Chadwick was not surprised when he was ordered to RAF Hawkinge for "Temporary Duties." When he arrived, he was told by the wing commander that he was the new commanding officer of 613 Squadron. Squadron Leader Danfield had been killed the day before. Chadwick was shocked by the news and quickly found the two flight commanders. He told them he had met Squadron Leader Danfield just a couple of weeks earlier at Ringway. Both men appeared mildly shell-shocked. The loss of their C.O. was just one more blow in the daily battle. The squadron had been stood down until the new commanding officer took over.

Chadwick discovered that they had twelve serviceable Spitfires and sixteen pilots, including himself. Two replacement pilots from a training school were expected in the morning. He asked the adjutant to organize a meeting for all the officers and pilots. Nearly half the pilots were not commissioned and wore sergeant's chevrons.

Before the meeting he had a long discussion with the engineering officer, a capable man who had initially trained at Halton, been commissioned six years earlier, and was now a flight lieutenant. Chadwick was assured the ground crew could keep the planes flying if damage was not too devastating, and replacements were coming in quickly. The ground crew was stretched but surviving, the shortfall was pilots.

Chadwick next talked to the warrant officer who supervised armaments. Although he had over 200 hours flying the Spitfire he had never fired the guns. He was satisfied that he understood the reflector gunsight and the corrections allowed for gravity drop. He expressed the opinion that thirty-caliber bullets were on the light side. The warrant officer agreed and told him the Spitfire later models would have twenty-millimeter cannons.

The air in the hangar was thick with tobacco smoke when Chadwick rose to address the squadron. "Good morning, chaps. I'm Squadron Leader Allan Chadwick. I was deeply shocked to learn of Squadron Leader Danfield's death. I had the pleasure of meeting him just a few weeks ago at Ringway. I know you all will miss him."

He paused for thirty seconds before continuing. "I won't mince words. Britain is facing a crisis, and we are in the front line. I am sure you heard or read the Prime Minister's speech after Dunkirk. We are alone at the moment but gearing up to help is the British Empire and I believe America is going to join us in due course. Our equipment is better than the Jerries and we have Chain Home to get us into battle at the right place and time.

"I have recently been involved in the testing a new four-engined bomber, the Lancaster. Believe me, chaps, when we get squadrons of them over Germany they will wonder what hit them. So we just have to hold on and victory will come. A few details now. New members of the squadron will fly as wingmen to the more experienced pilots. Stick to his tail like glue. Don't get ideas of taking on a Hun. Just keep your leader's tail clean and your chance will come. If you get separated, rejoin as fast as possible but watch your back. If rejoining is not on, get down to the deck and head for home. Happy hunting!"

Chadwick asked the pilots to stay for a few minutes. "I want the old men to discuss the advantages and weaknesses of the Me 109 for the benefit of the new chaps."

A long discussion followed with plenty of dissensions. Everybody's experiences had been different. Some men were excitable and moved their arms violently to simulate planes in motion around each other. It was agreed that below 10,000 feet, the Messerschmitt had a slight speed advantage. The Spit could out-turn the German plane, but using this to advantage was hard. Everyone agreed that deflection shooting was difficult. When attacking Stukas, wait till the dive was finished and attack from behind, keeping slightly below the target. The rear gunner could not respond as his field of fire was blocked by the tail. When diving to escape, roll into it. A bunt stops the engine for a second.

The meeting broke up with new pilots looking a little shaken. Chadwick asked the two flight commanders to stay for a minute. When they were alone he addressed them very seriously. "We must be very clear on the squadron battle tactics. It is my understanding the Fighter Command official guidance is that a close formation attack is not working. Comments?"

Flight Lieutenant Kirk spoke up immediately. "It's bloody stupid. You can't fly in close formation and watch your arse at the same time."

The other commander agreed. "The wing man should be a hundred to a couple of hundred yards away."

After some discussion, the three of them agreed that pilots would be qualified to lead pairs or fours. The flight commanders would lead scrambles involving flights of six planes. Pairs would fly separated by 200 yards from another pair. After an interception, pairs would operate independently, with the wing man sticking to his leader like glue. Chadwick asked the flight commanders to brief their pilots and to keep him informed of any difficulties.

"There are two things we must accomplish," he concluded. "Maximize Jerry losses, and keep our own pilots alive."

Chadwick contacted the wing commander and told him 613 Squadron was ready to be added to the "available" list at the Chain Home interception centers. Chadwick himself was a little apprehensive about how he would handle an interception. In the past, the shoe had been on the other foot. He had been attacked in Iraq by fighters, now he was going to attack an enemy.

A scramble came the next day, just after sunrise. The 613 Squadron was given the call sign "Bathtub," and two flights of six Spitfires, Red and Blue Flight, were ordered to make angels fifteen on a heading of one-seven-zero degrees.

Chadwick led Red Flight; Blue Flight flew on his right, spaced about a quarter mile. Visibility was good but the sun was a problem, although not quite in their eyes. Chadwick hoped they would be higher and south of the German formation so that they could turn north and attack with the sun on their right. Pilots had been briefed not to use the voice short-wave H.F. radios they carried, except in an emergency. Getting the attention of the flight leaders was done by briefly pushing the transmit switch, known as "blipping." This was done to fool enemy direction-finding receivers on the French coast.

Chadwick heard three quick blips, very loud, in his earphones. He searched the sky intently and spotted the swarm of Messerschmitts on his left at the same height. Then he saw the bombers, stacked 1,000 or 2,000 feet below. His duty was to get the escorting Me 109s, while the bombers would be left for the attention of the Hurricanes.

The German pilots spotted the Spitfires at the same time and turned toward them. The two fighter wings were flying toward each other at a closing speed of nearly 600 knots. In seconds, he had a German plane in his gunsight, but before he could press the trigger it had flashed behind him. He wrenched his plane in a hard turn and soon spotted another Messerschmitt half a mile ahead. The throttle was jammed to the end of the quadrant. Chadwick was overtaking the left side of the target and he tried to concentrate on putting the gunsight rings a little ahead of the German plane. His whole being was concentrated on the image in the sight. He pressed the trigger and the plane shook with the recoil. The German pilot suddenly realized he was under attack and banked and climbed with violent movement. He disappeared out of Chadwick's vision in a split second.

Chadwick throttled back slightly. The Merlin had been racing at full power, and the Germans were descending to attack the Hurricanes, which were attempting to intercept the bombers. He put the nose down and dived after the nearest German plane and pushed the throttle back to full power. This time he decided to attack directly from behind. He was lucky. The German didn't know he was under attack until Chadwick's bullets struck his machine. He made the mistake of diving and Chadwick was easily able to keep him roughly in the gunsight while keeping the trigger firmly depressed. He saw a piece of the German plane fly into the air and then his guns stopped. He had blasted away all his ammunition.

He glanced at the fuel gauges, and both were showing nearly empty. He reckoned he had less than ten gallons. Time to go home. He could see the White Cliffs on his right and streaked for Hawkinge. When he landed, he discovered his wing man had stayed with him. He climbed down from the plane and found he was drenched in sweat. He told the intelligence officer during the interrogation that he had damaged a 109. All the pilots came back from the sweep and none claimed any victories. While the planes were being refueled and re-armed, he conducted an informal debriefing. Chadwick confessed that the speed at which events happened was bewildering.

"Planes are a lot faster than when I flew in Iraq," he joked wryly.

The squadron was scrambled again just after lunch. This time the vector given them was one-two-zero, angels eight. They were after bombers attacking the numerous RAF airfields in the southeast of England. Chadwick spotted a large formation of German bombers, and he immediately recognized the distinctive twin tail of the Dornier 17. He was approaching the enemy from their left and put his sight on a leading plane with distinctive markings. He was too far away to open fire but closing the gap rapidly.

Suddenly, he heard a shriek in the earphones. "Red one, break right." Just as he jammed the stick over and hauled back, he gunned the engine. The Merlin responded with a surge of power but the plane shuddered as bullets thudded into the wing near the root on the fuselage. An Me 109 tore past on his left with his wing man in hot pursuit. As Chadwick watched, mesmerized, the Spit opened fire and smoke and flames burst from the stricken German as it plunged earthwards.

Chadwick shook his head violently. He knew that watching the fireworks was the way to get killed. He made a careful scan all around and then realized he was losing fuel, the shot in the wing had ruptured a tank. He turned northeast, and could just make out the runway at Manston. He decided to head for it while the engine was still running.

But as he approached, he found the airfield was under attack. Waves of Dorniers were dropping bombs on the field. It was too late to change course. He was committed. He pushed down the undercarriage lever but only got one green light. Somewhere in his mind while he concentrated on the approach was the thought that the hydraulics were shot. But as he swept over the fence and put down full flap, he instinctively lifted the undercarriage lever and turned off the ignition—an action that probably saved his life. Seconds later, the Spitfire landed on its belly with terrible crash. The good wheel was unlocked and the plane skidded without cartwheeling.

Chadwick was shaken but unhurt. When he slid back the canopy, the strong smell of hundred octane fuel overwhelmed his nostrils and he scrambled to the ground and started running. He heard a voice shouting—"Look out, get down!"—as a German plane dived toward the ground, its machine guns stuttering. The earth a few feet away was violently disturbed and then it was all past. It seemed suddenly quiet. A fire engine which had been making its way toward the fallen Spitfire stopped by him. "You all right, Sir?"

A wave of euphoria swept over Chadwick. "Yes, right as rain. How about a lift?"

Chapter Nine

Chadwick got back to Hawkinge in time for a late dinner. The peacetime facilities had been completely overwhelmed by the influx of fighter squadrons, and aircrews were eating in a large tent. He spotted the pilot who had been his wing man that afternoon, Sergeant Evans. "Taffy, you saved my hide. I reported the 109 you nailed to the intelligence wallah at Manston, and you'll be credited with a confirmed kill. I could eat a horse. Where's the grub?"

"Thank you, Sir. I saw that you managed to prang at Manston. Things were pretty hot. Glad you got away with it. And I think horse is just what you'll be eating."

Chadwick tucked voraciously into an anonymous stew and boiled potatoes. It tasted delicious. He discovered the squadron was stood down until 0600 hours. After the meal, he loitered outside the tent as the light left the sky. The men were gathered in small groups, most savoring a last cigarette before bed.

One of the flight commanders came up to him, Flight Lieutenant Kirk. "Do you have a moment, Boss?"

"Of course, Tom."

The officer motioned Chadwick to a quiet spot. "I just want a word with you concerning Flying Officer Sillitoe."

"Yes, I remember him. Met him when I delivered a Spit a couple of weeks ago. What's he been up to?"

"Just after you met him he went on a week's leave. He was pretty broken up by the death of a friend who died after crash landing his Spit. He seemed to be much better when he got back. He flew today's sweeps as my wing man. Particularly this afternoon, we were in the thick of it, bouncing those Dorniers. You know we have one Dornier confirmed down by the Observer Corp, along with the 109 that Taffy clobbered. It was a good sweep. I came back with no ammo left. But the chief armorer told me after we landed that Sillitoe's guns had not been fired. The canvas was unbroken."

Chadwick understood the implication of Kirk's story. Each time a plane was re-armed the armorers pasted a strip of canvas over the gun ports. The purpose was to keep out cold air at altitude, which sometimes caused the ammunition belt to jam. The first bullet discharged always tore the canvas away.

"Yes, that's a bit odd," he said to Kirk. "There was plenty of opportunity I take it?"

"Oh, yes, bags. Those Krauts held the formation as we tore in. He could easily have attacked a plane next to the one I was blasting."

"Leave it with me, Tom. I'll have a quiet word. Thanks for bringing it up."

Chadwick went into the old peacetime building that now served as an area to relax and get a drink. He pushed his way to the bar and eventually managed to get a pint of bitter. Rank counted little in the struggle to get to the bar.

Flying Officer Sillitoe was sitting on a bench by an open window. He was not drinking. Chadwick made his way over and greeted him. "How goes it, Peter?" There was such a hubbub that Chadwick could not catch the young man's mumbled reply.

"Let's go outside, where it's quieter," he suggested.

They walked onto the grass. "It's getting chilly, now the sun's set." Standing silently for a minute they looked at the last vestige of orange in the western sky. Finally, Chadwick spoke. "What's the problem, Peter?"

"Sir, I really love flying. That's why I joined the Auxiliaries. And the Spitfire is the most wonderful plane ever made. I am so lucky to be able to fly it."

"Yes?"

"Well, it's just that when my friend Stephen Bradley was killed, the squadron doctor told us he was wounded by a German plane but was able to fly home. His injuries weren't fatal, but then the Spit crashed on landing and burned. Well, it's a bit hard to explain, but I felt that taking the life of a man flying a modern plane was, well, sacrilegious, sort of. It's like using a finely wrought statue to bludgeon a man to death."

"Um, are you religious, Peter? I mean really religious? Do you believe in the story of Jesus Christ?"

"I'm Church of England, Sir, just like everyone else. But I don't like the medieval mumbo jumbo they wrap religion in. I teach science, and I know the earth is just a speck in the vastness of the universe. Somebody made it, so let's call him God."

"Peter, at the moment we're defending Britain from an evil dictator. If we fail, everything we hold as 'British' will disappear. A thousand years of tradition, not to mention the 'blood, sweat, and tears' Churchill talked about. We need your skill and training to put a bullet where it will do the most good. At the moment we're the scalpel. We shoot as precisely as we can to defend our island. But based on what I was doing before I joined 613, I can tell you the Air Force will become the butcher's cleaver in the future. It's going to take a strong will to stomach what we will have to do to win this war."

"What do you mean, Sir?"

"Assuming the Jerries don't beat us into the ground and we can hold air superiority over the Channel, the war will change to attrition just like the last war. But instead of troops shooting and artillery shelling just yards apart, the killing will be done by huge formations of heavy bombers, probably killing more civilians in cities than troops in trenches. It's coming. It will be done by both sides."

"That sounds horrible. Pilots would never bomb innocent women and children."

"Peter, the Germans did it in the so-called civil war in Spain that just ended. I know at the moment the Germans are aiming at our airfield, planes, and RDR centers. I wonder how long it will last?"

"I still believe in the chivalry that fighter pilots showed in the last war."

Chadwick sighed, "I don't know how much of that was actually true, or a newspaper myth. Anyway, all I'm asking you to do is fly your fighter aggressively, just like those chaps in '14 to '18, if that's what makes you feel chivalrous. You are fighting men armed with similar weapons, intent on conquering us. Can I count on you to do your duty?"

"Yes, Sir, and I'm sorry. Stephen's death upset me a lot, but you've helped me set my mind at rest. You can count on me."

"Jolly good, Peter. Sleep well, I think we're on call again at six-ack-emma, to use a phrase from the war you admire. Good night."

Chapter Ten

Across the Channel, the Luftwaffe struggled to get airfields operational that were close to Britain. A military aircraft requires a substantial amount of support and it took time to set this up. The first units to become fully operational were Stuka squadrons. Because they were organized to move fast to keep up with the Panzers, they formed an airborne artillery. But they were vulnerable flying to and from the target, they were relatively slow, and poorly maneuverable compared to a Hurricane or Spitfire. However, once in position, they were deadly accurate, and they dived at over 300 knots, their bombs were released at low level by an automatic system which also pulled them out of the dive, as the pilot was usually "blacked out" by the high G-forces. Raids by Stukas were limited until the Luftwaffe could get fighter squadrons in service to protect them.

Because a bomb had such high momentum, it was not greatly affected by the wind, and accuracy depended solely on the pilot's skill to keep the target in the bomb sight. In addition, the plane was fitted with a siren energized by the airstream, which induced a psychological fear factor in those on the receiving end. In the early stages of the battle to gain control over the English Channel, the Stukas concentrated on ships and RAF airport structures, such as hangars and control towers. The importance of the RDR radar system to direct British fighters onto attacking German planes was not fully appreciated by the Luftwaffe, and so attacks on RDR facilities were rare. Also, the huts containing the cathode ray receivers looked run-down and nondescript. The towers for the aerials were steel lattice structures which were very hard to bring down.

The Royal Air Force studied the Ju 87 carefully and issued guidance for planes attacking these dive-bombers. Assuming the protective fighters could be dealt with by Spitfires, the

Stukas were easy meat for Hurricanes either before or after a bombing dive. The rear-facing gunner had a field of view hampered by the tail and was unable to deal with attacks carried out from beneath the plane. As the days lengthened before the solstice, Chadwick's squadron had fierce duels with swarms of Ju 87s and their protective umbrella of Me 109s, and sometime Me 110s.

In one epic day, 613 Squadron was scrambled four times to deal with raids by Stukas. Chadwick was credited with a kill when a twin-engined Messerschmitt, which had been attacked by his wing man, dove under his Spitfire and then climbed, giving him a beautiful shot with no deflection. All eight guns poured lead into the German, as he had an almost plan view of the victim. The Messerschmitt blew up and the two British planes flew through a cloud of smoke and debris. At the time Chadwick was excited and elated, but when he recounted the incident to the intelligence wallah after landing he felt suddenly saddened and sorry for the German pilot.

Two days later, Chadwick snagged a Stuka that had just completed a bombing dive on West Malling airfield. As the Stukas climbed away and the speed fell off, their underside was totally exposed, making it easy for a well-placed fighter to wreak havoc.

As the Luftwaffe pulled itself together, the size of the bomber fleets increased dramatically. The bombers continued the assault on airfields but also attacked aircraft and engine factories and ports. Chadwick flew on most of the squadron scrambles, and within a few weeks he was feeling exhausted. One day, he asked Tom Kirk how Peter Sillitoe was getting on.

"He's joined the ranks of the converted, boss. Whatever you said to him worked wonders. I'm thinking of recommending him as a leader of four. I think he nailed an Me 109, but it probably went down in the Channel and we couldn't confirm it."

"He thinks he's a knight in shining armor on a warhorse, but don't disillusion him. I'll be happy to sign a recommendation of promotion to leader of a flight of four."

An hour later, the whole squadron was scrambled, vector one-eight-oh, angels fifteen. There was cloud at 9,000 feet, and when the squadron broke through at 12,000, Chadwick saw their target some distance ahead and slightly higher. The squadron continued to climb; the waves of bombers stretched far to the south. He had never seen so many planes in the sky at once, and he estimated the bomber fleet at over 100 aircraft.

German fighters immediately spotted the British planes and dived to attack. The sky became a confused melee of twisting, turning planes, but the German bombers attempted to hold formation and pressed on, heading north. Chadwick spotted an Me 110 ahead and banked violently to get it in his sights. He knew he was pulling far too much "g" to get a shot, but then the German turned toward him. He quickly leveled the wings and, as the planes thundered toward each other at nearly 700 knots, closing speed, he fired all the guns, his eyes concentrating on the cockpit of the approaching plane in his gunsight. The Messerschmitt flashed under him and he wrenched a turn to the left to try to keep it in sight. He was pulling so much "g," This vision began to fail, and he found himself staring down a tunnel.

Chadwick eased off the bank and quickly recovered his sight. There was no sign of the German fighter, but he was close to a Heinkel 111, flying ahead of him and on the right. He immediately began a curving attack so that as he approached the target, he was line astern. The ventral and upper turret guns of the German bomber blazed away as Chadwick opened up with the plane, filling the gunsight rings. He flew over the bomber with feet to spare. And then the forward gunner on the Heinkel, forewarned by the turret gunner, raked the Spitfire and Chadwick felt the plane shudder as bullets plowed into it. The throaty roar of the Merlin changed to a mechanical cacophony. The Spit lost speed and thick, black smoke blanketed the windshield. Chadwick could feel the heat from a burning engine, he rapidly slid back the canopy, unplugged the earphone cord and oxygen hose, rolled the plane over and hit the harness release.

A few seconds after leaving the plane, Chadwick found himself falling in dense cloud. He could feel the wind on his cheeks, but he was completely disoriented. He did not know if his head was up or down. It was a strange feeling; there was no gravity. After what seemed like ages, he popped into daylight again. He seemed to be alone. There were no planes in sight. Flailing his arms, he managed to get his head up and search for landmarks. Eventually he spotted the coast, and realized he was going to drop into the Channel. It seemed safe to pull the ripcord, he had no desire to make himself a target for a roaming German fighter. The 'chute opened with a crack and he surveyed the sea beneath him, looking for ships. It appeared to be deserted.

Chadwick racked his mind to think of the possible disasters awaiting him. He prayed his wing man, Sergeant Mike Derbyshire, had got off a position report on the H.F. wireless. It looked too far to swim to shore. He debated with himself the possibility of becoming entangled in the 'chute and shrouds when he fell into the sea. He decided it would be best to fall out of the harness just before impact and he turned the locking ring of the harness release in preparation. He was descending quite rapidly, and judging when to press the harness release was tricky.

Suddenly he found himself in the water. The 'chute was streaming to leeward and he pushed the release, which functioned perfectly. He swallowed a mouthful of salty seawater and coughed violently. His hand desperately searched for the tab on his Mae West and to his relief, the life jacket inflated, bringing his head above the waves.

Chadwick's wing man, Sergeant Derbyshire, saw his flight leader exit the plane. He immediately gave an emergency call on H.F. to Hawkinge Tower. They got a bearing with the direction finder and checked with Chain Home, which provided a fix. The air-sea rescue coordinator called the Folkestone lifeboat.

"This is the Royal National Lifeboat, Folkestone."

"This is Air-Sea Rescue. We have some business for you. Pilot parachuted into the Channel."

"Better speak to the duty coxswain, hold on."

"This coxs'n Abel Trevik. Please give me the details." He carefully wrote down the bearing and fix.

"What time did he enter the water?" The coxswain had sailed the English Channel nearly all his life. He knew the current ran strongly and changed direction four times a day. He moved to a desk with a chart and looked up the tide tables. Trevik walked to the dock, the duty crew was already aboard and had the engine running. The coxswain took the wheel and when clear of the breakwater he briefed the crew. "We're looking for a single pilot, he's not going to be easy to spot. I reckon he'll be about two miles east of where he went in. We'll start a square search in twenty minutes, so keep your eyes peeled, and warm up a blanket on the engine."

The sea was fairly calm. The waves were perhaps a foot high, but Chadwick could see nothing except the grey sky above and the next wave. He was still wearing his flying boots, gloves and leather helmet, he decided to keep them on because, at least for a few minutes, they provided a small amount of insulation. But the seawater was cold and as the water seeped through his clothes to his skin he began to shiver. After twenty minutes, he was shaking violently and lost feeling in his hands and feet.

After an hour, the shaking stopped, and a kind of lassitude clouded his brain. He did not hear the rough voices shouting, "There he is!" He could not raise his arms to fend off the white wooden hull which bumped into him. Men pulled him over the gunnels into a capacious boat, hands searched his clothes.

"He's Raff, one of ours. Not a bloody Jerry."

Another voice cried, "Ay we throw them back," and laughed.

Chadwick was stripped naked by the seamen and wrapped in a blanket which had been warming on the engine coaming. Slowly he began to understand he had been rescued. The "thump, thump, thump" of the diesel engine was comforting.

The coxs'n shouted to one of the men, "Billy, run up the signal for 'Ambulance needed'."

A seaman fastened a colored pennant to a rope on a short mast and pulled it to the top. On shore a look-out at the Lifeboat Station saw the signal through his telescope and called the hospital. Emergencies like this were happening almost every day.

At the dock, Chadwick was carefully lifted into the waiting ambulance. He could only dimly understand what was happening. Before the vehicle left, a seaman threw in Chadwick's soggy clothes, wrapped in a blanket. At the hospital, a young doctor looked at Chadwick casually and said, "Let me have a rectal temperature, nurse, please."

A nurse inserted a long thermometer and after a couple of minutes said, "Ninety-three point seven, doctor."

The doctor, who had been examining Chadwick's body for wounds said, "He seems to be in one piece, just mild hypothermia. Put him in bed with lots of blankets. If he wakes, give me a call. Oh, and please get housekeeping to deal with his wet gear."

Chadwick came to his senses early in the morning. A nurse noticed his eyes were open. "Oh, you're awake. How do you feel, Sir?"

Chadwick grinned, "Just tickety-boo."

"Please roll over, Sir." She inserted a thermometer. A doctor approached and raised his eyebrows, "Ninety-eight point two, doctor."

"Well, well, you seem to be recovered. Are you feeling better?"

"Yes. Nothing wrong with me. I think I ought to be getting back to my squadron. Where am I?"

"You are a guest of Folkestone Infirmary. All in good time. I think some breakfast is in order, and then we'll see about getting you back to—where is it?'

"Hawkinge, Doctor."

"That's just up the road. The matron will arrange a meal and your transportation. Before you go I want one of our specialists to listen to your heart."

The matron showed up after a few minutes. "This early we only run to warm porridge. Do you like milk and sugar?"

"Yes, that would be fine. Same with the tea." Chadwick looked over the matron carefully. She seemed to be in her late forties, and had a large bosom encased in a starched shirt. Chadwick felt an urge in his loins he hadn't experienced for some time.

A nurse brought his breakfast on a tray. She pointed to a bundle. "Your clothes are on the chair, Sir. They've been washed and dried. We couldn't do much with the leather things. I think they may be ruined. You can have some felt slippers for the ride to your station."

After he swallowed the porridge and sipped some tea, an elderly doctor listened with a stethoscope, ordered some deep breaths, and examined his tongue. "I think you're well enough to be discharged, young man."

The ambulance driver was told to take Chadwick to the sick bay, but en route Chadwick countermanded that and went directly to his room when they arrived at Hawkinge, and changed into a uniform, and then he walked over to the squadron orderly room. He was greeted with restrained clapping, "Hear you went for a swim, Sir."

"Yes, Sergeant. Damn cold this time of the year."

Chadwick gave the note to a clerk that the doctor in Folkestone had pressed on him. "Please give this to Doctor Lever, and on the way back, please change my flying gear for new ones." He pointed to the bag given to him by the matron. Then he went to the crew room and talked to a flight commander.

"We lost two kites including yours, Sir. One of the new pilots also parachuted from his Spit but died after he was picked up. But here's the good news. We claimed four Jerries shot down, all definitely confirmed. Your wing man, Mike, got a Dornier."

"Bravo! That's great news," Chadwick said, and then looked around. "That reminds me, Tom, where is Mike ? I have to thank him for the timely wireless call when I bailed out. He saved my bacon."

"He's around somewhere, I'll tell him you're looking for him. We're on standby at the moment. We have nine kites serviceable and pilots assigned for the next scramble. Mike isn't in this batch."

"Jolly good. When can we expect new kites?"

"Two expected this afternoon. A twelfth machine should also be repaired in a couple of hours, so we'll be back to full strength."

The scramble came an hour later, and when the planes returned, Chadwick discovered they had shot down two more Stukas and damaged a Messerschmitt, which probably crashed in the Channel but nobody saw it go down. As the dogfights developed in intensity, pilots could not afford the luxury of watching their victims go down. They had to keep a ceaseless watch on their back.

Chadwick was in the crew room after lunch when the replacement Spitfires arrived. Two planes came in low, broke sharply to the left, dropped the wheels flying downwind, and landed neatly after a curving approach. He watched the pilots climb down, and then he almost exploded.

"My God!" he said, and then ran to meet the visiting pilots, stopping in front of them as they walked toward the control tower. Both were women. "Hello, Penny," Chadwick said. "Welcome to the front lines."

The young woman in slightly grease-stained white flying overalls stopped in amazement. "Allan Chadwick! Well, you're not dead yet!" She turned to her companion. "Dorothy, this is a prewar friend of mine, Allan Chadwick. Squadron Leader, I should say. It's probably due to him I learned to fly."

"Penny, this is fantastic. Looks like you're getting in the flying hours you always wanted. Where did you fly from?"

"I'm based at Castle Bromwich, delivering Spits. Generally make two or three flights a day. You chaps keep pranging 'em." She started walking toward the tower, "Got to keep moving. ATA keeps us busy. There should be an Anson here soon to take us back."

Chadwick walked with them to the door of the tower. He grabbed Penelope's hand and pulled her toward him and gave her a kiss. "It's wonderful to see you. We must keep in touch. Remember me to your mother."

Penelope's companion stepped up to Chadwick and planted a wet kiss on his lips. "Don't I get one too?" The women walked into the tower, chuckling as they started to lightly climb the stairs.

Chadwick went back to the crew room. He was quite excited to see Penelope again, although in those heady days before the war, when they dashed about in his old Bentley, he had never found her particularly attractive.

Chadwick led a flight when the order to scramble came, forty-five minutes after he left Penelope. Mike Derbyshire was again his wing man. The dispatcher ordered the whole squadron into the air, divided into three flights of four aircraft. *There must be a whopping Jerry show heading our way*, Chadwick thought to himself.

They bored off over the Channel to 20,000 feet. The Chain Home operators had positioned the squadron perfectly—they were directed to turn north and found the German planes directly ahead and down sun.

"Tally-ho," Chadwick shouted into his microphone.

About forty Ju 88 medium bombers flew below. Chadwick was too experienced to swoop immediately onto the Germans. He knew if they could see bombers, there were fighters nearby. Staring intently he glimpsed the German fighters below and to the right. The British timing was propitious. The Germans had spotted a formation of Hurricanes climbing to attack the bombers and the escorting fighters were diving to intercept them. They were too intent to notice the Spitfires lurking up sun.

Chadwick selected a German flight leader and Mike Derbyshire focused on the leader's wing man. They caught the Germans completely by surprise, Chadwick opened fire almost directly behind his victim at a range of 300 yards. Derbyshire opened up at the same time. Both planes began to smoke and within seconds the canopy flew off Mike's target and the pilot launched himself over the side. Chadwick's target started an increasingly steep dive and disappeared from view, trailing thick black smoke.

Chadwick noticed with surprise they had crossed the coast. The sky had become full of planes milling about in seeming chaos. But the German bombers, displaying iron discipline, had maintained formation. Chadwick wondered what target they were aiming for. He knew the countryside beneath them intimately.

When he saw bombs falling, he realized the Germans were aiming at the Vickers factory at Brooklands. For the moment he could see no German fighters within range, and he chose a Ju 88 and started a curving attack. It was a deflection shot and when he saw his tracers arcing ahead of the bomber, he applied a touch of rudder and his bullets began to pepper the side of the German plane. As he crossed behind the target, the rear gunner put a long burst into his Spitfire. The gunsight and the upper part of the instrument panel disintegrated.

Chadwick felt a strong blow to his head. He found his vision was clouded over and for a panicky moment thought he had been blinded. His oxygen mask had been knocked askew. On his lips he felt the salty, metallic taste of blood. Without thinking, his left hand flew off the throttle and pushed up his goggles. With an overwhelming feeling of relief, he found he could see perfectly, but there was warm blood pouring down his right cheek. The windshield was still there but a large hole allowed a blast of air to funnel into the cockpit. He banked sharply left and then right. He could see no planes, British or German nearby. But as he peered down the tilted wing he saw a familiar sight, the airfield at Farnborough.

Then the engine began to run roughly and, as he juggled the throttle, he found he could not control the engine rpm, which refused to change. Keeping a careful eye open for a potential attacker he began a dive toward the airfield. He was moving far too fast and to regulate his speed, Chadwick turned off both magnetos, the airspeed tapered to 120 knots and he selected undercarriage down. The increased drag and the change of trim seemed to indicate the wheels had lowered and to his relief he saw two green lights. He started a curving crosswind leg, but then needed power and so he flicked on a magneto for a second. The engine gave a surge of power with a loud backfire and Chadwick concentrated on lining up and getting the airspeed below a hundred.

Things were happening too fast. He selected full flap and then realized he still needed some power and he switched a magneto on and off for a couple of seconds. The Spitfire thudded onto the runway halfway down its length, mainwheels first. Chadwick delicately squeezed the brake handle on the control column to avoid clipping the propeller, which had stopped turning. The plane stopped just before the Spitfire ran off the end of the runway.

"Not the best landing I've ever done, but as the joke goes, any landing you can walk away from is a good one," he shouted out loud. He switched off the electrics, raised the flaps, and waited for an ambulance. Blood was pouring down the side his face.

Aircraftsmen carried him into the sick bay on a stretcher, and male medical orderlies stripped off his bloody clothes and cleaned him up. A doctor examined his scalp, Chadwick was quite conscious when the doctor said to him, "Not as bad as it looks. Head wounds tend to bleed a lot. A few stitches will put you right. How do you feel, Squadron Leader?"

"My head hurts. Otherwise, never felt better."

"It looks like you were hit by glass, but your flying helmet took most of the damage. We'll shave a little hair and I'm going to add some antiseptic, which will smart, and then a few stitches. Let me know if it is too painful."

Chadwick gritted his teeth and endured. Then he was wheeled into another room where a technician x-rayed his skull. Within an hour he was tucked up in a hospital bed with a bandage that resembled an eastern turban.

"I don't see any damage beyond the scalp laceration," the doctor told him. "I'm going to give you a sleeping draught and we'll see how you feel in the morning."

The next day Chadwick awoke as sunlight streamed into his room. He felt on top of the world. An orderly entered with his breakfast on a tray. "We got a message from 613 Squadron last night, Sir. You are credited with two confirmed kills—a Messerschmitt109 and a Dornier, which crash-landed in Kent. Congratulations, Sir."

"Thank you, Airman. Please get someone to call the squadron and find the total score for the squadron and the butcher's bill."

"I'll pass that on to the adj, Sir."

Later the station adjutant stopped by. "I called your squadron, Sir. They claimed six Jerries downed in the scramble you took part in. One Spit was shot down and two badly damaged. The pilot didn't survive, I'm sorry to say. The squadron was scrambled again in the late afternoon and claimed two kills with two of the squadron aircraft damaged. One pilot wounded. You chaps are certainly giving the Jerries what for," he said with relish.

The next visitor was an old friend, Wing Commander Codrington. "Good morning, Allan. You always did like the Spitfires. I see you brought one for us."

"Good morning, Sir. Always nice to be back at Farnborough."

"The M.O. thinks you ought to stay in bed for a day or two, Allan. I'll send someone to Hawkinge to pick up your uniform, so you can join us in the mess. I think you'll recognize a few old faces."

"I don't want to tire you now, but while you're here I would love to hear about how things are on the front lines of Fighter Command."

"Thank you. I look forward to getting back on my feet."

"By the way, I called your old boss at Boscombe, Wing Commander Rowley, to let him know we had an unexpected guest and he's threatening to come over tomorrow. If you're interested, your Spit is a Cat Four. A Queen Mary is coming later to take it to a maintenance unit."

Several acquaintances from his days at Farnborough stopped by Chadwick's room to congratulate him. But by the late afternoon he felt fatigued, and even though his uniform was retrieved from Hawkinge, he stayed in the sick bay for a simple supper.

The next day Wing Commander Rowley was an early visitor. "Good morning, Allan. I just popped over in the Rapide to wish you a full recovery." Exaggerated tales of the blood-soaked cockpit of Chadwick's Spitfire had reached Boscombe. "I look forward to you rejoining us when this phase is over. Getting the Lancaster in the air is not being easy. We need your charm to deal with Avro."

"You use the word 'phase.' What does that mean, Sir?"

"The War Office believes the German air effort will die down by the end of September. Intelligence claims they can't sustain the losses they're taking for more than two months. Either the invasion will come within that period or it will never happen. Weather in the Channel in October and thereafter will be too bad and in 1941 we will be militarily too strong for the Germans to invade us. So then we'll shift to mass bombing, and we need the Lancaster for that, by the hundreds. There are a couple of items I want to bring to your attention."

"Yes?"

"The first concerns those Merlin engines you filched from Vickers. It won't be necessary to return them."

"I'm glad to hear that, Sir. It would have been a complication. What happened? Is Scotland Yard onto us?"

Rowley laughed and shook his head. Chadwick quickly said, "Dennison let Embry win at golf?"

Rowley laughed again. "You can thank your friends across the Channel. They dive-bombed the Supermarine factory at Southampton. The bay containing Merlin engines was completely destroyed. According to the paperwork, our four engines were still there."

Chadwick chuckled, "Well, it just goes to show, honesty isn't always the best policy. What was the second point you wanted to discuss?"

"The Air Ministry has ordered twenty Boeing Fortresses. They'll be delivered before the end of next year, but Boscombe will get one model for evaluation early next January. This gives us time to decide on changes to match operational expectations before the planes are constructed. Your experience with the Lancaster modifications should be helpful there."

"That sounds wonderful. Maybe there's a trip to America in it."

"I wouldn't count on it, Allan. You know those Ju 87 bombers were astonishingly accurate. The raid was surveyed by some of the Boscombe experts; the Supermarine plant was attacked by twelve planes, and all the bombs landed within a two hundred-yard circle. Results like that could never be achieved by horizontal bombing."

"That's something we should talk about when I get back to Boscombe. Although the Ju 87 is deadly, it's also deadly for its crew. How many of the twelve planes you mentioned made it back to France?"

"I don't know."

"I'll wager only nine got back, or perhaps even fewer. A well-equipped defender—someone with modern fighters—can pick off the Stuka like ducks in a shooting gallery. They're absolutely dependent on a fighter escort if they want to live. I was involved in some bombing trials when I was at Farnborough. The fundamental reason why the Stukas are so accurate is that the pilot could see the target and get very close to it. Of course, horizontal bombers must fly at great heights to avoid flak. Also, above twenty thousand feet, the maneuvering ability of an attacking fighter falls off due to the thin air. Because the ground is usually obscured, high-level bombers can never be dependent on a visual sighting. Accuracy must come some other way—I suspect with an accurate aiming system, bomber heights could easily be twenty-five or thirty thousand feet."

"I must say, Allan, you have knack of getting to the heart of a matter. What do you suggest?"

"Ah, well, that's why we need experts, like the boffins at Bawdsey who built the first Chain Home RDR. It will have to be some parallel development using wireless. Either the bomber and or the target must be located by wireless. The trick is to connect the two. These methods must be ready when the Lancaster fleets take to the air."

"It's always a pleasure talking to you, Allan. I hope you're soon mended. Please let me know when you'll be returning to Hawkinge. I'll send the Rapide."

"Thank you very much, Sir. I would appreciate that."

After lunch Chadwick found it had turned into a pleasant summer's day, and so he put on his uniform and took a walk around the Farnborough site. He was feeling rather stiff from two days in bed and the exercise was invigorating. He noticed with some surprise that air raid precautions had been taken far more seriously at Farnborough than Ringway, or even Hawkinge. Sandbags protected doorways and a couple of squat brick air raid shelters had been erected.

One fresh development that puzzled him was a two-foot square board on a post that was painted green. He passed several on his walk and then discovered by asking a civilian that the paint turned red if poison gas was detected, and then everyone was supposed to don a gas mask. In fact, he suddenly realized that all the civilians he passed had been carrying gas masks in government–issue cardboard boxes or in homemade containers.

When he returned to the sick bay the doctor examined his head, changed the bandage to a large plaster, and carried out some eye tests. He was told he could return to Hawkinge in the morning and he made a phone call to Boscombe Down to arrange a pick-up by the Rapide.

At Hawkinge he first stopped by the squadron orderly room to make his number and then visited the wing commander. He was told that the two days of his absence had been very busy. The Luftwaffe was throwing every bomber they had in a frenzied attempt to destroy the RAF. The 613 Squadron had been scrambled seven times in the two days, and were getting desperately short of pilots. Some had flown four sorties in quick succession. Two pilots were killed or missing and two severely wounded. They had been replaced by two pilots straight from flying training school.

"On the bright side," the wing commander said, "if you can call it that, you've been recommended for a gong, the Distinguished Flying Cross. Your wing man Mike Derbyshire is up for the Distinguished Flying Medal, and Tom Kirk will also get a Cross—613 Squadron has certainly earned its laurels. Congratulations on your leadership, Squadron Leader Chadwick."

"Thank you, Sir. I had better be getting back to find out just what the manpower situation is. Looks like I'll be writing a few letters."

"Before you go, Allan, I should mention that I have a friend in Air Intelligence who told me they were interested in the Ju 88 you downed over Brooklands. Apparently your shots severely wounded the pilot but he managed to crash-land and the plane is in good shape. On board they found some electrical gubbins that were being tested under battlefield conditions. It's believed to be part of a target locating system the Huns are developing. The crew is being interrogated but I think the pilot is close to death, so he won't be much help."

Chadwick found that it made him feel very sad to hear a pilot he had shot was dying. He hurried to the crew room and was greeted by some good-natured bantering about taking two days off while they were getting walloped. He laughed along with the fellows but under the humor he felt enormous tension in the room. *We are reaching some kind of limit*, he thought to himself. *These chaps are ready to explode.*

The telephone jangled loudly and interrupted his thoughts. "Two flights scramble" someone called out and a rush of bodies left Chadwick almost alone in the crew room. He saw Sergeant Derbyshire sprawled in a chair and went over to him. "Congrats, Mike, I hear you got a gong."

"Thank you, Sir," Derbyshire replied wearily. "But if this keeps up, I doubt I'll get a chance to pin it on."

Chadwick went to the office he shared with another squadron commander. The paperwork he had to deal with had accumulated while he was immobilized at Farnborough. The pilots of 613 returned in an hour. They had downed three German planes and suffered one lost, but the pilot bailed out and survived. After lunch Chadwick rounded up the two new pilots and took them to the office.

"I'm Squadron Leader Allan Chadwick. For what it's worth, I try to run 613 Squadron, although it must seem rather chaotic to you chaps. What are your names?"

"Pilot Officer John Unsworth, Sir."

"Pilot Officer Christopher Pearson, Sir."

"How much flying time do you have, John?"

"Eighty-four hours, Sir, mostly on Magisters."

"Have you flown a Spitfire?"

Unsworth replied enthusiastically, "Yes, I've had three trips. Great kite, Sir."

"And you, Chris, how much time?"

"Ninety-one hours twenty minutes; one hour, forty minutes on Spits."

"I gather you were posted straight from flying training school. You haven't been on an OTU course?"

Both the young men nodded.

"It can be dangerous up there, I want to keep you alive as long as possible, so please listen carefully. Talk to your flight commanders. Get as much advice as you can. You will fly as wing men on a leader, hang back to one side about a hundred yards and keep your eyes peeled. Your job is to keep the Jerries off your leader's tail. You'll be given a call sign. If Jerry hangs on, give your leader a shout on H.F. to break. The Spit carries a very limited amount of ammo—fifteen to twenty seconds if you keep the tit pressed, so short bursts. If you lose your leader, head for the deck and hurry home. But watch your back. Do not attempt an interception yourself. It is very difficult to hit a plane except from directly behind. So don't bother trying unless you find yourself behind a fat Ju 88, and then you can depend on it that there will be one-oh-nine on your tail. Talk to as many pilots as you can. Any questions?"

Pearson spoke up. "I have a thousand, Sir, but I assume they will all be answered when I am on a scramble."

Unsworth looked thoughtful but said nothing.

"Right-oh. Dismissed." Both men saluted and left the office.

Chadwick sighed. *The slaughter of the innocent,* he thought to himself, *and I'm the butcher*.

Next Chadwick turned to a task he had been putting off. He had to write to the next of kin of both pilots killed the day before. Neither was married but he didn't really know them personally. He was too honest with himself to write the same letter to both families and he struggled for over an hour to produce drafts that a clerk could type for him in the morning. He felt too depressed to venture into the mess for dinner, and he telephoned the mess manager to send over a sandwich and a bottle of beer.

As he walked back to his room he could hear loud singing coming from the bar. He knew that pilots stressed by war broke the tension by getting drunk. It had happened to him in Iraq. The RAF had a long tradition of drinking songs, and often the singing went on for hours without repeating. He could hear the refrain of "The Ball of Kurriemuir" and he softly sang to himself, *Four and twenty virgins came down from Inverness, and when the ball was over there were four and twenty less.*

The odd thing was that suddenly he felt a good deal more cheerful. But he knew as the night progressed the boys would get drunker and drunker and start to play mess games, which usually resulted in a lot of broken furniture. *You're only young once*, he thought, and then he couldn't stop the next thought from gathering in his mind. *A lot of these young chaps, they will never be old.* And that dispelled the cheerful mood he had felt for a moment.

The squadron was placed on standby after six a.m. and a scramble came for the full squadron at seven. Chadwick was surprised, as it was barely light. The Germans must have been gathering over France in the dark. They were ordered to make 18,000 feet. The controllers had placed the squadron a little east of a huge wave of German bombers. Scores of Messerschmitts milled above them, but the defenders had the advantage of height and the sun behind them. Chadwick decided they were probably heading for Southampton again.

The German planes were the usual mix of Junkers, Dorniers, and Heinkels but he could see no Stukas. An Intelligence Summary which had been posted on the 613 notice board stated that examination of downed aircraft showed the Ju 88 in particular was heavily armored and the cockpit and nose should be the aiming point, which was also true of the Dornier 17. Chadwick had smiled when he read that. Pilots were lucky to get a bomber in their gunsight at all, let alone select what part to aim for.

By now the Spitfires were almost on top of the Messerschmitts, Chadwick picked a plane that was leading a flight of four and dived to attack. The German was alerted at the last moment and began to dive, but Chadwick had poured three seconds of lead into him and saw pieces fly off the plane. He banked sharply and climbed. His wing man was one of the new pilots, John Unsworth, and Chadwick spared a glance to his right to see if Unsworth had stuck with him. He saw that his wing man had dropped well astern and as he watched for a second, he saw a Messerschmitt banking to get a bead on the new man.

Chadwick yelled on the H.F., "Red two, bank left." Unsworth never deviated and Chadwick saw to his horror the German plane open fire. Chadwick wrenched his plane round and lost sight of the action behind him, and seconds later he saw Unsworth's Spitfire diving steeply. He was trailing a thick black plume. "Red two bailout," he radioed. But it was to no avail. Unsworth's fighter pilot career had lasted a mere twenty-five minutes. Chadwick felt a white, blinding anger and pushed the throttle to full power to get behind another Messerschmitt.

The sky was full of planes, twisting, diving, and some going down in flames. The fighter on fighter crowd had tended to fly past the bomber stream, which was under attack from Hurricanes, but Chadwick felt bile in his stomach. He vowed to himself to send a Hun to his death in revenge for poor innocent John Unsworth.

He dived and turned so that he was facing the oncoming bombers. He chose a Dornier 17 and commenced a head-on attack. The closing speed was over 500 knots, but he kept his gunsight on the cockpit and withheld squeezing the trigger until the target filled the sight. Somewhere in the back of his mind was the thought he was behaving stupidly and he knew the front gunner on the Dornier was blazing away. But sometimes in the heat of battle man behaves irrationally.

That's how heroes are made. Chadwick pushed the trigger with all his might, and the Spitfire shivered, both from the recoil and the impact of German bullets. In a split second he had zoomed past the Dornier. The engine stopped and a stream of black oil covered the windshield.

Chadwick knew there was no chance of starting the engine. He turned off the magnetos and the fuel line. He looked through the side of the canopy, and realized he had crossed the coast and was over land. He could make out the distinctive headland at Dungeness. The Spitfire was down to 5,000 feet and descending at 400 feet a minute. Chadwick banked and looked ahead through the other side of the canopy, but his vision through the windshield was completely blocked.

The countryside ahead seemed to be fairly open. He opened the canopy and loosened the shoulder straps. By leaning over he was able to see a little past the edge of the windshield but oil was still spraying from the engine and his goggles were splattered. He ducked back inside the cockpit and re-tightened the straps.

Chadwick lowered the flaps and watched the view through the side carefully. He just prayed there was not a substantial building or tree in his path. Judging his height purely by the view from one side, he eased the stick back and glanced quickly at the air speed indicator. He was flying at seventy knots when the left wing struck a tree, spinning the aircraft round causing it to strike the ground. It skidded with a tremendous noise and stopped with its nose down in a ditch. Chadwick was shaken but unhurt. Nothing was on fire but there was a pungent smell of petrol. He had been lucky.

He unfastened the straps, dropped the side panel and climbed out of the machine. He walked to the front of the plane, and saw that the engine cowling was riddled by bullets, but the mass of the engine had protected him in the cockpit. One wing was canted up slightly, and so he sat on the leading edge at a comfortable height for his legs until some farm workers ran up and volunteered to take him to a police station.

Chadwick arrived back at Hawkinge by sunset. He was told his Dornier had been watched by the Observer Corp crashing on Romney Marsh. The squadron had downed four German planes, two bombers and two Messerschmitts. Pilot Officer Unsworth was the only casualty, although Chadwick's plane was a write-off and two other Spitfires were badly damaged.

Chadwick went to his office. Unsworth's death had deeply troubled him and he wrote a sincere letter to the young man's parents. He mentioned their son had been flying as his wing man and had given his life to ensure the Germans never got control of the airspace over England and the Channel. Then he wrote a bitter letter to the wing commander, pointing out that posting untrained pilots to front-line squadrons in the present critical battle was a death sentence.

Whether his outburst had any influence or not is unknown, but a little later the commander of Eleven Group issued orders that pilots needed at least two weeks experience at an Operational Training Unit before posting to a front-line squadron, which was little enough. Eleven Group included RAF Hawkinge and was taking the brunt of the Luftwaffe attacks on Fighter Command.

There was also concern about morale. Both pilots and ground crew were stressed to the limit as the RAF airfields were often under attack by the Luftwaffe. Pilots tried to get some rest, and ground crews struggled to repair and rearm fighters. To this end, wing commanders were told to grant forty-eight-hour stand-downs to squadrons on a rotating basis, consistent with maintaining a minimum strength available for scrambles.

Chadwick was still at his desk when the squadron engineering officer knocked on his door. "I take it, Squadron Leader, that you want rearming and refueling pit stops to be as quick as possible."

"Of course," Chadwick replied.

"Then I have a simple request—pilots must not use the oxygen in the cockpit on the 'emergency' setting."

"Explain, please."

"Pilots are going to the planes and sucking oxygen through their masks to cure hang-overs. In the normal position the masks provide oxygen when the pilot breathes in, but the chaps are breaking the thin copper wire on the switch position and shifting it to 'Emergency,' which then pumps a full stream of unregulated oxygen into the mask. They believe this will cure their hang-over affliction. But it depletes the tank in one flight, whereas with normal use a tank lasts all day. The problem is that the oxygen technician cannot refill the tank while the plane is being refueled. This adds at least fifteen minutes to a turn-around."

"I'll see what I can do, but you're asking me to debunk a long-held myth, Flight Lieutenant." And they both laughed.

Chadwick signed a few more papers and made his way to the mess for dinner. Drunken singing emanated from the bar, the scandalous words of the "Good Ship Venus" echoed in his ears as he sat down to soup and roast chicken.

T'was on the Good Ship Venus,

By God, you should have seen us.

The figurehead,

Was a whore in bed,

And the mast the captain's penis.

There was an outburst of ribald laughter and more scabrous verses followed.

When Chadwick had finished his meal the singing had died down and he pushed his way to the bar. The boys were indulging in mess games, and "High Cockoloram" was in full swing. Half a dozen chaps, head between the legs and arms around the waist of the next fellow were lined up at right angles to the wall. Another bunch was attempting to scramble on their backs and touch the ceiling. The ones underneath writhed to toss them off and there was frequently the sound of tearing cloth as shirts and jackets were ripped. Then they started to clear away tables and chairs to make a space for "Bar Rugby."

Chadwick decided this was not a good time to mention the engineer's concern about the use of oxygen. He reckoned if he opened his mouth they would have had his pants off and run up the flag pole at the entrance to the base, while ordering the guards on duty to salute them. It was a ritual he had seen inflicted in the past.

There was a heavy German raid the next day, and 613 Squadron was scrambled just after eight a.m. They intercepted a fleet of at least a hundred bombers at 15,000 feet over RAF Manston in Kent. The airfield was being bombed, but the Luftwaffe did not deviate as the fighters pressed home attacks. Chadwick thought it looked like they were heading for the London docks.

The Messerschmitts fought as tenaciously as ever, but Chadwick got a 110 in his sights and gave a long burst as it turned to evade him. He saw pieces fly off but then lost sight of his victim in cloud. The squadron returned to Hawkinge and found the field had been bombed and the hangars machine-gunned. Smoke was rising from several buildings and planes parked outside. All the pilots managed to land despite the craters, and they claimed two German fighters shot down.

Another scramble was called in the afternoon. Chadwick looked over the list of pilots available for standby and chose twelve he thought were still in good shape. But most of the pilots were showing signs of irritability and the "twitch," a slang word for combat fatigue.

The squadron climbed to 16,000 feet and ran headlong into the biggest German armada he had ever seen. The scramble had come a little late and the squadron was just able to intercept some bombers by chasing them at full throttle. German fighters fell on them like a wolf on the fold, and Chadwick had to use all his flying skills to dodge the Messerschmitts. A hasty glance behind showed he had lost his wing man sometime during the melee. At the same time, bullets thudded into his plane. So, he tried an old trick—yanking the throttle back for a second. It worked. A 109 flashed past him and he was able to trigger a short burst without any deflection the German went into a steep dive trailing smoke and Chadwick saw him crash into a field.

He was down to 10,000 feet when he noticed one fuel tank was empty. He reckoned the bullets he took had punctured the tank—fortunately, without catching fire. He recognized the countryside below and made a beeline for RAF Biggin Hill while the Merlin was still running. The airfield had been attacked and burning buildings cast a pall of smoke. *At least I know the wind direction*, he thought grimly to himself as he searched for a reasonably flat area to make a short landing. He managed to stop on the very edge of a crater, and needed some ground crew to push the machine round so he could taxi to dispersal. When a bowser came, he had them fill only the good tank, and then he took off and made the short hop back to RAF Hawkinge.

In the mess that night he listened to the BBC News, and was surprised to hear that central London had been bombed. Until then, the Germans had avoided bombing purely civilian targets. *I bet it was that crowd we attacked this morning that seemed to be heading for the docks. They must have over shot the target. The vis was pretty poor.*

Whatever the reason for the attack, the Prime Minister, Mr. Churchill, was incensed and ordered a retaliatory raid on Berlin. Wiser heads tried to dissuade him. RAF bombers could hardly reach Berlin with any kind of bomb load, and almost certainly the Germans would retaliate. Churchill prevailed, of course, and a small force of Hampden bombers made the long trip to Berlin and dropped a few bombs. Damage was slight. Some planes were lost due to enemy action, and some ran out of fuel. It was a deep psychological blow for Hitler, who demanded retaliation by bombing London. RAF Bomber Command had been carrying out raids against port facilities and for the past months had concentrated on bombing barges and tug boats being assembled in France, Belgium, and Holland for the invasion of Britain.

The RAF Fighter Command was reaching a critical point due to attrition of pilots. One day when Churchill visited RAF Uxbridge to watch the plotting board direct fighters to counter Luftwaffe attacks, he was told all available squadrons were in the air or refueling. There was no reserve to deal with additional Luftwaffe raids. The margin was that slim.

Similar emotions of confusion, frustration, and anger stalked the corridors of power in Berlin and London. Hitler was upset because he confidently expected the British to seek peace, as they were facing certain defeat. When they did not and insolently bombed Berlin, he ordered the Luftwaffe to flatten London, which caused confusion. Their priority until then had been the elimination of RAF Fighter Command. Hitler was frustrated by the British intransigence because his real desire was to attack the Soviet Union, but he needed to pacify his west flank. His generals were angry because using Messerschmitts to defend the bomber streams tied them to tactics which hampered fighting the British planes.

On the British side there was confusion because of political in-fighting among higher commanders about the best way to use Fighter Command's dwindling resources. Some favored swift attacks by rapidly assembled small flights of fighters, while others believed large wings of two or three squadrons would be more effective. There was anger in Bomber Command at the high losses suffered by attacking Berlin with inadequate aircraft.

The war as seen through Chadwick's eyes had simply co-alesced into a grim daily battle to get as many 613 planes into the air as possible when they were scrambled. Once in the air he struggled to keep inexperienced young pilots alive in the split second encounters against the blazing guns of battle-wise German pilots. On the ground the crews were weary. They had been bombed and machined gunned for weeks while try-ing to keep as many squadron planes as they could in ser-viceable condition. Chadwick himself developed a sixth sense about the competence of pilots he was flying against. Almost as soon as they made a move, he knew if he was nailing a begin-ner or a crafty old fox.

He flew his Spitfire as though it was an extension of his body. The guns seemed to fire themselves at precisely the right moment. He returned from a mission drenched in sweat and occasionally smelling of pee. Twice he had to make a forced landing with his Spitfire shot to pieces, but he miraculously avoided injury.

When the wing commander dropped into the crew room one day he was horrified at Chadwick's appearance. He had lost weight and his tension was betrayed by a slight tremor in his hands. When he spoke, Chadwick gave the impression of a man overly concerned with petty details, but he ran the squadron competently and he had downed three more planes in the past week. Bombing attacks on the airfields had almost ended as the Luftwaffe turned its attention on London. The wing commander ordered 613 Squadron to stand down for seventy-two hours.

The mess was quiet at dinner time. Chadwick ate and then decided to have a drink in the bar. No sooner had he propped himself up at the counter with a glass of bitter when there was a noisy arrival, as some pilots from another squadron marched in leading a German pilot in a muddy flying suit.

"Look what we found in jankers. This Jerry was waiting to be taken to the authorities, but we rescued him."

"What's going on?" Chadwick asked.

"Well, Sir, this chap pranged this afternoon, but he managed to evade the Bobbies for a few hours until he was caught just down the road. They put him in the jankers at the gate, but we thought he needed a drink."

"Is someone on the way to collect him?"

"Oh yes, Sir, the MPs are coming."

Chadwick looked at the young man, "Do you speak English?"

"Ja, yes, a little."

"Some beer?"

"Danke, yes."

The barman passed him a glass. "Prosit."

"What were you flying?"

"My name is Heinrich Stolz, Leutnant."

"Name, rank, and serial number, right? We are pilots, just interested in your plane."

One of the RAF pilots spoke up. "He was flying a Messerschmitt 109, and did a belly landing in a field near Standen. Then he scarpered. Bobbies found him in a hen house and left him with the guards at the gate."

Chadwick stared at Stolz with interest. He looked similar to the chaps in 613 Squadron. Then he said slowly, "Which is better, Messerschmitt or Spitfire?" and laughed.

The pilots in the bar picked up on Chadwick's question, "Yes," they shouted, "which is best, Messerschmitt oder Spitfire?"

Someone said, "Mehr besser?"

The German's face cleared. "Ach, Messerschmitt, naturlich. Viel, besser." He put his empty glass on the counter, and Chadwick signaled to the barman to give the German another.

The German took a long pull. "Danke, sie sind sehr Freundlich." And then he slowly said, "Very kind. When I here after invasion, I buy you drink."

It took a moment for his heavily accented words to sink in.

There was a roar of disapproval, and then laughter. Someone shouted, "He's got some balls."

Chadwick wondered if they were going to scrag the chap but fortunately two beefy military policemen with bright red caps and white puttees showed up at the door of the bar.

"Over here, gentlemen," Chadwick shouted. "We're just entertaining your guest."

The policemen looked at Chadwick with disapproval but saluted, grabbed the German by each arm and marched him out saying, "Thank you, Sir."

Chapter Eleven

When Chadwick awoke the next morning at the usual time of five a.m., he reviewed the day and realized he had nothing to do. The squadron was on stand down. He didn't have to order inexperienced young men into fierce air duels they were scarcely ready for. He suddenly felt as if a ten ton weight had been lifted from his shoulders. He was so unused to having spare time that after breakfast he wondered what to do. *London. That's it,* he thought. *I'll take the train to London, maybe call on Doug Larson.* He made his way to the wing orderly office and spoke to the flight sergeant in charge.

"Flight, I'm thinking of going to London for a couple of days. Is there an RAF mess you can book me in to?"

"Yes, Sir, there's a Transit Mess for senior officers on official business. "

"That should fit the bill. I'll pop into MI5 while I'm there. Where is it?"

"The 'Official Business' is not strictly needed, Sir. We can draft an order to cover you. The mess is on Horse Guards Parade, near Whitehall. I think they share a building with the Army. I'll type you a travel warrant. Don't forget your gas mask."

"Thank you, Flight. You know where to find me if I'm needed."

When Chadwick had gone, the sergeant turned to a companion in the office, "I heard the Wingco talking about his squadron on the telephone. He said 613 Squadron was near breaking point. I think the poor blighters should get a month off, not a blinking three days. That's the mob for you."

Chadwick donned a blue Gabardine raincoat and caught the train from Folkestone to London, St. Pancras Station. He took the Underground Victoria line to Green Park and walked to the RAF Transit mess from there. The weather was mild, with rain threatening. After unpacking, he called his friend Doug Larson at MI5 but when he learned Larson was unavailable, he left a message.

Walking along Whitehall, Chadwick was startled by the air raid siren. Air Raid wardens began directing pedestrians into an underground shelter. He looked at his fellow detainees. They were mostly well-dressed men, probably civil servants from the many government offices nearby. Nobody spoke. One man lit a cigarette from a match. An older man ostentatiously fumbled in the bag he carried and put on a gas mask. The silence was palpable. The only noise was the quiet murmur of a fan and the crump of exploding bombs far away.

After thirty minutes, the "All Clear" sounded. Outside, the street seemed just the same. Chadwick thought the raid must have been on the East End, near the docks.

As Chadwick was close to the offices of MI5 he decided to call in person and see if Doug Larson was now available. It turned out that he was, and he was soon sitting down with his old friend.

"What are you up to, Allan?"

Chadwick was in the process of shedding his raincoat, and as he turned, Larson cried, "Wow, Allan, you've got another medal, the DFC. Congratulations! Where are you stationed?"

"I'm at Hawkinge. Decided to come up to town for a couple of days."

"Hawkinge—it's taking a pasting, I hear." Larson took a close look at Chadwick.

"Yes, the squadron just got a three-day stand down."

"Allan, if you don't mind me saying so, you look fagged out."

"Doug, I'm running a squadron with mostly young kids. They should be in flying school, not tangling with the Luftwaffe. I don't mind telling you, Fighter Command is on its last legs, and we're desperately short of pilots. I was talking to a Jerry pilot last night—he just got shot down with his Me 109. The bastard offered to buy me a drink after the invasion. Talk about confident."

"Well, on the intelligence side, his confidence was overblown. Our experts think the time has just about passed for Hitler's invasion. Certainly by the end of September his chances are slim. MI6 tells us there is major confusion in the Luftwaffe. Their intel predicts Fighter Command is down to a handful of planes, yet the pilots complain all the bomber raids are met with swarms of British fighters. They don't know what's going on. I'll tell you one thing, our deception of RDR has really helped. The Krauts have no idea the system is so good. There's been very little bombing of RDR aerials and buildings. That caper you pulled off in Cromer in '38 has really paid off. How is Melanie, by the way?"

"I haven't seen much of her since the shooting started. Her ancient manse was taken over by the Army, so she's not too happy. And, of course, I've been tied down—first by bomber trials, and for the past few weeks, lending a hand to Fighter Command."

"We had a briefing by MI6. They have a good network in Poland. Things are very bad there. It makes you pray the Nazis will never gain our shores. In the west, the SS is killing innocent civilians by the thousands if they're Jewish. In the east, the KGB is killing politicians, high ranking officers, and intellectuals by the thousands. All in all, it's a bloodbath. Look, we've had enough of war for the moment. What are you doing tonight?"

"Nothing planned, Doug. Are you busy?"

"Nothing special. I have a vague date with a friend at her local pub. We just knock back a couple of drinks. There's usually a bit of a sing-song. Tell you what, she has a nice friend. They both work at the same office. Let's make it a foursome."

"I didn't bring any civvy clothes, Doug. You know the rules. 'In the current emergency service members must travel in uniform.' Bit of a bore."

"Don't worry, the place will be packed with Pongos. There are a lot of anti-aircraft gunners stationed nearby. I have to finish a few things before I can leave. Maybe you can look after yourself for a couple of hours and then take the Tube to Aldgate, on the Circle line. When you come out of the station, turn right into Houndsditch. Walk north about two hundred yards, and look for the Cotton Tree on the right. Shall we say half past seven?"

Chadwick left the building and walked north to the Strand and then past St. Martin in the Fields. He drifted into the National Portrait Gallery without any plan in mind but he was always fascinated by the images of great men in the past. Many had been vicious and cruel and he tried to see it in their faces, but without success. He walked back onto the street through a wall of sandbags, bought a newspaper, and settled for a quiet read and a pint of bitter at a friendly pub that wasn't too crowded. Later he ordered another pint and a plate of fish and chips. For reasons he didn't understand, that kind of food was not rationed.

The war news was not cheerful reading. With Italy in the war, Mussolini was making moves against the British in the Sudan. German submarines were sinking a lot of British merchant ships in the North Atlantic. Bombers were attacking London and other cities whenever the weather was fair, and the raids had been mostly in daylight.

It was still quite light as Chadwick fought his way along the crowded streets to the Underground. He found the Cotton Tree without difficulty and spotted Larson immediately when he entered.

Larson rose to greet him. "Allan, I want you to meet Deidre and Mary, friends of mine. Ladies, this is Allan Chadwick, one of our noble defenders."

Chadwick mumbled, "Hello." It was warm in the pub. He undid the buttons of his rain coat but did not slip it off.

"What are you drinking, Allan?"

"A pint of bitter would go down well. Thanks, Doug."

When Larson went to get him a drink, Chadwick turned to the two women. "Do you work with Doug?" he asked.

They both laughed. Mary said, "Oh, you know, Doug is a spook. We both work for the London Port Authority. We log ships in and out. When we notice a ship bound for the Caribbean or America we wish we could climb on board." They both laughed again. Chadwick noticed that both wore wedding rings and appeared to be in their thirties. Mary had a robust figure, while Deidre was slim and had a rather sallow face.

Larson returned with Chadwick's beer. "Mary was just saying she hoped to stowaway on a ship to America," Chadwick joked.

"Wouldn't we all?" Larson said. "But I think America will be in this war before long."

"It's possible," Mary answered, "but still, nobody's going to bomb them. We only have twenty miles of the Channel to keep the Germans away, but they have three thousand miles of the Atlantic Ocean on their doorstep."

"I went to the flicks last night," Deidre announced. "I saw a new Walt Disney called *Fantasia*. It was really clever and funny in parts."

"I don't care much for cartoons," Mary said, "but there's a new film due anytime with Cary Grant and James Stewart. Fancy that, two dream boats for the price of one."

"What's it called, Mary?" Doug asked.

"I've forgotten. I saw the trailer, but I can't remember the title."

"You know, Cary Grant is English," Deidre said.

"Getaway! He sounds American," Mary countered.

The two women continued to argue amicably about film actors.

Chadwick was about to say that it was months since he last saw a picture, but then changed his mind. That was an obvious opening for one of the ladies to invite him to go with her, a step he did not want to take.

Chadwick noticed his companions had emptied their glasses, and so he offered to buy a round.

"A gin and tonic for me," said Deidre, "and slice of lemon if they have it."

"A G and T is just fine. I doubt they have any lemons. They're scarce," Mary said.

"A pint of Watneys will do the trick, Allan."

Chadwick made his way to the bar, and found that it was crowded.

When Chadwick left the table, Mary said to Doug Larson, "He seems nice, your friend Allan, but he's very quiet."

"He's a deep one, Allan is," Larson told them. "Just at the moment he's under a lot of stress. He was flying only yesterday, and just got a couple of days off, so be nice to him."

"If he wants to take me home, I can be very nice to him," Mary said with a smile, and Deidre gave her a jab in the ribs, "Your hubby Jack wouldn't like that, Mary."

"Oh, but Jack would never know. We all 'ave to do our bit for the lads that are fighting for us."

Chadwick returned with drinks and shortly after, the crowd at the bar erupted in song.

We're going to hang out washing on the Siegfried Line,

Have you any dirty washing, mother dear.

Mary and Deidre joined in noisily, and Chadwick found himself humming the tune. He was tone-deaf and didn't sing well—probably the result of spending hundreds of hours sitting next to two thundering Rolls Royce engines. When all the verses and choruses were exhausted they found another tune.

Bless 'em all, bless 'em all,

The long and short and the tall.

You'll get no promotion,

This side of the ocean,

So cheer up my lads. Bless 'em all.

Many verses followed, some of which may have surprised the original composer.

The pub was getting noisy, but Chadwick found he was enjoying the camaraderie when to everyone's surprise the air raid siren started its mournful warble outside.

"That's strange," Larson said, "The Jerries generally leave us alone at night."

Chadwick glanced at the watch on his wrist. It was nearly half past nine. The barman raised his voice, "Them of you that live nearby just scoot 'ome. The rest can follow me into the cellar." He led the way to a small door underneath the staircase. "Down you go." He ushered people downstairs in single file. The cellar did not have a high ceiling and was cluttered with beer barrels. People dispersed themselves as best they could.

"I do hope this doesn't last too long," Deidre said, "It's not very nice down here, and it's going to get stuffy."

In the silence that followed they began to hear the muffled noise of exploding bombs. The explosions sounded closer and then, suddenly, there was a tremendous crash, an ear-splitting roar, and the sound of debris falling on the floor over their heads. The lights went out. It was pitch dark. Striking a match, the barman went to the stairs and shook the door at the top, it was firmly jammed. IIc struck another match. "We can get out through the loading door at the back."

Someone called, "You had better stop strikin' them matches mate. I can smell gas."

A collective moan filled the space. It was frightening in the pitch dark.

"I know my way round this place; I'll push my way to the back and get the door open."

There was the sound of people stumbling and a quiet "Sorry luv, can't see where I'm putting my feet."

A woman was quietly crying somewhere. With much jangling of iron bolts the door opened and cool air wafted into the cellar. The barman called out, "There's bricks and stuff all over the place, so be careful."

Chadwick and Larson held hands with Mary and Deidre. Outside the sky was lit by searchlights and the flash of exploding anti-aircraft shells. The air was thick with dust. In the distance they could hear the explosion of more bombs. It was difficult to make out any details, but the four of them managed to find their way by scrambling over shattered walls to the main street, which was illuminated by the headlights of emergency vehicles.

"Breathe through some cloth," Chadwick said. "Pull up your shirt or blouse."

An Air Raid Warden approached them. "It's safer off the street. I suggest you walk over to the Aldgate Tube station."

They began to walk toward the station. The street was littered with every kind of debris and hoses from the fire engines. Water gushed from a shattered fire hydrant.

Chadwick cocked his ear toward the sky. "I think the aero engine noise is getting weaker, so maybe the Jerries are finished for tonight." Just as he said that, a building a few yards away erupted with a violent explosion, throwing them all off their feet. Missiles of brick and glass flew over them. Chadwick levered himself up; his ears were ringing.

Larson stood. "My God, where did that one come from?" he asked.

"Delayed action," Chadwick replied. "Let's help the ladies up." Mary staggered up but Deidre lay supine, a rapidly growing pool of blood gathering under her body.

Mary ran over to Deidre, "Oh, Jesus Christ, love, what's the matter?"

Chadwick seized Deidre's shoulders and gently turned her over. A gaping wound in her left arm, near the shoulder, was pumping out deep red blood. "Doug, go find some first aid people as quickly as possible. We need an ambulance. I'll put a tourniquet on her arm."

He searched around for a second, looking for some cord, and then with a cry pulled the belt out of his raincoat, dropped to his knees and wrapped a few turns on Deidre's arm above the ragged wound. He drew it tight and was gratified to see the blood flow slow down. But she had already lost a lot of blood. There was a pool on the pavement, slowly running toward the grid.

Within a few minutes Larson was back, "How is she?"

"Not good, Doug. She's lost a lot of blood. I have the flow under control but she needs urgent medical attention. Is there an ambulance coming?"

"Allan, it's chaos back there, but I pulled rank. I have a Metropolitan Police warrant card, so an ambulance will be here as soon as possible."

They waited half an hour. Mary was getting distressed at the delay. Deidre never regained consciousness. Finally, they heard the clanging of the ambulance bell and Larson stepped into the road to flag it down. Two men quickly loaded Deidre onto a stretcher. One of them asked Larson if he knew who she was. He quickly wrote down her name on a roll of sticking plaster and taped it to her good wrist. "Helps them in the Accident Clinic," he explained.

"Where are you taking her?" Larson asked.

"Royal London Hospital, Whitechapel Road, mate."

Larson shouted to Mary, "Did you get that?"

She nodded affirmative.

He turned to Chadwick. "Mary will look after you. I'm going back in the ambulance. I think the Tube is out here, but I should get something further north. Keep in touch."

He told the ambulance driver he would ride in the back. When the man looked dubious, Larson produced his warrant card again. Bell clanging, the ambulance slowly made its way through the littered street.

Chadwick turned to Mary. "Looks like we're on our own. Let's just go the Underground station and see if trains are running." As he spoke the "All Clear"' sounded, and soon people who had been sheltering in the Underground station came bustling round the corner. At the station, a policeman confirmed the trains were not running on the Circle line, as the electricity supply had been cut.

"What now?" Allan said to Mary. "Looks like I am in for a hike." The thought depressed him. He was feeling fatigued after the excitement of being bombed and then tending to Deidre.

"You must come to my place," Mary said. "I only live a few streets away. Besides, you look a total mess. You need cleaning up."

She was right. His trousers and Mackintosh were soaked in blood. His face was covered with ash and soot. "All right, Mary," he said, "lead the way."

Within minutes, they climbed a flight of steep stairs to a small flat. It basically had two rooms—a bedroom and a kitchen and dining area, as well as a tiny bathroom.

"I'll get a fire going," Mary said as she entered. She flicked a switch but the lights did not come on. "No elec," she said, "but we have candles. While I light the fire you get those bloody clothes off. Cold water will get the blood out if it's fresh." She lit a couple of candles and in the dim light passed an old dressing gown to Allan. He sat in a battered arm chair in front of the fire she had started.

"Here, Luv." Mary passed a warm bottle of beer.

"Thanks, just the thing, Mary."

She dumped his trousers and Mackintosh in a large sink and scrubbed vigorously with soap powder. "At least, they haven't shut the water off," she said cheerfully.

When she was satisfied with results of the washing, she pulled a mangle from a recess under a shelf and squeezed Allan's clothes. Next she unfolded a small clothes rack and draped his clothes so that they got some heat from the fire. "They'll be dry in the morning," she announced, "I'll run an iron over them before I go to work, we should have the elec back by then."

Mary fetched another bottle of beer and settled in the only remaining chair. "Now we can relax."

"It's very nice of you to look after me, Mary," Allan said. "What happens now? I got the impression you were married."

"Oh, aye, chained for life," Mary replied with a laugh. "My hubby, Jack, works for a company that repairs ships. He was an artificer in the Andrew and retired after twenty years in '36. At the moment he's in Scotland working on submarines. He wouldn't mind you being here. He's used to my little ways."

"Such as?"

"Well, I think I can be frank with you. A man who faces death every day must be wise to the ways of the world."

Chadwick couldn't imagine what she was referring to, but he said nothing.

"Well, when he met me I was making a few quid on my back. I was never a street-walker," she said with emphasis. "I knew a lot of gentlemen, mostly on the older side, who just needed a little pokey now and then without the expense of a wife."

Chadwick still remained silent.

"They were dears. They did it to convince themselves they were still young. I had to help them along a bit, sometimes, you know, a little play-acting." She paused for a minute, "Times were hard. Jack didn't always have work, and as they say, two can live as cheaply as one."

Chadwick finished his beer, "I'll just use the bathroom to get my face clean, I look a mess."

"I'm afraid there is no hot water in the tap, I could warm up some in a pan over the fire if you like."

"Not necessary. I'll just be a minute."

Chadwick retired to the small bathroom, which just had room for a hip bath, a sink, and a toilet. When he returned to the kitchen, Mary rose and went into the bathroom. He heard water splashing about and the flush of the toilet. When she returned she was stark naked. "Brrr, it's cold even with the fire, I'm going to bed."

Chadwick studied her. Mary was well-built but by no means fat. She had gorgeous bulbous breasts without any sag. She caught him looking at her, "Well, what do you think? Not bad for a woman on the wrong side of thirty! Come on, Allan." She took his hand and went into the bedroom, "I won't bite you."

She led the way holding a candle, which threw the small room, dominated by a large double bed, into romantic shadows. Chadwick hesitated. It crossed his mind that he had never made love to a self-professed tart before. But then the excitement caused by the bombing and the alcohol he had drunk inflamed his mind and he thought, *She's probably satisfied any erotic fantasy a man can have. She'll probably do anything.*

He eagerly climbed next to her underneath a heavy, homemade quilt.

"Allan," Mary whispered, "just give me a little massage, you know, turn me on." She moved his hand to her crotch, and he kissed her beasts. They had both been celibate for a long time and their love-making was passionate.

Eventually they fell into a deep sleep. Mary slipped out of bed as soon as it was light. She went into the kitchen, found that the power was back and ironed Chadwick's clothes. She stirred up the dormant fire and crept back into bed. A suggestive whisper into Allan's ear aroused his dormant fire. They both enjoyed a tumultuous climax and then Mary looked at the clock on the dresser, "Oh, God, it's late. Allan, you need a shave. There's a razor in the bathroom. I'll get you some hot water."

Chadwick found the razor in the bathroom was a cutthroat. He had watched his father use one, but he had always shaved with a safety razor. He stroked the razor against a leather strap, hanging from the wall, as he had seen his father do. He stirred some soap in a mug, lathered his face and gingerly scraped off the whiskers.

When he went into the kitchen Mary had the table set for breakfast. "Not much to eat, I'm afraid, love. I'll make some toast. Pour yourself a cuppa."When they both left together thirty minutes later, Mary pressed a piece of paper into Allan's hand, saying, "There's my name and address. I don't have a telephone, of course, but I've put down the number at work."

At the Aldgate station they both got on the Circle line train heading west. Mary left at Tower Bridge with a squeeze of Allan's hand. Chadwick disembarked at Westminster and walked to the RAF mess on Horse Guards. He decided to retreat back to Hawkinge that very day; London was just too exciting.

Chapter Twelve

Chadwick arrived at RAF Hawkinge in time for lunch. In the mess he ran into the wing commander, who said, "Hello, Allan, I heard you had gone up to London. Back so soon?"

"London was just a bit too much, Sir. I was in a pub last night when we were bombed. Later a friend was badly hurt by a delayed action bomb."

"Yes, one of our squadrons was vectored onto that raid. It was getting late, just before ten was it?"

"Yes, that's the one. Quite a frightening experience, actually."

"Things are changing, Allan. Please stop by my office after lunch."

Once Chadwick was sitting with the wing commander, his superior said, "A few things we must discuss. First off, 613 is going to be rotated, going back to Ringway, I think. It has taken a beating. Should be quieter up there. I've been informed your personal score is ten confirmed, a double ace, Allan. Congratulations. You'll receive a bar to your Distinguished Flying Cross. You've done brilliantly.

"But the time has come to send you back to Boscombe. Rowley tells me they are truly up to their necks; the Lancaster is reaching an advance stage of construction and they expect to receive a model of the new American bomber, the Fortress, soon. But the thing that has Rowley on edge is an intelligence discovery that the Jerries are using some kind of radio beam to position their bombers over the target. This must be thoroughly investigated and methods invented to defeat it.

"In addition," he said, "the boffins must produce a British version for Bomber Command which must be jam proof. "

"Hmm, that's quite a list, Sir."

"That's not all. I'm afraid higher authority is fighting for your body. Wing Commander Codrington has formally asked for your posting back to Farnborough. Your combat role with 613 Squadron in the past two months and your past experience with the development of RDR make you a prime candidate for the program to develop an RDR system for night fighters. Intelligence has got Churchill really concerned that night bombing is going to be the priority of the Luftwaffe over winter. He is worried that prolonged night-time bombing will break civilian morale."

"Do I have any say in my future?"

"You know the service, Allan. The RAF tells you what your duties are and you do your best. I think in this case a friendly talk with wing commanders Codrington and Rowley may be helpful once you've decided in your own mind what would be the best way for you to make a contribution to this war—which, I suspect, is going to last a long time."

"Thank you very much, Sir, for the background chat. Forewarned is forearmed, they say."

"One last thing. Do you have a recommendation for someone to take over the squadron?"

"Tom Kirk has been a good flight commander. I can recommend Tom without reservation."

Two days later, 613 Squadron reassembled. Chadwick addressed the pilots in the crew room.

"Welcome back, chaps. Hawkinge has been busy while we were away, but I'm told the Jerries are bombing London instead of RAF bases. And I can personally testify that they're trying—I was bombed out of a pub on the first night of my leave. So I owe them one for the pint I lost. We have twelve functional Spitfires and I believe we've been joined by three new pilots. So we're not far from full strength. I would like to talk to the newcomers after this meeting. Any questions?"

Several pilots mentioned routine matters but nobody raised the question that was on everyone's mind—when would the squadron be posted back north? Chadwick walked to his office and asked the new members to join him. "Sorry I don't have enough chairs. Just sit on the desk. Please introduce yourselves."

A tall fair-haired young man volunteered first. "Pilot Officer Roy Cummings, Sir." Chadwick nodded his head at the man sitting next to Cummings. "Pilot Officer Fred Latham, Sir." The third pilot was a short stocky man with black hair, combed back from his forehead. "Sergeant Bill Huntley, Sir."

"Did any of you attend an Operational Training Unit?" They all shook their heads. "Are you all familiar with the operation of the guns and use of the reflector sight?" They were all silent. "I'll put it another way—who has not fired the guns on a Spitfire?"

They all spoke at once. None of the three had ever fired the guns. Chadwick swore to himself. The RAF was sending lambs to the slaughter.

"Mr. Cummings, how much time on Spits?"

"Three hours, ten minutes, Sir."

"Fred?"

"Two hours, forty-five minutes, Sir."

"Bill?"

"Two hours, thirty minutes, Sir."

Chadwick sighed. "You all need a little more training before I send you up to defend the King's realm. I'll arrange for you to fly with your flight commanders when the squadron is not on standby. That will include some gunnery practice over the Channel. Thank you, that will be all for the moment."

Next Chadwick talked to the two flight commanders. He mentioned the deplorable lack of experience of the new pilots and suggested that they send the new men up with more experienced pilots to engage in some mock dogfights, and blast off a few bullets into the sea. "Make sure they know how to turn on the arming circuit," he added, sarcastically.

Chadwick was still haunted by the fate of Pilot Officer Unsworth, who was killed only minutes after the start of his first operational flight while flying as his wing man. He decided to try something different. Instead of the new pilots protecting the tail of his flight leader, Chadwick decided he could protect their tail. A few days later, the flight commanders told Chadwick that the newcomers were as ready as they would ever be for a scramble. With only fourteen pilots to choose from, a full squadron scramble was flown by pilots who were dog-tired.

The next day Chadwick arranged for the three new men to fly with him as flight leader. They gathered by a fighter at the dispersal. "Please pay close attention, gentlemen. You are flying in Red Flight, the squadron call sign is 'Bathtub.' I am Red One. Huntley you're my wing man, Red Two. Formate on my left; two hundred yards' clearance. Cummings, formate on my right—Red Three, two hundred yards' clearance. Latham, you formate on Cummings, same distance, Red Four. Arm your guns after take-off.

"My plan is to attack the bombers. They're slower and not as maneuverable. I'll lead the flight toward a suitable group of bombers. This will certainly attract the attention of the Jerry fighters. They'll attack us from astern. You fellows are my bait. When I judge it right, I'll pull up and fall back momentarily. I will call 'Red Attack' on H.F. Huntley, you stay with me. We should be able to down the Jerry on the tails of Red Three and Four, who will attack the bombers. Try to shoot from line astern of your target—remember your guns are harmonized for four hundred yards. Aim slightly high if closer. If you're curving in, lead the target on the gunsight rings.

"It'll all be over in a few seconds," Chadwick concluded. "We'll try to reformate, but watch your backs. If you lose me, head for home. Any questions?"

There was a clamor of questions from the three pilots. When Chadwick thought they understood his plan he wished them luck and told them to wait in the crew room for a scramble.

The scramble came at ten o'clock. The sky was bright with high cloud. A large raid was developing with London as the target again. The German planes were heading northwest at a height of 12,000 feet. Numerous fighters flew above the fleet. Several RAF fighter squadrons were already vectored onto the raiders when 613 Squadron joined the fray. Spitfires had been ordered to engage the protective German fighters, but Chadwick made a beeline for a neat line of Heinkel 111 twin-engined bombers.

As he expected, the fighters above peeled toward the Spitfires. Chadwick kept a sharp look-out behind Red Flight. Praying that his judgment was right, Chadwick called 'Red Attack' on H.F. and simultaneously chopped the throttle for a second and pulled back on the stick. The plane dropped fifty knots of speed and climbed 500 feet in a second. Red Two was not so quick and zoomed ahead for a moment until Huntley collected his wits.

The attacking Germans were also caught by surprise and an Me 110 on Huntley's tail flashed in front of Chadwick. He put the nose down slightly, jammed on full throttle and for a couple of seconds poured lead into the Messerschmitt. Then, to Chadwick's surprise, he saw Red Two was in a good firing position and Huntley's guns belched smoke and tracers as he fired on the same plane that Chadwick had attacked seconds before. The Messerschmitt burst into flame and dived steeply.

Chadwick was impressed. He throttled back a touch so that Red Two could reformate. He then saw that Red Three and Four were engaged with more Me 110s and flew as fast as he could to help his team mates. When the Germans saw more Spitfires joining the scrum, they rapidly disengaged and climbed back to protect the bombers.

Chadwick led his flight to engage the Heinkel 111s. They had just a couple of minutes before they would be flying over the coast and leaving defense up to the anti-aircraft batteries. The gunners on the bombers kept up a continuous barrage of fire as the British fighter drew near and Red Three started to trail a stream of fluid. Chadwick decided they had done enough for beginners and ordered the flight home on H.F. Within a minute, Red Three reported he was overheating and Chadwick told him to land at Manston, which was clearly visible. He led the other three Spitfires back to Hawkinge.

When Huntley and Latham climbed down from their planes, clearly highly excited, Chadwick told them they had been 'bloodied,' and congratulated Huntley on his first kill.

The daylight attacks by the Luftwaffe on London began to taper off, and the number of night-time raids increased. By the end of summer the raids were occurring nightly, and the newspapers began referring to them as the "Blitz." The RAF had no effective night fighters at that time, so RDR could only warn the anti-aircraft gunners that a raid was approaching and alert the ARP wardens at the predicted target cities.

Fighter Command began to rebuild its strength, and 613 Squadron was now rarely scrambled as the days grew shorter. The wing commander personally announced the promotion of Tom Kirk to Squadron Leader, the new commander of 613. Squadron Leader Chadwick was warmly praised for his leadership and was posted back to RAF Boscombe Down. But before he left Hawkinge, 613 Squadron laid on a rousing sing-song in the bar. Other squadrons joined in and mostly everyone got drunk. Within a week, 613 squadron was relocated to RAF Ringway.

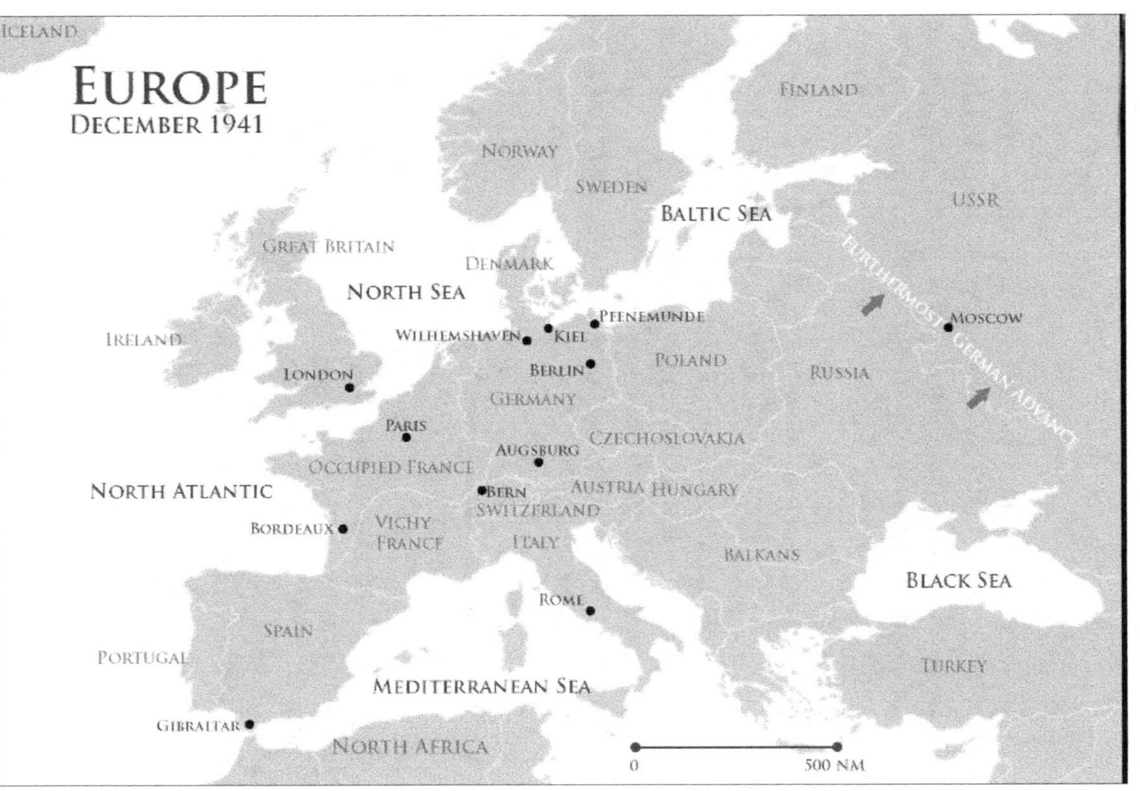

EUROPE
DECEMBER 1941
ICELAND
NORWAY
SWEDEN
FINLAND
BALTIC SEA
USSR
GREAT BRITAIN
DENMARK
NORTH SEA
IRELAND
WILHELMSHAVEN
KIEL
PEENEMÜNDE
MOSCOW
FURTHERMOST GERMAN ADVANCE
LONDON
BERLIN
POLAND
RUSSIA
PARIS
GERMANY
AUGSBURG
CZECHOSLOVAKIA
NORTH ATLANTIC
OCCUPIED FRANCE
BERN
SWITZERLAND
AUSTRIA HUNGARY
BORDEAUX
VICHY FRANCE
ITALY
BALKANS
BLACK SEA
PORTUGAL
SPAIN
ROME
GIBRALTAR
MEDITERRANEAN SEA
NORTH AFRICA
0
500 NM
TURKEY

Chapter Thirteen

Chadwick left Fighter Command with very mixed emotions. He knew the battle for air superiority over the Channel was of supreme importance, but he was sickened by the sacrifice of improperly trained pilots, thrown into air battles they frequently did not survive. Chadwick owed his life to his wide experience with the Spitfire, his years of flying and, of course, a little luck. He had been wounded twice, but he emerged with a stellar record—the Distinguished Flying Cross medal with bar.

Wing Commander Rowley, Chadwick's immediate superior at Boscombe, offered him the chance of two weeks leave, which he turned down. In his heart he yearned for Melanie, and could not bear the thought of two weeks adrift and alone without her companionship.

When they discussed the proposal from Farnborough that Chadwick assist in the development of night fighters, he expressed his feeling that the offensive phase of the war would soon be starting and for a while would be carried by Bomber Command. Chadwick knew that the equipment and size of the command were inadequate. His hope was to help get the Lancaster in operation as soon as possible and to help with development of electronic bombing aids to improve accuracy. Rowley suggested that he talk to the boffins in Air Intelligence about their investigation of German bombing raids involving wireless beams.

One afternoon he caught the train at Salisbury and traveled to London to meet Doug Larson, whom he had last seen in the middle of a fierce bombing raid on London. As usual, they met at a pub, and Chadwick asked after Deidre, who had been wounded by flying debris when a bomb exploded near them.

Larson said she was recovering and he was reminded to put his hand in his pocket and pull out a belt. "This is yours, I think, Allan. The doctors took it off of Deidre's arm at the hospital, and said it probably saved her from bleeding to death. I had it cleaned up—it was somewhat bloody."

"Thanks, Doug. Now the heat is off a bit, what's the word at MI5 about our trick with RDR?"

"I'm not directly involved in that aspect, Allan, but the word from MI6 is that the Luftwaffe is totally puzzled by the number of defending fighters, but has not linked that to RDR. So it looks like our deception worked."

"I think they'll figure it out soon, but it certainly bought us precious time. Now I want to touch on a new topic. Has Intelligence any whiffs of a German scheme using wireless waves to improve bombing accuracy?"

"Not my field, old boy, but I'll ask around. Tell me, how did you get on with Mary after I left in the ambulance? I was sorry to leave you but we have standing orders in MI5 to report to HQ when a raid develops. Some higher-ups believe spies on the ground are in touch with the bombers. Frankly, I doubt it. That's rather like standing in front of a firing-squad to improve their aim."

"Mary was very hospitable and let me stay at her place because the Tube had stopped."

"And...?"

Chadwick said nothing. They discussed inconsequential matters and Chadwick caught the train back to Boscombe. London was bombed most nights consecutively and he saw no point in staying in town.

However, two days later, Wing Commander Rowley ordered him back to London. He had been in touch with Air Intelligence, part of the Air Ministry, and had arranged for Chadwick to be briefed on what they knew so far about German schemes to improve bombing accuracy. Chadwick made his way to Whitehall and sat down with another RAF officer, Squadron Leader Trevor Morgan, a trim, precise sort of man, with no wings on his tunic. He was what aircrew disparagingly called a "wingless wonder."

After mutual introductions, Morgan looked at the ribbons on Chadwick's uniform and said, "Looks like you have had a fairly hot war so far, Allan."

Chadwick was dismissive. "Short posting to Fighter Command in the recent brouhaha. They hand out gongs if you save enough stamps."

Morgan laughed. "I understand Boscombe is interested in German wireless bombing systems. Well, we're just coming to grips with it from the examination of downed bombers, interrogation of crew and decrypts from the 'Y' service. It's early days, but something is going on, which we hope to pinpoint. One of our chief boffins, Dr. B.G. Smith—known to everyone as 'BG'—gave a briefing to the War Cabinet two days ago on this topic. Sorting it out was given a high priority by Mr. Churchill."

"Please give me a reasonably technical summary of what you know, Trevor."

"We only know part of the system. It consists of a wireless beam that crosses the target. It can be adjusted in azimuth at the aerials, which are in Belgium or France, so that different targets can be illuminated. The Jerries only turn it on just before a raid, so it's hard for us to find in the time available."

"But to provide any accuracy the beam must be very narrow. I understand from my technical friends that it's impossible to achieve," Chadwick said.

"With one aerial that's true. The Jerries are clever. They use two aerials, each broadcasting a signal on the same frequency. They're set up so the beams from each aerial overlap very slightly. Each beam is modulated so that a pilot flying in the intersection area hears a steady tone, but left or right of the intersection the receiver gets a series of dots or dashes. This tells the pilot which way to turn to get the steady tone. The area of the steady tone is narrow, quite adequate for good bombing accuracy. Pilots discussing it among themselves call it 'Knickbeine' in German—which best translates into 'Dogleg'."

"That's ingenious! But the area of steady tone only provides a line, a plane could be anywhere on that line."

"True. I was describing what we know at the moment. To define a fixed point requires a cross-bearing on the 'Dogleg' beam. We haven't detected the cross-bearing beam, but it must exist. The pilots talking to each other, not knowing we have wired a microphone in the room, call it 'X apparatus' or 'X marks the spot.' 'BG' has calculated that a plane exactly at the 'X' point could be within two hundred yards of the targeted geographical position."

"Thank you, Trevor. Let me think about this for the moment." Chadwick sat silently for a spell.

Morgan broke his reverie. "How about some tea while you're thinking?"

"Grand! Milk and sugar, please." Morgan went to the door and whispered to someone on the other side. An older woman in a floral frock knocked within a minute and entered with a tray bearing tea things.

Morgan poured a cup for Chadwick and one for himself.

"As I understand the system, Trevor, it only provides an accurate release point for the bombs, just like bombing on a perfectly clear day. Any errors accumulating after the bombs leave the plane are still present."

"You're quite right, old chap, but compared to our experience so far that's an enormous improvement. Photographs taken after raids by Bomber Command show they're lucky to get the bombs on the right city, let alone the desired target. And, in its defense, 'Dogleg' works at night and in bad weather."

"This also means the proponents in Bomber Command of celestial navigation are talking through a cocked hat. After all, they fly for another ten or fifteen minutes after the navigator takes his sights before he can calculate the fix. They're lucky to be only a few miles off!"

"Quite so. Our work has two objectives—one, to understand the Jerry system and find out ways to fool it, and two, design a better system for Bomber Command knowing the weaknesses in the Jerry method."

"Clearly, intelligence has to complete the investigation of 'Dogleg' and 'X Apparatus' and then come up with a defense, probably involving the Telecommunications Establishment and the RAF. On the other hand, Boscombe has to stay in touch while devising a bombing system for us. My own feeling is that an adaptation of the Jerry method won't work. The range to German targets is much greater than the range for the Luftwaffe to British targets. But the experts will decide. The main thing is to get moving on this as soon as possible."

Morgan pressed Chadwick to join him for lunch, but Allan begged off, pleading pressure of work. He was back at Boscombe in time to speak to Wing Commander Rowley the same day. Chadwick described the information he had gleaned from the intelligence people. He stressed it was in the early days and there was still a lot to discover about the German bombing aid. Nevertheless, it was time to get the technical staff at Boscombe fully immersed in the problem.

Chadwick pointed out the solution for Bomber Command would involve operations planners, experienced crews, and navigation experts. He suggested that he pay a visit to an operational bomber wing to get their input, based on raids conducted to date. Rowley agreed and Chadwick called his friend Wing Commander Harris at RAF Church Fenton.

It took several days before Chadwick could arrange a flight to Church Fenton when the squadrons based there were not engaged in operational sorties. The Rapide dropped him off one overcast afternoon and he signed in at the officers' mess. He met Wing Commander Harris in the bar before dinner.

"When I last saw you, Wing Commander, I had flown up the first Lancaster for your inspection. At the time you were pessimistic about daylight ops with the Wimpy. How is it going with the night-time raids?"

"Obviously, our losses are way down, perhaps on average two or three percent loss per raid. Very sad to lose anyone, but the higher-ups think just in terms of numbers, not young men, and they term it sustainable. I think we sank a fair number of tugs and barges intended for the invasion. On the other hand, the photos taken after raids show that we don't do much damage to facilities on the land."

"I hate to be persistent, Wing Commander, but is that because the bomb load was too light? Or you didn't find the target?"

"I would say a combination of both. That's what gripes me about our losses. We're losing good men but not achieving much."

"Boscombe is working hard to get hundreds of Lancasters into service. That will go a long way to solving the bomb load problem. But it's the second of your concerns that I'm involved with now, how to find the target. I hope while I'm here I can get a feeling about that from the crews."

"We're not flying tomorrow. How about if I arrange for you to meet several experienced crews? And in the meantime, how about some dinner?"

As Harris and Chadwick ate together, they talked about inconsequential matters—officers' mess ethics prohibited discussion of religion, the war, politics, and ladies.

In the morning, Chadwick sat down with three bomber crews. Between them, they had flown fifty-seven sorties. The first topic was enemy defense. Fighters hadn't been a problem on the night raids, but flak could be accurate. A pilot asked if the Germans had RDR, and Chadwick said he would look into that. One pilot made the comment that ack-ack was considerably more accurate if a plane was caught by two searchlight beams. This suggested the searchlights were linked to a central control, once the vertical angle of the lights was known, simple trigonometry would yield the plane's height, thus enabling the fuse for the shells to be accurately set. Chadwick made a note to follow up on that tidbit.

He then asked the men about navigation en route. All navigators were trained to calculate celestial fixes using the moon and stars. The general feeling was that this technique was of little value. One navigator said that the intensity of anti-aircraft fire was a better guide. From previous trips, crews learned what parts of the route were dangerous. All bomb aimers agreed that intense anti-aircraft fire made a farce of accurate targeting—pilots weaved to avoid areas full of bursting shells, which were always the heaviest directly over the target.

One pilot suggested, tongue in cheek, that perhaps Squadron Leader Chadwick should fly with them on the next raid. Chadwick turned the idea over in his mind and said that wasn't a bad idea. The crews clapped and stamped their feet.

"When's the next raid?" Chadwick asked.

"We're down for tomorrow night if the weather cooperates," Harris replied. "The moon is past first quarter and rises about sixteen, GMT. That should give us some moonlight between ten and midnight. Usually ports are selected under those conditions. Navigation is helped by reflection off the water."

"I'm on," Chadwick exclaimed. "Do you have a Wellington for me?"

"If you're serious, Squadron Leader Chadwick, I'm sure we can find one lying around for you. You'll need a volunteer crew—I'll work on that."

The next day, the destination for the next raid, as announced by Bomber Command, 452 Squadron, based at Church Fenton, was to attack the docks at Wilhelmshaven. Take-off was set to 1915 GMT, aircraft to navigate individually. Chadwick was introduced to his crew—the navigator, Flying Officer Charles (Chuck) MacIntosh; flight engineer, Flight Sergeant Tony Spinrad, who also manned a machine gun; the bomb aimer, Sergeant Bill Sharpton; wireless operator Sergeant John Kelsey (Sparks); and two turret gunners, very young leading aircraftsmen.

Chadwick dressed carefully for the flight. He drew extra clothes from stores and started with two layers of underclothes. He knew it would be bone-chilling sitting for hours at high altitude. The crew attended a briefing at 1400 hours. Navigational details, timing, and position of flak batteries were discussed at length. A hearty meal was laid on for 1700 hours. After that, crews collected flying gear, parachutes, and rations for the trip.

After a last minute trip to the toilets, the crews began to board their aircraft. Many carried lucky charms and peed on the tailwheel, a ritual good luck gesture. The plane's interior had originally been painted black, but the plane displayed the wear and tear of many missions. Bare aluminum showed where men had squeezed their way in the narrow fuselage. Movement was further hampered by long belts of machine gun bullets for the guns.

Shortly after the sun set, the tower fired a Very flare; time to start engines. In a sequence which had been explained at length in the afternoon briefing, the twenty-four planes began to taxi to the operational runway. The weather was clear, with a light southwest wind. The noise on the ground was tremendous, with the roar of forty-eight Pegasus radial engines and the shrieks from the brakes. Chadwick detected a brittle cheerfulness in his crew as they plugged into the intercom and checked their microphones.

At 1915 hours, another Very flare signaled the start of a rolling take-off. Chadwick carefully counted, and when it was his turn he followed the navigation lights of the plane ahead, checked both engines, and waited the allotted time before pushing both engines to full power. He climbed at about 800 feet a minute. Chuck MacIntosh started his dead reckoning plot and passed the initial course to Chadwick. The blacked-out countryside displayed few lights but the waterways and lakes glowed softly in the moonlight. After thirty minutes, the navigator announced they had crossed the coast. Chadwick turned off the navigation lights and told the gunners to fire a few rounds. He adjusted George, the automatic pilot, to hold 15,500 feet, and set the compass heading given to him by the navigator.

The crew was now facing a leg of about 200 nautical miles over the North Sea. The navigator announced they should see the coast in little over an hour. After twenty minutes the navigator carried a bubble sextant to the small astro dome and took some sights on the stars and the moon. The delicate knobs were icy cold and the navigator wore silk gloves. He then retired to his desk, pulled down the copious tables from the shelf and began to calculate their position at the time of the sight. When he had a fix computed, he compared it to the dead reckoning position and calculated a new correction for the wind. When the navigator passed the amended heading to the skipper, he suggested that the initial approach would be over the sea, which minimized anti-aircraft fire.

Chadwick asked to see a more detailed chart of Wilhelm-shaven, as he knew it was a major Kriegsmarine port. After some thought, he suggested they make a landfall south of the town, turn north parallel to the docks, and release the bombs as they crossed the port. And then they would head for home.

The plane droned on through the night. A gunner brought Chadwick a cup and a thermos, and he poured some hot tea. Chadwick unclipped his mask and shouted his thanks over the roar of the engines. The gunner passed over half a bar of Cadburys Fruit and Nut Chocolate. As Chadwick sipped the tea and crunched on the chocolate, he realized he could just make out searchlights ahead. He alerted the navigator, who came forward for a look through the windscreen, and then suggested a few degrees turn to the left.

Within minutes, flak and fires on the ground were visible. Shells began to explode around them. They couldn't hear the noise above the engines unless it was a near miss, which scattered shrapnel through the fabric sides of the fuselage. They flew down the east side of Jade Bay and ran into plenty of flak from anchored ships. Turning west, the Wimpy made a landfall south of the town.

Over the shoreline, Chadwick headed north and ordered the bomb bay doors open. The bomb aimer confirmed the course was good and the target was in the field of view of the bomb sight. The plane was rocked by flak exploding nearby. A particularly loud explosion under the left wing caused the Wimpy to violently bank right, but Chadwick quickly corrected. The left engine began to backfire and run roughly. The bomb aimer swore over the intercom yelling, "Hold her steady, steady … bomb's gone!" The laboring plane leapt skywards as 2,000 pounds of bombs plummeted earthwards.

Chadwick ordered the doors closed. "Flight Sergeant Spinrad," he said, "can you do anything with the port engine?"

"I'm trying, Skipper."

Chadwick increased power on the right engine. They were now over the sea and the flak diminished. He called over the intercom, "Keep your eyes peeled for fighters. Now the guns have stopped, this is their chance. Sparks, send the 'mission accomplished' signal."

The engineer spoke on the intercom, "Skipper, I think we have a leak in the left tank and the feed to the left engine. I'm transferring fuel to the right tank. I suggest feathering the left prop."

Chadwick acknowledged and spoke to the navigator. "Chuck, calculate fuel use to the nearest RAF base, please." As he spoke, a stream of bullets ripped through the plane and the rear gun turret burst into life, followed a second later by the front turret. Chadwick barely saw the fighter as it flashed by on the left. What caught his eye were the flames from the exhaust. "Any casualties?"

The navigator came back calmly, "Our best bet is Leconfield. If we're still flying, we can press on to Church Fenton, but that's another ten minutes. I think Sparks was hit by that gunfire. Here's the course to Leconfield—two eighty-nine, magnetic. When things settle down I'll calculate the time using the lower ground speed. Tony is looking after Sparks."

"Spinrad here. Sparks has had it. Gone for a Burton. Severe wound in the chest. We have a hundred, forty-five gallons remaining."

"This is MacIntosh. I calculate with ground speed of one hundred and twenty knots, we should sight the coast in one hour, fifty-five minutes. We're using forty-five gallons per hour. Provided we don't lose any more fuel we should make it to Leconfield, but we should watch it. If the head wind picks up, it's going to be tight."

The crew continued to nurse the wounded Wimpy home. When they had crossed the German coast, the navigator started a dead reckoning plot. After an hour, he clambered to the astrodome and took a sight on the moon. He asked the engineer to note the fuel level. When he had finished his calculations, his heart pounded and he carefully went over the penciled data again. There was no mistake, the ground speed in the hour since leaving the coast was only eighty-five knots. The plane was bucking a headwind of about forty knots.

MacIntosh called the flight engineer for the fuel use since leaving the coast. It was the same rate, about forty-five gallons per hour. His calculation based on the position line obtained from the moon sight showed they still had two hours flying ahead of them, or about ninety gallons of fuel.

"Tony, what's the current fuel level?"

"About ninety-five gallons, but these gauges are not so accurate. Could be ten gallons, either way."

The navigator called Chadwick on the intercom to discuss the frightening fuel situation. Chadwick called Spinrad to find out the rpm for most economical cruising and he adjusted the throttle and mixture controls. He asked the navigator to confirm the heading. MacIntosh checked the almanac and decided he could get a cross-bearing on the moon position line from the planet Jupiter, which he could see shining brightly in the south-southwest. He was too fatigued to shoot any stars for additional position lines. The fix over the North Sea yielded a distance of 141 miles to RAF Leconfield and required a course correction of six degrees left. The navigator decided they would use a further eighty gallons. The gauges showed ninety gallons, so it was going to be touch and go.

Chadwick came on the intercom. "Guns, is there any tea left?" The drone of the engine on the long leg home was hypnotic.

Flying Officer MacIntosh was a busy man. He took another sight as the yellowing moon approached the western horizon. With such low angles, the correction for refraction was tricky. The sight confirmed the wind was down slightly, a common effect at night. With any luck they would land with a few gallons in the tank. He called the Chadwick, "Skipper, the fuel is going to be very tight, but we should just squeak home, I reckon. The good news is that there will be some light when we arrive, so you don't have to pull off a single-engine landing in the dark."

"Let me know when we're twenty miles off the coast. I'll switch on the navigation lights. Without Sparks, the Chain Home people may scramble an interception if we don't announce our arrival."

"Skipper, this is Flight Sergeant Spinrad. I'll see if I can coax the 1154, 1155 H.F. sets to make a voice transmission. What is our ETA at Leconfield, Flight Officer MacIntosh?"

The bomber was in serious trouble. The moon had set and there would be no clear indication they had crossed the English coast. The flight engineer had not been able to contact RAF communications. The navigator took another sight on Jupiter, which had moved to the west. His fix put the aircraft twenty miles east of the coast.

Chadwick turned on the navigation lights. "How's our fuel state, Tony?"

"Banging on the empty pin, Skipper."

Chadwick turned over the options in his mind. If the engine stopped because of fuel starvation the best bet was to bail out over land.

The front gunner suddenly shouted over the intercom, "Skipper, I can see some dim lights dead ahead."

The navigator scrambled past the pilot to the turret. He tapped the gunner's shoulder, and pointed to the right and slightly down. Despite the black-out, he could see signs of life. Straining his eyes he tried to discern a distinctive pattern. In the first glimmer of twilight he could see the white of breakers on the shore. As he searched, the right engine emitted a short series of explosions and stopped. Chadwick corrected the swing and ordered everyone to get their parachutes ready.

"We're at ten thousand feet," he announced over the intercom. "I'll glide to the west—" and then he spotted a Pundit which had miraculously sprung into life far ahead on the nose.

The navigator saw flashing "DFD" pundit through the windscreen. "Hurray! That's Driffield."

Chadwick came onto the intercom. "Spinrad, dump the door. In two minutes everyone out, and I'll be the last." He trimmed the Wimpy for a smooth descent of 600 feet a minute and an airspeed of 100 knots. "Chuck, fire a red Very, then get everyone out." The altimeter slid below 3,000 feet, and Chadwick yelled, "Go, go!" and unbuckled from his seat. When he got to the door, the crew had already abandoned ship. He flung himself into the dark, chilly air. His groping hand found the ripcord and the 'chute opened with a crack.

As he swung gently in the harness he looked down past his feet. It was impossible to make out anything. He crossed his arms over his chest and flexed his knees. Suddenly he had the impression of something shooting by and then he received a violent blow, which winded him. Chadwick reckoned he had definitely made contact with Mother Earth, and he twisted the harness release and fell awkwardly to the ground. After a few minutes he cautiously stood up, and as his eyes adjusted, he could make out a few shapes nearby.

The dawn was blooming rapidly, and after ten minutes, Chadwick found he was in a small wood of slender trees. He abandoned the 'chute and marched to the north, at first using the stars as a guide. An hour later he came across a tarmac road and sat on an old stone marker that had "Kilham VI" chiseled on it. He was feeling very hungry.

The first vehicle to come along took him to the police station at Bridlington, where he wolfed down a delicious breakfast of bacon, eggs, fried tomatoes, and toast. Ultimately, he was scooped up by the RAF and taken to Leconfield. Chadwick discovered all the crew had survived with nothing worse than scratches and bruises, apart from poor Sparks, whose body rested in a battered wreck in the hills.

Eventually, the crew assembled back at Church Fenton with the squadron intelligence officer and Wing Commander Harris. Crews had removed the body of Sergeant Kelsey from the wreck of the Wellington and salvaged the in-flight navigational log compiled by Flying Officer MacIntosh, who listed the important times during the flight. Chadwick described the impact of the flak and Spinrad gave details of the damage to the wing and engine. Wing Commander Harris asked Chadwick for his general impressions.

"The celestial sights were useful to confirm dead reckoning fixes and to manage fuel use when we lost a tank over Wilhelmshaven. But they didn't provide the accuracy needed to put the plane directly over the target. Fortunately, we had enough moonlight to do that. We were lucky to make it back to Blighty before running out of fuel. Without the wireless operator to transmit for a fix, bailing out over the sea would have meant the chop. I must commend Flying Officer MacIntosh and Flight Sergeant Spinrad for the efficient way the return leg was accomplished."

The gunners mentioned that they were surprised by the fighter attack and they doubted their return fire hit the target. Harris commented that an assessment of the raid by Group intelligence indicated some damage to machine shops and warehouses at the naval dockyard. RAF losses were light. Chadwick's plane was the only Category Five, and Kelsey was the only fatality.

Before he left Church Fenton, Chadwick had a private word with Wing Commander Harris. "There is no doubt we need a wireless navigation system. This will provide course corrections to and from the target, and it will place the plane over the target with an accuracy of a few yards. The RAF desperately needs the heavy bombers if we're going to justify the losses versus the damage inflicted on the German industrial and military structure.

"By the way, Flying Officer MacIntosh was top notch. A good navigator and never flustered."

"Squadron Leader, you realize you got our best man, I hope." Harris chuckled.

Chapter Fourteen

When he returned to Boscombe Down, Chadwick relayed the same impressions to Wing Commander Rowley, who suggested he become familiar with the effort to provide wireless navigation to a distant target. Chadwick got in touch with the development people in Bawdsey. He discovered his old friend, Dr. Bostock, who had a major role in the development of RDR, had been packed off to the United States to work on high frequency radar.

Chadwick arranged a lift to RAF Woodbridge in the Rapide. When he landed and made his way to the tower to telephone Bawdsey, he was overwhelmed by a wave of nostalgia that took him back to those golden prewar days when he was helping to get RDR under way. So much had happened since, especially flying Spitfires out of Hawkinge, that he knew he would never again be the carefree young pilot he was then. Death had hardened and changed him.

At Bawdsey, he was introduced to Dr. Starret, who supervised the work on the new navigational system. He explained the work was carried out by several overlapping entities so that when a design was completed, the equipment could be put into production with no loss of time. Private industry was providing much of the development emphasis. He confirmed that the German system, 'Knickbeine,' or 'Dogleg' system, was not suitable for the much longer range needed to bomb targets in Germany. An entirely different technical approach to the problem was under consideration, Chadwick was told.

Chadwick mentioned that the German system had several operational drawbacks. "The 'Dogleg' and 'X Apparatus' are very limited because they only define one target, and the beam tips off the enemy to the intended target."

"Yes, you're quite right, Allan. The RAF wants a universal navigational system which provides assistance to and from the target. The price to pay for that is some loss of accuracy, but we think we have an answer for that. The system under consideration uses the time difference between synchronized wireless signals to form a grid on a chart not unlike latitude and longitude. The technicians call it 'Gee,' short for 'grid.' It requires a number of transmitters to be operated in various parts of the British Islands. Fortunately, we can steal a lot of technology first designed for the early RDR. Some receivers have been made but they are not suitable for airborne trials. That must come soon, as we need to establish the maximum range obtainable at different heights. This work has a very high priority. Now, the next step, how to get target accuracy. To be honest, the original idea is Jerry's. We plan to copy it from 'Dogleg'."

"I would be very interested to hear about that, Dr. Starret."

"The Germans used highly trained crews with specially-equipped planes to mark the target with colored flares or bombs. The fleet following these planes simply bomb the designated area marked out first. They call the marker planes 'Pfadfinder,' or 'Pathfinder.' For this system to achieve accuracy of targeting, the error must be measured in feet, not miles. The Gee system is replaced by the triangulation of two distance measurements from RDR stations in Britain. Thus, it works for one specially-equipped 'Pathfinder'."

"It sounds exciting, Doctor. But suppose the Pathfinder is shot down?"

"At a meeting I attended, that possibility was raised. Apparently, a new, very fast fighter/bomber is in the works and will be flying within a few months. It has a ceiling of nearly forty thousand feet and a top speed of three hundred and sixty knots. Thus, it should be almost immune from flak and German fighters. It was proposed that specially-equipped versions would form a Pathfinder nucleus. The new plane is mostly made of an impregnated wood, and is almost invisible to RDR. It's called the 'Mosquito'."

"It seems like a lot of thought and work has already gone into solving the problem. How can Boscombe Down help?"

"I believe Boscombe will be responsible for early flight trials once we have some receivers suitable for a high altitude environment. Perhaps after lunch, Squadron Leader, you would like to visit our laboratory where we're working on the receiver display unit, which will be carried by aircraft."

Dr. Starret led Chadwick to the familiar lunch room. Allan mentioned that he had frequently eaten there with Dr. Bostock when the Chain Home RDR system was being devised. "Oh, really?" Starret commented, and then, "Before my time." This made Chadwick feel like an old man.

In the laboratories Chadwick met no one he remembered from the old RDR days. The place had clearly expanded a great deal. He examined prototypes of the Gee receivers, although they were just for bench testing. A design that met military construction standards was being designed by a large electronics company. The equipment consisted of a cathode ray tube that displayed the time difference from "Master" and a "Slave" transmitters. This was measured on the horizontal trace of the 'scope.

"It's very similar to the display used on the Chain Home receivers," Chadwick observed. "The problem with them was noise, which disturbed the trace."

Starret was impressed. "That's a perceptive remark, Squadron Leader. Are you an engineer?"

"Yes, I attended Cranwell College—quite a few years ago, though," he added reflectively. "I picked up some rudimentary electronics knowledge working with the RDR people."

"Well, you're right. Noise will bring errors into the measurement of the time difference and thus errors in the perceived position. To explain in a little more detail, the measurement of a pair gives a position line. To get a fix, a second pair must be measured. Another position line, crossing the first position line, then provides a fix. We are producing charts with grid lines superimposed for incremental time differences. The navigator simply plots the measurements on the chart. The system will cover the British Islands and much of Western Europe. It will be one of Boscombe's jobs to determine just what the usable range will turn out to be."

"Remind me again, Dr. Starret, how much time difference corresponds to how much geographic distance."

"The wireless wave travels about a thousand feet in a microsecond, a millionth of a second."

"To get any reasonable accuracy you must measure fractions of a microsecond? The diameter of the cathode ray tube screen is only three inches. How long is the trace in microseconds?"

Starret looked at Chadwick, thinking *This chap is just too sharp.* "It's adjustable by the operator," he answered in exasperation.

Chadwick begged to be excused for a few minutes and called Boscombe to arrange a pick-up by the Rapide. He discovered he was too late for a rendezvous that afternoon and would be taken back to Boscombe in the morning. He thanked Dr. Starret for an illuminating discussion and predicted they would meet again.

Back at RAF Woodbridge he signed into the officers' mess and idly wondered if Squadron Leader Wilson was still the "Station Master." An orderly confirmed that Wilson was indeed the station commander and Chadwick picked up a phone and asked to be connected.

"Good afternoon, Squadron Leader Wilson, this is Allan Chadwick. How are you? Perhaps you remember me when I frequently visited Woodbridge to take care of business at Bawdsey. Before the balloon went up."

After a slight pause Wilson replied, "Of course, you're the RDR expert. Is that why you're here?"

"Not exactly, Sir. I'm visiting Bawdsey, but working on different—er—things."

"Wonderful! I'll tell you, Woodbridge had been in the thick of the attacks by the Luftwaffe, and squadron commanders constantly praise the advantage that RDR gives them. Perhaps we can meet before dinner, in say thirty minutes in the anteroom?"

"I'll be there, looking forward to it."

Chadwick bought himself a beer and settled into a comfortable chair, he was soon joined by George Wilson. "Judging by the fruit salad on your tunic I don't have to tell you about the incredible strain Fighter Command has been under. DFC and bar, eh? Did you command a squadron? I remember now you were very fond of the old Spit."

"I was squadron commander of 613 Squadron, mostly based at Hawkinge. Yes, we were flying Spits."

"Hawkinge? My God, you were right on the front line, about five minutes from France, right? Gives the bogeys plenty of time over your zone."

"We were busy, that's true, Sir."

Wilson looked at Chadwick keenly. "Sounds like things really got to you, Allan. It was a bloody awful time. I've never attended so many funerals, one after the other. It was just like the first shindig, young kids, lucky to last a few hours."

"I agree, it was murder, but who is the murderer? Things are a little quieter now. Gives us time for some rehabilitation."

"Tell you what. Come and have dinner with Barbara and me. You must remember meeting her, what, over three years ago?"

"I would be delighted, Sir. Shall we say seven o'clock?"

"Yes, I'll give Barbara a tinkle, warning her I'm bringing a distinguished guest."

As was his style, Chadwick knocked on the door exactly at seven, and was soon sipping sherry with Wilson and his wife. When Wilson introduced Chadwick to Barbara, he said, "Squadron Leader Chadwick commands a squadron at Hawkinge, dear."

Chadwick quickly corrected him, "That was true last week, but I've been posted to Boscombe Down, George. Sorry, when you asked about the Spits I should have mentioned that the posting was to replace a squadron commander who was unfortunately downed, but it was just temporary. I was there a little over two months, and now I'm back looking at bomber problems."

"It's so nice to see you again, Squadron Leader. So much has happened since we last met."

"Please, call me Allan. Yes, 1938 seems like another world. Did you receive much bombing here at Woodbridge?"

George Wilson answered, "Mostly on the airfield itself. Stukas plastered the hangars and maintenance shops. We only got a couple of hits on the housing area."

"How are your children?"

"All healthy and happy. I didn't tell you about a stroke of luck we had. An old friend, retired wing commander, passed away just before the war started. To make a long story short, his widow sold his house in Felixstone to us. We just picked up the mortgage with some financial adjustments, she went to live with one of her children in Devon. At the moment, my son and daughters live there. He works in Ipswich, the girls are working in Felixstone. When the RAF decides they no longer need my services, Barbara and I will move there."

He stopped and looked at Chadwick. "What about you, Allan? Still single and fancy free?"

"Oh, yes. The past year has been pretty busy. When this nastiness ends, maybe I can settle down."

Barbara rose from her seat, motioning for the two to continue without her. "Please excuse me, Allan, while I finish cooking our meal."

When Barbara retired to the kitchen, Wilson asked, "What bombers are you concerned with Allan?"

"I spent a lot of time since we last met working with A.V. Roe, up in Manchester. They're building a new heavy bomber, four engines, two-thousand-mile range and load of fifteen thousand pounds."

"My God, makes the Vimys you flew look pretty ancient."

"There's no comparison. This is the beginning a new aerial war." After a little more chit-chat Barbara called them into the dining room, where the conversation centered on the domestic problems of living with the war.

Chadwick returned to the mess well pleased with the evening. It was a touch of domesticity he truly enjoyed.

When Chadwick returned to Boscombe he asked Wing Commander Rowley how the development of the "Gee" system was managed.

"There's a committee with permanent members and temporary members. It's chaired by a fellow from the Air Ministry, which is logical. They pay the bills. I represent RAF Bomber Command. The chap you met, Dr. Starret, is the Telecommunications rep. There's a man from the A.C. Cossor Company; they're gearing up to build the airborne receivers.

"Let's see, um, there's someone whose name I forget who's in charge of the transmitters and ground-based aerials. There's a temporary member who handles navigation from Calshot. Occasionally we have temporary members dealing with supplies, such as charts, valves, electrical gubbins, and so on. I regard you as my number two, dealing with the actual installation in bombers in the coming months."

"That sounds perfect, Sir. I will immediately contact Cossor so that I can see the actual receiver and display as it is planned at the moment. Then I think visits to Vickers, Avro, De Haviland, Handley Page, and Short Brothers are in order. But first I'll get to Cossor, and see how the electronic gear is coming along."

Wing Commander Rowley put Chadwick in touch with the Cossor representative on the Gee committee, who invited Allan to visit the company's laboratories in London. He traveled the next day and was received with some pomp at the company's factory. Rowley had impressed on Cossor the importance of Chadwick's position at Boscombe.

The equipment to fit into bombers consisted of two units—a receiver and a cathode ray tube display. Chadwick expressed surprise at the size of the display unit. The display screen seemed relatively small. An engineer explained this was the first time they had built a display for use at high altitude, typically 20,000 feet and above. The air at that height is quite thin and the cathode ray tube requires a high voltage. Tests on a unit placed in a tank and evacuated to the corresponding pressure, caused the high voltage circuit to "flash over," the engineer explained. The thin air behaves like a neon tube and ionizes, he said.

Chadwick did not fully understand and pressed him for details.

"Ionization causes atomic nuclei to be stripped of electrons, forming a short circuit to earth. The most frightening example is lightning," the engineer said. "The cure is to keep all high voltage parts well away from the metal case, which increases the size, though."

Chadwick nodded. "What is the highest altitude you've simulated?"

The engineer turned to a colleague who was standing nearby. "What is it, Joe?"

"About thirty-five thousand feet, a pressure of about four pounds per square inch, Sir."

Chadwick asked, "Will all production units be tested under low pressure?"

The engineer answered, "Based on the performance of samples, we will make that decision later, Sir."

Chadwick turned to the Cossor representative on the Gee committee. "This equipment is presumably top secret. Is there any provision to destroy it should the plane carrying it possibly fall into enemy hands?"

"That has not been decided, Sir."

Chadwick asked about the aerial need for a Gee receiver. Would it be a separate installation on the plane? After looking at a simulation of a Gee navigation solution using the trace displayed on the cathode ray tube, the party retired to a conference room for tea and a discussion.

Chadwick pressed the Cossor people for dates, especially when prototypes would be sent to Boscombe and when production units would be available for installation in aircraft. Finally he was able to get a promise of three fully flyable prototypes within a month. He suggested outline drawings and power requirements for the two units be sent to the aircraft manufacturers. He was concerned that space on the navigator's desk would be unduly squeezed by the Gee equipment. When he left he took this information with him to Boscombe Down.

Chadwick pressed Wing Commander Rowley for a decision on the type of aircraft to be used for the first airborne trials. It had to be capable of cruising at 25,000 feet, with a range of at least 1,000 miles. It was expected the trials would take place occasionally over German territory, and so a good defense was needed. He convinced the wing commander that trials using the three promised prototypes must be carried out concurrently, so that changes that might be needed would be in time for the introduction of the Gee navigation in operational bombers. Rowley brought up the question of supplying three operational bombers at a meeting of the Gee Committed, and the Air Ministry allocated three Wellington bombers for the first trials.

Chadwick flew to Brooklands to make sure the planes would be able to accept the Gee equipment. He checked into the officers' mess at RAF Farnborough, anticipating a stay of a few days with Vickers. His old friend, Wing Commander Codrington, was delighted to see him again. He was surprised to learn Chadwick was back with Bomber Command at Boscombe and congratulated him heartily on the awards he had earned with 613 Squadron.

Sitting alone in the mess after dinner, Chadwick was gripped by a wild impulse to call Melanie Fitzgibbon at Pangbourne. Muttering to himself, *To think is to act,* he went to the phone in the lobby and called the familiar number. After some delay he pushed button "A" and found himself talking to Myrtle, the housekeeper. She was astounded to discover who was calling and told him Lady Fitzgibbon was living in an apartment over the stables. The British Army had taken over the house. Unfortunately, there was no phone in her apartment, Myrtle informed him.

Chadwick thought rapidly, and then told her he would call again at eight p.m. on the following evening, and perhaps Lady Fitzgibbon could be waiting for his call. Myrtle promised to pass the message on.

Chapter Fifteen

Chadwick spent a full day with the engineers and technicians at Brooklands. He explained the intention of using wireless navigation to the test pilots. He found there was simply no room in the navigation space of the Wellington to site the Gee display on the navigator's table. As a temporary compromise, the receiver and display were placed on a shelf over the table.

A Vickers car dropped him off at Farnborough in time for dinner in the mess. He telephoned Clair Court Hall at eight and found Melanie was waiting for his call. Chadwick apologized for the long period between his rare appearances, and Melanie seemed pleased to hear from him. When he explained he was briefly at Farnborough, she suggested a meeting in Reading. Neither of them had a car but both could catch a train to Reading Junction. They agreed to have dinner and Chadwick said he would call back and leave word with Myrtle about a possible date and time. When he replaced the telephone he felt a frisson of romantic energy after hearing Melanie's voice.

The next day at Brooklands, Chadwick was surprised to find the pilots he had talked to the day before were skeptical of the bombing tactics he had outlined. He listened and then trumped their objections by describing his sortie to Wilhelmshaven in a Wellington. He mentioned how useful continuous fixes would have been for the return leg when they were desperately short of fuel. He conceded the system did not provide precision bombing but was a big step in the right direction.

Two technicians were told to modify a Wellington and Chadwick could inspect it about two days. Chadwick borrowed a Bradshaw from an office secretary and called Myrtle with times for a rendezvous with Lady Fitzgibbon.

He discovered that Farnborough had a Spitfire that was not being used for a few hours. In the morning he persuaded the wing commander to authorize a flight to RAF Ringway, and on arrival he chatted with Squadron 613 commanding officer, Squadron Leader Tom Kirk. He was told that Fighter Command was modifying the battle plan for interceptions and the German "Finger Four" battle formation was recommended. It was very similar to the "two pairs" formation he had discussed with Kirk when he took over the squadron.

He wandered into the crew room and heard they had been scrambled a few times for raids on Manchester and Liverpool, but Ringway was not positioned too well and they may move to a base on the east coast. He congratulated Pilot Officer Sillitoe on two confirmed kills.

Chadwick flew back to Farnborough before lunch, bused to Farnborough station and caught the train to Reading. Melanie was waiting for him in the Kardomah Café. Coffee was unavailable but they were serving tea, so Chadwick ordered a pot along with a scone. "You're looking very well, Melanie," he started.

"I'm not sure I can say the same thing about you, Allan," she countered. "You're looking a trifle pale."

"True, I don't get outside much these days."

She stared at his uniform. "Is that another medal they've given you?"

"Oh, yes, I've pranged a couple of Spits, but walked away. Very good for Supermarine's financial balance sheet."

"You're too flippant, Allan. I know you. Sounds like you're lucky to be alive."

"I hear the Army has taken over Clair Court. How is that working out?"

"They're ruining the place! Ugly great Nissen Huts going up in the lawn next to the driveway." "How is the apartment? A trifle confining? Do you do your own cooking?"

" I often sneak over to the main house and eat with Myrtle and Cedric."

"Plenty of handsome Army officers around, I suppose."

"What am I detecting, male insecurity?"

Chadwick laughed. "You always could see right through me, Melanie." He toyed with the scone, which was slightly stale, and finished his cup of tea. "Are we going to eat dinner in Reading, Melanie?"

"If you want to. It's not too chilly, let's take a stroll down to the river and work up some appetite."

Chadwick stood up and helped Melanie into her over-coat. He shrugged on his RAF greatcoat and paid for his tea at a cash register near the door.

In the street they turned north and walked past the old Abbey ruins. "Why did you call me, Allan?" Melanie asked, even-tually.

Chadwick thought for a minute. "It must have been nos-talgia. I was back at Farnborough for a day or two, and it had pleasant memories of those golden days before the war. I will always associate you and the green machine with RAF Farn-borough."

"Oh, thank you. What do you think of first? Me or that great noisy Bentley?"

Chadwick smiled and said nothing. After a few minutes they came to the river bank and sat on a bench.

"I must say, Melanie, it's a pleasure to talk to someone who is not in the service. The last few months have been difficult. I've ordered young men into Spitfires they are hardly qualified to fly and watched them die under the German guns. Do you remember meeting Doug Larson on our mad drive to Cromer a couple of years ago? I looked him up when I was in London a while back. He's involved in intelligence matters in some way. He told me that reports from agents in Poland describe mass killings of innocent civilians by the Germans, and by the Russians too, in the east. It seems like the war is knocking down all notions of civilized behavior. We were in a pub with two of his lady friends when it was bombed, and one of them was badly injured."

"Poor you, you escape death and destruction in the air, only to be bombed on the ground."

Chadwick looked at her sharply. "It's made me think. Now I'm heavily concerned with Bomber Command. I'm helping to maim and kill civilians in Germany. The Jerries are evil, but are we any better?"

"My God, Allan, you really are serious. Sorry, I was a little glib a moment ago. Sounds like you are suggesting the world is too complicated and perhaps a roll in the hay is the answer."

Chadwick looked at her, suspecting that somehow she had divined from his ramblings that he had slept with Mary. "No, it made me realize that you were right, to stop while we still loved. If either one of us were killed, it would be too grievous for the other to bear."

They were silent for a few moments as the afternoon began to fade. Suddenly Chadwick asked, "Do you ever see Dorothy now, Viscountess Addenbury, or Freddy?"

" I haven't seen any of the Isbell's Insiders since the war started. I heard that the government had requisitioned Addenbury's country estate." She paused and then said, "Speaking of your concerns over bombing German women and children, you have to remember the first rule of the jungle—survival. We simply can't let Germany win this terrible war. To do that innocent people, bags of them, are going to die. Do you feel better for talking to me?"

"Yes, Melanie, I do. I've nobody else I can really talk to."

"It's getting chilly. How about a stroll along the river and we'll find some cozy place for an early dinner. We can be good friends, Allan, without the baggage of a love affair. If circumstances put us in the same bed, it won't be for the first time. I think you are like the captain of a great ship, isolated and with no one to share the responsibility. Am I right?"

"Yes, in some ways you are, my dear."

"Well, then, whenever you can get away and you're at your wit's end, come to see me. Is that a welcoming little hostelry I see down that lane?"

They pushed open the door of a small pub and were greeted by a blast of warm air from a roaring wooden fire. The place was crowded. A sign on the bar said, "No Spirits." Chadwick ordered a beer for himself and a glass of cider for Melanie. They stood against a whitewashed wall away from the direct heat of the fire. Eventually a couple rose from a small table and Allan and Melanie slipped onto the warm chairs.

"I don't think they're serving food, Melanie," Chadwick whispered to her above the clamor of the crowd.

"I think we can get something to eat at the station, Allan," Melanie said. "In the old days the restaurant there was not bad."

They slowly emptied their glasses and ventured into the night. It was quite dark as they made their way to Reading Station. Despite the war it still retained a slight aura of the Great Western Railway. They verified the train times at the destination board.

In fact, it was just as easy for Melanie to take a bus instead of a train to Pangbourne, but she wanted to keep Chadwick company until he returned to Farnborough. They were able to sit in a decent restaurant that still had linen serviettes, in plain rings. They both ordered an omelet with chips. Before he left to walk onto his platform, Allan squeezed Melanie's hand and gave her a light kiss on her cheek. "Let's stay in touch, Mel," he whispered.

The next day, when Chadwick returned to Brooklands, he felt a renewed confidence, and also satisfaction that the break with Melanie had, to some extent, been patched over. He told the works manager that three Wellingtons would be needed at Boscombe within two weeks. They must be modified for the Gee equipment, including power and aerial connections. The manager protested the works order did not include those changes and Chadwick assured him the paper to cover everything would ultimately arrive from the Air Ministry.

He flew back to Boscombe the same day and brought Wing Commander Rowley up to date. He suggested they immediately recruit volunteer air crews for the three Wellingtons and start to train them on the use of Gee. Rowley told Chadwick to take charge of the small test flight unit, with the goal of establishing the three-dimensional volume of height and range over Britain and Europe in which the Gee equipment performed satisfactorily.

Three Wellingtons were delivered to Boscombe within a week. The volunteer crews were briefed and sent to Cossor for training on the equipment. They would fly with no guns or bombs to minimize weight and thus push the maximum ceiling achievable. After a busy week, one plane with crew was sent to the north of England. The remaining two planes remained at Farnborough; one was used to plot Gee performance over southern England and part of France.

Chadwick himself piloted most of the flights over Germany. By flying very carefully he was able to coax the bomber to

29,000 feet, although the indicated airspeed showed the plane was almost on the point of stalling. This height was well below the ceiling of an Me 109, but it took the fighters so long to climb to that height they were never intercepted.

The navigator was delighted to get reliable Gee fixes up to a range of 400 nautical miles. Often a signal would be lost from one pair of a chain, but the other pair still provided a position line. Within a month the results were accepted by Bomber Command and a directive was issued for all the command planes to carry Gee. During the period that Chadwick had commanded the test flight unit they had made sixty-two sorties and lost no planes due to enemy action.

Engineers at the Telecommunications Establishment had proposed another form of wireless navigation using RDR stations, which promised a very high degree of accuracy, and the Boscombe Flight Test Unit began to work with the developers to test a prototype. All the test flights were carried out over Britain, as the equipment was so experimental the authorities could not take the chance of a trial receiver falling into German hands.

After a few weeks Chadwick began to feel he could make a better contribution to the war effort and he persuaded Wing Commander Rowley to give him a new task, which was to assess how well operational squadrons were using the new Gee receivers which were entering service.

Chadwick's way of assessing the performance of Gee was to fly with a crew on a raid, make a note of the Gee coordinates and wait after the raid for some photographic reconnaissance. On one scary raid to Essen in the Ruhr, he flew with a squadron that was operating the twin-engined Manchester out of RAF Scampton. He remembered the plane from the days when he flew with Avro test pilots to get the Lancaster bomber under construction. The Manchester he flew then had been extremely unreliable, and suffered the loss of one engine.

He talked to the pilots in the crew room of the squadron he planned to fly with. They had discovered the plane's weak points and carefully flew to minimize them—for example, prolonged operation at a specific engine rpm often resulted in failure, so these engine speeds were marked on the gauges in red and avoided, except for brief, unavoidable periods. The squadron had visited Essen before. It was a center for coal mining and steel works.

Before the raid, the squadron chief navigator briefed the aircrews on the route, with special emphasis on the anti-aircraft gun sites. With Gee it was feasible to fly a twisty, zig-zag route that avoided flying over the worst flak. They would take off and land in complete darkness. The moon was in its last quarter and would rise after the attackers left the target area. The length of the raid was about 800 nautical miles, of which about 360 miles would be over Germany or enemy-occupied territory.

Chadwick chatted with crew before take-off. He sensed the brittle bonhomie. The pilot was Flying Officer Derek Rigby, and the navigator was Pilot Officer Selwyn Yardley. Yardley told Chadwick that the Telecommunications people from Malvern had installed an experimental receiver to detect enemy RDR transmissions, which they expected to hear as they approached the German border. The wireless operator and flight engineer were sergeants, and the three gunners were leading aircraftsmen. The navigator also acted as bomb aimer. As they approached the plane, which was looming in the darkness like a giant bird, several struggled to unfasten their flying suits and there were the usual jokes about the size of a member needed to pee on the tailwheel and not on one's flying boots.

Chadwick dressed warmly. When their turn for take-off arrived, he stood behind the pilot's seat. The plane was carrying 8,000 pounds of bombs, a mix of 500-pound high explosive and incendiaries. They slowly climbed to 14,000 feet over a blacked-out England. At 11,000 feet they entered a wispy cloud layer which persisted to their cruising height. The Gee equipment was working perfectly and the pilot gave permission to test the guns after Yardley confirmed that they had crossed the coast. The pilot throttled back to yield a cruising indicated air speed of 175 knots, which was a true air speed of about 225 knots, Yardley said they had a tailwind of 22 knots. He calculated the ground speed was nearly 250 knots and they would cross the Dutch coast forty minutes after leaving the English coast. The preflight briefing had suggested a strip with little flak between Rotterdam and Amsterdam.

When they crossed into Holland, Yardley waved Chadwick over to his desk and plugged his helmet into a jack. A faint buzzing noise was evident, and it grew louder as they progressed east, "German Freya RDR," Yardley explained, and he pointed to a dial. "Two hundred and fifty-one megacycles per sec, that's the freq they use, much higher than Raff RDR."

There was little chatter on the intercom, except for brief conversations between the navigator and the pilot. To Chadwick it seemed like crossing the North Sea was over in a few minutes and then there was spotty flak as they flew over Holland. The navigator was busy for thirty minutes as he ordered twenty degree course changes in a winding approach to the German border. Rigby warned the gunners to keep a sharp eye open for German fighters, which were directed by the Freya operators.

However, as the intensity of flak increased when they approached Essen, the danger from fighters diminished. Essen was visible from about thirty miles away. Fires started by earlier bombers flickered on the ground but there was no disguising the glare from the blast furnaces at the steel works. The flashes from anti-aircraft shells were almost continuous and the gunners had the height fused correctly. Rigby warned Yardley to move to the bomb aimer's position and said he would dive slightly to lose a thousand feet and increase the air speed.

Searchlights ahead focused on a bomber and it twisted in the glare to escape. Suddenly the left wing of the bomber disappeared as shells burst on the plane and it began a death spiral, illuminated by the search lights. Nobody bailed out. When

Yardley made his way forward, Chadwick slipped into his seat and began to note the Gee readings on a pad. Yardley was making a visual attack on the target and called corrections to Rigby. When he called, "Bombs gone," Rigby made a tight turn and streaked for the border.

Chadwick noted the exact Gee reading at the moment of bomb release. He switched to the signal from the Freya receiver, which was very loud and intense. He rose and made way for Yardley to regain the navigator's seat and after a few minutes, Yardley called a new course to the pilot and mentioned their ground speed was now about 200 knots. Scattered flak persisted but none came close.

They crossed over the Dutch coast and the wireless operator sent a signal to ensure Chain Home was aware of their position. The plane had not been fitted with IFF at that point. Once over the North Sea Chadwick poured himself some tea and moved round the plane filling mugs for the crew. He asked Rigby if he wanted a breather and slipped into the pilot's seat for an hour. He was quite impressed with the Manchester. So long as the Rolls Royce Vulture engines kept turning, the plane was a satisfactory medium-to-heavy bomber. Rigby took over as they approached Scampton. It was an airfield Chadwick knew well. It had one heart-stopping attribute—the runway was built on a gentle hill and until a plane crested the rise, it often seemed to be running out of tarmac.

At the de-briefing Chadwick turned over his notes to a specially prepared officer who would correlate them with photographs of the target taken later. Chadwick ate breakfast and then slept until two-thirty in the afternoon.

Chadwick made several bombing flights with different squadrons and found the navigators warmly welcomed the Gee receiver. It provided reasonably accurate fixes in any kind of weather, allowed safer transit of German-occupied territory, and was especially useful on returning to base, when the signals were strong and the effects of German jamming not so noticeable. The people at Air Intelligence who worked with Chadwick to determine bombing accuracy confirmed his opinion that Gee would certainly put a bomber over the right city but could not guarantee a hit on a precision target.

One day Wing Commander Rowley mentioned that three squadrons had been formed to fly the newly-imported American bombers, the B-17, with the RAF designation "Fortress I." Perhaps Chadwick would like to accompany one on a daylight raid?

The three squadrons flying the Fortress were based in Northamptonshire. Each squadron fielded six bombers. They were an early version of the Boeing B-17, and were not considered ready for combat by the U.S. Army Air Force. The Fortress lacked a tail gunner, and it was planned to fly six planes in close formation, thus providing protection from fighters with mutual gun cover. An upper gun placement at a rear extension of the cockpit protected the rear, but the field of fire was limited by the stabilizer fin and tail.

The lead plane for each squadron had been equipped with a Gee receiver. Chadwick was dropped off at RAF Polebrook and spent a few days talking to the crews and inspecting the planes. All the crews had been trained at McChord Field in Tacoma, Washington State. They had been overwhelmed by the generosity of Americans while over there. They told stories of flying over the Tacoma Strait and seeing a huge suspension bridge that had suffered a spectacular collapse in a strong wind. They had flown the planes to Britain in stages, carrying no bombs but loaded with extra fuel.

Chadwick's raid would be their third daylight attack. He was to fly as second pilot in the leading squadron, while the other squadrons were formatted at the rear, forming a wing of eighteen aircraft. When they assembled for briefing before daybreak, Chadwick smiled when the intelligence officer unveiled a map of Wilhelmshaven, the main German naval base. He had been there before. The plane captain was Squadron Leader Roland Jones, referred to as "Rolly" on the intercom.

The lead squadron took off first and slowly climbed to 30,000 feet in a box formation. The other squadrons formatted to complete the wing, with each squadron separated vertically by 500 feet. The planes flew through thick cloud, which began at 18,000 feet and persisted to 23,000 feet where they broke into brilliant sunshine. They saw no flak but as soon as the navigator announced they were over Germany, they spotted a large formation of Me 109 fighters approaching them head-on.

Jones called the three squadrons to close up and provide covering fire. The bomb aimer could not see the target. The navigator stared at the Gee equipment and directed the pilot over a precalculated point, at which stage the bombs were released. The sight of all the bombers releasing their deadly cargo seemed to drive the Luftwaffe pilots into a frenzy. Wave after wave attacked the Fortress. The plane shook as five gunners opened up on the attackers. Bullets thudded into the sturdy plane as Jones made a turn to the northwest.

Chadwick swiveled in his seat to catch sight of the other squadrons. Two thousand feet below, a German fighter was diving with black smoke pouring from the engine. The RAF squadrons were holding good formation and muzzle flashes showed the gunners were firing almost continuously. The flight engineer came up on the intercom. "Rolly, number four engine is hit—oh, boy, it's on fire."

The captain came back, "Okay, flight, shut it down. Feather and extinguish."

Chadwick glanced along the starboard wing. The engine was smoking but it died down as the rpm slowed and the extinguisher got a bite. Even in the heat of battle Chadwick smiled to himself—the crew had picked up a lot of Americanisms. Jones's "Okay" had sounded exactly like Humphrey Bogart.

The German pilots had seen the smoking engine and renewed the attacks on Chadwick's plane. *Like sharks going for a wounded whale*, Chadwick thought as bullets crashed into the cockpit. The control column suddenly gave a violent jerk and Jones gave a cry of pain. A bullet had penetrated the cockpit, hit Jones's shoulder and shattered the yoke.

The plane shuddered and Chadwick grabbed the control column on his side to correct the lurch. He looked at Jones; blood was running freely down his arm.

"Captain, I have control. Navigator, give me a course for home then get up here. Rolly is hurt."

Chadwick eased up the boost of the remaining good engines to maintain air speed. The navigator and flight engineer entered the cockpit. Chadwick slipped off his oxygen mask as the navigator bent to put his ear close. "See what you can do for Rolly. I'll fly from the right-hand seat."

As the squadron left the German coast, the Messerschmitts withdrew, and Chadwick called the other squadrons on H.F. to get reports of battle damage. All of them thought they would get home but two planes had had the hydraulics shot out and would have to crash-land. Four had suffered serious injury to crew members.

"Sparks, get our ETA off the Nav and clear us with Chain Home."

The flight engineer injected Rolly with an ampoule of morphine. One of the gunners brought round mugs of hot tea. It was very cold in the cockpit, as a frigid wind was whistling through the bullet hole on the port side. Ultimately, the flight engineer stuffed a life jacket in the hole, which helped.

Chadwick's hands grew so cold he could not feel them, but fortunately the automatic pilot was functioning and he was able to take his hands off the column and warm them inside his flying suit. Frostbite at this altitude was a real threat.

Eventually, the three runways at RAF Polebrook came into view and Chadwick called the planes carrying injuries to land first. The rest of the wing landed in turn and then the two planes with no undercarriage crash-landed on the grass. Rolly was taken to the sick bay, along with the other wounded crew. The rest assembled for the debriefing .

The next morning Chadwick shared his feelings with the wing commander—the Fortress was a strong, durable plane but it lacked the defense needed to fight off attackers in daylight. The bombload was not significantly higher than a Wellington, but it could operate at a higher altitude. In Chadwick's opinion daylight raids were too costly and night-time raids were mostly inaccurate. A wireless targeting system with an error not exceeding a hundred feet would help to get heavy bombers into the right position for a heavy load to affect the strategic balance of the war.

The wing commander pointed out the raid had cost two "Forts," as they were deemed Category Five write-offs after their crash landings due to hydraulic failure, which in turn, was caused by Luftwaffe attacks.

Chadwick returned to Boscombe Down where he began to get fully acquainted with the successor to Gee, a system that used RDR stations to provide accurate coordinates for a bomb release point, albeit at a high altitude and thus still prone to errors as the bombs descended. The code name for the new system was "Oboe." The useful range from stations in Britain was somewhat over 200 nautical miles, thus many targets in Germany were beyond its reach. To test its effectiveness under operational conditions, a few raids were carried out using early prototype

Oboe wireless transponders over dock facilities in France used by the German Navy.

Chadwick was captain of several heavy bomber sorties used for these trials. On analysis, an interesting pattern emerged. Although the bomb grouping was very good with bombs usually within a 200-yard circle, the circle itself was often displaced from the intended target. It took quite a number of trials before the reason became obvious—British charts had a different datum for the lat/long grid.

One afternoon Chadwick found himself with time on his hands when a meeting he had attended at the Air Ministry in London ended early. On impulse he called his old friend, Doug Larson at MI5, and within an hour was sipping a pint of bitter at Larson's favorite pub.

"What are you up to these days, Allan?"

"I'm still nominally at RAF Boscombe Down, but I've been flying a lot with bombers operating out of Devon. We've been giving the French Atlantic ports a lot of attention. The reason is secret, though."

"Flying a lot over France, eh? That reminds me of something that came up in a meeting with MI6 a few weeks ago. The French résistance has a well-developed network and as our bombing raids increase, they are funneling quite a few downed crews back to Blighty. Anyway, the idea was bandied about that maybe RAF crew should carry fake identification papers, as getting good ones made in Frogland is hard, and we can make perfect versions here. Of course, the idea fell through because most RAF crews don't speak French or German. And if they were caught with false papers, they might get shot as spies."

Chadwick laughed, thought about it for a minute, and then said, "Still, the ones that do have a good knowledge of a European language might benefit, like me."

"You're really interested, Allan? I could fix you up tomorrow—unofficially, of course. Are you staying the night in town?"

Chadwick hadn't given it much consideration. An idle thought flitted across his mind. He still had the scrap of paper that Larson's friend Mary had given him with her telephone number at work. He glanced at his watch and saw that it was ten past four. He could probably catch her. He had fond memories of Mary, especially when she had confessed without apologies that she was a former working class courtesan.

"What are your plans, Doug?"

"Well, to be honest, I have to get back to the office, at least for an hour or two. If there's a raid I'm stuck with the firm. Can you look after yourself?"

"Yes, of course. I'll see you in the morning. What time would be convenient?"

"Drop in about half past eight. I'll get things organized so we're ready."

Larson finished his drink and left. Chadwick debated with himself about spending the night with Mary. She had certainly been very friendly the night they were been caught in a bombing raid. Now that winter was well advanced, the raids on London had been sporadic. *Nothing ventured, nothing gained*, he thought to himself. He had a few overnight things in a small blue canvas satchel, along with his gas mask. He had originally thought he would not get away from the Ministry meeting in time to get back to Boscombe Down. *Oh, what the hell, I'll play truant. The blighters owe me a lot of time!*

He abruptly rose and walked out of the pub to a public call box on the street. He inserted the pennies and dialed the number Mary had given him.

"London Port Authority," a crisp female voice answered. He pushed button "A."

"Mrs. Mary Hancock, please."

"Personal calls are not allowed. This is a government phone."

Chadwick thought rapidly. "This is Sergeant Atkinson, Thames River police. I would still like to speak to Mrs. Hancock to report a ship departure delay."

"Just a minute, Sir."

After a delay Mary came on the line. "Mary Hancock," she announced in a slightly puzzled voice.

"Hello, Mary. Is that harridan within earshot? Say 'go ahead' if no."

"Go ahead."

"This is Doug's friend, Allan. You may remember we met in a raid a few months ago?"

"Yes."

"I'm stuck in London again. Are you free?"

"Yes."

"I told your harridan I was reporting a late ship departure. I hope that covers you."

Mary picked up at once on the game. "You hope to make the next tide, Sir, I understand."

"Can you meet me at the news kiosk at Aldgate Tube at six?"

"Yes, I'll report that to your agent. Thank you, Sir. Good day."

Chadwick hung up the phone, laughing to himself. He pushed button "B," but no money came back. It rarely did.

Chadwick walked to Charing Cross station and ordered a beer at a congested bar. He glanced at his watch. It was nearly five, and he had to kill an hour before meeting Mary. He could catch the Tube to Aldgate conveniently from the station. He idled away thirty minutes drinking his beer and then pushed his way on the crowded platform to some steps, descended, and searched for an east-bound Circle line train. The train was packed, many riders were smoking, and after half a dozen juddering stops, he alighted, climbed the stairs, and spotted Mary waiting by the W.H. Smith counter.

"Hello, Mary."

"Hello, Allan. To what do I owe this pleasure?"

"A meeting I was at finished early, but too late for me to get back to my base. So I thought of you."

"That's nice, but the last time there was a raid on, people had their heads down. Now things are quiet, and a lot of people around here know me and Jack. We have to be careful."

She walked to the street. There was a large double-decker bus slowly making its way in the traffic thronging High Street. "Come on." She darted across the road and stood in a short queue to get on the bus. Chadwick followed. She whispered, "We'll just put a couple of stops between us and Aldgate."

There was only standing room on the bus. Chadwick handed a three-penny bit to the conductor and waved his arm to include Mary. After ten minutes, Mary plucked at Allan's arm and indicated they should get off.

"Where are we?"

"We're just behind Leadenhall Market. I know a nice pub."

She led the way to a public house with large window boxes which supported some dispirited plants. Inside it was warm and fairly quiet. Mary slid behind a small table and Allan asked, "G and T?"

"Yes, please,"

"Who was that I talked to when I called?"

"That was our office manager, Miss Prudence Gamble, a frustrated virgin. Did she make a fuss?"

"I told her I was a policeman."

Mary laughed. "Anyway, we managed to get together. I take it you are looking for some cheap lodgings, with a doxie included."

"Something like that," Allan replied.

"Jack was home for Christmas but he's back in Scotland. Let's have a few drinks and go home. I was able to get a nice bit of meat today at work. We can have that, fried."

"At work?"

"Well, you know, there's always breakage when they're unloading ships. Some of the dockers were unloading an American ship when a case broke, scattered tins all over the place the dockers said."

"Tins?"

"Yes, the meats in tins. It's called Spam. It's really tasty — you'll enjoy it. I've a few spuds to go with it."

"What do you have to drink, Mary?"

"Just tea."

"Let's stop at an off-license and get a couple of bottles."

"Lovely."

They chatted in the pub for an hour or so. Mary complained about the raids, which had been almost nightly until Christmas. Now they occurred once or twice a week.

"People get used to them," she said. "I don't even bother to go to a shelter."

Chadwick was surprised at her phlegmatic attitude. He asked after Deidre, her friend who was wounded in the raid when he met them with Doug Larson. She's back at work, Mary told him.

After a couple of "G and Ts," Mary announced it was nice and dark and they should be on their way. She led him south and they stopped to get some bottled beer at an off-license on the way to the Underground station near the Tower of London. It was only one stop to Aldgate. As they walked out of the station, Mary said, "I'll walk ahead. Take a left at the lamp post, second right, number twenty-five, second floor. I'll leave the door off the latch. Don't knock."

Chadwick slowed and watched her walk down the street. The lamp was not illuminated because of the black-out. Within a minute he was sliding into the door of her small flat. Mary was waiting and gave him a generous kiss, saying, "Take your coat off, I'll get some supper moving."

Soon the chilly air warmed up as she got a fire going in the grate and she opened a couple of bottles. Mary reached into her handbag and pulled out a rectangular blue tin, "Here it is—manna from heaven, whatever that means. Let's see how you like it." She busied herself at the stove and Chadwick savored the appetizing smell of fried onions. She plonked two plates on the kitchen table. "There you are, love. Fried onion and potato with fried Spam, a meal fit for a king. There's some HP sauce if you want."

Chadwick tucked in. He was quite hungry. The Spam was, indeed, delicious. The bottled beer fitted in nicely. When they had finished, he helped Mary soak the plates in hot water, which she got from a kettle, as the flat did not run to the luxury of running hot water.

"What's on the program for tomorrow, love?"

"I think I must be on my way about eight."

"All right, you can leave a few minutes before me. There's some Spam left. Do you want a bit for breakfast? I'll have it ready while you shave. Now there's the night's entertainment to round off a perfect evening."

Chadwick excused himself for a minute and ducked into the tiny bathroom with his satchel. He took a pee and cleaned his teeth and put his razor on the sink for the morning. Mary squeezed in and to his surprise picked up his toothbrush and gave her teeth a vigorous polish and then sat on the toilet. This was a level of intimacy he had not known with Melanie.

He backed out and waited for her in bed. She soon appeared, stripping off her clothes as she climbed between the sheets. They kissed fondly and Mary said, "You know what I like. Earn your supper, Allan."

Chapter Sixteen

Chadwick presented himself at Whitehall on the dot of eight-thirty. Doug Larson was waiting. "I want you to meet a few specialists, Allan. They'll decide on the details of your new identity." They walked down a corridor with small offices on either side. Larson knocked on a door and poked his head inside. "Marcel. I have our candidate here."

"Come in, come in, Monsieurs."

Chadwick was introduced.

"Monsieur Chadwick, I would like to have a short conversation in French with you. This will enable me to best determine your home address." He chatted to Chadwick about the weather, the possibility of a German raid and the quality of the food since rationing was introduced. Chadwick held up his end of the conversation as best he could.

"Décor, Monsieur Chadwick" Marcel said. "You're not going to fool many Frenchmen, but you could probably convince some thick-skulled Boche. Your accent is terrible but you could be from the northwest, perhaps Basque country or Brittany. What is your name, eh? We will use the same initials, how do you like Alain, er, er Clemente? How does that sound? Now to find you a home."

He turned to a tall bookcase full of travel guides. He selected one, flipped through the pages, and then said, "Here we are. Bernay. A small town twenty kilometers south of Le Havre. On the River Charentonne, about eight thousand souls, cloth production, agriculture, timbered old center. Can you remember that? Big enough to hide you in, I think. Monsieur Larson, this is not a comprehensive ident, n'est pas? Just a casual level."

"Yes, Marcel. Good enough to pass inspection on, say, a train."

"Bon. Now an address. Monsieur Chadwick, it is better for you to use an address you will remember, in French, naturellement."

"I live at thirty-two Chestnut Road."

"Wonderful, trente-deux, rue de Chataigne, Bernay, Eure. I will pass this along to the printer."

Larson took Chadwick to another specialist. "Just a few more minor details, Allan. Profession, ingenieur. Height, one-seventy-seven centimeters. Weight, sixty-seven kilos. Eyes, blue. Hair, brown. There you are, Allan, you're a new man."

He walked into a larger office, where several people were at work. "Here's our registry. You will be listed here. If there is any contact from France, registry will automatically alert me and a duty officer. We still need to decide on the class of travel permit."

Larson talked quietly to a short, balding man with thick glasses. "Allan, this is Hymie Synder. He's originally from Vienna, where he was a printer of government documents. Now he does that for us. He suggests a Guest Worker pass. Hymie is an expert on European paper. Your permit will pass inspection by the Gestapo."

On hearing that word Chadwick felt a momentary twinge of fear, as it brought back the feeling he had when arrested in Berlin years ago.

"The permit will need a date and a signature. Hymie can arrange that. Let's date it about a month ago. Leave things with me. I'll contact you at Boscombe Down when you can pick it up. If you ever find yourself in France under the Nazis, you will also need a work permit. Obviously, we can't issue one, but the French could manage that. I think it's time for tea."

Chadwick undertook the tedious rail journey to Salisbury and soon forgot about the fake travel permit. Experts working on Oboe had concluded the British maps of France needed the datum shifted by 410 yards to the east and sixteen yards to the south. Chadwick went on several Oboe raids using the new charts. The results were only slightly better. Chadwick sat in a meeting of people from Bomber Command, Telecommunications, and Boscombe Down.

After a raucous meeting, it was agreed the remaining errors were largely due to the high altitude of the Pathfinders and the bomber following in their footsteps. Chadwick volunteered to make a Pathfinder sortie at low level using the first Mosquito plane to be delivered to Boscombe.

To start, he organized a series of mock raids on British targets. He placed dummy marker flares on airfields near Plymouth, Falmouth and Weymouth. These had some similarity to typical French Atlantic ports. He decided to make the drops at a thousand feet, and approach from the seaward.

During these trials, the RDR operators developed a technique of guiding the Pathfinder along one position line from a conveniently situated transmitter that passed over the target. A second position line crossing almost at right angles gave the crossing point for the flare release. They called it "Cat and Mouse." Stalking along the first line was the Cat. Reaching the second line was when the Cat pounced on the Mouse.

After a couple of weeks of intensive flying, Chadwick, his crew, and the RDR operators felt they were ready for a bombing raid over German submarine pens at Nantes. The track of the Cat and the Mouse over the target was carefully plotted using the new charts. Precise time delay measurements were calculated to the nearest tenth of a microsecond, corresponding to an error of a hundred feet.

Timing was critical. Chadwick's Mosquito flew on a curving path approaching the French coast from the Bay of Biscay. The bombers flew at high altitude over the Cherbourg Peninsula and made a last minute turn toward Nantes above Angers, arriving only a minute after Chadwick had marked the target with phosphorus flares. The intended target was thus not obvious to the Germans until the last minute.

Chadwick took off in partially cloudy weather from an airfield near Penzance just before midnight and flew south skirting Ushant. His navigator picked up the Cat line about fifty miles from the coast and they barreled eastwards with the two Merlin engines at full throttle, 340 knots on the air speed indicator, and 900 feet on the altimeter. The navigator called slight course changes to Chadwick and a second navigator gave warning of the rapid approach of the Mouse.

The Mosquito roared over the coastal defenses before the startled gun crews could react and the second navigator pressed the bomb release a split second after the shore flashed under the plane.

Fifty seconds later a fleet of Wellington and Manchester bombers glimpsed the flares and pounded the naval dockyard. Although the pens were protected by massive concrete roofs, the bombs destroyed much of the supporting infrastructure, and submarine maintenance was interrupted for weeks.

Chadwick zoomed up to 30,000 feet as soon as the flares were released and made a night landing at Chivenor thirty-five minutes later. Photographs taken by the bombers using flash bombs were examined by the photo reconnaissance experts and it was deemed as accurate a bombing raid as had ever been achieved in the past.

No bombs fell on the French houses clustered beyond the walls of the dockyard. There were no British losses, Churchill himself was informed of the success the next day, and there was great celebration in the Air Ministry that many problems of night bombing had apparently been solved. Nobody told Churchill that the Oboe technique did not reach as far as Germany.

Avro began to sporadically deliver Lancaster bombers. The test team at Boscombe took over the assessment and the preparation of "Pilot's Notes" with a sense of urgency. It was hoped to field a few squadrons before the end of the year. A great deal had to be done, not only for the flying crews but also for the maintenance technicians on the ground.

One day Chadwick volunteered to fly a Lancaster, which had been under test, back to Woodford because he was familiar with the Avro airfield and the people there. He flew with a skeleton crew of a flight engineer and wireless operator. The weather closed in after they arrived, and the Rapide planned for their return was grounded, so they settled in at RAF Ringway. Chadwick's old squadron, 613, was no longer stationed there.

In the morning, the forecast was for more of the same and he arranged travel warrants for the three of them to return to Boscombe by train via London. They caught the express to Euston at Stockport station, but the train was delayed en route by damage to the tracks from a German raid the night before. It was after nine in the evening when the train finally staggered into London. The Railway Transportation Office, or RTO, at Euston gave them vouchers for hotels and hostels in the area and Chadwick finally got to bed near midnight.

He met the two sergeants at Waterloo station in the morning and got them on a train to Salisbury. He decided to travel on a later train, as he had unfinished business with Doug Larson. Larson was pleased to see him and showed him with great delight the travel permit MI6 had made for journeys into occupied France. The permit had the German Eagle balanced on a swastika at the top. Larson assured Chadwick the signature corresponded to that of a high Nazi official. The paper had a slightly worn look, as though it had been jostled many times in someone's pocket. Larson mentioned that Mr. Synder had told him the paper was not quite right—it would pass inspection but the Germans had been forced to cheapen paper due to the difficulty of importing trees from Scandinavia. In an envelope with the permit was some greasy French money.

"Not a word to anyone about this, Allan," Larson warned. "This is just an arrangement between you and me. Just keep the envelope tucked inside your flying suit. If you need it—well, you never know. It might get you back home in one piece." Chadwick thanked him warmly and made his way to Boscombe.

Wing Commander Rowley mentioned that several improvements had been tried to make Oboe easier to use. He suggested Chadwick set up a few trials similar to the ones he did earlier with the original Oboe equipment. The need for two navigators was eliminated by having the pilot hear a signal which indicated if the plane was left or right of the path for the Cat. Once settled on that path, a series of "squeaks" increased in crescendo as the moment drew near for the Cat to pounce on the Mouse—the point at which the two Oboe paths intersected over the parget. After some initial problems and a lot of flying involving trial and error, the electronic wizards got it working fairly well.

Rather than lay on a complicated large raid with a Pathfinder, Chadwick proposed the first trial over France could be a single bomber flying low to deceive the German RDR, and bombing a military target which could be photographed later to assess the accuracy. He was given permission to equip a Wellington for the raid. The new Oboe equipment was installed with an internal explosive charge to destroy it should the plane be forced down. Air Intelligence chose a target which had not been bombed up to then—the flying boat marine center at Brest. A sloping ramp ended at a large concrete apron, on which flying boats were hauled on a cradle for servicing on land. It made an ideal target.

The Oboe experts set up the Cat and Mouse signals. The actual release point for a thousand pound bomb would be about a mile from the target. The bomb would continue along the Cat path as it fell a thousand feet before impact.

Chadwick took off at midnight with good visibility and a cloud base of 4,000 feet. He started the turn onto the Cat path well over the Atlantic and swept in over the port of Brest before the anti-aircraft gunners could react, even though their guns were directed by Wurzburg RDR. He maintained the same low altitude over the Gulf of St. Malo and the Cherbourg Peninsula and landed once again at Chivenor on the south coast of the Bristol Channel. The runway lights were turned on briefly when his arrival was predicted by RAF RDR. In the morning, a Spitfire photo reconnaissance plane took a picture from 30,000 feet, and the apron showed a distinct crater slightly north of the center.

In France on the same morning, a young Leutnant in the Luftwaffe Intelligence Center pondered the routine report that was made of enemy activity in the previous twenty-four hours. Why did the British send a high-speed single bomber along the Channel coast to plant one bomb on the sea plane base, which was hardly a target of great military importance? It came to him as he was eating lunch in a pleasant French chateau which had been commandeered. It was obvious. The Tommies were testing a bombing aiming system. It must be similar to "Knickbeine."

After lunch he explained his deductions to an intelligence officer concerned with signals, and he agreed that a search must be made immediately for the wireless signals that the British had used so that methods of jamming could be devised. The Luftwaffe kept a continuous log of frequencies that were scanned automatically, twenty-four hours a day. It did not take long for the Luftwaffe signal specialists to find traces of transmissions from England corresponding to the times of the raid. Far more interesting was the discovery that the aiming system required the bomber to make a series of short transmissions as well, which opened up the possibility of tracking it before it reached the target.

Analysis of the results of Chadwick's raid were received with great satisfaction by Telecommunications, Malvern, and Bomber Command Operational Planning Group. The equipment he had carried in the Wellington was a prototype which had been hastily wired together. The transmissions from England were done under manual control and that side of the improved Oboe needed to be redesigned for automatic operation. But the result justified the effort, without the British realizing that the single aircraft raid had tipped their hand and the German Luftwaffe was on to it. Their research engineers suggested a fighter could be equipped with a receiver tuned to the British bomber frequency using a directional aerial, and then the fighter could simply home in on the bomber. Development went ahead.

Chadwick was still quite unhappy with the overall picture for carrying the bomber campaign to Germany. The precision guidance systems hardly penetrated German air space and Chadwick was concerned that the bombing of Germany would simply consist of area bombing of cities. He still felt that deliberate bombing of civilians was immoral. He concentrated on understanding the detailed technical features of Oboe, which used short bursts of wireless waves from RDR aerials, called pulses, to measure distance to a bomber which returned a similar short transmission when the pulse was received, what the boffins called a transponder.

Thinking hard about the system in the evenings, Chadwick suddenly had an inspiration. Suppose the pulse directed to the bomber was sent from a plane flying at 30,000 feet? Excited, he grabbed a book on trigonometry and calculated the range for a line of sight to the horizon. He worked the numbers and decided the range could be over 400 miles between a plane flying at 30,000 feet in England and a bomber over the continent at 20,000 feet.

Brimming with enthusiasm, he wrote a brief description of the system, and in the morning got hold of Wing Commander Rowley as soon as he could.

Rowley listened, not grasping some of the technical details, but when Chadwick had finished, he said, "Allan, you certainly have a bee in your bonnet about bomber precise guidance."

Chadwick stopped short, thought for a minute and replied, "Yes, Sir, I suppose I do. But my motive is not necessarily to drop bombs where they should go but to not drop them where they shouldn't."

"I think you should explain this idea to the boffins. Let me think—fly over to Bawdsey and see if you can sell the scheme to Dr. Starret."

Chadwick made some arrangements. The Rapide ferry from Boscombe Down had been replaced by an Anson, which carried more passengers but tended to be slower. All those people wanted to be dropped off at different RAF bases. Chadwick found Woodbridge was the last stop. His meeting with Dr. Starret was the following morning after his arrival at RAF Woodbridge. He wondered if he should call the station commander, Squadron Leader Wilson, but decided against it. He spent the evening polishing his presentation.

Bawdsey sent a car for him at eight, and by nine Chadwick was sitting with half a dozen senior engineers and physicists. He started off by explaining that his goal was to extend the range of Oboe so that targets in Germany could be attacked. An operational range of 600 nautical miles would do the trick, he suggested. He conceded that some loss of accuracy would be sacrificed. He outlined the scheme using an intermediate aircraft as a relay for the transponder signals and suggested the relay would fly in a closed pattern about 300 miles from the RDR bases in Britain.

Chadwick acknowledged the scheme needed four additional relay planes—two for the Cat track and two for the Mouse track. He also acknowledged the additional relays introduced time delays which were not precisely known, and so precision would suffer. His presentation took nearly an hour, and Starret arranged for some tea to be brought into the room and they take a short break.

After tea, Chadwick faced a barrage of doubts and questions, led by Dr. Starret, who started off by criticizing the vast man-power and equipment need for just one bomber. Chadwick countered by saying that one bomber could be a Pathfinder for a fleet of up to 500 Lancasters. There were shouts indicating skepticism at the mention of 500 and Chadwick realized the boffins probably had no knowledge of the scale of the vast bombing campaign planned for later that year. "That number is secret," he said with a grin.

Dr. Starret pointed out the aerials on the relay aircraft would be nothing as efficient as the aerials on the ground stations. Chadwick riposted by claiming the extra height would make up for that. The boffins spent a long time debating among themselves how to compensate for the delays introduced by the flying relays.

Finally, Starret announced it was time for lunch. He looked very thoughtful over the meal and in a private meeting with Chadwick afterwards, told him the idea had merit and it would receive further analysis at Bawdsey and probably also by the Telecommunications people at Malvern. Chadwick flew back to Boscombe on a late flight, well satisfied with the way things had gone.

He had been the trigger for the scheme to extend the range of Oboe, but he did not have the expertise to carry the idea further, and so he was not aware that, as the experts discovered and then solved problems with the proposal, that it became an important development activity and was crucial in taking the bomber offensive to German targets.

A small test flight was set up using the three Wellington bombers originally used in the testing of Gee. It was based at RAF Honiley for the airborne trials of Oboe developmental equipment.

Chapter Seventeen

In the late spring, the British Government was surprised when the German Army was unleashed on the Soviet Union. MI6 agents in Poland had warned of suspicious German Wehrmacht maneuvers and Churchill even arranged for Stalin to be informed, although an exact date could not be foretold.

Chadwick heard about the attack, as usual, from the BBC News. For several months he had been involved in getting new Lancaster bomber squadrons activated and trained. Ten new Lancaster bomber squadrons were formed using squadron numbers that had been inactive since 1919. Each squadron fielded twenty aircraft in two flights. The Air Ministry felt this was the best way to expand the RAF to incorporate the new heavy bombers rather than re-equip existing squadron with older planes such as the Handley Page Hampden, which could be replaced later.

There was a great deal of learning to be accomplished, and for several months Chadwick visited them all with guidance on formation flying, bombing tactics, and advice on getting the best performance out of the Lancaster. A crucial problem was how to avoid collisions over the target. This was solved to some extent by using Gee where possible to separate bombers into streams, not formations, at the start of the attack. Aircraft were timed precisely and assigned different altitudes. However, in trials at night, accidents did occur.

Chadwick was temporarily at RAF Duxford when he received a message, passed down from Boscombe Down, to contact Dr. Starret. When he telephoned the research establishment, the doctor asked if he could possibly get to Bawdsey within the next day or two. The subject he wished to discuss was too secret to be mentioned on an open phone line. Intrigued, Chadwick easily persuaded the squadron he was visiting to fly him to RAF Woodbridge. When he sat down in the untidy, book-lined office with Dr. Starret, the scientist again warned him the topic was most secret.

"For the past six months, we have been energetically developing the SuperOboe bombing aid using airborne relays to extend the range, an idea you first suggested."

Chadwick scratched his head. "I did? Yes, I vaguely remember."

"To work properly, the system requires tedious calculations to be made very quickly, and for that we developed a mechanical calculator. Numerous trials have been carried out over the British Isles. Our superiors have decided it is sufficiently mature to try it over Germany. I am now in a position to ask you if you would like to fly in the Pathfinder as an observer. This experience will be valuable for your present duties, I am told."

Chadwick could appreciate the thinking that had obviously gone on somewhere in Bomber Command. "Yes," he said. "It's possible. Where and when is the raid?"

"The raid will be in about a week, depending on the weather. I was simply asked to get your reaction. If you agree, you will be thoroughly briefed by Bomber Command. However, I know from the rumor mill that it will be the RAF's biggest exercise of the war up to now. All the new Lancaster squadrons will be involved. The Pathfinder will be a Wellington, which has been specially modified to work with the system. It has dedicated aerials and some pretty complicated electric gear, which the crews have been working with for about a month."

"Right-oh, I'm on. Who is my contact?"

"Please visit Group Captain Hearne at Bomber Command, RAF Uxbridge."

Chadwick smiled to himself. He had met Hearne nearly three years earlier, when there was some concern about the number of bomber wings he needed to simulate raids on Britain to train RDR operators. Chadwick called Boscombe and was in time to book a flight on the Anson ferry to RAF Farnborough, which was conveniently close to Uxbridge.

When Chadwick stopped by Hearne's office, the group captain enthusiastically seized his hand and pumped it up and down. "Squadron Leader Chadwick! Welcome. When I heard the name I wondered if it was the same chap who stole all our planes to play with Fighter Command." He looked at the battle ribbons. "I see you're having a busy war. Well, Bomber Command has a big one coming up. I'm told you'll be observing the Pathfinder performance and passing the word back to the operational squadrons."

"I'm still a bit in the dark, Sir. What's the target?"

"The target is the Messerschmitt factory at Augsburg, in southern Germany, a range of about nine hundred miles. At the moment it's the major source for the Luftwaffe Bf 109 fighter, a worthy target, I think you'll agree. The raid requires elaborate planning, a feint will be made for Munich, but the main force will hit Augsburg. I think Dr. Starret has recommended this flight for you because of your initial contribution to start the development of 'SuperOboe.' Perhaps tomorrow you should fly into Honiley and meet Flight Lieutenant Dennis Scofield, who's in charge of the test flight. I'll send an order to Honiley outlining your duties."

Chadwick left Northolt the next day, sorry he hadn't been able to see Lady Fitzgibbon when he was so close to her house. *But that's the war*, he consoled himself. He had fond memories of RAF Honiley anyway. He had been stationed there for the very first trials that led to his involvement with RDR. He remembered a very attractive barmaid at a pub near Honiley. *What was her name? Esmeralda?* But for the life of him he couldn't remember where the pub was, or its name.

Flight Lieutenant Scofield was delighted to meet Squadron Leader Chadwick. In the arcane world of electronic warfare, Chadwick had achieved a somewhat legendary reputation. He introduced the two navigators who flew with him—Flying Officers James—Jim—Jackman and Dick Ramsey. "Jim's primary job is to navigate with Gee when we depart and link up with the Cat signal, which doesn't start until we are about a hundred miles from the target. Dick is the Mouse monitor and bomb aimer. Everything must be done according to a strict time schedule, so they're pretty busy. Come and look round our special Wimpy, and we'll be flying tomorrow, Sir."

Chadwick went with him to dispersal and climbed aboard the familiar Wellington. The interior had been substantially modified; two navigation desks carried racks of electronic gear. Chadwick noted that they carried yellow and black striped switches under protective covers. He pointed to them.

"Yes, Sir. Throw those and we'll probably set fire to the kite," Ramsey said with a laugh.

"Explosive and thermite," Scofield added. "The boffins really want to keep this stuff away from the Jerries."

The next day Chadwick attended a navigation briefing for the Pathfinder and wing commanders. He was impressed by the amount of careful thought that had gone into the planning of the raid and the feint. Besides this attack on Augsburg, Bomber Command had laid on another attack on Kiel by Wellingtons and Manchesters at the same time. The idea was to keep the Luftwaffe busy. The forecast looked favorable for the attack in forty-eight hours. Take-off for the Pathfinder would be 2215 hours, Greenwich Mean Time.

The night of the raid, Chadwick listened to the final briefing, mostly the latest weather forecast, and then started his preparations. He ate heartily, emptied his bowels, and dressed warmly. His flying boots were a new issue that were designed to be converted to normal-looking civilian shoes by cutting away the fur-lined tops, although they still looked pretty bulky to him. He put the envelope that Doug Larson had given to him in an inside pocket. The crew made the usual strained jokes when they were dropped off at the aircraft. Once plugged in to the intercom, each acknowledged good audio and waited for the Very signal from the tower.

Chadwick stood behind the pilot as they surged down the runway, delineated by dim smudge pots. During the climb, Chadwick asked Scofield what height they would be cruising at.

"Thirty-two thou," was the reply.

Chadwick expressed mild skepticism, and Scofield told him the engines were specially modified, with new super-chargers. "We've had the old girl up to thirty-five thou," he said proudly.

In advanced RDR stations in France, operators of the Luftwaffe Kammhuber line soon detected massive RAF flights heading for targets in Germany. Obeying special orders, a twin-engined fighter, the Me 110, was put on alert. Later it was ordered to climb to 10,000 meters. This plane had been modified after Chadwick's raid nearly a year earlier on the seaplane base at Brest. The wireless emissions that were part of the Cat and Mouse system had been analyzed by Luftwaffe experts and the Me 110 had been adapted to home in on the British planes by displaying the patterns to an observer in the rear seat, who gave directions to the pilot. They called the homing device "Boobytrap." It was an irony that no one would ever know that both the Cat and Mouse signals and the Boobytrap's detector owed their existence to Chadwick, who was now being tracked by the very device he had inadvertently caused to be created.

Jackman confirmed he was receiving the Cat signal when they approached the German border and Ramsey slid into the forward bomb aimer's position, where he heard both the Mouse and Cat signals. Scattered flak lit up the sky. In the Me 110, twenty-five kilometers behind the Wellington, the observer, Ober Leutnant Gunther Schneck, excitedly called his pilot on the intercom,

"Hauptmann, I have a target on the ranging apparatus. Target is twenty-three kilometers ahead, on our left. I am not receiving the signals from them yet."

The pilot, Hauptmann Werner Hochberg, muttered, "Good. Keep an eye on it. It is like flying in treacle at this altitude."

The German fighter slowly overtook the Wellington, which was approaching the bomb release point. The flak at the Messerschmitt factory was very heavy. The Wimpy rocked from near misses. Chadwick listened on the intercom to Dick Ramsey as he called the timing of the Cat pounce. At the same time, the crew in the Me 110 were homing in on the same signals.

"Up a hundred, right five degrees—whoa, too much!" Schneck called out to the pilot as he stared intently at the screens in his cockpit.

"Dammit to hell," Hochberg yelled over the intercom. "I have to move the stick like I'm stirring plum pudding."

At their altitude, the plane's control surfaces did not have a good bite on the thin air. Anti-aircraft fire was also exploding near the German plane.

"What's the range, Schnek?" Hochberg demanded.

"Just over two 'k,' Hauptmann, but the echo is blurry at these short ranges."

"Keep trying."

On board the British plane, Ramsey was counting down. "Steady, steady—bombs gone."

Scofield was also listening to the Cat and Mouse signals on the intercom. "I think we got a perfect fix, gentlemen. We should see the flares explode soon. Turn off the Oboe gear, Jim. No point in broadcasting any longer than necessary."

Jackman flipped off the switches on the electronic equipment littering the navigator's desk. On the German plane, Schnek cried out, "God in Heaven, the damned signal has gone."

"Well, it's getting a little hot," Hochberg replied, as two shells exploded near the plane. "Time to head for home." He initiated a steep diving turn.

"What's our course home, Jim?" Scofield called on the intercom. "Try two-ninety for twenty minutes. That will keep us south of Stuttgart. Then three zero fiver should do the trick. We'll be over France when you make the turn. Maybe the flak will be less."

At the Oboe Control Center in England, the sudden cessation of the responses from the Wellington indicated they had shut down, and presumably the flares were burning. Another officer coordinating the Lancaster stream commented, "First Lanc will be over target in two minutes. We'll get a sighting report."

There was a palpable feeling of relief aboard the Wimpy once the flares had been released. They had done their part, and now it just remained to get safely home. In fact, nearly 400 miles of hostile territory lay between them and the safety of England. In about ninety minutes flying time, they would be over the North Sea.

Jackman called the turn south of Stuttgart. "I'm getting sporadic Gee signals. We'll be over France in a couple of minutes."

Then the plane was wracked by exploding anti-aircraft fire, which was particularly well-aimed. They were re-crossing the Kammhuber line and the guns were directed by the Freya RDR system. A violent, noisy explosion threw the plane into a steep bank as a shell detonated ahead of the left engine. Scofield wrestled with the controls. The left engine kept running but began to make loud, ominous noises. The pilot saw that the engine temperature was leaping up and the rpm falling. A blast of cold air swept into the cockpit from the forward hatch.

"Squadron Leader, please check on Flying Officer Ramsey, that last one was awfully close to his office."

Chadwick snapped "Will do" into the microphone and then unplugged and squeezed his way into the nose cone. It was a shambles. Ramsey was prostrate besides his seat, his body lacerated by dozens of shrapnel fragments. His head sagged, and Chadwick could see he was practically decapitated. The 200-

knot wind howling through the shattered Perspex was already freezing the blood solid.

Chadwick backed out and yelled into Scofield's ear, "Dick's had it. No hope, skip."

Scofield nodded. He was furiously trying to keep the bomber level as the left engine gave up the ghost.

Chadwick went back to the navigator's desk and plugged in. "How bad is it, skipper?"

"Left engine dead, won't feather. I can just hold her with full rudder and aileron. Christ, just looked at the fuel gauges, left tank is empty. Right tank about half full. We're sinking about three hundred feet a minute. We're going to have to bail out within a few minutes. Jim, press the destruct switches on the Oboe stuff."

The self-destruct charges included a thirty-second delay. Chadwick watched with interest as Jackman reached across, flipped up the covers, and pressed the switches. Shortly after, there were a series of sharp detonations, but more surprisingly, a loud shriek as gases escaped through gaps in the equipment cases and dense white smoke began to fill the fuselage.

"Squadron Leader, jettison the door. Should clear that smoke."

"Dennis, how do you plan to evacuate while you're holding full rudder?"

"I'm the captain, last to leave the ship. Isn't that the drill?"

"I suggest you throttle back on the right engine. That will relieve pressure on the rudder bar. We will just descend a little faster, that's all. But we can all get out."

Scofield did as Chadwick suggested and found the plane was gliding nicely at 120 knots, 600 feet a minute vertical speed.

"Try turning George on, Dennis. Match the speed and heading first, then set an altitude five or six thousand below our present height."

"My God, Squadron Leader, I think she's stable for the moment."

Chadwick mentally thanked Mr. Pemberton of Farnborough for making sure there was a good reserve of pneumatic pressure to run George. Then he wrenched his mind to the dire situation they were facing. "For reasons too difficult to explain, I must not bail out near the point you fellows leave the ship. I suggest the crew bail out now. I'll stay by the hatch. When George shows signs of instability, I'll go then. Remember— name, rank, and serial number only. Do not mention my presence. I was never on this flight." He chuckled, trying to ignore the seriousness of the fate awaiting all of them. "Happy Landings."

Despite their misgivings, the crew flung themselves into the inky void over France. The Wellington continued to glide almost silently earthward. Somewhere a cover was banging in the slipstream.

Chadwick waited a full ten minutes after the crew left and was about to exit the plane when he had a better idea. He made his way to the cockpit with difficulty, the parachute hanging off his back hampering his movements. He glanced at the altimeter and the height set on George's control panel. They were passing 11,000 feet; the height set was 10,000. He quickly readjusted the height setting to 4,000 and struggled back to the hatch. George would now be able to control the crippled plane for another ten or twelve minutes. The Wellington would inevitably crash many miles from where Chadwick landed.

He launched himself into the blackness.

Chapter Eighteen

Chadwick tumbled helplessly as he fell earthwards. But the stars showed him which way was up, and by extending his arms he stabilized and pulled the ripcord. He slipped his goggles over his eyes. Apocryphal RAF horror stories of bailing out at night flashed through his mind. *I might land on a church steeple, or plummet down a factory chimney. Suppose the furnace is still lit? How about landing in a pig sty?* His musings were cut short by a sharp blow from some wooden stakes and he rolled into what seemed to be a thin bush. His 'chute was caught on some vegetation and he worked blindly to wrap the cloth into a ball and secure it with the shrouds.

It was pointless to move until there was a trace of dawn. He could see no lights nearby. Chadwick leaned against the parachute. He felt quite warm, and even dozed off, and then suddenly came to his senses, hearing the shrill cry of birds and seeing a trace of orange on the horizon. Gradually, he realized he was surrounded by a wide field of grape vines. Although it wasn't light enough to see far, when he stood up, he could tell there was no habitation nearby.

Chadwick unzipped his flying boots and pulled out the small penknife he always carried. He began to snip away at the stitching in the upper part of the shoe to detach the calf-length fur-lined top. He then picked at the hundreds of small pieces of thread still showing on the shoe. After an hour's work he donned the shoes, not sure anybody would be fooled by them.

The wintry sun had not risen far above the hilly landscape, and it was getting light enough for him to think about his next step. He was saved from making a decision by the appearance of an elderly man in the track between the vines. He slowly approached Chadwick, who saw that the man wore large leather gaiters, brown corduroy trousers, and a pale blue shirt under a leather jacket. His unruly white hair poked out from a black beret. His face was deeply tanned, and his white beard was neatly trimmed.

"Good Day, Monsieur," Chadwick said in the best French he could muster.

The old man replied in accented French, pointing with a gnarled stick. "You have ruined a few of my grape vines, young man."

"I am terribly sorry, Sir. Perhaps the cloth in the parachute has enough value to compensate you."

The old man fingered the cloth. "Perhaps. Who are you. What is your nationality?"

"My name is Allan. I am English. The plane I was flying in was shot down last night."

"Oh, the war." The Frenchman said it as though it explained everything.

"Could you please tell me where I am?"

"You are in Lorraine, about a hundred kilometers from Nancy."

"Are there any German soldiers nearby?"

"We don't see them in the country too much. They stick to the towns and cities. Do you want to meet one?" There was a glint of humor in the old man's eyes.

"Not particularly. I would like to get rid of these flying clothes."

"I will take you to my house. It's about a kilometer from here. Leave most of your things. I'll bring a small cart later. My name is Pierre Fournier."

He started to walk down the track and gestured for Chadwick to follow. After a short rise, the field began to slope down and as they rounded a shoulder, Chadwick caught a glimpse of a substantial farm. Three sturdy white stone houses surrounded a square, and behind were long sheds with steel chimneys.

"My wife died ten years ago," the old man said gruffly. "I live with my two daughters. I have a son but he was called up in 1939 and I have no idea what has become of him. We have farmed here for many generations. You need have no fear that you will be betrayed."

"You are very kind, Monsieur. I am obviously lucky to meet you."

"No, you were lucky you landed in the west of Lorraine. This part of France is called Alsace-Lorraine. Most people speak German and French and even a language of our own. Until the war with Prussia it was French. Then it became German. They built a lot of factories, mostly in the east. Then it became French again. Now they tell us it is German. Mostly the French live in the west and farm the land just as we have always done."

The old farmer opened a heavy wooden door with an iron latch. They walked across a stone flagged floor to a wide room at the back. The old man thrust open the door. A well-built, buxom woman turned in surprise. "Madeleine, we have a guest. This is Allan, who just dropped in."

The woman looked at Chadwick with shrewd eyes.

"Madeleine is my eldest daughter. My son Jean was born next and then my youngest daughter, Charlotte, who is around somewhere."

Chadwick mumbled a greeting in French.

"Madeleine, how does Allan compare to Jean in size?" The woman looked at Chadwick.

"He is not as tall and he's thinner."

"That's what I thought. Monsieur Chadwick. I think we can make you look like a Frenchman. We can find some old clothes of Jean's, and Madeleine can tailor them a bit."

"Do you require to measure me, Mademoiselle?"

She replied shortly, "No, there is not much difference."

"Madeleine, can you find a little something for Allan to eat. I'm sure he is hungry."

"Sit down, Allan, our food is simple farm produce. For breakfast, bread and cheese, with our brand of white wine."

"That would be wonderful, Monsieur." Chadwick was soon tucking into a hunk of home-baked bread with a thick slice of cheese. When he tasted the wine it had a slightly sweet flavor. "The wine is very good," he remarked. "It reminds me of a Riesling."

"The wine was made here with the grapes you squashed this morning. Riesling, I think, is a German wine also made in Alsace-Lorraine."

"How much wine do you make every year, Monsieur Fournier?"

"About two thousand liters, just for our own use and a few friends. We sell most of our grapes to much larger yards. That is where the farm income comes from."

"Monsieur Fournier, I don't want to be a burden to you or your family. We were told in England that the French résistance is very active and tries to return airmen like me to Britain."

"Perhaps. First we shall look after your immediate needs. Madeleine, please prepare a bed for our guest. Come with me."

Fournier led the way to some narrow wooden stairs and on the landing opened the door of a pleasant room. There was a bed with a striped mattress and a chest of drawers. On the dresser was a deep bowl and a pitcher. "You can wash here. One of the women will fill the jug with warm water. Look through the window." Fournier pointed to a small building at the back of the house. "There is the WC."

Chadwick was beginning to feel a little overwhelmed by the casual way Fournier was fitting him into the family life.

"When Madeleine has some clothes for you, we will harness the donkey and go to get the parachute and other stuff."

Just then his daughter entered with an armful of Jean's things. "I have shortened the pantaloons. The other things will take more time, but will fit all right, I think."

Chadwick was left to change. When he went downstairs Fournier clapped his hands. "Bravo, my brave Musketeer. Come, we'll wake up the donkey." He led Chadwick to a barn. Inside was a donkey, a horse, and two morose-looking cows. They harnessed the donkey to a small cart and made their way back to the spot where Chadwick had so suddenly landed in Fournier's life.

The farmer took some new stakes out of the cart and passed a couple to Chadwick, "Please remove the broken stakes and insert these new ones."

Chadwick looked at the vineyard. He had left a trail of destruction about a hundred feet long as he was pulled along the ground by the parachute after touching down. He started to repair the damage by cutting the coarse twine on the broken stakes and tying the bedraggled plants to a new stake. As he was working near the farmer, he heard him talking softly in an incomprehensible language. He was swiftly tying a broken vine to a stick and as he leaned close to the plant, he whispered and stroked the leaves.

"It looks like you are talking to the vine, Monsieur," Allan said with a laugh.

"I am indeed. My father taught me that all living things can understand feelings and emotions. I told the vine I was sorry for the injury but all will be well soon. It will tell the others."

Chadwick decided the old man was mad. "How will it do that, Monsieur?" he asked.

"Why they talk to each other through the roots. Underneath where we are standing, the roots intertwine and talk to each other."

When they had finished the repairs, they put the 'chute and Chadwick's flying clothing in the cart, along with the broken stakes. Back at the house they carried the parachute inside and Chadwick said to Miss Fournier, "I hope you can make something nice from the cloth. Perhaps underwear at least."

Madeleine stroked the material, "It will make good sheets."

Just then another woman entered the room.

"Look what our guest has brought us, Charlotte, some beautiful cloth."

Fournier cried, "Charlotte, this is Allan. He will probably be staying with us for a little while."

Chadwick extended his hand while looking at Charlotte with amazement. It was hard to believe she was Madeleine's sister. She was a gamine, slim and pert. She smiled at Allan and skipped lightly out of the room.

"I think I will go up to my room, Monsieur," he said to the father.

"Yes, Madeleine has made up your bed. Relax, we'll have some lunch in an hour."

Chadwick found his bed had been made up with a thick quilt and a bolster. He washed his hands and removed the envelope that Larson had given him from inside his shirt. Some instinct warned him not to mention the fake identification to Fournier, but he took a few notes of paper money from the pile and put them in his pocket.

Chadwick went downstairs for lunch and showed Monsieur Fournier a hundred franc note, "We carry a few notes in case we are forced down, Monsieur. I would like you to take this money to cover the expenses you have been forced to bear by my arrival."

"We do not use much money nowadays, Allan. But there are some things I have to buy occasionally when I am in the village. Thank you."

"The next time you are there, please find out quietly if there is a resistance group that could get me back to England."

"Yes, yes, I will look into it. But do not worry, you're quite safe here."

A week went by but Fournier did not leave the farm. Chadwick helped with farm chores—mucking out, feeding the animals, chopping wood. The Frenchman even took the opportunity to carry out some repairs to the wooden sides of the barn, now that he had an extra pair of hands for help. Chadwick ate with the family; the meals were simple but nourishing, mostly derived from Madeleine's small garden. Meat was rare, but once they had a kind of sausage stuffed with rabbit meat and onions.

One evening after Chadwick had retired, the old farmer suddenly spoke to his daughters in the special argot used for centuries in Lorraine. "Madeleine, has Allan tried to get into your bed? Or have you tried to climb into his bed?" Madeleine said nothing.

"Papa," Charlotte cried, "you are being disgusting."

"Not really, my love. I am being practical. Farms need a young man around, and see what heaven has sent us. It would be different if Jean was here, but only God knows where he is."

One day, a postman pedaled up the muddy lane to the farm with a letter for M. Fournier. It bore a German stamp and the old man regarded it with suspicion.

"Open it, open it," his daughters shouted. "I think it is Jean's handwriting."

Fournier carefully slit the top of the envelope with his knife and extracted a single sheet. His daughters crowded round, excited. Fournier glanced at the signature. "Yes, it is from Jean. He sends his love."

"What else? Tell us."

"He is in a labor camp, building airfields. He says he is fine. Because he speaks German he is a foreman. The sergeant, though, has told him to act stupid, or he may be drafted into the Wehrmacht."

"That is wonderful, father. One day when the silly war is over he will be coming back."

Fournier considered carefully what she just said, thinking, *The Germans were doing well in Russia, and were nearly at Moscow. The war should be over soon, except for the perfidious Albion.* These thoughts settled the doubts in Fournier's mind about Chadwick and shortly after lunch, he harnessed the horse to a carriage and drove into the small village of St. Evrard en Marne. He took Madeleine, who came to make some small purchases. He warned her to say nothing about their guest to anyone.

In a bar, he ordered a glass of absinthe and chattered with friends he had known since childhood. There was one man in particular he wished to meet. He passed the word and shortly after, a tall man entered and greeted him warmly. "Pierre, how are you? Time on your hands this time of the year, eh?"

They chatted and Fournier said quietly, "I have an angel who fell to earth and wants to fly home." His friend passed a stubby pencil and a small notepad under the table. "Put the name here, I will pass it on."

When Fournier returned to the farm he told Chadwick that wheels were in motion.

Chapter Nineteen

There was a great deal of consternation at the Oboe Control Center when Chadwick's plane failed to return from the raid on Augsburg. The concern was at several levels. The first was to determine if the secret Oboe equipment had been destroyed before it fell into enemy hands. The second concern was Chadwick. His report on the success of the Oboe-directed mass bomber raid would be invaluable before another similar raid was planned. And then there was concern that Chadwick knew a good deal about Oboe and under interrogation may give away vital secrets.

It was decided to make a priority of finding Chadwick's whereabouts. Someone brought up the question of what to inform the next of kin, not only Chadwick's but the six crew flying with him. "That's a tricky issue," said the wing commander who was running the meeting. "We also lost three Lancasters in the raid. It was strictly 'Most Secret.' I think the decision has been made to post the crew of those missing Lancs as MIA without any details about the raid itself.

"So, Squadron Leader Chadwick and his fellow crew members are also categorized as MIA. There was a Wellington raid on Kiel that same night, I think officially we will say their Wellington went down on that raid. Concerning Chadwick's disappearance and the site of the crash, we'll leave that to Air Intelligence, who will no doubt pass it on to their spooks in MI6."

Doug Larson was routinely informed two days later, because of the trigger against Chadwick's name, that MI6 had been asked to locate Allan Chadwick and the crash site of the plane he was flying when it went down somewhere over Germany or France. He decided their precaution in equipping Chadwick with paper had been a good move. Presumably "Alain Clement" would appear somewhere if he was alive.

M. Fournier harnessed up the horse again and drove into the village with Madeleine, it was a week before Christmas and he had given her a small sum to spend on holiday extras. The letter from Jean had made him think about the role of Chadwick in the family's farm. If Jean returned shortly, then his half-formed plan for Chadwick could be abandoned and the flier consigned to the arms of the résistance network.

He entered the bar feeling jubilant and asked for his friend with contacts. He detected an air of depression among his drinking pals. "Happy Noel! You all seem like you lost your purse."

One of the drinkers spoke up. "Pierre, you live in isolation on that farm of yours, so you probably don't know that America has entered the war on the British side, against Germany."

M. Fournier was shaken. His euphoric feeling disappeared instantly. He was an intelligent man and he knew that in the last war when America entered the conflict, Germany was defeated a little over a year later. All his assumptions evaporated. He realized now that the war would not end soon. Jean was probably not coming home. And he had initiated Chadwick's escape back to England, which compounded his dilemma.

On the way home, he sat glumly next to Madeleine on the front seat of the carriage. "Did you hear the news when you were in the village? The war has just got a lot worse."

"Yes, I heard, Papa. But we will survive on our little farm."

"I don't think Jean will be coming home soon, my dear. The Germans will need every man they can find to fight the war now." Fournier sat in silence for a few minutes as the horse plodded up the muddy lane. "I know this is an embarrassing topic, but really, what do you think of Monsieur Allan Chadwick?"

"Like all English, he is stuffy, I think."

"This is lot for a father to ask of his daughter, but the future of the farm is at stake. Our family has owned our farm for many generations. I do not want to lose it now because of this war."

"What are you saying? You want me to sleep with Allan? That is crazy, Papa. Pregnancy is hard to achieve. And even if that happens, the chances are we will have another girl to feed."

"I am sincerely sorry, my love. We live in perilous times. Difficult decisions have to be made. It is my understanding of breeding, that like cows, there are certain times that are usually successful."

Madeline looked at him in disbelief, and then turned away, embarrassed by the discussion.

"As for a grandson, the Good Lord will take care of that. Allan is young, probably feeling lonely and the nights are cold." They sat in silence as the farm came into view. "Perhaps in a few days we will make another trip to the village. You can talk to the midwife. I will find out if the escape plan for Allan is working. You go inside, I will look after the horse."

From London questions went out to the French résistance, requesting information on all RAF crashes on the night of the raid, with emphasis on whether the plane burned and if there were casualties or survivors. The résistance had good rapport with most police departments, where records of aviation crashes were kept.

The report to England went a circuitous route through Spain to the British Embassy in Madrid. Here it was encrypted and sent by telegram to London. Within ten days MI6 was informed that three planes crashed in France on the night in question. The report noted that two planes were four-engined heavy bombers, and one was a two-engined medium bomber. Referring to the four-engined planes, the report noted that one crashed with all on board killed and was destroyed, and six bodies were retrieved. It continued, noting that four airman escaped by parachute from the other heavy bomber and were arrested. Their plane was seriously damaged on impact, but did not burn. The medium bomber went down near Joinville and burned. Five airmen parachuted to safety and were arrested. One man was found dead in the plane; the coroner's opinion was that he was dead before the crash.

Each incident on the report ended with the same instruction: refer to the Appendix for the names of the deceased and the fuselage number. Air Intelligence quickly checked the names against the authorization log of Chadwick's trip, and found that Flight Lieutenant Scofield, Flying Officer Jackman, and the non-commissioned fliers were prisoners of war. Flying Officer Ramsey had been killed. So where was Chadwick? He seemed to have disappeared. Officers pored over detailed maps of France. The plane had crashed at Joinville, and Scofield and Jackman had been arrested near Charmes. It was a reasonable supposition that Chadwick had bailed out somewhere between the two places. A message was passed on to MI6 to alert the résistance to scour that area.

A day after they returned from the village, Madeleine sat down for a confidential talk with her father. "I will follow your advice, Father," she said. "I will seduce Monsieur Chadwick if I can. I cannot say he has shown much interest up to now, though."

"Bless you, child. It is the only way I can see for saving our farm in this currently insane world. There is some urgency, because when the résistance plans his escape, he will have to go with them. And it might be soon."

"In that case, I must talk to the midwife in the village. We must go back tomorrow."

"I will say we forgot to buy flour on our last visit."

Both Charlotte and Allan were surprised to see them leave early again the next day, but Charlotte was not taken in. "They are up to something," she told Allan. And before long, she put two and two together and concluded their visit must be related to her father's incredible suggestion about creating an heir. Then it crossed her mind that the heir would inherit the farm, and resentment suddenly sprang up. *Why should Madeleine's child be the lucky one?* she thought. Charlotte was not a virgin; farm children grew up too close to the animals to be unaware of the facts of life. She had coupled with a few of the itinerant workers that came to pick the grapes each summer. They were rough, coarse men who were not skilled in the arts of love. She decided she knew enough to outsmart Madeleine if she moved fast.

Chadwick first took care of a few chores in the barn, which by habit had become his responsibility. Then he went to his room and washed and shaved. It was a cold day and he was happy to flop down in a large chair near the fire. There was an ancient bookcase against one of the walls, and he selected a French mystery to read.

He was barely into the first chapter when Charlotte approached, saying, "There's room in that chair for two, *cherie*." She squeezed herself into the space next to Chadwick. Chadwick was surprised. Charlotte had not shown much interest in him previously.

She chattered on, "It's a frigid morning. They are going to be so cold in that carriage, and with the state the lane's in, it will take them at least an hour and half to get to St. Evrard. We must warm each other." She put her hand inside his shirt.

A willing invitation was a definite aphrodisiac and Allan found himself getting aroused. Charlotte moved her hand lower. Suddenly he stood and picked up Charlotte in both arms. She was a slight girl. "My room, I think," she whispered.

On the way to the village, Fournier talked seriously to his daughter. "There is another aspect. Once you raise the subject with the midwife, we are exposing the whereabouts of the airman at our home. Tongues will wag."

"We can't avoid that unless I say you are the problem."

"My God, that would never do."

"I shall ask her how to avoid pregnancy, but it will give us the guidance we need, I think."

The midwife, Madame Bonfleur, had delivered both the Fournier girls, and naturally when Madeleine questioned her about avoiding pregnancy she enquired the reason. "Don't you live alone after Jean left?"

Madeleine was forced to confess they had an unexpected guest. Madame Bonfleur knew better than to ask too much. Instead, she explained the importance of tracking the menstrual cycle, telling her conception was more likely just before or after ovulation, Madeline was still puzzled and the midwife told her to count the days after the start of a period. She also mentioned that her temperature might rise a little during ovulation. Madeleine was not sure if they possessed a thermometer, but she said nothing.

"I'll put it simply—keep men at arm's length in the middle of your period." Madame Bonfleur also suggested a sponge soaked in olive oil and inserted before the brute of a man had his way could be effective. As Madeleine was leaving, Madame Bonfleur shook her head. *The girl knows nothing. I'll be delivering another Fournier around the time of the Celebration of the Birth of the Blessed Virgin Mary*, she said to herself.

On the way back to the farm, Madeleine racked her brain to remember just when her last period had started, and then it came to her and she counted forward—thirteen days. "Tonight's the night, I think, Father."

That night, shortly after everyone had settled down to sleep, Madeleine crept into Allan's room. "It's so cold tonight, Allan, do you mind if I join you?"

Chadwick was surprised, to put it mildly. *What has everyone been eating?* He thought. But he moved the bolster and made room alongside him. He thought of all the jokes about commercial travelers sleeping with farmer's daughters, and began to wonder if perhaps there was a grain of truth in them.

"You're very beautiful, Madeleine," he said, and kissed her firmly on her lips. Chadwick knew that women needed to be loved before attempting intimacy. He had had plenty of practice with Melanie.

When Madeleine finally fell asleep, she decided seducing the stuffy Englishman had its rewards.

In the morning, they both went downstairs together. Chadwick went to the barn and Madeleine set the breakfast table—and then got the thought to go back and straighten the bed. When in Chadwick's room she opened the drawer containing his meager possessions and discovered the envelope with papers inside. She held the thick wad of French money, more than she had ever seen at one time before. Then she saw his RAF identification card and the fake Guest Worker permit with swastika at the top. She was totally confused. *What on earth was Allan doing with a German document and how did he get it?*

Her father was the only person she could turn to. She knocked on his bedroom door, but he was an early riser and had already left. Madeleine put the envelope back in Chadwick's room just as she had found it and went to her own room. She started to cry. Life had suddenly got so complicated, and she wasn't used to it. She didn't understand what it all meant.

Over breakfast Monsieur Fournier pointed out that tomorrow was Christmas Eve, and so a slap-up dinner was traditionally called for. He proposed to kill a chicken, and Madeleine said she would bake a sponge cake, called the "yule log." Fournier reminisced about Christmases of many years ago, when he was a child and the family much larger. He told Chadwick how they would arrange shoes in front of the fire for "Pere Santa" to fill with presents for those who had been good. "This part of France belonged to Germany then," he mused. "And they knew how to have a good Christmas."

Madeleine told him later in the day of her discoveries in Chadwick's room. "I already know," he said. "His Air Force gave him money and documents in case he was forced down. Don't worry, he will be gone soon. Did—er—you get him to leave something with you?"

"Yes," she said shortly and started to cry again.

"Be brave, my pet," he consoled her. "This is the worst of times. It will improve."

The fact Chadwick had a German work permit was actually news to Fournier. He wondered if he should inform his résistance contact, but there was no easy way to do it.

Later that day Chadwick asked Madeleine if she had any colored crayons. She found him a few, relics of her childhood. Then he begged a few inches of cotton thread, and she handed him a bobbin from her sewing box. He went to his room to make three small presents for the Fournier family. He cut out two girl's silhouettes and one boy's from blank paper. He colored them appropriately and using the thread fastened the feminine outlines to a rolled up hundred franc note. The boy's figure he tied to two notes.

Both the women avoided eye contact with him during the evening meal. He half expected a visitor during the night but it was quiet.

The next day after breakfast and the usual chores, he joined in preparations for the evening's festivity. The wine flowed freely and Monsieur Fournier promised something stronger for dinner. Darkness enveloped the countryside and inside the farmhouse they lit the candles.

Fournier began to sing some French and German carols. They roasted chestnuts at the fireplace and Fournier produced a bottle of Champagne which he had bartered for some of his own wine. They made a toast—"To happier times"—and then presented the presents as they sipped the Champagne from thick glasses. On behalf of the whole family, Fournier gave Chadwick a small silver crucifix which he said had belonged to his mother.

Chadwick protested vehemently. "I could not accept something so precious and treasured." But they all insisted he must take it. A perilous journey lay ahead and the crucifix would bring luck.

Then with great fanfare, Madeleine brought out the roast chicken, along with an assortment of vegetables and sauces, and sweetmeats were served as they finished the dinner. The Champagne was long gone but there was plenty of Fournier wine, and Chadwick tottered off to bed after a chilly sally into the back yard feeling pleasantly intoxicated.

In the morning a small boy, no more than ten years old, appeared at the door with sealed envelope for Monsieur Fournier. He was given a piece of the sponge cake and a glass of milk while Fournier carefully opened the envelope and read the message. He turned to Chadwick. "You are off this afternoon, Allan. The résistance will meet us at a nearby farm and you will travel in a lorry to Nancy."

Fournier added a message to the bottom of the note giving Chadwick's name on the fake Guest Worker's permit. He resealed the envelope with a touch of hot wax and instructed the young lad to deliver it without fail to the same man who had first given it to him.

Chadwick and Fournier left just after lunch. The farmer insisted that Chadwick take a few of Jean's clothes, which Madeleine packed in an old canvas bag. Chadwick gave him a thousand francs in exchange. He kissed Madeleine and Charlotte, and promised to visit them when the war was over. Fournier led the way along narrow paths across the field and through small woods. These byways go back hundreds of years, Fournier commented. The farm they were heading for was only about half a kilometer from a paved road, which is why the résistance chose that rendezvous.

A man was waiting for them. "I expect a lorry within half an hour," he muttered.

When they heard the engine in the distance Fournier grasped Chadwick's hand. "Good luck, Allan, and don't forget this." He pressed the crucifix into Chadwick's fingers. Allan had left it on the chest of drawers in his room. He again protested he couldn't take the valuable family keepsake, but Fournier was adamant. "Bring it back when you visit after the war is over."

A man swung down from the cab of the lorry. "Chadwick?"

"Yes."

"Get in."

Inside the cab, three men were crowded together. The driver never opened his mouth.

"You can call me Emile," the other man said. "I am the driver's helper. You are cadging a ride to Nancy if we are stopped. You have a German Guest Workers pass I understand. Use that. You have been fired from your job at a firm that made mining equipment. Here is a ration card. The story is that from Nancy you hope to ride to Paris."

It was uncomfortable in the noisy, crammed cab, but the journey was over in an hour, and they were not stopped along the way. In the city, Chadwick was fascinated to see German soldiers walking in the streets, his first sight of the enemy since the war began. Emile took him to an ugly building containing numerous apartments. They climbed two flights of stairs and Emile knocked on a door in a long corridor of identical doors. Chadwick was greeted inside by a suave Frenchman with jet black hair combed back over his skull.

"I am Alphonse. I need a few details from you, Monsieur, so that we can send the correct information to London. You will stay here until orders come from Paris. Please ask for anything you need to be more comfortable."

Later, Alphonse warmed up a stew which had vestiges of meat in it and tore lumps off a baguette to wipe his plate. Chadwick followed suit, and they finished a bottle of red wine between them, although Alphonse drank most of it.

The apartment had a wireless set which was tuned to Radio Paris. In the late evening Alphonse turned down the volume and picked up the BBC, broadcasting in French. Chadwick was depressed to learn of the sheer volume of ships being lost in the Atlantic due to U-boats. Alphonse told him the main problem for the average citizen was food. The Germans had requisitioned so much agricultural production that the official ration wasn't adequate to sustain a flea, Alphonse said. The result was a thriving black market, but food on the black market was expensive. Many women wasted hours in queues when the availability of something became known.

Chadwick wondered whether to mention that he had a hoard of French money, but kept his mouth shut for the time being. He learned that the general attitude to the occupiers was "live and let live." There was little overt resistance in Nancy, but collaboration was coldly polite. Chadwick asked if it would be safe for him to walk around the town in the morning, Alphonse considered this and said someone would have to go with him, as his French was a give-away.

Chadwick remembered Larson's comments on the civilian killings in Poland. "Have there been any mass killings by the German Army, Alphonse?"

"No, there's been no reason for them. You know, the résistance here is poorly organized. The Communists haven't recovered from Stalin's pact with Hitler earlier. The so-called Free French aren't accepted by most Frenchman. The organization such as we have comes from the British Secret Service, and their main goal is to get airman returned, for which they pay well."

Chadwick digested this surprising information. "What about you, Alphonse?" he asked. "What do you think?"

"I am a special case. My mother is Jewish. From what she hears from relatives in Germany all hell is going to break loose once the Boche have knocked off the Russians, defeated the British, and they control Europe. I have to hope a miracle occurs and Germany loses this war. Maybe the Americans will make a difference."

A friend of Alphonse, Charles, took Chadwick on a tour of the city center in the morning. There were very few German troops to be seen, and most pedestrians walked with their noses buried in a scarf. Chadwick observed long queues at shops selling food and tobacco and saw that most of the vehicles on the road belonged to the German Army. Occasionally a crowded bus passed by.

They walked onto a grand square, and his guide pointed to an ornate building. "The Town Hall. The German administrator resides there. Would you like some coffee?"

On a chilly morning that sounded attractive to Chadwick. The small patisserie was crowded and thick with cigarette smoke, which smelled dreadful to Chadwick. "What on earth are people smoking, Charles?"

"Better not to ask," his guide replied with a laugh. The coffee in a tiny cup was bitter, but fortunately there was sugar available. "The coffee is made from roasted acorns, Allan. But it is warm, anyway."

On the way back to the apartment they passed a cinema, and Chadwick stopped to read the poster advertising the show. "The Assassination of Father Christmas," he said out loud.

"That is a film made under German supervision," Charles explained. "But I think it has a hidden message."

"Can we go to see it?" Chadwick asked.

"Why not? But there is only one showing a day—tonight at eight. At least the cinemas are warm with so many people packed in."

Alphonse had made a thick soup for lunch, which they all enjoyed with the ubiquitous baguette. Chadwick glanced at a paper they had picked up in town. It was full of resounding praise for the victorious German soldiers in Russia. There was no mention of any RAF raids. Chadwick began to get depressed by the seemingly unstoppable might of the German armed forces. If they went to see the film he would miss the BBC broadcast that night, but still, Chadwick urged Alphonse to pay for two of them to see the film.

Charles and Allan went early to get good seats. As the place filled up, the air was polluted by the smell of homemade cigarettes. The show started promptly with a German newsreel with French subtitles—"The German Weekly Review." After a stirring portrait of the German Eagle, it started with a wounded soldier in hospital getting awarded a medal with his wife watching. Then there were shots of artillery raining shells down on Moscow and Leningrad. Chadwick looked at the amount of snow in the pictures and decided it couldn't have been much fun for the ordinary soldiers.

The black and white film was of high quality and sometimes featured appropriate background music. Chadwick compared it to the Gaumont newsreels shown in British cinemas and felt it was of somewhat better technical quality, but the message was plainly propaganda. When the newsreel ended, he expected to see some local advertisements but there were none. The main film began right away. It was filmed in the mountains of France and depicted a small, poor village beset by a series of misadventures, culminating in the death of Father Christmas, witnessed by two children. The photography was stunning and some scenes shot in chiaroscuro were technically very effective. Charles whispered the plot had a subtle meaning only a Frenchman would understand, but the German censors had allowed it to be shown anyway.

It was a relief to be back in the pure but frigid air after the show was over. Chadwick decided the average Frenchman was trying to conduct his life as normally as possible in the circumstances but artists were inspired by the tension in the air. He felt it was a fragile balance and bound to collapse as world events unfolded.

Life in the apartment settled into a routine. After breakfast Chadwick read for a while and usually went for a walk accompanied by Charles if it wasn't too wet. A woman showed up once a day with food, and sometimes cooked. They listened to the BBC after dinner. The cryptic messages that followed the broadcast were for the résistance leaders, who knew the coded statement's meaning.

One day Chadwick and Charles witnessed an altercation between some young Frenchmen and the police. The men were standing on some steps in the medieval part of the city making speeches. The protests were about food shortages and the fat profits made by black marketeers. Some pushing and shoving developed which got out of hand. Police whistles brought more policemen and eventually a squad of German soldiers, who freely used their rifle butts to subdue the rioters. Half a dozen were led away in handcuffs.

"What will happen to them, Charles?" Chadwick asked.

"A stiff fine or jail if they don't have the money."

Finally, Alphonse informed Chadwick he had been told to transfer him to Paris. He had been ordered to ensure Chadwick's papers would pass muster if he was stopped on the way. The permit issued by MI6 was judged to be acceptable and he already had been given a ration card in the name of Alain Clemente. Chadwick was given two crumpled envelopes addressed to him at a fictitious address in Nancy with trivial letters inside. "Makes you look genuine," Alphonse told Chadwick, "if you are searched."

Chadwick and Charles boarded a train at a little after ten in the morning. Policemen on the platform were making random inspections, but nobody bothered Chadwick. "The trip to Gare de l'Est in Paris should take about two to three hours," Charles told him. "Sometimes there are delays, as military trains have priority."

The train stopped at several towns on the way to Paris. Frequently, SNCF ticket inspectors boarded the train at these stops. At Epernay, a police inspector entered Chadwick's compartment. "Papers please," he announced as he moved from one person to another. When Chadwick handed over his Guest Worker permit the inspector asked, "You worked in Germany?"

"I worked in Alsace-Lorraine," Chadwick replied. "It is considered part of Germany now."

"Interesting. And you come from Bernay?"

"Yes, Sir."

The policeman rubbed the permit between his forefinger and thumb. "Nice work," he said in English.

"Pardon, Sir. I didn't catch that," Chadwick replied in French.

"Have a good trip. Paris is the next stop."

Watching from his seat across from Chadwick, Charles was terribly scared and had difficulty controlling his bladder.

At the bustling station, Charles made contact with another emissary and Chadwick was told to follow him. He led the way to the Metro and passed Chadwick a ticket. "You are staying in the Eighteenth Arrondissement. Monsieur, follow me, my name is Henri. You will like it, there are plenty of girls."

After changing trains twice, Chadwick and Henri emerged on a busy street with elegant, tall apartment blocks. Henri dived into a warren of narrow passages and then entered a slightly decaying hallway. A fat, slatternly woman rose from a chair.

"Alain, I would like you to meet our concierge, Madame Marie Limoges. Marie, this is Alain. He will be staying with Bernard and myself for a few days, or possibly longer."

Chadwick extended a hand. "A pleasure, Madame."

"Don't think because I am fat and ugly that I am stupid."

Chadwick was taken aback, and after a pause he said, "I would never think that, Marie."

"It's a climb to our rooms, Alain, four flights. I hope you are fit."

Chapter Twenty

Two weeks after the raid on Augsburg, Bomber Command laid on another large attack on the Junkers factory at Dessau, southwest of Berlin. Another long flight from England. Two hundred and twenty bombers formed the attacking force, mostly Lancasters, but this time the losses were much higher than the raid on Augsburg. Ten bombers went down over Germany or Holland and eight more were severely damaged. Three were written off as Cat Five.

An intensive analysis of the raid was carried out by Bomber Command and Air Intelligence. The Pathfinder using "SuperOboe" had been accurate and about a quarter of the factory was revealed in photographic reconnaissance to have been leveled. Interrogation of crews and close examination of surviving but damaged planes pointed to a curious fact—heavy caliber bullets, twenty millimeters, had struck the planes from underneath.

Earlier, first interrogation of returning crew had discounted reports by air gunners that they had seen other planes of their squadron, illuminated briefly by search lights and fires on the ground, being attacked by fighters from underneath. Careful examination of bullet holes on some of the bombers clearly indicated the attacking fighter had been flying beneath the bomber and fired upwards.

This produced a lot of head scratching. The representative from Air Intelligence said they would pass the word to agents on the ground to sound out contacts with the Luftwaffe and aircraft companies for work on fighters that would enable them to fire upwards. The whole idea met with skepticism but there was no denying the evidence from returning, damaged bombers. The attrition rate of five percent actually lost, and three percent more written off, was marginally acceptable if it did not get worse.

When experienced fighter pilots were asked how such an attack could be made, they said it was almost impossible. The attacking plane would collide with the target, especially at night. They mentioned the tactic used by Spitfires to clobber Stuka dive-bombers as they climbed after a bombing run. It required very skillful flying to get in a burst under the Stuka and avoid a collision, and that was in daylight.

Several officers were told to investigate further and MI6 alerted agents to pursue the subject. The group met again within a week. One officer reported that in the first world war BE-2 fighters had been equipped with forward-firing guns that could elevate up to sixty degrees and were effective in shooting down Zeppelins. The new Defiant fighter was mentioned—the twin guns in the turret could elevate but they could only point rearwards.

The most interesting new information came several weeks later from MI6. Luftwaffe pilots were talking freely of "Schrage Musik," translated as "Strange Music." This was the German code word for the modified Me 110 fighters, equipped with twin twenty-millimeter cannon which could fire upwards, at angles of as much as seventy-five degrees from the horizontal. The project was top secret; squadrons so equipped only flew from airfields inside Germany.

It was difficult to come up with a counter to this new development. The length of a Lancaster bomb bay precluded adding a turret to the underside of the plane. Experts suggested a close examination of a modified Me 110 would be helpful, but even if downed by fire from a bomber the wreckage would land in Germany, which was not too accessible.

Then someone from MI6 spoke up. "We discovered that older Me 110 fighters are being modified to accept the Schrage Musik guns at the old Marcel Bloch factory at Talence, near Bordeaux." The MI6 informant added, for the benefit of the RAF attendees, "Marcel Bloch, or MB as they were called, made many French fighters before the war, but since the occupation they've been involved in Luftwaffe repair and modifications. It is part of the Occupied Zone of France." The MI6 man was pressed to provide more details and he promised another report in a week.

When the group met again, the representative of MI6 had a little more information. "The French factory works on two Me 110s at a time, and modifying each one takes five to six weeks. But the guns are not fitted in France. They're added by the Luftwaffe when the plane returns to Germany. Apparently, the airframe requires strengthening to absorb the recoil of the guns. Also some kind of electronic device is added. We don't know its function. The planes are worked on in a section of the factory that's sealed. We have a fairly good network in the Bordeaux region but they don't have lot of aviation background."

A second man from MI6 spoke up. "Maybe we should send that RAF pilot we're jockeying around down to Bordeaux. Just joking, of course."

An RAF wing commander asked, "Who is that, Six?"

"A pilot on the Augsburg raid parachuted into a rather remote farming area. We finally got him to Paris in preparation for an escape back to Blighty, but a snag arose which is delaying our plans."

"And what was that?"

The man from MI6 was a little reluctant to go into details. "The résistance situation in occupied France is complicated. There are two major groups operating against the Nazis—the Communists and the Free French. Basically these groups were politically antagonistic to each other before the war, with the Free French representing the conservative, nationalistic parties. Now that they have a common enemy their cooperation is, let's say, patchy. The current snag is because the Communists have accused the Free French of turning over one of their men to the German counter intelligence, the SD. So Six is keeping its head down and waiting for things to blow over. The chap in question already had an alias because of pre-vious connections with British Intelligence, so he's just cooling his heels in Paris—all at the expense of Six. He's been there nearly a month."

"Can you say who it is?"

"I won't mention his alias, for security reasons. He might be known to a few of you RAF chaps—Allan Chadwick."

The wing commander exploded. "Allan Chadwick! I know him. Chadwick is swanning round in Paris? 'Stradinary! Doesn't he know there's a war on?"

There was burst of laughter at this remark.

"Seriously, Chadwick would be a good man to get involved with this Schrage Musik stuff. He's an experienced pilot and has been involved in some technical developments over here."

Six said he would discuss with French liaison leaders and get back to them. "I have to assume you RAF fellows regard the Schrage Musik threat as serious?"

"Very. It could undermine our whole concept of night-time strategic bombing in the next stage of the war."

"You understand a move to Bordeaux would put Chadwick under considerably more risk than he presently faces hiding out in Paris?"

Nobody replied.

In the next meeting, MI6 reported on communications be-tween leaders of the liaison with the French résistance. "If this committee thinks the RAF escapee they are presently looking after in Paris could help with finding out more about Schrage Musik, he could be taken to Bordeaux. If the decision is made to do that, they would alert the Six leadership in that region of France and stress the importance of his mission. Bordeaux is not far from the Spanish border and perhaps C could be returned to Blighty via Spain when this is over."

For the first two weeks in Paris Chadwick was enjoying himself, although the weather was cold and damp. Henri found him some warm, second-hand clothes that were more suitable for a city dweller than the clothes he had received at the Fournier farm. There were not many German soldiers on the streets during the daytime, but in the evening Wehrmacht troops thronged the bars and risque strip clubs. It amused Chadwick to sit down at a café for a morning drink and have a burly German soldier plunk himself at the next table and order a drink in bad French. Chadwick often raised his glass in salute and the German usually responded in kind. But as the novelty wore off he felt he should be on the move.

Many French citizens were ambivalent about the German occupation as it was widely believed that Germany would control Europe for the foreseeable future. Henri was told to meet with some résistance leaders and he was informed Chadwick was to be transported to Bordeaux, although the reason was secret. They discussed the best way to get Chadwick to the south. Inspections were rigorous for people traveling to or from the Vichy zone, and so it was thought best to stay in the occupied region. Police inspections were also much more thorough on trains leaving or arriving in Paris, so the decision was made to send Chadwick to Nantes by road and then take a train to Bordeaux from there.

When he got back to the apartment, Henri told Chadwick to skip shaving for a few days, as he would be traveling to Nantes as a lorry driver's helper. Chadwick realized his days as a "tourist" in Paris were coming to a close, so he attempted to squeeze in as many sights as he could.

Henri usually traveled with him and sternly forbid such obvious tourist traps as the Eiffel Tower. There were no French tourists, and so they traveled by Metro and visited less well-known but free attractions such as the catacombs. Chadwick was surprised at the open way prostitutes solicited in Montmartre, especially around the bordellos that clustered near the famous Moulin Rouge. Henri told him the daring dances, such as the "can-can" had become far more pornographic and the girls frequently wore no underclothes.

The curfew meant that they had to be off the streets by 9 p.m. and shops and restaurants closed at 8 p.m. They walked under the Arc de Triomphe and on Avenue Foch, Henri pointed to an ornate building with tall windows. "The Headquarters of the SD. We must not get caught by those bastards."

Chadwick recognized the familiar, black Mercedes Benz automobiles parked outside. He couldn't resist telling Henri that he had been arrested by the Gestapo in Berlin before the war. Henri was deeply impressed. A sprinkling of the pedestrians had yellow stars stitched to their clothes. Henri explained that all Jews were forced to be identified in that way.

Henri gave Chadwick a new identification card. He mentioned several reasons for the new identity. The first was that "Guest Worker" cards were much more common in Germany, and French engineers sent there rarely came back to France, so that kind of card was unusual at home. Another reason was that Chadwick was traveling as a driver's helper, stating his profession as "engineer" was suspicious. His profession was listed instead as "skilled worker." He could claim he was there to keep the engine running.

The lorry they drove had been modified by the substitution of a tractor engine, which ran on kerosene, but slowly—their maximum speed was fifty-five kilometers per hour, preferably downhill. They carried a load of antique chairs in a covered rear section. The chairs belonged to a senior German officer, which is why the driver had permission to drive to Nantes, and his papers were all countersigned by the German authorities. They were frequently forced to the side of the road by police on motorcycles to permit military convoys to zoom past. Their papers and identification documents were examined twice in a fairly casual way.

The journey took from sunrise to sunset, about seven hours. The driver knew that Chadwick was "on the run," but to everyone else involved, he was just the helper, slightly dull-witted. When they arrived at a warehouse in Nantes, they helped unload and then were given a substantial supper and invited to sleep on two steel cots.

In the morning after breakfast, a member of the résistance detached Chadwick and took him to an apartment in the city center. Here he cleaned up, shaved, and donned some better clothes. It was planned to send him on to Bordeaux the next day by train, a four-and-a-half-hour trip if not delayed by Army trains. Chadwick was escorted to the train but left to make the journey by himself. He was given a red scarf to wear and that was the recognition cue for the person who would meet him at the other end. His one-way ticket and new identification was examined by a French official without comment.

When he stepped down from the carriage, Chadwick was surprised that a woman gave him the correct password and escorted him out of the station onto a tram. In the fifteen-minute trip, he noticed many German soldiers in the streets. They alighted on a pleasant avenue with trees planted on both sides of the road, and walked to an apartment block. Chadwick was getting used to climbing stairs and made a comment to his guide.

"The electricity is only on for an hour or two each day," she explained. When she closed a door behind them she wiped her brow. "Whew, I was scared. There aren't many men of your age on the streets. The Germans sweep them up to work on the submarine shelters they're building at the docks. But you should be safe here, inside," She went into a small kitchen and came back with a bottle of white wine. "This will make us feel better, of course, though it's not chilled." She poured a generous glass for both of them. "My name is Helga."

Chadwick introduced himself.

"Alain, pleased to meet you. Thanks for meeting me." She began to chat and told Chadwick that Bordeaux was crowded by refugees from further north. It had been bombed by the

Germans at the start of the occupation. The border with Vichy France was only ninety kilometers to the east, but it was forbidden to cross without papers, which were very hard to get. Helga told Chadwick there was a fresh baguette in the kitchen and some cheese. He was welcome to finish off the wine.

"Our leader will be coming to meet you tonight, so make yourself at home." With that, she wished Chadwick "bon jour" and departed.

It was after dark when the door to the corridor opened and a tall woman in a stylish overcoat entered the apartment. Chadwick had dozed off on a couch and awoke with a start.

"Good Evening, Alain," the woman said with a flawless English accent. "I use the name Boadicea."

"Good evening to you, queen of the ancient Brits."

The woman gave a pleasant laugh. "In the present climate, it's better not to know too much about your friends." She placed a large carrier bag on the table. "Here is your supper and more liquid sustenance. As you have no doubt been told, Six made a special request to have you sent down here so that your flying expertise can be used to dig into some details about work at the Bloch factory. My understanding is that the work is secret and impossible to see. But there is man who is sympathetic to the English who works at the field and refuels the German planes before they leave for Deutschland. If you wish, I can arrange for you to interview him. As soon as that is done we'll slip you into the Spanish pipeline. You should be home by Easter, with luck.

"I also have some information for you sent by Six which spells the outline of the questions Six needs answers for." She fished out a crumpled piece of flimsy paper and straightened it out. "Sounds dramatic, but I could swallow this message if stopped and searched. Here are your questions."

Chadwick took the paper and examined it closely. "I'll study this before meeting your man."

"Let me tell you something about the situation here, Alain. To be honest, one of my concerns is that your appearance will not rock the boat. I have a French father and an English mother. I grew up spending time in both countries. My father owned considerable property in Bordeaux, some of which has been seized by the German authorities. My parents are living in Vichy France at the moment, but they are getting very old. We have a network that works with Six. The primary function is to smuggle airmen like yourself into Spain. We also provide observations of the submarine docks, now under construction. We do not engage in random killings of German soldiers or sabotage of railway lines, as that would bring retaliation from the Nazis. Life for the average Frenchman here is tough, with little food, electricity, and fuel. I do not propose to add to the burden by having hostages shot for acts which are annoying to the Germans but in reality have little impact on the course of the war. I think this year, '42, will see a clarification. Either Herr Hitler's Thousand Year Reich will really seem possible or the war will turn and begin to mark the end. Then some tough decisions will have to be made."

"Thank you, Boadicea. I have to say that since I arrived in France nearly three months ago, I have come to realize what war really means for the average person. Flying is an entirely different kind of war."

They continued to chat about inconsequential matters for a few minutes and then Boadicea rose to leave. She smiled to herself. The little speech she had made to Chadwick about not rocking the boat was almost the same as the one she made to the German Uberkommandant when she became his mistress.

It was three days before Boadicea showed up with the worker from the Bloch factory. Chadwick had used the time to become familiar with Schrage Musik information sent by

MI6. Each day one or more people showed up at the apartment with food, drink, something to read and simply for a chat. He heard that it was safer for men to travel in the early morning or late afternoon, when they might be expected to be traveling to or from work. Chadwick was introduced as Alain to a visitor answering to the name Hugo. He was a muscular man of medium height; he appeared to be in his sixties. He told Chadwick that he did not particularly like the English, but he hated the Boche. He said he had seen enough of them in the last war and it was extremely galling to see them strutting about Bordeaux.

Chadwick asked him about the twin-engined German fighters that came to the factory for special modifications. Hugo told him the work was carried out in a sealed part of the factory. "All the inspectors and engineers are German. Only the technicians are French. It is impossible to see the planes before they fly back to Germany."

Chadwick pressed him for details and then, after a pause, Hugo mentioned that the planes were sometimes left in the transit hangar on the night before departure the next day for Germany. Hugo operated the refueling lorry and said the planes were always full before they took off. Usually a single Luftwaffe pilot was flown in to take them back. He made a test flight and often it was too late for a flight to Germany that day. Hugo topped off the tanks and watched them put the plane in the transit hangar. He said talk with technicians left him with the impression that the pilots deliberately tried to organize things so that they could spend the night in Bordeaux.

Chadwick asked him if the plane flew with a co-pilot.

"No, the rear seat does not have a set of controls, there is just the console with a screen." Hugo confirmed that the guns were not fitted at the Bloch factory.

Chadwick asked a number of questions to which Hugo could give no answer, and so he told the man that the next time there was Messerschmitt in the transit hangar he would like to take a look at it.

Hugo was extremely dubious. "Although it is not a sealed part of the site, there were routine security patrols."

Chadwick told him it was important for the British to learn if the angle of the guns could be adjusted in flight, and the only way to answer that question was if someone could examine them.

Hugo whined that his job was to climb on the wings and put fuel in. He never actually entered either cockpit, but he could look at them from the wing.

Boadicea had not taken part in the conversation with Hugo, and so Chadwick called her over. "We must be going soon," she announced. He told her he had discovered the planes were probably accessible on the night before they left for Germany, and he wanted to take a look. At first she raised strenuous objections, but Chadwick argued he had come this far and the job should be done properly.

"Let me talk to some others that work on the airfield and I will let you know," were Boadicea's parting words.

The next day a rather elderly man showed up with some food and an old English newspaper. "In the Group I am known as the 'The Prof'," he announced in good English.

"Were you a real professor?" Chadwick asked.

"Oh, yes. I taught at the university here for many years. But now it's shut, so I eke out a living by making translations. I speak and read a few languages."

"What did you teach, Sir?" Chadwick asked.

"Well, it was called philosophy, but that was a catch-all. I'm interested in science, history, mathematics, you name it."

"How did you get this old *Daily Mirror*, Sir?"

"The German coastal patrols intercept neutral ships and bring back reading matter they think may be of interest to intelligence, and that's where I come in. That came from a Portuguese ship that had visited the West Indies. I think the readers of that rather racy paper were more interested in bosoms than bombs."

"For a student of history and philosophy you're living in a fascinating period."

"Yes, your remark reminds me of the ancient Chinese curse—may you live in interesting times—and I can certainly appreciate the cynicism in it."

"I would be very interested in your assessment of how the war is going, Sir."

"I think Hitler's push into the Soviet Union is faltering, Alain. It was assumed German forces would be safely ensconced in Moscow when General Winter entered the picture."

"General Winter? Oh, I see what you mean," Chadwick said. "The same General Winter that dished Napoleon."

"Precisely. From what I hear on the BBC, the Soviets have launched a counter attack in the middle of winter and caught the Nazis by surprise. The Russian Bear is a slow-moving creature, but once it gets going it is unstoppable. I'm enjoying our conversation, Alain, but before I forget I must pass on a message from Boadicea. Your attempt to inspect a Messerschmitt at close quarters has been approved, but to minimize risk while you're on the move you'll be quartered at a farm in Talence, near the airfield. Hugo believes a plane will be ready to fly to Germany in about six days, so you'll be moved sometime in the next three days. The penetration of the airfield will be carried out on the night before it leaves. We're trying to find a small torch for you to use, but batteries for that kind of thing are very hard to find."

"That sounds wonderful, Prof. You must thank Boadicea for the organization, and if we are successful I am sure Six will be delighted."

"I ought to mention that Boadicea is in two minds about your mission. This kind of overt spying is somewhat above our usual level of resistance. If you're caught, her philosophy of not aggravating the Hun is in jeopardy."

"If I am caught I won't betray any of you."

"Brave words, Alain, but I'm not sure you're dealing with gentlemen when it comes to the SD."

Chadwick wondered whether to mention the incident in Berlin four years ago, but decided against it. "What do you think will be the impact of the Americans joining the war, Prof?"

The professor went into a long discussion, mostly one-sided, about the economics of war and asserted the longer it lasted, the more likely the Germans would lose. After a glass of wine and a cheese sandwich for lunch the professor left, saying he had greatly appreciated their conversation.

Chapter Twenty-One

After another two days in the apartment, Chadwick was moved one night to the farm in Talence. Hugo accompanied him to the farm and introduced him to the farmer and his wife. Their children were long gone and, like the Fourniers, they lived a life of poverty. They had a few chickens, but their cattle had been taken by the Germans. Hugo came every night with some food, which they all shared.

Then Hugo announced that the following day a recently completed Messerschmitt would be ready for a test flight. If things went as usual, the next night would be the one for Chadwick's reconnaissance. The airfield was clearly visible from the farm and Chadwick spent hours outside watching for the flight. He saw the plane take off a little after noon and return two hours later. When it did not take off again, Chadwick decided his escapade was on. He returned to the house blue with cold. The old woman tut-tutted and came back with a beaten-up old greatcoat.

"This was my husband's when he was in the Army, but he never wears it now. You must use it when you go out."The old couple had not been told of the plan to infiltrate the airfield and were fast asleep when Hugo slipped in and led Chadwick across a field.

The boundary mark consisted of a fence that was easy to climb through, and Hugo led the way to the hangar. "There is a German guard," he whispered, "but they don't go inside the buildings, except the one they use as a guardhouse. I think they mostly snooze in there."

Hugo produced a key and they entered the hangar through a small side door. Several planes stood silent in the gloom. There was a strong chemical smell mixed with the odor of aviation fuel. Hugo walked up to a plane that loomed over them. A complicated aerial was attached to the nose, but Chadwick could not make out any details in the dark.

"Hop on the wing, Alain."

Chadwick was feeling quite nervous and pressed his cheek against the metal skin. It was bone-chillingly cold. He climbed up and after a minute of fumbling asked Hugo, "How do you open the damned canopy?"

"It's in two parts. The first over the pilot's seat and the second over the observer. Push the colored plate and slide the canopy back."

Chadwick did as he was told, and in the dim light of the torch his eyes swept the console of the observer's space. He noticed there were no flight controls in the rear cockpit, but a few dials showed the familiar faces of an altimeter, and airspeed and heading indicators. The German instruments looked similar to the British instruments. Then he focused on the gun positions, located on either side of the fuselage. The mounting assembly was between both cockpits. A one-foot wide track on the floor led from behind the observer's seat. *Ah,* he thought, *that's where the magazine is placed.* He wiggled back and found the seat tilted forward, exposing a large volume where the bullets were stored. He went back to the observer's cockpit but he could not make sense of the numerous controls attached to the electronic cabinet. He shut the canopy and stepped into the pilot's cockpit. He decided the cockpit had a fairly conventional layout for a twin-engined machine.

Hugo was crouching on the wing. "I think it is time we were off, Alain."

Chadwick shut the forward canopy and slid off the wing onto the concrete floor. "Lead on, McDuff," he whispered. Hugo opened the side door and then quickly ducked back in. "Guards are making a round," he whispered. They quietly stole back into the hanger and hid behind a metal cabinet. After ten minutes,

Hugo said all was clear and they walked back to the farm without any trouble.

"When is the next Messerschmitt ready for flight tests, Hugo?"

"I'm not sure. This one and another came about the same time, so I imagine it will leave in the morning. The next should be ready within a day or two."

"I would like to inspect that one too."

"I'll have to ask Boadicea, Alain."

"No. I've decided. Just tell her it's important for me to clarify a few things once I've thought about what I learned tonight."

An idea was forming in Chadwick's mind. It was so audacious he pushed it into the back, but the next day he began to plot his next move. At first he thought he could use some rope. In prowling around the old barn he found rope that was rotted, so he rejected it. He cast around, not quite knowing what he was looking for, when he spotted a reel of baling wire. "Two mm diameter," he could just make out on the side of the reel. On the top lay a hefty steel tool, slightly rusty, about twelve inches long that combined pliers with a side cutter. He cut off several feet of wire, coiled it up and put it in a capacious pocket on his greatcoat. The tool went in another pocket.

When Hugo showed up in the evening with some food, he mentioned the next Messerschmitt would probably be ready for a test flight in two or three days. Chadwick asked him to arrange a visit from the Professor, as he needed some help with German.

The Professor showed up the next day. He mentioned that it was more difficult for him to visit the farm than the apartment, but he had borrowed a bicycle. "Heaven help me if I lose it or it is stolen," he said.

Chadwick suggested he wheel it inside the front door of the farmhouse, out of sight from the road.

"Now, how can I help you?" the Prof asked.

"Please give me the German words for common aviation terms, such as 'undercarriage,' 'flap,' 'pitch,' 'mixture,' and so on." They went through a comprehensive list with Chadwick making notes. Chadwick asked the professor if he knew the latitude of Bordeaux, and the professor guessed it was a little south of forty-five degrees north. He was eager to continue his discourse on the war, and Chadwick found he was enjoying the conversation with an intelligent man. Although the news seemed pretty bad at that time, the professor was optimistic that France would be liberated one day.

When Hugo showed up, he told Chadwick their inspection of the Messerschmitt would be the next night. "Boadicea is not pleased with all this subversive work. She says after this visit you will be on your way to Spain within two days."

They met the next night and made their way through the fence to the transit hangar. When Hugo opened the side door, Chadwick pulled him inside and told him to listen carefully. "I have to make a lot of measurements if my report is going to be of any value to the British. It will take several hours. You should go back and I'll let myself out. The door will lock behind me. I'll be very careful, but you have to be back early when the airfield opens, and you need your sleep."

Hugo protested adamantly that he was responsible for the Britisher and would stay. Chadwick asked for the torch and then literally threw him out, saying they would meet at the farm after the plane left. Once he had got rid of Hugo, Chadwick crossed over to the Messerschmitt, climbed aboard and slid open the rear canopy. He took off the greatcoat and tried to arrange a comfortable perch for himself behind the rear seat. He put the coil of wire and cutting tool within easy reach. In time he fell into a restless sleep.

Chadwick was awakened by the grinding of the hangar door and the slow creeping of daylight into the building. In a while he felt the plane move as several men pushed it into the dispersal area. After a tense wait, the forward canopy slid back and the pilot climbed aboard. There was some guttural conversation and then the engines started, one after the other. Without a flying helmet, the noise was overwhelming. Chadwick sank into his coat and pulled up the collar, pressing the cloth against his ears. He felt the Messerschmitt taxiing and then came the engine run-up, each throttle pushed to full rpm while the pilot checked the instruments. The engines settled back to a steady tick-over and then Chadwick felt the plane turn swiftly on one engine, and then the other opened up smoothly as the plane accelerated. He felt the thump as the wheels retracted and he glanced at his watch. *Come hell or high water,* he thought *I'm on my way.*

It was cold in the rear cockpit and he was grateful for the old coat. The plane continued to climb and the air got colder. Suddenly, Chadwick had a frightening thought, *If the pilot climbs much above ten thousand feet, I'll pass out due to lack of oxygen.* That thought steeled him to begin his attack on the pilot. He put the coil of wire and the pliers in a pocket so that they were easy to reach and then pushed open the seat and climbed into the ammunition track. He could just make out the top of the pilot's flying helmet above the armor plate at the back of his seat.

He looked through the canopy. The plane was flying in thick cloud. Rain drops coated the Perspex. He inched forward until blocked by a strut between the front and rear cockpits. Chadwick reckoned he could just reach far enough to swing a blow down on the plot's head with the pliers. He had no idea how much force to use, but he decided the pilot was protected to some extent by his helmet and he swept the pliers down with all his force. The German's head lolled and the plane suddenly jerked as his hands tightened on the control column. Chadwick climbed over the strut and looked at the pilot. He was out cold.

The plane started a gentle dive to the left and the speed increased. Chadwick grabbed the column and began to regain straight and level flight. A glance at the instrument panel showed they were flying at 3,200 meters. The pilot was wearing a mask connected to a black, rubber tube. Chadwick took off the mask and helmet and hung them on a knob on the instrument panel.

Now he was faced with the seemingly impossible task of getting the pilot off the seat while keeping the plane flying stably. With the plane slowly oscillating in height and turning randomly, Chadwick unfastened the seat harness and then the parachute buckles. Somehow he had to get the unconscious pilot into the empty space where the guns would be mounted behind his seat, but there was just enough room between the seat back and the inside of the canopy. Chadwick knelt on the strut and reached for an arm of the inert pilot. Desperation gave him strength, and with all his might, he got the body out of the pilot's seat. It was now wedged between the seat back and the canopy.

The plane had commenced an increasingly steep dive. Chadwick scrambled back and crossed over to the other side, darted forward, seized the stick, and hauled back. The "G" load forced him to his knees and then he eased the pressure on the stick. The bunt lifted the prone pilot off the seat and Chadwick pushed the pilot back with one hand while holding the stick with other. Things were getting out of control, but there was now just enough room on the seat for Chadwick to squeeze in beside the pilot and stabilize the motion of the plane.

He was breathing heavily and sat for a moment to gain his breath. He glanced at the instruments. He was down to 2,600 meters. He trimmed carefully for level flight and then got his shoulder under the armpit of the German and heaved him into the space behind the seat. For a moment, the body was wedged under the canopy, but a determined push caused it to fall behind the seat. Chadwick carefully adjusted the controls to bring the plane onto a heading of true north and a height of 3,000 meters.

Next came the most important part of his attack. The pilot had to be immobilized before he woke up. Chadwick snipped eighteen inches off his coil of wire and twisted the ends around the pilot's wrists using the pliers to make several tight turns. He passed the wire though a hole in a bracket before fastening the end on the other wrist. Then he pulled out more wire and looped it round the poor fellow's neck, and twisted the end with the rusty tool. He twisted the other end of the wire around a handy pipe. He was breathing hard, and a glance at his watch showed nearly an hour had passed since they took off.

Now, Chadwick thought, *I'm facing one of the most challenging navigational exercises of my career. I don't know where I am and I don't have a map that includes my destination. And I'm not sure we have enough fuel to get there anyway. Not only that, I'm flying a plane I'm not familiar with, and it has Nazi insignia, so the British will be only too happy to fire at it.*

Chadwick turned his attention to the solution of the navigational problem. He slowly climbed to 5,000 meters and adjusted the pitch and boost for an indicated air speed of 330 kilometers per hour. He estimated the true airspeed was 430 kilometers per hour, or about 250 knots, in more familiar units. The professor had told him Bordeaux was just south of forty-five degrees north latitude. He knew from years of flying over England that the south coast, from Kent to Cornwall, was about 200 nautical miles long and was just north of fifty degrees north latitude. *Seems like a target I can't miss* was Chadwick's thinking.

The real problem was when to let down in cloud. The difference in latitude was five degrees, equal to 300 nautical miles. Assuming that the average wind at altitude was thirty knots from the west, then to fly true north he must compensate for about thirty miles of leeway while flying about 300 miles—simple: one in ten is six in sixty, thus fly six degrees left, applying mental navigation he had been taught at Cranwell many years before. He decided to fly ten degrees to the left, as it would be safer for a let-down, as the Channel was wider to the west.

Chadwick wondered how "Fritz" was faring. Perhaps he had awakened. He wasn't sure if the German was getting enough oxygen, but no matter. He would be descending soon. Forty-five minutes after setting course to the north, Chadwick began a slow descent. He was still above cloud, and he had flown off the edge of the Luftwaffe map, but he assumed he could safely descend to a thousand meters. He fervently hoped there was no high ground ahead.

At a thousand meters he held the height for a few minutes and then slowly descended again, he began to see fragments of snow-covered ground through wispy grey cloud. He maintained 500 meters height and to his delight spotted storm-tossed water ahead.

As he crossed the French coast Chadwick thought about the Chain Home RDR. They would have his echo on their 'scopes. He wondered if they would vector an interceptor for a single intruder. That thought was soon answered. Two Spitfires dropped out of the clouds and began a curving attack from the west. Chadwick knew he could not out-fly a Spitfire in the Me 110. When flying with 613 Squadron the summer before they had clobbered many of the twin-engined German planes, Chadwick himself was credited with a couple of Me 110s.

He banked toward the attackers and throttled back. He felt the plane shudder as bullets found their target, but his plane was well-armored and continued to fly normally. Surprised by his reduction in speed, the Spits swept past and began a bank to the left.

Chadwick decided he was flying slowly enough to safely lower the undercarriage and he also applied full flap and pushed the throttles to maintain a 170 kilometers per hour indicated air speed. The Spitfires swept in from the east for another attack, but when the leader saw the Me 110 had its wheels down, he chopped the throttle and flew alongside. Chadwick waggled his wings and pointed downwards with his fingers. The Spitfire pilot nodded his head vigorously and pointed down. Chadwick nodded and he formatted on the Spit as he flew over familiar countryside.

North of Portsmouth the Spitfire turned gently west and for a moment Chadwick thought he was going to land at Boscombe Down, but the Spitfire descended quickly and flew parallel to a runway at an airfield Chadwick did not recognize. In front of the control tower, he saw the letters "MW" and realized he was going to land at RAF Middle Wallop.

He performed the downwind checks and bled off some height. The wheels were already down. He made sure the brakes were free and touched the main wheels first on landing. He taxied clear of the runway and after a few minutes, a Crossley appeared with a couple of airmen carrying rifles. They signaled for him to follow and he taxied to a dispersal area and stopped the engines when an airman made the throat-cutting gesture.

This is going to be fun, Chadwick thought to himself. He opened the forward canopy and climbed down, and then he donned his French Army, World War One greatcoat.

An RAF car drew up and a squadron leader emerged. He walked up to Chadwick and looked at him with amazement. "Who the devil are you?"

"Squadron Leader Allan Chadwick, returning from a spot of French leave. I think Air Intelligence and MI6 would be interested in this Luftwaffe kite." Chadwick suddenly grasped that he had made an outrageous pun and reaction set in, he broke down with uncontrollable laughter. Between gales of mirth he managed to say, "The German pilot is up there. You'll need metal cutters to get him down. I think the M.O. should see him."

The pilot of the Spitfire that had intercepted Chadwick had landed nearby and walked over. He fully expected to meet a Luftwaffe pilot who was deserting. When he heard Chadwick talking in normal English he was staggered. "Excuse me, Sir, but how did you get your hands on an Me 110?"

"In a nutshell, I pinched it," Chadwick replied. "And thank you, by the way, for not shooting me down."

The Spitfire pilot slowly comprehended what Chadwick had told him. "It's an honor to make your acquaintance, Sir. I'm Flying Officer Fitch."

Chadwick extended a hand. "Chadwick."

He realized the joke could get out of hand, and so turning serious, he told the squadron leader that that this was a highly secret caper put together by MI6 and that the plane should be put under cover as soon as possible. In addition, all the personnel who had seen the German plane should be sworn to secrecy.

Chadwick remembered he still had some clothes at RAF Boscombe Down and the squadron leader who had greeted him arranged for someone to go over and collect them. He introduced himself as Nigel Perry, commander of 615 Squadron. Chadwick suggested a bath and a drink of Scotch would be very welcome.

Just then a couple of mechanics who had been told to bring down the German pilot emerged carrying the limp body. One went up to the squadron leader and waved a piece of baling wire. "He was trussed up like a Christmas turkey, Sir, but that's not what did him in. There was blood all over the place."

"Ah," said Chadwick, and turning to the Spitfire pilot, he said, "I think your burst killed the turkey. The M.O. will be able to find out what killed him."

The squadron leader realized that some action was needed quickly. He arranged for the Messerschmitt to be placed under guard in a hangar. Nobody was allowed to see it until the experts were informed. He asked Chadwick who he should call at MI6, and Chadwick could only remember the telephone number of Doug Larson.

"Please take me to your office, Sir, I'll have to speak to the person at this number in private."

Perry left him at his desk with the telephone, and as he was dialing the number, an orderly appeared with a stiff Scotch and a soda water bottle. "Import Export," came the familiar greeting. "Doug Larson, please." To his relief the receiver was picked up right away, "Good morning. Larson here."

"Good morning to you, Doug, this is Allan Chadwick."

There was a long silence, and then Larson said, "My God, Allan, unless you're calling from Paris, I guess MI6 managed to spring you."

"Well, not quite, I managed to borrow an Me 110 and fly to Blighty. Just landed twenty minutes ago."

There was another long silence, and then Larson said, "You flew here in an Me 110? Awfully nice of the Luftwaffe, I must say. Is the plane in good shape?"

"Apart from a few bullet holes, it's as good as new."

"Allan, this incident has to be kept under strict secrecy. I've been to a few briefings by Air Intelligence since you went down. The Air Ministry thinks the Me 110 night fighter is a real threat to our Lancaster fleets. You may have just provided the answer. Where are you, exactly?"

"I'm at RAF Middle Wallop, quite near Boscombe Down."

"Let me talk to some senior people, Allan, and I'll get back to you. Bye."

Chadwick put the phone down and savored his Scotch. *How lucky I've been and how unlucky that poor Luftwaffe pilot has been. Just chance,* he thought. Then he had an impulse and called Clair Court Hall.

"Clair Court Hall."

"Hello Myrtle, how are you? This is Allan Chadwick."

"Mr. Chadwick, what a surprise!"

"Is Lady Melanie available?"

"She was here a few minutes ago, having a cup of tea, please hold on. I'll try to find her."

After a long delay Melanie picked up the phone. "Allan? You bloody blighter. I've been going batty trying to get news of you. Where are you?"

"Well, dear, I've been abroad. Really sorry I missed you over Christmas. It was just impossible to contact you. But I'm back in England now. I'll definitely get in touch as soon as I can." Just then there was a discreet tapping on the door. "Got to fly. Bye-bye for now."

Chadwick put the telephone down and Perry poked his head round the door. "Sorry to interrupt you, Squadron Leader, while you were talking I had a word with Group. You have really put the cat among the pigeons. Once they understood what I was telling them, they want you in London as soon as possible. Sorry, I had to pass this up the chain."

"Can't be helped. I know how important this is going to be. Tell you what, please call Wing Commander Rowley at Boscombe. Give him a brief outline of events and ask for the Anson to pick me up at, say three p.m. I hope my clothes will appear soon, but next, I think, a nice warm bath—my first in several weeks. Thank you for the drink, by the way. It was just what I needed."

Perry took Chadwick to the officers' mess and showed him to a bathroom on the second floor. "Here you are, Squadron Leader. Soak in here as long as you like. I think your uniform will be here soon."

Chadwick took off his French greatcoat, saying, "Could you look after this, please? It's a souvenir I wouldn't want to lose."

Perry took the coat, felt the weight and pulled the steel pliers out of a pocket.

"Ah, yes, wouldn't want to lose that tool also," Chadwick said. "You never know when you have to deal with baling wire."

Perry decided that Chadwick was too deep for him. He asked an orderly to make a brown paper parcel of Chadwick's clothes. When Chadwick's uniform was delivered from Boscombe he arranged for some new underwear to be requisitioned from the quartermaster. Chadwick still needed shoes. Perry waited until Chadwick emerged from the bathroom, warm and clean-shaven, and determined the size of shoe needed and suggested a drink before lunch.

When Chadwick put on his jacket, Perry looked at the battle ribbons and said, "You seem to be having an exciting war, Sir. I would imagine there's another gong in this caper."

"Never thought of that, Nigel. Perhaps you're right. Tell you the truth, I feel really bad over the Kraut pilot who was shot by Flying Officer Fitch. He didn't deserve that."

"It could have been you, Squadron Leader. Chances of war. Let's head for the bar."

The wildest rumors had been circulating, and a respectful crowd parted to make room for Perry and Chadwick to approach the bar. Perry looked around, and announced, "This is Squadron Leader Chadwick. That's all you need to know. The events of this morning are super, super secret and must never be discussed with anyone."

With a drink in hand he turned to Chadwick. "What squadron were you with, Allan?"

"I commanded 613 at Hawkinge last summer."

The pilots barraged Chadwick with questions about the fighting over the Channel a year before.

The Anson showed up on time and Chadwick was greeted by Wing Commander Rowley. "We are off to the Air Ministry, Allan. There is intense interest in your escapade of this morning. I am nominally your commanding officer, and you are officially still on the strength of Boscombe Down, and so I had better come and provide some support. Besides, I'm dying to hear your story of how you managed to pinch an Me 110."

Chadwick thanked Squadron Leader Perry and the pilots of 615 Squadron. On the way out of the mess Perry handed him an RAF greatcoat. "Someone left this in the mess months ago. You'll need it in London, and here's a hat someone left. Good luck. It's been an honor to meet you, Sir."

The Anson landed at Croydon airfield and Chadwick and Rowley were whisked to the Air Ministry by a waiting car. The meeting was held in a secure auditorium, with guards at the door. Once Chadwick and Rowley were seated, the meeting was started by an air commodore. "For the past few months Bomber Command has been plagued by unacceptable losses of the night-time bombing formations attacking Germany. Many losses have been attributed to a new Luftwaffe tactic which permits our heavy bombers to be attacked from below by fighters firing almost vertically upwards. I will now turn the meeting over to a representative of MI6. No names, no pack drill."

A slight man in a business suit rose to his feet. "My section is primarily concerned with cooperation with résistance units in occupied France. A frequent task is to organize the transfer of downed RAF air crew who have not by apprehended by the German authorities, back to Britain. French resistance at the moment is a little spotty. The majority of Frenchmen seem to prefer to sit on the fence and wait for developments in the war. I think it's fair to say that many think Germany will rule Europe for a long time. For that reason we don't make outlandish appeals to patriotism, but rather we pay hard cash in gold to Swiss banks for help in getting our men back.

"Toward the end of last year we were informed that a pilot involved with a raid on Augsburg that included experimental apparatus had apparently been shot down and may be roaming around free. At the time, his assessment of the experimental gear would have been valuable. He was eventually located, by which time his report would have been passé, but we started plans to get him back. He was moved to various safe houses and then when he was in Paris, we learned of the RAF interest in the new German night fighter developments and, more importantly, that a French aircraft company in the south of the country was providing technical help to modify the Me 110 aircraft for the new night fighter role. It seemed like a good idea to move our pilot to the vicinity of the French company so that he might uncover some aspects of the German work that would assist in the production of countermeasures.

"Accordingly, the French résistance groups we work with spirited him to Bordeaux, near the French factory, and found workers with some knowledge of what was happening. Probably with that background you will now understand better the report by the officer himself. I must conclude by reminding everyone that this subject is classified as 'Most Secret.' If the Germans get hints of the windfall you are going to hear about they could make changes that would undermine our efforts to counter the Me 110 night fighter. Our heavy bomber strategic bombing campaign is one of the most important British initiatives in the war to date. Its success must be guaranteed. This subject is an essential cog in that chain."

The air commodore gestured for Chadwick to take the podium. "I will start by my arrival in Bordeaux. At first I stayed in a nice apartment, and met the leader of the résistance cell, a woman, and she told me a worker at the airfield had useful information. One night I talked to him. Usually, he said, two Me 110s were undergoing modification. The work was done in a sealed part of the factory with German engineers and inspectors. The technicians were Frenchman who worked for Marcel Bloch Aircraft Company before the war. When I questioned him closely he admitted the planes that were being returned to Germany often spent their last night in a transit hangar. He implied that pilots tried to arrange things so they could spend the night in Bordeaux."

There was a ripple of laughter from the audience.

"I told him I'd like to inspect a Messerschmitt in the transit hangar if at all possible. He told me later that the woman in charge of the cell had reluctantly agreed, as she did not want to cause trouble with the Germans that could result in brutal retaliation on French citizens. After a few days I was moved to a small farm located next to the airfield. It was run by an old farmer and his wife. They were very poor. Résistance workers came every day with food.

"Then a man came to say a Messerschmitt would be tested the following day and would probably spend the night in the transit hangar. The next afternoon I kept the airfield under observation from a field and arranged to take a look that night. The old lady gave me a greatcoat that had belonged to her husband who had served in the French Army in the Great War. It was very useful, as the weather was cold. When it was dark, I climbed through the airfield fence with the French worker and hopped onto the Messerschmitt in the hangar.

"I only had a small torch and it was difficult to see much, I noticed the rear cockpit had no flight controls and housed some electronic gear. There were no guns fitted that could point almost vertically upward, but the mountings for two guns were on either side of the fuselage between the pilot's and observer's seats. Tracks for ammunition led back to a large space behind the observer's seat, which tilted up for access. We had to let some German guards pass by before we could return to the farm."

Chadwick stopped to take long swallow from a glass of water. "I haven't talked so much in months," he joked. "Well, in thinking it over, I decided I had a lot of questions and we should repeat the inspection on the next Messerschmitt to come our way. The lady boss of the cell was reluctant but agreed for one more inspection. However, the idea had formed in my mind that it would be possible to hide in the empty ammunition locker and take over the ship. I asked the French worker if they sometimes flew back with someone in the rear seat, and he couldn't remember that ever happening. So I had to solve the problem of overpowering the pilot. I prowled round the barn at the farm looking for rope and a weapon. All the rope was old and rotten, but I found a reel of baling wire and a tool to cut and twist it. I did not tell anyone I was going to steal the plane.

"Once the next Messerschmitt came down the line, I told the worker I had some complicated measurements to make and sent him home. Then I hid behind the rear seat until the Luftwaffe pilot was flying at about ten thousand feet. I sneaked along the ammunition tray on the port side and conked the pilot on the head with the baling wire tool. Then I fastened him securely behind the pilot's seat using the wire and turned my attention to flying the crate to England. We were in cloud but when I judged it safe I slowly let down, making a course of roughly north true. Fortunately, I broke into the clear at about fifteen hundred feet and found I was over the English Channel. I was intercepted by two Spits from Middle Wallop that got in a burst, but I lowered the wheels and signaled I was landing. Unfortunately, the poor German pilot lying behind me was killed by shots fired during the interception."

The air commodore rose. "Thank you, Squadron Leader. That is one of the most amazing stories I have ever heard in my twenty-four years in the Royal Air Force. I think Six has a few more words to add."

"Were any other Luftwaffe planes overhauled at the airfield?"

"A Ju 52 took off while I was watching and there were two more in the hangar."

"Thank you. To return to the subject in hand, I think you realize, Squadron Leader, that your flying in the future must be over the British Isles. There must be absolutely no possibility that you fall into enemy hands if you happen to be shot down again. Of course, Six will inquire about your whereabouts in a few days, that would be normal. We will not issue any calls to look for Me 110 crashes, the disappearance must remain a mystery for the Germans as well as the French. Under normal circumstances, the death of the Luftwaffe pilot would be reported to the Red Cross, but of course that would tell the Germans everything. We're going to give the unfortunate man a burial with full military honors as an unknown Luftwaffe pilot who was killed attacking Britain. His identity papers were destroyed. Now I would like to introduce the man who leads the investigation team of the bomber losses."

A young man with wild, woolly hair, dressed in slacks and a sports jacket, stood up. "We've been intensively studying the bomber losses for the past two months. Analysis of the bullet paths suggested a gun at a fixed vertical angle, but we had no idea how it was aimed, especially at night. The gift horse provided by the squadron leader should give us the answers. With a fixed angle the fighter must get into a specific position relative to the bomber. Once we know more, we can possibly direct counter fire to that position. As I speak, the Messerschmitt is being flown to Boscombe Down, it will be repainted with RAF rondels, and I suspect most observers will think we are testing a variant of the Beaufighter. I will report our conclusions to this group, hopefully, within a few weeks.

"Before I finish, I must congratulate the squadron leader on his astonishing coolness in seizing a German plane in flight and his skill in bringing it to England in conditions of thick weather. It is definitely the key we needed to solve this problem."

There were loud shouts of "Hear, Hear!" from the audience and sporadic clapping.

Wing Commander Rowley grasped Chadwick's arm. "You look absolutely shot, Allan. I suggest we repair to the mess on Horse Guards for a good meal and an early bed for you."

The next day Rowley met Chadwick over breakfast. "I've talked to many people since the meeting. Your escapade will go down in history, except nobody can be told about it. The air officer commanding Bomber Command would like to meet you. There's a car laid on for Uxbridge at ten a.m. In case you've forgotten, the commander is Air Vice Marshal Stevenson."

"Thank you, Sir. Yes, I remember him. We met a year or two before the war. He was concerned by the number of bombers I was commandeering for RDR development. I doubt he'll remember me, though."

When they arrived at Uxbridge, Chadwick and Rowley were taken immediately to meet Air Vice Marshal Stevenson. "I've just been getting a report of the meeting yesterday at the Air Ministry. Squadron Leader Chadwick, my experts tell me you might have just saved our bacon." He looked at Chadwick keenly. "Don't I know you?"

"We met briefly in '38, Sir. I was organizing targets for RDR development. I had an old Bentley."

"Of, course, I remember you. Wonderful thing you did. Our bomber losses are getting too much. I'm told you may have saved the day. Wonderful."

Stevenson turned to Wing Commander Rowley. "I'm going to recommend the Distinguished Service Order for Squadron Leader Chadwick. I trust you concur, Wing Commander."

Chadwick and Rowley flew back to Boscombe, seated side by side. Rowley said, "Allan you have accumulated pay and leave during your sojourn in France. Why not take a week or two off to unwind?"

"Thank you, Wing Commander. I'll see what I can arrange. But first I want a word with the scientist who was running the counter measures program."

"Good idea. His name is Dr. Trevor Thomas. I'm sure he would appreciate any help from you. I'll introduce you to him when we arrive at Boscombe."

The next day a bus carried officers and airmen to Middle Wallop. They wore greatcoats over their Best Blue uniforms. A squad from RAF Middle Wallop fired a one gun salute as the Luftwaffe pilot was lowered into the ground in a quiet corner of the old Norman churchyard. Chadwick looked into the grave and saluted. He was keenly aware that his freedom had resulted in the young man's death and he could not escape a feeling of guilt.

Chadwick got on well with Dr. Thomas. He left the flying of the Messerschmitt and the Lancaster target to pilots already assigned to the team, but sat in as results were discussed. The radar in the night fighter was thoroughly dissected by experts from Bawdsey and was given high marks. A summary was presented one day by a Bawdsey engineer.

"The observer in the rear cockpit can direct the pilot onto a bomber by viewing echoes that yield up-down and left-right information. We estimate from trials that the fighter can be positioned to better than a mile with good accuracy. But to hit the target, the bomber must be seen through the gunsight, which is ingeniously designed for the guns firing at about sixty degrees from the horizontal. Most of our tests were conducted in daylight, but when we flew night interceptions, the genius of the design became apparent. The gunsight emphasizes infrared radiation and the image from the engines greatly helps the pilot center the guns on the target."

Someone raised the question of how accurately the radar measured range as the plane approached the bomber. Here again the engineers from Bawdsey could only admire their German counterparts. "As the fighter approaches the bomber, the rate at which transmitted pulses are emitted goes up, so that as the range shortens the resolution of returning pulses is enhanced." The engineer could not keep the admiration for the design out of his voice.

Dr. Thomas spoke up. "That is a clever bit of circuitry, but it is also the Achilles heel of the system. For our countermeasures we needed to know how far away the fighter was, so that prepositioned guns on the bomber can fire before he does. Measuring the pulse repetition rate of the German radar tells us exactly that. We hope to have a working prototype of the countermeasures tested, at night, within a week—using cameras instead of live ammunition, of course," he added, to sound of laughter from the group.

When Chadwick checked his mail in the officers' mess one day he found an envelope of heavy, white paper addressed to him from the Central Chancery, Buckingham Palace. There was to be an investiture at which he would be awarded the Distinguished Service Order by His Majesty the King. There were instructions on entering the palace grounds, and he could invite up to four guests.

Chadwick decided to invite his parents, and perhaps this was a chance to completely heal the breach with Melanie. He telephoned Myrtle at Clair Court Hall and arranged a time for Melanie to call him at the mess. When they eventually made contact he asked her if she would like to go to a shindig at Buck House. He confessed he was about to get another medal.

To his surprise she was not overjoyed, and in fact she became almost angry. "So, that's what you have been up to. Sticking your neck out! You're going to get yourself killed, Allan. That is exactly why we decide to call things off when the war started."

Chadwick floundered on, "I've invited my parents to come down from Liverpool, and wouldn't you like to meet them?"

"Would it be appropriate for your parents to meet their son's mistress and the King at the same time?"

Chadwick attempted to turn her remark into a joke. "We don't need to tell my parents or the King the exact circumstances of your presence, dear. I thought it was a nice excuse for a few nights at a good hotel in London, but I have to book early. From what I read, the American Army is flocking to London and booking all the rooms."

Melanie was silent for a few moments. "This means a lot to you doesn't it, Allan?"

"Not the medal, exactly, but if I'm honest, I guess I like the respect."

"Book a room for your parents and for yourself. Whether we will share it can be decided later. We still have a few weeks before the ceremony. I don't suppose you can tell me what you did?"

"No, I'd get shot at dawn if I did." Chadwick felt desperately that there must be something he could use to win over Melanie without breaking the Official Secrets Act. "I did travel a lot, and I can say, the Folies Bergere is not what it used to be."

"Please let me know the dates for the room when you have them. As Tommy Handley would say, 'Ta Ta, for now'." And with that, Melanie hung up.

Chadwick attended a briefing given by Dr. Thomas. They had converted the pulse repetition rate into separation distance by taxiing the Messerschmitt behind a Lancaster on an unused runway. A "black box" designed by the electronic engineers displayed the distance between the two planes once the German radar was detected. Thomas suggested the guns could be fired by one of the crew at an appropriate distance. Chadwick pointed out that during an actual bombing raid with fighters attacking, the crew were usually too busy to watch a dial or meter and they would have to come up with something that was automatic.

A week later Dr. Thomas unveiled a new black box. "This one flashes an alert signal when German radar pulses are detected. If it is in the 'armed' mode, selected by a switch, the twin twenty-millimeter cannon pointing aft fires automatically when the pulse repetition rate corresponds to a separation of eight hundred yards, which we believe is before the fighter reaches its firing range. The guns on the bomber are pitched at an angle, assuming the fighter is crossing the eight hundred-yard range and climbing slightly. There must be some trial and error to optimize those settings. Look at it from the Luftwaffe pilot's viewpoint—this fellow is firing bullets into a bomb bay loaded with ten tons of high explosive. A very fine judgment is needed to open fire to destroy the bomber without blowing yourself out of the sky. So we chose eight hundred yards from the bomber before the fighter reaches its firing point of four hundred yards. Some concerns were expressed by the armaments people that guns were fired by a machine—that is, not triggered by a human being. I suspect this is the wave of the future."

Twenty Lancasters were modified to incorporate the rear firing guns and the aircraft took part in a 250-plane fleet that bombed Dortmund. The results were inconclusive. Ten British planes were lost, and the modified bombers never fired the rear-pointing guns. As a deterrent, it was understood that all the bombers must carry the defensive system if it was to be effective, and modifications were carried out as fast as possible on the remaining aircraft.

Chadwick was able to book two double rooms at a pleasant hotel near the British Museum. As the date of the investiture drew close, he telephoned Melanie. "I've got rooms booked for four days, Melanie. Gives us a day before the royal shindig and a couple of days after. My parents are staying at the same place, but on a different floor. Are you on?"

"I've thought a lot about your invitation, Allan, and I am very proud of you. But the facts I raised over a year ago are still pertinent. If I meet your parents under these circumstances, it is a de facto declaration of some kind of affiliation. I am too scared to do that. I am terribly sorry."

Chadwick was hugely disappointed. Things had seemed to go so well since he returned to England. He had assumed that Melanie would fall in line. He tried a last line of attack. "The ceremony doesn't begin until eleven a.m. How about coming into town for the day by train? You'll only meet my people at the Palace, and maybe for lunch afterwards. You'll meet the King—your friend Freddy would be impressed."

"I haven't seen Freddy for ages, Allan. In fact, I've seen no one who belonged to the entire Isbell's bunch. It seems so long ago. You really want me to be there, don't you? I will see if there is a train I could catch. Don't forget I have no car nowadays, so getting to the station is not that easy. I'll call you at the mess tomorrow evening, TTFN."

Melanie agreed to come to the ceremony. She planned to make her own way to the Palace from the station, and Chadwick made sure she was on the guest list. He met his parents at Euston the day before the investiture, and they took a taxi to the hotel. Chadwick's mother thought Allan was looking thinner, and he agreed that he had not put back all the weight he'd lost in France. Mrs. Chadwick had had her hair permed for the occasion, and she came down to breakfast in her best clothes, a smart two-piece suit. His father wore a sharply pressed three-piece suit with a waistcoat. A gold chain was draped across his budding paunch.

Chadwick arranged with the concierge for a taxi to take them to the Palace at quarter past ten. His mother commented on the bomb damage as they made their way, adding, "Not as bad as Liverpool." The taxi made its way through shattered streets covered with boarding to prevent people falling into the gaping cellars.

The damage in central London wasn't as bad as it was on the East End, due to the proximity of the docks and oil storage tanks there, Allan told his mother.

"What's all this about then, lad?" Chadwick's father asked.

"Just a typical wartime incident— flying, you know."

His father seemed to be satisfied with that facile explanation.

They entered the Palace grounds through a side entrance. Chadwick told his parents the Palace was bombed during the Battle of Britain. When they climbed out of the taxi, their identification cards were compared with the guest list by a burly police sergeant.

The investiture was held in the Palace ballroom. Footmen in magnificent uniforms stood against the walls. The guests were seated some distance from a solitary high-backed chair. The two dozen or so awardees were seated separately, equerries in uniform questioned each one, and the awards were placed on velvet cushions with their names. The equerries fastened small hooks to the uniforms of the awardees, "Makes it easier for the King," was the whispered explanation. The Lord Chamberlain announced, "His Majesty, the King," and then the King walked into the room flanked by two officers of the Gurkha regiment. He was dressed in the uniform of an Army General. A small marine band played the National Anthem and everybody stood. When the King sat, so did everyone else.

The Lord Chamberlain addressed the audience. "We are gathered this morning to recognize acts of gallantry by members of the armed forces. I will mention their rank and names one by one. They will advance to the King to receive their medals. At the completion of that part of the ceremony, there will be a reception with light refreshments."

The Lord Chamberlain then commenced to read the names and honors. Each stepped forward and saluted, and then the King took the medal from a cushion held by an equerry and hung it on the recipient's uniform. The King made a few remarks to each man, not audible to the audience. When Chadwick's name was called, he stepped up to the King, and as he reached to hang the white enamel cross the King whispered, "Good show, Squadron Leader. I received a confidential report on your exploits. Try to stay alive." Chadwick said he would try, and saluted. He stepped back and the equerry gave him a case for the medal.

Later, the Lord Chamberlain announced the reception would commence and Chadwick went in search of Melanie. When he found her, he took her hand and introduced her to his parents. "Perhaps you can have lunch with us, Lady Fitzgibbon," he said.

"That would be delightful."

The band softly played selections from Gilbert and Sullivan operettas. Servants were passing with glasses of wine and small, cucumber sandwiches. In due course, the King disappeared through a small door, and once out of sight of the crowd in the ballroom, the King turned to an aide, "Quick, give me a cigarette. I'm dying for a drag."

Taxis were lined up in the courtyard and when the Chadwicks and Melanie climbed aboard, Allan told the driver to take them to the Ritz. He had already made a lunchtime reservation. During lunch Melanie chattered away about her son who was serving in the Army in North Africa. Mrs. Chadwick interrupted the flow to ask her how she met Allan. "Let me think, I don't really remember, do you, Allan?"

"We have a mutual friend, Lord Lowestoft. He was very interested in my experiences in Iraq and invited me to a gathering you were at, Melanie."

"Yes, that's it. And then you brought a German student to my place in Pangbourne. Oh, that reminds of Clair Court Hall. Do you know, Mrs. Chadwick, the Army has taken over my house? I'm reduced to living in the stable."

Allan smiled when his mother replied, "How shocking. What do the horses think?"

Melanie wasn't sure if Mrs. Chadwick was being straight forward or pulling her leg.

Allan moved the conversation on by suggesting they choose some of the famous desserts at the Ritz. Later, when they parted at the door, Melanie said she would take a taxi directly to Paddington Station and thanked Allan formally for the invitation to the Palace.

Allan suggested to his parents that they walk to Piccadilly Circus. The famous statue of Eros was protected by a mountain of sand bags but they continued to the Thames Embankment. Chadwick managed to snag a taxi back to the hotel. His mother insisted on sewing the dark red and blue ribbon of the DSO onto his jacket.

The next day he had tickets for a matinee performance of "Lilac Time," a cheerful musical set in Vienna in the last century. Allan got the distinct impression that his mother did not like Melanie. She made references to Allan's "high falutin" friends and "Lady Muck" as they said their good-byes at Euston.

Chapter Twenty-Two

Chadwick spent his last night in London alone at the hotel. A great believer in the notion that you make your own luck, he had counted on Melanie to spend it with him, but she had a mind of her own. Back at Boscombe, he asked Wing Commander Rowley what his duties were, cognizant of the warning from MI6 to stay out of European air space.

Rowley suggested trouble-shooting for the Thomas group. "Until bomber losses start to fall we haven't fully capitalized on your amazing theft of a Messerschmitt," was his comment. Thomas suggested a visit to squadrons using the newly-installed rear firing system for their comments.

Chadwick called Bomber Command and found eighteen squadrons were using the defense system. Armed with a list he telephoned the intelligence officer at each squadron for results of the installation. He was disappointed to find that there had been no reported downings of attacking fighters. He decided to make a visit to the Avro factory at Woodford to witness the installation of the rear-pointing guns.

His old friend, Phil Donovan, was still the chief test pilot but production had increased so much that Donovan now managed a team of over twelve test pilots, including a few seconded from the RAF.

On his second day there, Chadwick noticed the commercial version of the device invented at Boscombe carried a "Receiver Type 4571" nameplate and was plugged into aircraft wiring which terminated at the wireless operator's desk. He spoke to an engineer who was responsible for the electrical system.

"As I understand it that unit connects the aerial to sensing circuits that close a relay and fires the guns when the unit decides a fighter is within range, correct?"

"Yes, Sir, that is essentially the way it works."

"How are the sensing circuits calibrated?"

"That's done by the manufacturer. Avro does not calibrate it, and it's pre-tuned, as they say nowadays."

"Hmmm. Would it be possible for me to take a few back to Boscombe? They'll be returned, of course?"

"I don't see why not. I'll have four units put in a cardboard box for you to take back."

Four days later, after a fruitful visit to many of the Avro satellite factories with Donovan, Chadwick returned to Boscombe with the four black boxes. He asked Dr. Thomas's group to test them, for both aerial sensitivity and accuracy in determining range from the pulse rate count.

A technician gave Chadwick and Thomas the results two days later. Three units had poor sensitivity; one was up to specification. Based on the Boscombe formula that related range to the pulse rate, the units operated the gun trigger at ranges 637 yards, 815 yards, and 951 yards. One unit never activated the trigger.

Thomas was appalled. "These were specified to be within one percent of the ideal figures, I don't understand it."

"Who is manufacturing these devices, Doctor?"

"I don't know. There was such a rush to get things moving, the order was left to the procurements people. They probably gave it to the low bidder."

It took Chadwick a full day to sort through the procurements summary provided by the Ministry of Supply. The Type 4571 unit was built by two companies that submitted bids to build a device to specifications prepared by Boscombe Down. They were to be calibrated before shipment using test sets supplied by Boscombe. Chadwick decided he should witness a test at Boscombe before carrying the investigation further.

An engineer had the 4571 unit on a bench. He was dressed in a lab coat and wore thick glasses. He introduced himself, "Rich Lomax, Sir. I have terrible eyesight." He touched his glasses and smiled in a deprecatory way. He showed Chadwick how to connect the test set. A thick coaxial cable plugged into a sturdy socket on the front. Lomax called it a "UHF connector." The other connection was made by a plug with many pins that went into a socket on the back.

Lomax explained, "First turn on the test set." A small light glowed on the front. "This provides power and simulated signals to the 4571 unit." Then he flipped the power switch on the unit under test. A light glowed on its panel. He pointed to a second switch on the 4571. "The crew must activate it by setting the switch here from 'Safe' to 'Armed.' Now it's sensitive to incoming signals. We simulate that by turning this knob on the tester labeled 'RF.' As you can see, a meter shows the level set, calibrated from one to ten."

Lomax slowly turned the knob, and at level four, a different light glowed. It was labeled 'Alert.' "That shows the unit is picking up radar signals of sufficient strength. Once it's in the 'Alert' mode it will count the pulse rate frequency and convert that to distance." He turned another knob on the test set and a meter labeled 'Distance' flickered to life. The dial was calibrated from 500 to 1,000 yards.

"Watch as I change the simulated distance," Lomax told Chadwick. The meter read one thousand yards. As the engineer turned the control knob, the meter needle moved to the left, landing on nine and then eight. At that point Chadwick heard a loud 'click' inside the 4571 unit and another light glowed. This one was labeled 'Fire.'

"The unit has closed the trigger circuit at eight hundred yards, firing the guns," Lomax continued. "Provided the unit detects RF below level five, and fires the guns at eight hundred yards, give or take ten yards, the unit is acceptable. I would expect an inspector to certify the test, depending on the way the company handles quality control. Boscombe has given two testers to each manufacturer—one for use during production, and one to certify performance. We specified each must be returned to Boscombe monthly for re-calibration. Dr. Thomas was not sure the eight hundred-yard distance is set in concrete, so to speak, and may be changed as operational experience is gained."

Chadwick was delighted to have a demonstration by such an intelligent engineer and thanked him profusely. He brought Wing Commander Rowley up to date and suggested a visit to the factories making the 4571 unit as the next step. Rowley suggested taking Rich Lomax along and another test set, so the factory equipment could be verified. Rowley said he would clear the visit with the Ministry of Supply, as they were sensitive to the services interfering in the procurement process.

Using the Anson flight to the nearest RAF field, Chadwick hoped to get the visits out of the way in a day. The first factory was a subsidiary of a large organization. Their records followed a standard company format and corresponded with the Ministry of Supply paperwork. A 4571 unit picked at random performed flawlessly within specification, using both factory equipment and the Boscombe tester brought along by Lomax.

The second visit was to a small private company at Shrewsbury, near RAF Shawbury. From there a service car dropped them at a medium-sized building in an industrial park. They were met in the lobby by the managing director, a nervous individual in a grey suit.

"I'm Cyril Underwood, Managing Director. The Ministry called to explain your visit, Squadron Leader. Our quality control is under the supervision of a first-rate gentleman you'll meet in a few minutes. Please come into my office. I can offer you some tea and biscuits while I give you a little history of the company.

"Drummond Radio was started by Mr. Drummond after a visit to America in the 1920s," the managing director began. "He was convinced wireless was the technology of the future. He raised capital and hired designers and production experts. He started with domestic wireless sets that ran off the mains wiring, no accumulators for him. With the war, we no longer make domestic receivers. Our main lines at the moment are the 4571 receivers. We make forty a month. We also make an aircraft intercommunications amplifier, a hundred a month. Please let me know how I can be of help."

"We would like to see the 4571 receiver production and test line, please."

Underwood led the way into the main assembly area, showing them how the mechanical assembly began the fabrication process, then the chassis were passed to a dozen workers, all women, all armed with soldering irons, which they used to fasten components to the chassis.

A male technician with a Boscombe tester adjusted the units before the case was screwed on. Lomax explained to Chadwick, "He adjusts the tuned circuits connected to the UHF connector to get a sensitivity better than five on the tester, and then he adjusts a small internal potentiometer to set the firing count corresponding to eight hundred yards."

Mr. Underwood interrupted Lomax. "Precisely. Once it is within specification, he screws the cover on and passes it to inspection, and then it goes to shipping. It takes a day or two before the unit is inspected. We shall go to inspection next. This way, gentlemen." He directed them down the hall.

They walked into a small room where they saw a technician and a middle-aged man, who rose to greet them. Underwood introduced him, "Mr. Sean McDermott. Mr. McDermott, these gentlemen are from Boscombe Down, where the 4571 Receiver was designed. They're helping the Ministry maintain quality control."

"What can I do to help, gentlemen?"

Chadwick said, "We'd like to test a receiver against our own equipment and the tester you use."

"We send our test units to Boscombe on a regular basis for verification," McDermott explained. Then he turned to the technician. "Tommy, pop into shipping and see if they have any 4571 units ready to go out."

The technician returned with one of the units, and placed it on the lab table.

Lomax looked at it and asked McDermott to show him the inspection log. He ran his finger along the serial number on the nameplate and stared shortsightedly at the logbook. "This receiver was inspected two days ago, passed satisfactory."

Lomax then spoke to the technician. "Please take off the cover before we test it."

McDermott said, "We don't test with the cover off."

"I understand, but please humor me," Lomax replied.

The technician removed six small screws and handed the chassis to Lomax, who ran his fingers over the internal parts. He then connected the tester and adjusted the controls. "Sensitivity three-point-seven, range seven hundred and ninety-three yards," he announced.

"There," Mr. McDermott said, a trifle loudly. "A good unit."

"Please put it back together," Lomax said, looking at the technician.

Chadwick and Lomax returned with the managing director to his office. Lomax tugged on Chadwick's sleeve, and when Underwood walked ahead, he whispered, "Find out if our visit was announced to the staff before our arrival."

When they sat in Underwood's office, he pressed them to stay for lunch.

"Sorry," Chadwick replied. "Love to, but our schedule is very tight and a little chaotic. I wasn't sure we were coming to your factory until the last moment. Did you get notification we were coming?"

"Yes, we actually got a phone call from the Ministry early this morning, so we expected you."

"If I may use your telephone, I'll call Shawbury and we'll be on way. Thank you, Mr. Underwood. You run a tight ship here, obviously."

When Chadwick and Lomax were seated in the RAF car on the way to the airfield, Chadwick asked, "What was all that about?"

"Well, Sir, I may have terrible eyesight but I am sensitive to touch. When I picked up that receiver it felt warm, and by taking the cover off I could feel the valves were definitely still hot, that unit had been operated before we saw it."

"Which is why it passed our inspection with flying colors, eh? Good work, Rich! I think MI5 should pay more attention to Drummond Radio."

Chadwick told the wing commander of their concerns. "Lomax firmly believed the 4571 unit we inspected was recalibrated just before our visit. The valves which run very hot in operation were still warm when we inspected it. I think all 4571 units from Drummond Radio should be impounded and retested."

"That's up to the Ministry, Allan. Suspicious activity concerning equipment procured for the government is not uncommon. The Ministry has a group that deals with it. I'll give them a call today and forward your comments."

"If it's all right with you, Sir, I'd like to mention this matter to my friend at MI5. It's not that Drummond is making any money by the deliberate miscalibration of the receivers, but RAF aircrew could well be killed when a good receiver could save them."

Rowley thought for a minute. "Probably not a bad idea. But too many cooks spoil the broth, y'know. The Ministry is used to downright financial shenanigans, but this does smack of sabotage, so let your friend poke MI5's nose into it."

The next day Chadwick flew to Croydon and took a train into central London. He met Doug Larson in his office in White-hall. He gave Larson the thinking that went into the defense against German fighters with vertically firing guns. Then he described his visit to Drummond Radio and the engineer's quick-witted detection of the attempt to cover miscalibration of the critical receiver.

"There's no illegal money in this, so far as I can see. It seems like plain sabotage."

Larson jotted down the details and said someone would look into it. Chadwick told him the Ministry had been informed and that his wing commander thought that their fraud squad would look into it.

"That's fine," Larson said. "We operate on a different level. We won't interfere with each other."

They chatted for a while and then Larson suggested lunch. "How about if I give Will Viney a call, see if he's free? Will is in MI6. You met him at Cromer when you clobbered that Nazi spy."

The three of them adjourned to an expensive hotel bar near the Embankment. "It's a trifle pricier here, Allan," Doug explained, "but it is fairly secluded."

When they had their drinks, Larson said, "Allan has been having a very adventurous time since you saw him last, Will."

"Oh? I've signed the Official Secrets Act. Pray tell."

"Should I give him the short version, Allan?"

"Of course. I always like to hear how the story grows in the re-telling."

"It all started when he got himself shot down in a bomber over Germany, or France, linked up with the Free French, and was on his way home when Six heard of a German fighter that was getting some interesting modifications they wanted to know more about. So, Allan was diverted so that he could inspect it. Instead he sneaked a ride and brought the plane to England with a dead German Luftwaffe officer as his co-pilot."

Chadwick laughed out loud, but Viney looked at him with eyes wide open in admiration. "My God, Allan, Doug wasn't exaggerating. I'm in awe." He looked at Chadwick's uniform. "See you have a DSO. I trust it was for that little escapade."

"Yes, and the receiver I've been telling Doug about is a direct result of laying our hands on the German plane. It will alert and even shoot down the Nazi night fighters when they attack our Lancaster fleets."

The three men sat in silence for a few minutes, sipping their drinks. Then Chadwick said, "Will, how is the war going from your spook vantage point?"

"I think Hitler has finally met his match in Russia. He's turned his forces on capturing the Baku oil fields, but if the Soviets stop him, he's like a man on a branch with someone sawing it off—he's out on a limb, as the saying goes."

"About the involvement of the Americans—what differences will that make?"

"The Americans are pouring a tremendous fortune into establishing the Eighth Air Force in England. They have the same strategic vision as Bomber Command, which is to destroy the

German ability to make weapons and fuel. I don't know how well that will work. Now we're dealing with economics. But the Yanks have a lot of money. They'll win in the end, I think."

"Funny you should say that. A professor I was talking to recently said the same thing."

"Oh, who was that?"

"You wouldn't know him. It was when I was in France."

Viney laughed. "So while you were planning to steal a German plane, you were discussing high-level strategic policy?"

"He was a nice old chap. Brought me the *Daily Mirror* to read one day."

Viney suddenly looked serious. "Unfortunately, once you put the war in economic terms, then the Americans will come out on top and the British will lose their empire. We can't afford this war in the long run."

Chadwick didn't really believe him, and said, "If the Americans are putting such an effort into their bombing fleet, I hope someone in RAF HQ is giving them the benefit of what we've learned in the past almost three years."

"Good point, Allan. You should get involved."

They chatted for a while longer and ordered sandwiches and later parted on the steps of the hotel. Viney grasped Chadwick's hand and said, "What you did was fantastic, Allan. With courage like that we're going to win this war. Congratulations on the medal. You richly deserve it. It's an honor to know you."

Chadwick was a trifle embarrassed and gruffly muttered something.

When Chadwick returned to Boscombe he mentioned the liaison idea with the new U.S. Army Air Force to Wing Commander Rowley, who said he would follow up on it.

Larson called him a few days later. "The situation at Drummond Radio is almost laughable," he said. "Allan, the Ministry conducted tests on the receivers and more than half failed to meet requirements. A check of the records showed that these had all passed through the Drummond inspection department. Special Branch Bobbies confronted McDermott, who immediately confessed it was his idea of helping the Irish Republican Army.

"No need for us to get involved, but it was very interesting. The chap I talked to from the Ministry was annoyed because of all the paperwork required to get the units recalibrated. That was more important to him than the fact that defective receivers could have resulted in many deaths. Incidentally, McDermott was charged with conspiracy and so was his technician, who turned out to be his son. They'll be put away for a few years. This is something else the RAF owes you for, but you've probably got enough medals to be going on with, eh?"

Chadwick sat down with Dr. Thomas and told him the story of the defective 4571 receivers. "Incidentally, Dr. Thomas, there is something about the receiver I keep meaning to ask you every time I see one tested."

"Yes, what is it?"

"When the 'Fire' circuit is completed and the light comes on, it extinguishes a few seconds later. What happens after that?"

"The armorers warned us that a four-second burst was safe for twenty-millimeter cannon, but longer bursts may lead to overheating, so the trigger circuit has a timer to disconnect the relay."

"And then?"

"The unit won't fire another burst if the range to the German radar climbs above eight hundred yards. Assuming the

'Alert' circuit is still primed, it will repeat the burst in the usual way when the distance drops back to eight hundred yards."

"Thank you for the explanation. I'm staying In touch with squadrons fitted out with the 4571 unit, I hope soon we'll start to see downing reports of Nazi night fighters."

Chapter Twenty-Three

Wing Commander Rowley called Chadwick into his office. "I've been in touch with the people in the Air Ministry who are involved with setting up the U.S. Eighth Air Force in England. Frankly, the effort going into this is staggering. They plan to have about a hundred airfields in operation before the end of the year, mostly in East Anglia. Some will be RAF fields turned over to them. Others will be built as quickly as possible. Almost all the liaison with the Americans has been concerned with infrastructure—roads, communications, fuel depots, maintenance centers, that sort of thing.

"However," Rowley continued, "the idea of having you discuss operations was well received, and they gave me the name of the officer who's starting to put together their operational planning. He is Colonel John Butzke, known as 'Buzz' to his friends. He's a career officer, went to West Point. He has over a thousand hours of four-engine time, but hasn't flown in combat. We're holding back no secrets, you're free to discuss Gee, Oboe, Pathfinders—whatever he's interested in. He's based at their headquarters in High Wycombe. He's been informed that an RAF officer will be in touch to familiarize him with RAF experience.

"I think you're going to have to be diplomatic, Allan," Rowley cautioned. "The Americans are charging in like young lions, and we don't want to discourage them by appearing as the wise, old uncle who's seen it all. Please keep me up to date on how it goes."

Chadwick made an appointment to meet Colonel Butzke, and flew in the Anson from Boscombe to RAF Northolt. He was sitting with the American by mid-morning.

"Good morning, Squadron Leader, a pleasure to meet you! How about coffee and some Yankee cookies?"

"That would be wonderful, Sir. I haven't had coffee in a long while."

"Really! You know Churchill made FDR promise the arrival of the Eighth would not strain British food supplies. I'm told that food, sundries, bombs, and ammunition fill two ten-thousand-ton freighters every month, just for us. The Air Force wouldn't function without coffee." He laughed. "I may have misremembered, but someone said it took twenty freighters to carry the vehicles we need to start the Eighth—fuel trucks, fire engines, ambulances, jeeps, heavy trucks.

"To get down to business—" and at this point, Butzke's tone became much more serious. "The Army Air Force made a detailed study of Raff and Luftwaffe tactics until we got embroiled. The conclusion was that neither organization was ready for a war of attrition—and I mean not of men, but resources. This is an industrial war. The ability of the enemy to forge the resources of war must be destroyed. The small fleets of Wellingtons, Hampdens, Ju 88s, and Dorniers could only inflict pin-pricks, which wouldn't significantly affect the production of war material.

"Now the British did wake up and the Lancaster fleets coming into service will affect the balance in the long run," he conceded. "The Luftwaffe has not made a similar disposition of their assets. And now they're paying for it in Russia. Those crafty Soviets have moved their factories east of the Caucasus and the Krauts can't reach them.

"These studies formed the basis of the Eighth battle plan," Butzke continued, "daylight precision bombing by massed fleets armed to deter fighters. This is the plan that was sold to Congress, which has come up with the funds to implement it. We hope to have at least five hundred heavy bombers operational by the end of the year and a thousand bombers by the middle of next year. The latest model, the B-17G will have more turrets. You appear to have seen this war from the pointed end, Squadron Leader. What do you think?"

Chadwick was feeling a little overwhelmed by the arguments put forth by the colonel. "I flew on some raids in a Wellington, and you're right—the bombload will never stop German production. That's why the Lancaster was produced."

The colonel pounced on Chadwick. "Right, but you failed to provide deterrent for fighter attacks, which is why the Raff raids are at night. Bang goes precision."

"That raises a topic I wanted you to be aware of, Sir. Our bombers are equipped with a wireless aid to navigation which place a bomber's position to within a mile or two, at night in any weather. I have been authorized to say that it is available for your planes if you wish to use it. We have also developed a much more accurate system to precisely locate targets, but it's limited to one or two aircraft, which mark the target. We call them Pathfinders."

"Wonderful, Squadron Leader! Before you leave, make sure I have some names and I'll get our signals people onto it. All our planes are equipped with the Bendix direction-finding radio. I think so far it is felt that the Bendix will be sufficient to get the boys home, but time will tell. From your experience, what do you see as the weakness in the battle plan?"

"I flew in one of the prototype B-17s which the RAF purchased a couple of years ago. Although it had plenty of guns, I still think that's the weakness. The German fighters are very good. They soon work out the vulnerable areas of a plane and train their pilots to exploit it."

"That's the reason we train to fly in close-knit groups— one plane protects another. My goodness, Squadron Leader, you've finished your coffee, please have some more. And we call these cookies Oreos." He pointed to the circular black biscuits. "You've gotta try one. And please call me Buzz."

"Thank you very much, Sir—Buzz. It's very good, and the cookie is delicious. And please call me Allan. Also, I think I should mention that all worthwhile targets in Germany are heavily defended by flak. Twisting and turning to avoid bursts totally destroys any idea of precision targeting."

"We gave that a good deal of thought, Allan. Beside a very sophisticated bombsight, the plan calls for the pilot to turn control of the aircraft over to the bombardier during the run-up to the target, using the autopilot."

Chadwick suddenly had a vision of Flying Officer Ramsey in the bomb aimer's position of the Wellington when a shell burst near the nose just after they had dropped the flares on Augsburg. Cruel, sharp fragments of the shell had ripped his body to pieces. "The bombardier will be very vulnerable, Buzz," he said to the American colonel, "especially with the plane holding a steady course for a minute or two."

"Jesus, Allan, you look like you've seen a ghost."

"In a sense I just did. On my last raid over Germany, the bomb aimer's office was close to exploding flak, and the aimer was killed. Sorry, the image just flashed into my mind."

"That bad, eh, Allan? Sherman got it right—war is hell."

"What about target planning?" Chadwick asked.

"Oh, we have a big group looking at that—strategists, economists, experts of every type. They just provide the facts. The decisions are taken way above our rank, Allan."

"What about photos for target analysis after the raid?"

"Some planes carry cameras, tripped by the navigator, I think."

"We tried that. Doesn't work very well. We have dedicated photo-recon planes, with good cameras. That's the only way to get information about the success of the raid. Another point— have your signals people been in touch with Sixty Group to make sure the IFF signals are compatible with Chain Home RDR?"

"That's been done and tested on planes arriving from the States via Iceland."

"Buzz, this is going to be a learning experience, like we went through in the late thirties and early forties. It won't be fun. The Germans are awfully good. When the flak stops, the fighters are onto you in seconds. I suspect your group formations will be in tatters at that point. Are you planning on joining a few raids yourself?"

"Sure. You can't lead from the back. If it turns out to be as bad as you suspect, the guys in the squadrons will want to know that headquarters knows what it's all about."

"One last thing I almost forgot to mention, Buzz. The RAF has organized a fairly good air-sea rescue service for planes ditching in the Channel. Please speak to your signals people about plugging into that network. I can give them a name to contact. They once pulled me out of the water after a couple of hours. Took me a day to warm up!" He laughed, and Butzke joined in the laughter.

"Allan, I'm beginning to get the impression you're like a cat, with nine lives."

Chadwick reluctantly turned down an invitation for lunch and returned to Boscombe. He had started to send the contact information he had promised to Colonel Butzke when his telephone rang. An excited voice identified himself as the intelligence officer of a Lancaster squadron.

"Wonderful news! A plane landed in the small hours, and the armorers reported an average of forty-two bullets had been fired by each of the two rear-facing cannon, and the wireless op said the 'Alert' light on the 4571 unit went on and then off. I think we just downed a Messerschmitt, Sir."

Chadwick agreed this was wonderful news, and passed the news on to Dr. Thomas. The scientist told him about a request that had filtered down from some squadrons equipped the 4571 system—they wanted a way to manually fire the guns. It was felt this would have a discouraging impact on Luftwaffe pilots stalking the giant Lancasters. Thomas pointed out that this would be easy to achieve by the addition of a push-button switch which bypassed the pulse counting circuit.

Chadwick thought about it, "Give it a try, Trevor, but make sure the four-second timer is still included in the circuit. In the excitement of the moment these chaps are likely to expend the whole magazine."

Chapter Twenty-Four

In the succeeding weeks two other planes reported the guns fired automatically and in one incident the destruction of a fighter was witnessed by the rear gunner of another Lancaster. Slowly the percentage of bombers lost on night raids began to fall, the residual losses attributed mostly to flak. The response was to increase the height of bombers, but there was an obvious correlation with the decreasing accuracy which resulted. A modification kit was put together that included a manually-operated trigger switch. It could be installed by technicians at the squadron bases.

Chadwick followed the results by questioning the intelligence officers conducting the debriefings. He began to suspect that Luftwaffe pilots were giving the Lancasters a wide berth— not what was originally intended, but satisfactory anyway.

He received a message from Colonel Butzke inviting him to visit High Wycombe again. The colonel greeted him with freshly brewed coffee, which Chadwick certainly enjoyed. On his desk was a new tin of Maxwell House ground coffee. Butzke pointed, "That's for you, Allan," but he could scarcely conceal his agitation. "Allan, this is not uncommon—politics has intruded on good military planning. I hate it."

"What's happened, Buzz?"

"Look at the calendar, Allan. Nearly the end of June. July Fourth is only a week away—Independence Day," he added for Chadwick's benefit. "Somebody in Washington felt the Eighth should make its presence felt on that significant date. In fact, we are almost ready to commence limited ops. Another two weeks should do it. But somebody picked up the July Fourth ball and ran with it. Now I hear six of our bomber crews are going to fly with a Canadian outfit on a raid that will be split with Canadians, using Lockheed Hudsons."

"Hudsons!" Chadwick echoed. "They're used for maritime patrol. They've nailed a couple of U-boats, I think."

"This won't be over the ocean, Allan. There's a raid planned on Holland. Six planes with American crews will go after shipping in the port of Haarlem; six planes with Canadian crews will bomb the railway marshaling yards near Amsterdam. They'll reform and fly back to England."

"What height will this raid use?"

"Five thousand feet."

"God!" Chadwick exclaimed. "The 109's will eat them alive."

"Allan, this boondoggle must've been put together in cooperation with Bomber Command. Please use your contacts to find out who authorized it and let's see if we can scupper it. Naturally, the American bomber crews are frustrated. They've been here a few weeks, some of 'em, and they want to fly. To them this is a big adventure."

"It's going to be a massacre, Buzz. Find me a quiet office with a telephone and I'll see what I can find out."

Chadwick called Group Captain Hearne at Bomber Command HQ and outlined Colonel Butzke's concern. He asked if Bomber Command had been involved in planning the Dutch raid.

"Only in general terms, Allan. Whitehall is very keen to get the Americans going at full steam, so our orders are to do anything they want. I believe an American general, let me see—Angus Blair—knew someone commanding the Canadian squadron, which is flying with Bomber Command. They fixed it up. He claims this is to get combat experience. Hope this helps."

Chadwick told Butzke that the raid had been planned by American General Angus Blair.

"Gus!" Butzke exploded. "That SOB. I should've known. He's a real operator. They have American newspaper men primed about the raid, and ready to submit glowing reports and pictures of the Glorious Eighth. Timed to be in the July Fourth editions."

The daylight raid took place on the second of the month, and the Germans were ready. Two of the six planes manned by Americans went down, and one plane flown by Canadians ditched in the Channel. The crew was picked up by German ships.

Colonel Butzke was waiting at the airfield when they landed. Most of the crews seemed to be in a state of shock. Several men had been wounded. Butzke forbid any interviews with reporters, instead giving the newspaper men a statement that a small raid on the continent by Eighth Air Force personnel had been completed. They claimed two Messerschmitts shot down. Photographs showed crew in flying gear standing under aircraft engines. Only experts would know the planes were not B-17s. Butzke told Chadwick the whole exercise could be considered "public relations," and he conceded it was important to keep the folks back home aware of the Eighth.

By August, the U.S. Army Air Force was able to assemble a whole group of three squadrons and mount raids against coastal targets in France. Gradually, the size of the attacking American force built up to over 200 planes, which enabled the underlying concept of mutual protection to be tested in practice.

Bad weather limited missions as winter developed, but the Luftwaffe was learning how to attack the massed fleets of heavy bombers. Attacks were made from head-on. The Americans could not bring as many guns to bear and the closing speed of nearly 600 knots meant accuracy was poor. It required nerves of steel on the part of the Luftwaffe pilot but some were successful, reducing the flight deck of formation leaders to a bloody shambles and disrupting the bombing run. Slowly, American losses began to climb, reaching five percent of the attacking force, an unsustainable situation.

Chadwick frequently visited Colonel Butzke to discuss the progress of the air war. One tactic they worked on saved a few B-17s that had been damaged and were slowly staggering back to England, lagging the fleet and becoming prey for marauding Luftwaffe fighters. Once these lost sheep came within range of British RDR, Spitfires were vectored onto the American planes to deter German attackers, which were often surprised, to their cost, by the sudden arrival of British fighters.

Chadwick and Butzke were both at RAF Tangmere when a badly shot-up B-17, trailing smoke, crash-landed on the grass parallel to the main runway. They went to the sick bay to talk to the American pilot, who was having some light wounds dressed. He was full of praise for the Spitfires, which shot down a German 109 just as it was attacking the American plane.

"God, were we pleased to see that Limey Spit. It saved our skins. We need them to be with us for the whole raid."

"That's not a bad idea," Chadwick and Butzke said, almost at the same time.

Back at High Wycombe the two officers discussed the problems of providing fighter escort for the American heavy bombers. Chadwick said, "The range of a Spitfire is just too small to escort bombers to targets in Germany. I don't think it's big enough to add extra tanks. It's really quite a light plane."

"How about 'drop tanks'?" Butzke suggested.

Chadwick thought about it. "No, I don't think so. If the pilots had to drop them as soon as they crossed the Channel they would still not have enough fuel."

They were both silent, then Chadwick said, "The Air Ministry placed an order with North American Aviation for a medium fighter bomber, called the Mustang. Now, I believe the U.S. Government had picked up the order. The plane is heavier than the Spit and has a range of about twelve hundred miles. It was intended to support ground operations. That might be worth looking at."

"What kind of guns does it carry, Allan?"

"Dunno. Let me make a few telephone calls."

Chadwick was soon back. "A real tank buster—six fifty-caliber machine guns. Can also carry rockets. Alison engine, about eleven hundred horsepower. A few RAF squadrons are equipped with that plane. I'll find out which and cadge a ride in one."

Chadwick discovered the plane had been used to support Commando raids on the French coast and to attack ports in Belgium and France at low level. He flew to an Army Cooperative field and after sweet-talking the commanding officer, strapped himself into a Mustang for a test flight over England. He was intimately familiar with the characteristics of a Spitfire and put the plane through a series of tests he would have used if he was air testing a Spitfire.

He found the Mustang was a versatile, good plane below 12,000 feet, but above that altitude the performance fell off rapidly. He knew that it was no match for a Messerschmitt 109 above 12,000 to 15,000 feet.

Back at Boscombe Down he talked over the problem with a senior engineering officer. "The Alison engine is exactly what it needs for ground support," the officer told Allan, "but it has a puny super charger. If you want performance at altitude it must have a two-stage supercharger."

"Would it be possible to add one to the existing engine?" Chadwick asked.

The engineer laughed. "Goodness no! The engine has to be designed from the crankshaft up to take the power from that much boost, like the Merlin Mark III."

Chadwick recounted the conversation he had had about the Mustangs to Colonel Butzke, who said, "Well then, the answer is simple. To get a good escort plane we just put a Rolls Royce Merlin engine in a Mustang. Just leave it with me, Allan. I'll put a firecracker up the ass of our procurement people."

Chadwick often visited Colonel Butzke at the Eighth Air Force HQ. He sat through numerous reviews of strike photos, and along with the senior officers he was disappointed at the average accuracy achieved by the bombers. Only a small percentage of the bombload fell within a mile of the target. Chadwick felt a growing awareness that the massed attacks both by the Americans and the RAF were killing and injuring a disproportionate number of civilians.

At Boscombe he examined copies of the U.S. photos through stereoscopic viewers, and felt anguish as his eye swept over the three-dimensional images of street after street of shattered houses, usually in working class areas near the factories. His conviction grew that such carnage was morally wrong, even though the senior strategists argued that workers were as legitimate a target as the factories they worked in.

"OK," he would counter, "but what about their wives and children?"

"Unavoidable casualties" was the pat reply.

The issue began to bother him so much that he had difficulty sleeping. He had helped to create the Anglo-American strategic bombing force, and now he agonized over the bloodbath it was making. Finally he went to talk to his superior, Wing Commander Rowley. Without exposing his moral scruples he told Rowley that the poor accuracy of both British and U.S. raids were resulting in far more aircrew casualties than originally anticipated, because the missions had to be repeated, sometimes over and over again, and the strategic goals of forcing a quick end to the war were in jeopardy.

Rowley grudgingly agreed. "But what alternative do we have until we can invade the continent?"

Chadwick had an answer, a solution that had slowly formed in his mind as he lay sleepless, night after night. "I think we can form a precision bomber unit, going after targets that are strategically important. The raid would be carried out at low level and would be very accurate and devastating."

"I think your concern is well-placed, Allan. Let me take it up with Bomber Command."

A few days later he called Chadwick into his office. "I spoke to Group Captain Hearne and mentioned your name and he was impressed. You have a lot of fans at Uxbridge. He said you must be prescient—a joint task force has just started looking at a proposal to bomb dams in the Ruhr Valley using a new kind of bomb. Just the kind of specific strategic target you had in mind. A new Lancaster squadron is being formed.

"But he also told me a new strike squadron is being considered for just this kind of activity using Mosquito fighter-bombers. Can I say you're very interested and would like to be involved?"

Chapter Twenty-Five

Chadwick was delighted to be told a few days later that he was going to be appointed the new commanding officer of 613 Squadron, which, of course, he had commanded two years earlier during the Battle of Britain. The number of Spitfire squadrons was being slightly reduced as Luftwaffe raids diminished, and 613 would get the new Mosquito, the Mark IV, which could carry a 1,500-pound bomb load at nearly 400 knots and with a range of nearly 2,000 miles.

Chadwick was used to moving around. He put most of his gear in his battered tin trunk and took a suitcase with him on the brief Anson ride to RAF North Weald. He was greeted by the adjutant and introduced to the support staff. None of the pilots that served with him in 1940 were flying with the squadron two years later.

He went to the crew room to introduce himself and found the pilots were all Spitfire trained and not too happy about flying a fighter bomber. He enthused about the Mosquito and told the fliers it was fitted with VHF wireless sets—"You simply 'push to talk.' No operator needed to tune and key the transmitter."

Chadwick tried to raise morale by describing the type of precision bombing sorties he had in mind. But first they all needed some training to fly a multi-engined plane, particularly flying on one engine. He was able to "borrow" four instructors from the Central Flying School for a week and made sure all the pilots got in some dual flying by strapping the instructors in the navigator's seat.

Twenty-four navigators arrived to fill out the two-man crews of the Mosquito. A few were experienced, but most came directly from training schools. Chadwick sat down with his flight commanders. "We have to get the squadron up to operational standard as soon as possible," he told them. "There's a lot of work to be done—low-flying navigation, low-level bombing, integration of two-man crews. But let's start by randomly picking names for pilot-navigator pairs. If any of the new navigators are pals with one of the pilots, let them choose him."

Intensive training started immediately. Chadwick selected lonely country houses as make-believe targets. However, the targets had to be changed frequently, as complaints poured into the local police from beleaguered homeowners.

Chadwick received a message to attend a meeting of the target evaluation committee in London, a two-day affair. He decided to combine it with a few days of leave, and dropped a letter to Melanie inviting her to stay in London with him. He told her he had been posted to RAF North Weald, which was an easy train journey to the city. As he left the mess to take an RAF car to the station, Chadwick noticed an envelope in his pigeon-hole addressed in familiar neat handwriting. He opened Melanie's letter when he was comfortably seated on the train.

My dear Allan, I know you will be terribly disappointed but I must decline your kind invitation to spend a weekend in Town. To paraphrase the good Dr. Johnson, I know the pleasure would be delightful but momentary, and the cost would be damnable and not momentary if I should lose you. So it is best to leave things the way they are. Perhaps when this dreadful war is over, things may be different, but they will never be the same as they were in the wonderful '30s. I hope you understand, and I remain your old friend, Melanie.

Chadwick scrunched up the letter and put it in his pocket. He brooded about women, and Melanie in particular, all the way to Whitehall.

The meeting at the Air Ministry was kicked off by a group captain, who told the participants the committee was a subgroup of the main target evaluation team and the topic was selection of low-level precision targets. A wing commander started to list the kind of targets that initially came to mind—oil refineries, power stations, railway tunnels, and bridges.

At this point, the speaker derided the bombing of railway lines. "They're quickly repaired. Rail companies always have depots of sleepers and steel rail stored at frequent intervals. But tunnels and bridges take weeks to repair. Maybe we should develop a skipping bomb that can be launched into a tunnel before exploding, an analogy of a depth charge. A good deal of Germany's transportation is by barge. Canals are hard to damage but locks if broken could produce immense delays."

The wing commander then introduced a speaker from MI6, a tall, beefy man he called Silas Kavanagh, who had a distinctive Irish brogue. "The targets we have talked about so far are rather obvious," Kavanagh began, "and are certainly important, but I want to talk about a subject that is just as important but far more subtle—morale. We receive plenty of reports from agents in Europe about the morale of the German people. It is good. For this we must credit Dr. Goebbels, who is a mastermind of propaganda. Mass bombings certainly affect the population under the bombers, but most of the German populations never hear about it. Hitler does not visit the stricken areas and there are no news reels.

"Now I am suggesting precision attacks which could affect how the average German citizen sees the war. One of the main instruments used by Dr. Goebbels is wireless. All the stations are under the control of the Nazi government. Destroying transmitting facilities would cut down on his influence. A clever idea was suggested to me recently. The tenth anniversary of the installation of the Nazi Party will occur in a few weeks, and ceremonies will be broadcast nationwide. Sounds of bombing raids at strategic targets might be beamed to the whole population by the government's own transmitters if timed right. We are working on that one. We must fight the war with words, as well as explosions."

Someone raised his hand. "What about targeting specific individuals?"

"You are talking about assassinations, Sir. Generally, individuals are too mobile to eliminate from the air. Many killings of this nature are requested by résistance groups in occupied countries. Frequently, MI6 agents receive requests to bomb Gestapo prisons, where captured résistance workers may betray vital secrets under torture. In fact, perhaps such targets should be added to the list of likely precision hits. But in general, assassinations are carried out on the ground. The killing of Heydrich, the Gauleiter of Bohemia, a few months ago, comes to mind. A thoroughly unpleasant person. He was fingered by local partisans who were dropped in by parachute and ambushed the SS General on his way to work.

"Suggestions to kill Herr Hitler are made frequently, and curiously enough, our psychologists are against it. Not only does it raise the question of creating a martyr, many of our military analysts are also against it."

Several voices were raised at this statement, demanding an explanation. "An analysis of Germany's early successes against Poland and France can be attributed two factors—surprise at German actions and outmoded tactics by the opponents. For example, France was fighting the Great War again, but faced a mobile, Panzer-led Army. Think of the Maginot Line. The Polish Army actually made a cavalry charge in the fight against the Germans. We believe Hitler is making disastrous decisions in the Russian campaign. Time will tell and we have no plans to deliberately target him, but from what our agents hear, quite a few German generals would like to do that. But we're getting off the subject, interesting as our discussion has become."

During cocktails before dinner, Chadwick button-holed Silas Kavanagh, and explained that he commanded a squadron newly equipped with Mosquito fighter-bombers specifically intended for low-level precise targeting. He asked for more details of the plan Kavanagh had outlined to disrupt the German celebrations of the ten-year anniversary of the Nazi regime.

Kavanagh explained, "The German radio network plans to broadcast across the whole of Germany a speech by the Reichsmarschall, Herman Göring, presumably extolling the giant strides made under Herr Hitler. In a speech a while ago, which most Germans are aware of, Göring said that the RAF was powerless against the Luftwaffe, and if Berlin was ever bombed, you could call him 'Meyer'."

Chadwick looked a little puzzled, so Kavanagh explained. "'Meyer' is a Jewish name. To call a Nazi a Jew is a deadly insult, so he's saying it could never happen. Now, if his speech is interrupted by RAF bombs while it is listened to by countless millions of Germans, the psychological impact would be fantastic."

Chadwick was intrigued. He told Kavanagh he would like to be part of that raid and asked if MI6 had all the details—time and place, for example. He was told MI6 was working hard on it and they would stay in touch.

He canceled his reservation at the hotel and traveled back to North Weald. He found his flight commanders had kept the squadron busy and he started to study the navigational problem of flying to Berlin in daylight. With Gee navigation it would be possible to fly a weaving course to avoid anti-aircraft batteries except on the outskirts of Berlin itself. He calculated the round trip distance was about a thousand nautical miles, quite feasible for a Mosquito.

When the targeting subcommittee approved the proposal made by MI6 to bomb the Berlin headquarters of the German Broadcasting System, Bomber Command selected 613 Squadron to carry out the attack. At the same time MI6 removed the ban on Squadron Leader Chadwick flying over Germany. They decided enough Lancaster bombers had crashed in Germany that the defense against the Luftwaffe night fighters could hardly be considered secret any more.

Experts at MI6 planned every detail of the raid. The broadcast would be made from the studios in the western end of Berlin. They were located in a fairly new building that also contained a concert hall. It was of a distinctive triangular shape which should be easy to identify. To assist in the low-level attack MI6 had commissioned model makers at the Elstree film studio to build a three-dimensional map of western Berlin, with emphasis on recognizable landmarks and their relationship to the broadcasting center. The scale was one to a thousand, and the model extended on the floor of a sound stage was nearly fifty by fifty feet, representing a ten-mile by ten-mile piece of the German capital.

Chadwick made the squadron practice hard. He decided to lead the raid himself. He would be accompanied by two other Mosquitos selected near the end of the training.

On several days, the crews visited Elstree studios. The model makers were very proud of their creation. Flying above the model was simulated by a platform suspended from an overhead crane. Viewers could lie on the platform at a height corresponding to 700 feet, about eight inches above the cardboard buildings. Once the crews tried that experience it brought home how difficult navigation would be at that low level. They memorized distinctive features such as the Reich Chancellery Building, the Brandenburg Gate, and the Rive Spree and how they lay with respect to the target. Experts from Bomber Command also used the model to suggest the details of the bombing run in consultation with Chadwick.

In the end they decided on an approach from the east, starting at a thousand feet above the ground and descending to 700 feet near the target. Speed would be about 200 knots. The model makers gleefully pointed out that it was easy for them to simulate fog, and so Chadwick tried a pass across the city with artificial fog rolling though the miniature streets, and he prayed it would not be too foggy on the day of the attack.

The significance of the date, Saturday the thirtieth of January 1943, had not escaped the American Eighth Air Force and they planned big raids over Nuremberg and Munich that day, cities that played an important part in the rise of the Nazi Party. Chadwick was glad to hear that, as he felt it would keep the Luftwaffe fighters busy.

MI6 put meticulous planning into the raid. An agent in Berlin planned to send the local weather conditions a few hours before the planes took off using a clandestine transmitter. The squadron was told the average height of Berlin was 175 feet, with no buildings or chimneys exceeding 550 feet. The planes were loaded with six 100-pound bombs, the first fused to detonate fifteen seconds after impact, the rest at three-second intervals. They were intended to make a lot of noise but not destroy the building, which had to keep transmitting if MI6's plan was to succeed.

The morning of the attack proved to be a typical grungy winter's day in England. It was bitterly cold, with a thick cloud cover and a ceiling of 2,500 feet. The report to MI6 from the agent in Berlin mentioned a cloud base of about two kilometers, a horizontal visibility of about four kilometers and also gave the local atmospheric pressure so that altimeters could be set accurately to show height above sea level.

Chadwick had a final briefing with crews before take-off. He mentioned the air pressure at the target and suggested with final height for the dive onto the radio station would be 825 feet above sea level. They would fly in a loose V-formation and close up for the attack. To avoid fighters, they would fly in cloud over the continent until the Gee fixes faded either due to range or German jamming. Then they would descend to just below the ceiling and fly using visual navigation. Communication would be via VHF, Channel 3; their call sign was "Battleship." Watches were synchronized—they planned to make the attack at eleven-naught-four, Berlin time.

The crews boarded their planes with plenty of time to get the engines warm and the Gee receiver adjusted before the strictly choreographed flight began. Chadwick's navigator, Flying Officer Nigel Sutton, climbed in first through the narrow hatch on the starboard side and settled in his seat on top of his parachute just behind and to the right of Chadwick. He swiveled to spread out a chart and arranged his long list of checkpoints on the tiny desk.

"All set, Nige?" Chadwick asked.

"Ten minutes to take-off, Skip."

An orange Very flare arched into the sky from the tower—the signal to taxi to the end of the runway and test the engines and perform the take-off vital actions. Should an engine be doubtful, a standby plane was already ticking over, to be called if needed.

Waiting at the end of the runway, the three Mosquitos idled until the green flare shot up exactly on time, with engines racing in fine pitch, the planes roared into the sullen sky and were soon lost in cloud. A voice blasted into Chadwick's ear, "Battleship Leader, Battleship two, please switch on glim lights. Cloud is rather thick. Over."

"Wilco, Battleship Leader. Out." Chadwick reached and flipped the switch.

"Course is naught eight six magnetic," Sutton said on the intercom.

"Naught eight six," Chadwick repeated.

As the plane gained height he adjusted the pitch and boost for an indicated air speed of 350 knots. Leveling off at 5,000 feet, the thick fog whirled past the windscreen. Looking left and right, Chadwick could just make out the rest of his flight, sticking closely on each side. Sutton made note in the logbook, and plotted a Gee fix. "Crossing the Dutch coast in seven minutes, Skip." After a few minutes he called a new course, "One naught three, magnetic."

"One naught three, magnetic," Chadwick intoned and made small adjustments to the rudder and ailerons. The heavy, deep roar of the two Merlin engines was almost hypnotic. Chadwick rubbed his eyes and glanced at Sutton who was busy plotting a line on the chart.

Sutton caught his look. "Wind is twelve knots, north-north-west, Skip. Just ease her left one degree." After a few minutes Sutton called again, "We should be crossing the Kammhuber line about now, Skip."

The small flight of three Mosquitos was clearly visible on German radar and remotely operated anti-aircraft guns opened up. In the thick cloud, the crews of the British planes saw nothing but the all-enveloping fog.

Sutton plotted a Gee fix. "Crossing the River Weser, Skip." He looked at his watch. "Puts us dead on time."

In the Luftwaffe Control Center, Colonel Erich Loeber looked at the plotting board. Two American raids were emerging, heading toward the south of Germany. An RAF raid had Hamburg in its sights. He was surprised. The British rarely bombed in daylight. But it was the small, high-speed formation heading for Berlin that attracted his attention. What was the objective of that incursion?

A highly intelligent man, Loeber was puzzled by the relatively small size of the formation. There had been no visual sighting, but the radar operators estimated the formation consisted of no more than five planes. He was used to strikes of hundreds of bombers. Compared to the thousands of kilograms of explosive unloaded by the average raid, what sort of damage could be inflicted by a handful of attackers?

Loeber's logical brain came up with the answer—they had a specific target in mind, but which one? Berlin sheltered many sensitive targets. He pointed to the plot of the Mosquito raid. "What is the estimated time for this raid to arrive at Berlin?"

A Leutnant fiddled with a slide rule. "Thirty-one minutes, Colonel."

"Warn them at Tempelhof to get some fighters in the air immediately. Low-level raid anticipated from the west. Give the Berlin anti-aircraft control a warning."

On board the Mosquito, Sutton tried unsuccessfully to squeeze a last fix from the Gee receiver. "Skipper, Gee has given up. We are about one hundred and eighty-four nautical miles from our turning point at Weissensee, about twenty-eight minutes."

"Thanks, Nige." Chadwick pressed the transmit button on the throttle. "Battleship, descending tuck in." He eased back the boost and started a gentle descent. After a minute, the Mosquitos streaked beneath the clouds. Only with the terrain in sight was it possible to grasp the speed they were making. Chadwick pulled gently on the column and increased the air speed to 360 knots.

Sutton peered through the windscreen. "Ha! There's the Midland Canal, just where it should be. That's Wolfsburg. Looks like the timing is perfect, Skip."

Black puffs of flak began blooming in the sky, none of it came close to the formation. "I'm getting good visual fixes, Skip. We just crossed the Elbe. Town called Rathenow is coming up. I'm looking for the lake at Weissensee. That's our turning point for the rate one onto two nine two, magnetic. When you start the turn, Skip, I'll slide into the bomb aimer's seat."

After fifteen minutes Sutton called that he could see the lake, and a few minutes later he snapped, "Start the turn, Skip. When you're steady on course you should see the Chancellery. That will give a good orientation for the wireless station."

Chadwick spoke into his microphone, "Battleship turning onto two nine two."

On the ground, Loeber was looking at the plot with some puzzlement, the mysterious formation had skirted the northern suburbs of Berlin, then he saw that it had started a turn. A sixth sense told him all was not right. The wireless set in the room tuned to the national network, began to play stirring martial music. All the men stood and raised their right arm in the Nazi salute as the Horst Wessel song, the National Anthem, blared from the loud speaker. Some men mouthed the words to the familiar folk tune, "The flag is high, our ranks are closed—" and then the implication hit Loeber like a thunderclap. "The bastards are going after the Reichsmarschall!"

Loeber could scarcely bear to listen, After the first verse the announcer intoned, "Ladies and gentlemen, the deputy leader of Germany, Reichsmarschall Herman Göring."

Loeber sat down weakly in a chair, his heart pounding. After a pause the deep voice of Göring fell on his ears, "Fellow German citizens, ten years ago on this auspicious date, the German people elected a new leader, Adolph Hitler, to bring the country from the chaos of the Weimar Republic and the threat of communism to the glorious state we are today, Masters of Europe, the shame of Versailles wiped out—"

Göring hesitated. Strange noises came from the speaker and then there was the crump of exploding bombs. A high-pitched, panicked voice intruded, "We're under attack." And then an engineer cut the feed. In the Luftwaffe control room, men looked at each other in amazement. Loeber stabbed the plot. "It's these bastards. They just bombed the Broadcasting Center in Berlin. Let's get some fighters in the air."

Sutton scrambled back into the navigator's seat and plugged in his intercom "Well, I think we got him in mid-sentence, Skip, assuming they started on time."

"Good show, Nige. I'm climbing to twenty-five thousand at full boost. With any luck the Gee will come to life soon. Give me a course for home."

As the Mosquitos streaked toward home, Reichsmarschall Göring walked through the halls of the studio. His face was livid with rage. Dust from the cracked plaster walls settled on his immaculate uniform. Sitting in his Mercedes Benz as they sped toward his luxurious hunting lodge, Karinhall, forty miles north of Berlin, his mind furiously turned over the options open to him to revenge the humiliation of the raid that had interrupted a nationwide speech to the German people.

The three Mosquitos landed at North Weald an hour after the attack, they encountered no Luftwaffe fighters and flak was scattered all over the sky without coming close. MI6 called after they landed. Their sensitive receivers had been monitoring the German transmission. "Wizard show," they said, in a parody of RAF slang for "congratulations."

Göring strode imperiously through the part of Karinhall built to match a French chateau. Walls reaching up to the high ceilings were covered by classical paintings in heavy gilt frames, looted from the countries conquered by the Nazis. Servants knew better than to approach him in the mood he was in. They lined the corridors with heads bowed. Flinging himself into a high leather chair behind a desk, Göring picked up the phone and snarled, "Get the head of the Abwehr up here as soon as possible."

The head of the Abwehr, Admiral Canaris, arrived at Karinhall by the late afternoon. Although a powerful man in his own right, he knew better than to antagonize Reichsmarschall Göring. Seated in the study, surrounded by souvenirs and pictures of Göring's life from his early years as a much-lauded fighter pilot before becoming the deputy leader of the Third Reich, Canaris offered his congratulations on Göring's escape from injury.

"They weren't out to injure me, Admiral. Their aim was to embarrass me in front of the people of Germany. I sense a personal animosity here. Someone in England planned the raid carefully. That is why you are here. I want a full report from your agents in England on who planned the raid on the broadcasting studios and who carried it out. They will rue the day they decided to make a monkey out of me."

Canaris replied, "The British desk is run by Dr. Kegel, as it was before the war. He has excellent contacts with numerous influential Englishmen. Many admired Adolph Hitler and the way Germany has recovered from the last war. At one point a negotiated peace was within our grasp, until that drunkard Churchill seized the reins of power. I'm sure we can get some names for you, although target planning within the Royal Air Force is carried out by a committee we have not been able to penetrate."

"I don't want a list of your failures, Admiral. I posed a couple of simple questions. I want answers. Then the Luftwaffe will teach those impudent Albions a thing or two. When can I expect a reply?"

"This will have the utmost priority, Herr Reichsmarschall. I cannot say when I will have the information you want, but we will stay in close touch with your staff."

Canaris drove to Hamburg that evening and was in conference with senior Abwehr officers by eight the next morning. He described the humiliation felt by the Reichsmarschall and his desires for an appropriate revenge. To achieve that he would need names of personnel and military units.

The chief of the Hamburg office, Conrad Nordemann, asked the head of the British desk, Dr. Gerhard Kegel, for his comments. Kegel pursed his lips. "Difficult, very difficult. We have no reliable contacts now with the British upper circles. I have a man who specializes in military affairs. He could probably get the name of the force attacking the studio. As for personnel involved, perhaps a clue lies in the animosity suspected. I suggest speaking to our friends in Swedish Intelligence. Göring's late wife, Karin, was Swedish, and there are many German sympathizers in the ruling classes. With your permission, Admiral, I will contact a few Swedish friends."

"By all means, shake every tree and let's see what falls out."

Nordemann addressed Dr. Kegel. "Contact your military man in England for any information on the raid. British propaganda will fully exploit the disruption of Göring's speech. There must be some chit-chat about it among RAF personnel."

That morning a short message on a specific shortwave frequency was received in England, not by the agent it was intended for but by British Intelligence, MI5, which had arrested the agent months before and "turned" him, using his transmitter to send misleading false reports back to Germany. The Double-Cross Committee carefully considered the request sent by the Abwehr. They tried to think of ways the unusual request could be turned to British advantage and in the meantime, sent a routine acknowledgment.

Kegel had more success with his Swedish contact. Politicians there had been concerned about the psychological impact of the raid on the average German citizen. Exports of machine tools and iron ore to Germany were an important part of the Swedish economy and any event that could affect the outcome of the war was studied carefully. At a cocktail reception in an embassy the next day, Kegel's acquaintance mentioned Göring's conviction that there was a personal animosity behind the disruption of his speech.

An elderly Swedish diplomatic pooh-poohed the idea, "I was stationed in England for years before the war. The upper class tried everything to avoid a war. They claimed to love Germany."

Someone murmured facetiously, "Love can turn to hate."

"There were meetings at an old country house which I occasionally attended. Called themselves the 'Insiders.' Some of those bigwigs could suggest a clever propaganda stunt like this one."

The matter was dropped but Kegel's friend contacted the intelligence chief in the Swedish Embassy in London to request whatever details of the raid that they could forage. A few days later he was able to send Kegel the identity of the squadron raiding Berlin—613, using the latest fighter bomber, the Mosquito. And the name of its commander was Squadron Leader Chadwick. As for planning, he suggested reviewing any files they had on the "Insiders" group that used to meet before the war.

Chapter Twenty-Six

The same RAF subcommittee met at the Air Ministry a week after the raid. Operationally, it was considered successful. Chadwick and the contributors to the planning were congratulated. The group captain introduced Silas Kavanagh of MI6.

"The intent was to embarrass Göring and the Propaganda Ministry," Kavanagh said. "Our agents in Germany report that this was brilliantly achieved. Dr. Goebbels, the Minister of Propaganda, was furious and, for once, had no comeback. Fifty million Germans heard the Reichsmarschall start his speech and then get rudely cut off by a bombing attack that he had claimed could never happen." Kavanagh chuckled. "Wonderful, but an opportunity to rub their noses in it will not come again for some time."

The group captain thanked Kavanagh and asked, "What have we learned ourselves from the raid? Before opening that question to the meeting, I'll attempt to answer it myself. A meticulously planned and executed raid can achieve surprise and seriously damage the enemy at small cost to the RAF and with low unintended casualties to civilians." He pointed to Chadwick. "Squadron Leader, what do you have to say?"

"Yes, it was carefully planned," Chadwick conceded, "but I have to say that we were lucky. If the visibility in Berlin had been any worse we could easily have lost the target, even with the excellent practice on the model at Elstree. I'm not sure if a pre-raid weather report will be practical in the future, because that means someone knows we're coming, and that may leak to the Germans. What I'd like to discuss has to do with future targets, especially more concrete ones like oil refineries and power stations."

"We'll certainly get to that, Squadron Leader," Kavanagh said, and then looked around the room. "Any more comments on the raid?"

A wing commander asked him if MI6 agents had followed the German attempts to intercept the raid.

Kavanagh sprang back to his feet. "Begorra, yes, Sir. We have receivers tuned to the Luftwaffe fighter control frequencies in the hands of our agents in Germany. Fighters were scrambled, but too late to catch the speedy Mosquitos. We heard complaints from the flak gunners that they could not depress enough to hit the planes on the approach to the target. And besides which, if they did open fire they would hit their own buildings."

Several other officers made comments, more to establish their own importance than to contribute anything useful, Chadwick thought to himself. The group captain turned to future raids, and it was agreed that more Mosquito squadrons trained in low-level attacks would be needed. A motion was made to ask the Air Ministry to commission two more Mosquito-equipped squadrons.

"Together with 613 Squadron that will make a very powerful wing," the group captain observed.

Two weeks later Chadwick was invited to Bomber Command Headquarters. He stopped in the office of Group Captain Hearne, an old friend.

"Allan, I must congratulate you on the Berlin raid. I'm told resistance groups in Germany were bucked up by that raid. The Air Ministry has directed us to form a new wing of Mosquito fighter-bombers, specifically for low level, precisely targeted objectives. Together with your squadron, 613, we're planning to convert 154 and 176 Blenheim squadrons to Mosquitos. They're stationed at RAF Northolt and RAF Bury St. Edmunds."

He paused and looked at Allan. "By the way, Air Vice Marshal Stevenson plans to appoint you wing commander, with appropriate promotion. I trust you have no objection?"

"I'm very flattered, Sir."

Secretly, however, Chadwick was not happy with the idea of being promoted to wing commander, although he had suspected it would happen after the meeting of the subcommittee. He knew coordinating the activities of three squadrons would entail a great deal of administration.

"I'm not familiar with 154 and 176 squadrons, Sir," he said to Hearne.

"I am not surprised, Allan—154 is a part of the Royal Australian Air Force, and 176 is a Kiwi unit, the Royal New Zealand Air Force. They're both first-class chaps, keen as mustard, but there is great competition between the Aussies and the Kiwis. Sometimes I would even use the word rivalry."

Chadwick groaned. "And you want me to forge them into an effective fighting force? Is that why they're based at different RAF stations?"

"Partly. At the start of the war we tended to mix the Aussies and the Kiwis until we learned our lesson. The repair bills to the officers' mess after dining-in night would have bought a new aircraft. So, you'll have to be diplomatic. Orders to create this new wing have been prepared."

"When the orders arrive I'd like personnel rosters for the two new squadrons in the wing," Chadwick said. "Someone is going to have to take over 613 Squadron. Are you planning to appoint a squadron leader or promote someone from the squadron?"

"Do you have a flight commander in mind that might merit promotion?"

"It's a tricky question, Sir. I've only had command for a few weeks and the Berlin raid was our first operation. I suggest I stay as squadron commander and wing commander temporarily until the wing is ready for operations with the new aircraft. By then I'll know the men much better and may be able to make recommendations."

"You're piling a lot on your shoulders, Allan. Let's aim for having the wing declared operationally ready in four weeks. Is that reasonable?"

"I suppose so. Precisely what support do I get for the wing admin?"

"The normal strength would be two admin bods, an adjutant, and supply wallah. Usually flight lieutenants and an office flight sergeant, plus clerks. We'll ask the station master at North Weald to find you some space."

When asked, the station commander replied there was absolutely no room in the old prewar buildings and hangars, which housed two fighter squadrons. Instead, he found space for the new wing in some temporary huts on the north side of the airfield.

When he returned to 613, Chadwick was met with some guarded criticism. New squadrons were joining the wing, but the flights in 613 had yet to make a combined raid. Chadwick called the targeting subcommittee; they had a target in mind— an oil refinery near the coast in Holland. However, MI6 had reported extensive anti-aircraft batteries protecting the place, sited especially to protect from an attack from seaward.

Chadwick invited the planners to visit North Weald and give a briefing. He also invited the commanding officers of 154 and 176 squadrons to attend, although their units were not yet ready for operations. It was the first time Chadwick had had the opportunity to meet the commanding officers of the Australian and New Zealander squadrons. The C.O. of 154 Squadron was a large, affable man with strong accent and a booming laugh, Squadron Leader William Pomfret. "Call me Billy," he announced. The C.O. of 176 Squadron was a quiet, retiring man who seemed to consider every word before he spoke, Squadron Leader Pope. They greeted each other warily.

"I want you to listen to this briefing for 613 Squadron so that you will get some idea of what we're planning. While you're still here at North Weald, I would like to discuss your squadron training plans before you leave. Let's go to the briefing room and see what we have in the future."

Chadwick introduced the visitors from the planning subcommittee to the audience. Both were flight lieutenants. They began with some slides. "Here are some photos of the Shell oil refinery on the outskirts of Oosterend. The refinery consists of a port for ocean-going tankers, extensive distillation columns, and a large tank farm. The whole facility is located on an offshore island north of the Zuider Zee called Texel. Refined products, mostly petrol and diesel fuel, are transported by undersea pipelines to Den Helder, about two miles away on the mainland, and from there, they are distributed by rail.

"Because ocean-going tankers are intercepted by the Royal Navy, the plant has been converted to refining crude made by synthetic fuel plants in Germany using coal as the energy source. The major product is fuel for the Luftwaffe. It is very heavily defended. The seas on both sides of the island are mined. There are extensive ack-ack batteries using Oerlikon twenty-millimeter cannon and eighty-eight millimeter rapid fire guns. Because it's an island, it's difficult to get an agent ashore for a look around. All the Dutch inhabitants, mostly fishermen and farmers, have been evacuated.

"Here is the plan of attack," one of the flight lieutenants from the planning committee said. "The squadron will be divided into three flights of four aircraft. The attack will be made from the south, making a landfall on the peninsula of North Holland at Bergen aan Zee. The flights will fly line abreast, with a north to south separation of about thirty seconds or two miles between flights, heading parallel to the shore following the railway line. The suggested height is two hundred feet above ground.

"The leading squadron will be armed with five hundred pound bombs. The target is the pumping station at Den Helder. The refinery itself is too well defended, but the plant can be shut down by destroying the pumping and valve house. The center flight and last flight will be armed with incendiaries. All flights will endeavor to suppress ack-ack with their forward-firing twenty-millimeter cannon. It is important for the leading aircraft to get the bombs on target, so that there will be plenty of fuel swishing about for the incendiaries."

Chadwick interrupted, "Perhaps as some insurance, the second flight—the middle flight—should carry a mix of high explosive and incendiary bombs."

"A good thought, Wing Commander. Once the bombs are released, the flights turn sharply left, to avoid overflying Texel Island—which, as I mentioned, is very heavily defended. The slides I'll run through show the approach and general target area, but from high altitude. Are there any questions?"

Chadwick spoke again. "I'll lead the first flight of four. The middle and rear flights will be led by Flight Lieutenants Eckersley and Porter."

After the meeting Chadwick sat down with the Australian and New Zealand fliers, and told them that when the raid on the refinery was accomplished, he would spend a few days with each squadron to review their training. It was his hope that within a month they would be conducting raids at full wing strength of thirty-six aircraft.

The raid was planned for a day of low, thick cloud. The meteorologist predicted weather like that from a low pressure cell heading for the Baltic, which he said would be in position in about two days. All the air crews attended a briefing. Navigation would be carried out using Gee. Take-off would be oh-eight hours. Radio silence would be maintained. Flights would take off at one-minute intervals, signaled by Very flares.

The day dawned with ominous, low gray clouds. Forward visibility at the base was about a mile and a half with light rain. Shortly after take-off, the squadron passed the English coast. The North Sea was tumultuous, and wind-lashed waves flung spray fifty feet into the air. Flying Officer Sutton reported that the wind was northeast, thirty-five knots, and almost on the nose. The Mosquito buffeted roughly in the gusty wind.

The Dutch coast flashed underneath the squadron forty-seven minutes after getting airborne. Chadwick turned smoothly on to a heading that kept the rail line just under the port wing-tip. He had to make several adjustments to compensate for the leeway. Sutton slithered forward into the bomb aimer's position, armed the bombs, and opened the bomb bay doors. Chadwick dived slightly to a height of 220 feet above sea level, and adjusted the speed to 350 knots. Seagulls flashed by the windscreen.

When the rails split into several branches, Sutton called that he had the target in sight. Scattered gunfire opened up. Chadwick pressed the trigger of the twenty-millimeter cannon in the nose, and Sutton shouted, "Bombs gone!"

Just as he called, there was a loud explosion and the plane swung violently to the right. Chadwick trimmed the rudder and increased power on the left engine. He glanced at the right engine. The cowlings were flapping furiously and black smoke poured out. He firmly shut the throttle, feathered the propeller and turned off the fuel feed to that engine. As flames began to lick out he pressed the fire extinguisher button. He eased back on the column, banked sharply to the left, and increased the pressure on the rudder bar until they were flying on a heading of southwest and sought the sanctuary of the sullen clouds.

Sutton struggled back into his seat and made some quick Gee observations. After a couple of minutes he called on the intercom. "Steer two-four-six magnetic. Our ground speed is three-eighty knots."Ten minutes later he asked Chadwick to call North Weald for a QDM.

They landed at ten–fifteen hours. Chadwick's plane was the only one with significant damage. The crews were highly excited and piled into the briefing room. The intelligence officer started by asking the rear flight what they had seen. They reported the target looked like a giant Guy Fawkes Night. Smoke and flames had made it impossible to see the actual pumping station. They thought the ack-ack was only moderate. The briefing officer said he would ask the engineering officer for a report on damage to all aircraft. Chadwick said the bar would open at eleven hours, and congratulated the crews on a disciplined attack.

MI6 made an assessment several days later. Fortunately, the weather had cleared enough to get some high altitude photographs. Agents on the ground had questioned Shell employees in Den Helden for a close-up opinion of the damage and the time to repair it. Their estimate was that the repair would take three to four months. MI6 believed the plant was producing about 1,000 tons a day. The loss to the Luftwaffe was about a 120,000 tons, equivalent to the fuel used by 60,000 aircraft sorties, perhaps as much as a third of average Luftwaffe fuel consumption. It was a mighty blow the Luftwaffe could ill afford.

A few days later Chadwick flew to RAF Bury St. Edmunds to review the training of the New Zealand squadron. The commanding officer, Squadron Leader Reginald Pope, was extremely deferential toward Chadwick, who found his attitude a little disconcerting. He tried to open up the conversation,

"What do they call you, Squadron Leader? Reginald or Reggie?"

"I'm usually Reggie to the troops, if they're being polite."

"Then that is what I shall use—Reggie."

The squadron assembled in a large briefing room, and Pope introduced Wing Commander Chadwick. "We're honored to have such a distinguished officer as our wing commander. He started his career at Cranwell and after that flew Vimy bombers in Iraq. On returning to the U.K., he was stationed at the Research Center at Farnborough, where he was involved in the development of autopilots, bombsights, and the Chain Home RDR system. When the war started, he commanded a Spitfire squadron and was awarded the DFC, with bar. Later, he was involved in the development of wireless navigation aids, such as Gee and was shot down in a bombing raid over Germany to refine the device. For that, he was awarded the DSO. He is now developing the ability of the RAF to deliver attacks on precise targets using high-speed, low-level aircraft. It is an honor to introduce Wing Commander Chadwick."

"Thank you Reggie," Chadwick said as he rose to speak. "In listening to your compressed version of my Air Force career, I realize that little has changed. In Iraq, I carried out low-level precision bombing raids. The new planes are a little faster and the bombs a little bigger. But otherwise, it's the same."

There was polite laughter from the audience, and then Chadwick resumed.

"The Air Ministry has put into our hands a wonderful aircraft, the de Havilland Mosquito. It's as fast as any German fighter and can carry a ton of bombs nearly two thousand miles. To fully exploit its capability we must train hard, which is why

I'm here for a few days. Pilots must become so proficient at flying on instruments that they won't even realize they've entered thick cloud. However, instrument training must be done in a safe way in clear weather. Pilots should wear blinkers and the navigator must keep a careful look-out for obstructions or other aircraft. With practice, a pilot should be able to hold a given altitude to within plus or minus fifty feet, and at the same time hold a heading plus or minus one or two degrees. Pilots must be competent to perform an overshoot procedure on instruments and to make a let-down based on QDMs and cross bearings.

"An attack on a precision target puts a tremendous load on the navigator," Chadwick continued. "In a high-speed attack, the terrain is flashing past the windscreen at nearly seven miles a minute. In claggy weather, a landmark may only be visible for a few seconds. He must rapidly shift his attention from the outside to the navigational aids, such as Gee and Oboe. He must recognize and discount German jamming. Often some evil-minded person is shooting at you. Finally, he is the chap who lines up the target on the bombsight and presses the button.

"I want to tell you about a raid recently conducted by 613 Squadron to interrupt Luftwaffe's fuel delivery. A refinery in Holland was too well defended to attack directly, but military intelligence discovered the refined fuel was transported in a pipe line across a narrow channel to waiting railway tank cars. Pilots and navigators had to deal with all the constraints I mentioned a minute ago—lousy weather, jamming, and ack-ack. We bombed the pipeline pumping station. And now, we've just been told by Intelligence that they estimate we disrupted about twenty percent of Luftwaffe fuel use for several months."

A hand went up. "Were any of 613's planes damaged or shot down?"

"The only plane seriously damaged was mine. I had to shut down one engine—which reminds me that all those piloting skills on instruments have to be accomplished using asymmetric power, one engine out, and possibly on fire."

There was a collective groan from the audience and Chadwick chuckled. "Believe me, on raids like this, both crew members are pretty busy."

Chadwick spent several days at RAF Bury St. Edmunds. He flew with half a dozen crew, both pilots and navigators. The Mosquito design did not readily permit a third person in the plane, so he displaced the pilot or navigator in order to fly with the New Zealanders. He found the pilots were weak on instrument flying. The only cure was constant practice.

The navigators were keen to discuss real problems, and he arranged for a handful of navigators from 613 to fly in and conduct a few one-on-one question-and-answer sessions. After dinner, the fellows usually gathered in the bar and sang traditional RAF drinking songs, but Chadwick sensed in a strange way that the New Zealanders felt themselves not quite up to the standard demanded of RAF fliers. At the same time, he knew what the cure for that was—a few successful missions under their belt.

Chadwick left Bury St. Edmunds with mixed feelings. They were a decent lot of likable chaps and he was urging them to get themselves killed. He found the rumbunctious Australians to be completely different—loud and probably too overconfident. Chadwick's description of the raid on Den Helder caught the squadron's interest but he got the feeling that they believed that they would have done a better job. The flights he made with both pilots and navigators proved the crews were competent, if inclined a little to cut corners. Chadwick felt both squadrons were close to being ready for missions and he next called on the targeting subcommittee to discuss possible operations. They said MI6 had been persistent in requesting attacks on Gestapo prisons, as many housed documents that should be destroyed. However, when the possibility of killing prisoners as well was raised, it was claimed the psychological benefit was worth the risk.

Chadwick was skeptical. *Has anyone asked the prisoners what they think?* was his immediate thought.

Finally, they reached a compromise. A raid would be planned against a notorious Gestapo headquarters and another against an electrical generating plant that mostly powered a port and armaments factories. The planners went to work. Chadwick attended some of their meetings when specific flying conditions had to be met.

The electrical plant was located west of Antwerp, and used cooling water from the River Scheldt. The planners proposed a landfall on the North Sea at Breskens on the southern bank of the river estuary. The ground was low and flat. A low-level raid had numerous good landmarks leading up to the coal-fired generating plant at Kallo. There were plenty of eighty-eight millimeter anti-aircraft guns in the region to protect the port of Antwerp, but these could not be deployed against low-level aircraft, the planners claimed.

Chadwick insisted a three-dimensional model be constructed of the south part of the Scheldt Estuary. Intensive training started for the Australian squadron, which Chadwick chose to attack the power plant. He went to Northolt for the days preceding the raid and sat in on the Met briefing and the latest word from MI6 on defenses. The Australians were full of confidence. All twelve Mosquitos would be deployed.

They left the airfield at sunrise and were back two hours later, but only ten planes returned. The intelligence officer quizzed the crews before they were dismissed for the day. They were brightly cheerful and made raucous jokes about a pilot nicknamed "Ned," whose plane had crashed because it struck a high crane in the port area. The other missing plane had flown into the ground and burst into flames. They were suffering from heavy machine gun anti-aircraft fire at the time. The opinion was that the pilot had been killed or severely wounded and lost control.

That night the officers' mess at Northolt laid on a sumptuous dinner, and after the last pilot staggered to bed at three in the morning, the mess orderlies started to clean up the wreckage. Chadwick had stayed around for a while, but when he heard murmurs about running the C.O.'s bags up the flagpole, he made a discreet exit.

A week later a chap from MI6 gave a report—Ned and his navigator had survived the crash, with injuries, and were in a hospital. There were plenty of jokes thrown at the speaker about the safety of the nurses. The plant itself had been badly damaged, the generators were beyond repair, and the coal depot was still burning, the MI6 fellow reported. Activities at the port had been curtailed due to rationing of electric energy—the local grid was not capable of completely replacing the power lost by the destruction of the Kallo plant. All in all, it was considered a successful raid and the death of two fliers was a regrettable but acceptable cost.

Chadwick attended a meeting of the subcommittee to discuss the proposal made by MI6 to attack the Gestapo headquarters in Le Havre. At exactly the same time, Dr. Kegel decoded a long message from Sweden in his office in Hamburg. Chadwick was blissfully unaware that he was the subject of the Swedish message mentioning him as the leader of 613 Squadron's raid on the Berlin broadcasting studio. His name triggered a memory in Kegel's mind about the exciting days in London before the war. Soon he had the files on the Isbell's Insiders and Allan Chadwick in front of him. He could not believe his good fortune.

Chadwick had been arrested by the Gestapo in the early 1930s and was a person of great interest to the Abwehr when he became involved with radar development in 1937. On the other hand, there was no information on the planners of the Berlin raid. The orders to mount spectacular raids on the tenth anniversary of the accession of the Nazi Party had apparently come down from very high levels to both Bomber Command and the U.S. Eighth Army Air Force. Dr. Kegel began to prepare a comprehensive report for his boss.

Chadwick sat in the meeting listening to the planners of a raid on the Gestapo headquarters in Le Havre that had just imprisoned several important members of the résistance movement. A desperate plea had been made to MI6 to attack the prison before the Frenchmen could be made to reveal details of their network at the port, which was a center for German naval torpedo E-boats and a thorn in the side of the Royal Navy. However, it became clear the French leaders did not care whether the prisoners escaped or were killed, so long as they were silenced.

The photographs showed it would be a difficult raid. The Gestapo building was in a heavily built-up area with schools and churches nearby. There was no time to build a model. The raid had to be laid on for the next day. Fortunately, there was good Gee coverage.

Chadwick recommended the attack be made by two squadrons, separated by two miles. The Australian and New Zealand squadrons gathered at North Weald in the afternoon for intensive briefings by MI6 and RAF navigation experts. They would arrive at the port just after sunrise, when it was expected the German officers would be at breakfast. Their living quarters had been clearly identified as a prime target. Other targets included the high wall around the prison and the cells themselves. A decision to proceed would be made by 8:00 p.m. and a coded warning broadcast on the BBC nine o'clock news so the résistance fighters could be in the street to assist escapees.

Just before eight, the meteorologists gave the raid their blessing. Chadwick attended the final briefing for the crews before they got some sleep. They would be awakened at five for a hearty breakfast with two eggs. Chadwick had assigned the New Zealand squadron to make the lead attack. The Australians would follow up about a minute later to clear up any missed targets. The attack would start in the south heading north over the docks. Chadwick felt in his bones that it would be a challenging attack. The region of the prison was heavily built up and the plan of the attack gave little time for the crews to become oriented with path marks to the target.

Chapter Twenty-Seven

At a meeting of the Double-Cross Committee, members hammered out a response to the request from the Abwehr for information on the planning and execution of the Göring raid. They offered no knowledge of the aircraft or squadron involved but, in the words of one member, it was decided to "set the cat among the pigeons" by claiming the specific idea of a raid when the Reichsmarschall was speaking over the wireless came from their embassy in Berne, at the instigation of a German contact, who probably had a personal reason to humble the Luftwaffe chief. They knew that high-level Nazi leaders had intense rivalries, based on staying in Hitler's good books, and if the Abwehr passed on their deception, it could cause a good deal of internal dissension among the enemy.

An analysis of the results obtained by the raid on Le Havre was very mixed. The immediate conclusion was that they had hit the target, but later it was reported by MI6 that a New Zealand Mosquito had gone down to the northeast of the target and the Australian squadron following behind, had mistaken the flames and smoke for the target and bombed the area, hitting a school. Some teachers and children were killed or wounded. After the Australian squadron had flown north, the local French résistance fighters climbed through the shattered wall of the prison and began to kill German guards who were wandering around in a state of confusion. They also set fire to records.

It was estimated that about twenty-five German officers or guards were killed by the bombing or the French Maquisards. Some thirty prisoners managed to escape but several had been killed in the bombing. MI6 reported the local résistance leader was delighted by the raid; his authority had been greatly enhanced by his ability to summon two RAF squadrons and many fresh young men had joined the ranks of the résistance. The 154 Squadron had lost the plane that crashed near the target, the crew was killed. Two Australian planes were damaged by German fighters on their way home.

In Hamburg, Dr. Kegel quickly assessed the information he had acquired about the Berlin raid. He judged the Swedish stuff to be reliable, and the suggestion to look at the old files on the group called Isbell's Insiders brought up useful facts about Chadwick, who had apparently commanded the attacking flight. The file mentioned his close relationship with Lord Lowestoft and a possible romantic liaison with Lady Fitzgibbon.

He looked at the message received via shortwave from the agent in England. He was skeptical about the suggestion that the planning had originated in Berne, Switzerland, but the man had provided solid information in the past and he decided to pass it on.

His summary report was approved by Herr Nordemann and sent by secure teletype to Admiral Canaris. He glanced over it, pleased the answers appeared relevant to Göring's questions and arranged to see the Reichsmarschall at his office in Berlin later in the day.

Seated with the Reichsmarschall, Canaris summarized the report, specifically naming the RAF squadron and commanding officer. He stressed that the idea the raid on the studio had originated in Germany was unlikely.

Göring disagreed. "I feel a personal motive in this action, perhaps coming from within Germany, and not England, is possible. I have many enemies, Admiral. Let me see the report." He read it carefully and then triumphantly placed his thumb on the paragraph about Allan Chadwick. "This is the kind of personal stuff I wanted. This man Chadwick needs to be punished. We can blast his squadron to Kingdom Come, but he would feel a personal loss if his lady friend was obliterated. Find out all you can about this Fitzgibbon woman."

Canaris was surprised at the pettiness exhibited by the Reichsmarschall, but he agreed to gather the information Göring wanted as quickly as possible. He assumed that he would be asked to arrange an assassination.

It was easy for the Swedish Embassy in Britain to find that Lady Fitzgibbon still lived at the family mansion called Clair Court Hall in Pangbourne. The informant missed that the Army had taken over the house and that Lady Fitzgibbon lived in an apartment over the stables. Göring was delighted with the news and immediately summoned the bomber group planners to his office. He wanted a massive raid laid on to obliterate RAF North Weald. He was frank with the Luftwaffe airmen that his motive was retaliation for the raid when he was delivering a speech to the nation. He was less frank when he also asked for a raid on Pangbourne. "This will show the damned English we are just as able as they are to lay on a low-level bombing raid," was his explanation to the airmen.

Within a few days a plan was explained to him. The raid on North Weald would be carried out in the waning night-time hours, combined with a raid on central London. Knickbein beams would be set up centered on the airfield. By carefully choosing the antenna location in Belgium, the same beam would also lie over Pangbourne, although the X-Gereat crossbeam could not be furnished for that target. By choosing daybreak for the raid, fliers would be able to visually identify the mansion house, as it lay in a prominent spot on the Thames River. They then faced 120-kilometer dash to the English Channel. The fastest bomber in the Luftwaffe inventory, the Ju 88, would be selected for the raid on Pangbourne.

Göring asked a few pertinent questions and authorized the complex operation to be made as soon as the technical factors were dealt with and the weather was suitable. The raids occurred a week later. Seventy-five bombers plastered the airfield at North Weald. Workshops, barracks, and the officers' mess were badly damaged. Eighteen Spitfires in the hangars were destroyed, mostly by fire. The Mosquitos of 613 Squadron, parked on the northern periphery of the field, were undamaged. There were many casualties among the RAF personnel.

Four Ju 88 bombers flew at high speed along the Knickbein beam at low level and bombed Clair Court Hall as the sun rose. Many soldiers in the main house and nearby Nissen huts were killed. Melanie Fitzgibbon had not sought shelter when the sirens blared and was badly wounded as the stables collapsed. She was taken for emergency surgery to a hospital in Oxford.

The gunners were ready after the German raiders turned south and two were brought down by anti-aircraft fire as they streaked across the English countryside for home. Spitfires were alerted on the coast and the two remaining Junkers were intercepted over the Channel. One ditched in the sea, though the crew was saved by RAF Air-Sea Rescue. The other crash-landed at an airfield near Cherbourg. The pilot died of his wounds. Göring felt vindicated by the raid, but there was considerable resentment among the German bomber crews that, of twelve airmen dispatched, only three returned after the meaningless raid on Pangbourne.

The three crew members rescued in the Channel were placed in a special interrogation center in London. The cells were fitted with microphones and often MI5 officers speaking fluent German were mixed with the prisoners. The pilot of the downed plane was distraught over the loss of his best friend. "I saw his damned kite go down, Hans," he said to a fellow crew member. "There's no way Rudi would have survived. We went through flying training together. He was my best friend. All for nothing, all because of that stupid Fat Man's ego."

"What do you mean, Erich? We all knew we could get killed any time."

"Yes, for a good reason. A friend told me the people in intelligence finally worked out the raid was in retaliation for the British raid that interrupted the Fat Man's speech on the wireless. Apparently, the girlfriend of one of the fliers lived in the house we bombed. What a waste! Nine men lost, including my friend Rudi." He choked back a sob. "Our exalted leader has a girlfriend of his own. What if the Englanders decide to go after her? That would put them right on top of Peenemunde and those rockets."

The German he was talking to looked confused. "What rockets, Erich?"

"Hans, do you live in a hole in the ground? Do you bury your head in sand? The mess was full of a story last week that Fatty's girlfriend, Hanna Reitsch, flew a specially modified rocket at Peenemunde to find out why it kept crashing. She worked out why and lived. Got a medal too."

"I have never heard of Hanna Reitsch. What is a woman doing test flying rockets?"

"Ach, she won hundreds of gliding competitions and moved up to test flying."

The conversation was transcribed and studied by an MI5 officer. Several points caught his attention. The first was the mention of a female target at Pangbourne. "I thought Pangbourne was Army anti-aircraft admin center," he muttered to himself and filed a request for a list of casualties. The name Peenemunde also intrigued him. Polish agents had reported unusual goings-on in that Baltic region, which had resulted in strange flying objects landing on Polish beaches. Later, he added the name of the woman injured at Pangbourne, underlined the words "Reitsch," "rocket," and "Peenemunde," and sent it for review by higher ranking officers.

A few days later it caught the eye of Will Viney, who oscillated between MI5 and MI6. The name of the injured woman, Melanie Fitzgibbon, triggered his memory straight away. He recalled standing by a wrecked Tiger Moth at a small airfield near Cromer just before the war. It had been rammed by an old Bentley just as it was taking off for a flight to Germany carrying a German spy. The car driver and his companion were Allan Chadwick and Melanie Fitzgibbon.

Further investigation soon revealed the true reason for the raid on Pangbourne. It was never to destroy the Army unit—the target had always been Lady Fitzgibbon, in response to Göring's twisted sense of revenge. After a few phone calls, Viney was connected to the commanding officer of 613 Squadron,

"Hello, Wing Commander Chadwick here."

"Good morning, Wing Commander. Will Viney here. I've been reviewing a prewar intelligence incident when you caused the crash of a Tiger Moth and some damage to your magnificent Bentley."

There was a pause and then Chadwick replied, "Well, Mr. Viney, that was a long time ago. What have you been up to since our lunch with Doug Larson?"

"Wing Commander, I won't beat about the bush. In the course of some official inquiries, I happened to come across the name of a woman injured in a recent German air raid. I regret to tell you the lady is Melanie Fitzgibbon. Naturally, I immediately thought of you, hence my call."

The mention of her name hit Chadwick like a bolt from the blue, and his heart sank. "You have a damned good memory, Mr. Viney. Is she badly hurt? Do you know where she is?"

"I'm not aware of the extent of her injuries, Wing Commander. But she's a patient at the Oxford General Hospital. She was injured when German planes bombed Pangbourne. I'm sorry to be the bearer of bad news. You can always get in touch with me through Doug Larson. I'll bid you good day. I'm sure you will want to call the hospital."

Chadwick put down the phone. His mind was in a whirl. Naturally, he was concerned about Melanie, but there was also lurking feeling that the call from Will Viney was not right.

Wilberforce Viney was a member of the Double-Cross Committee. He had not paid a great deal of attention to the discussion of how to respond to the intercepted message from the Abwehr, but now the full import struck home. It had been part of Göring's insane desire for revenge against the airmen who devastated his speech. He quickly arranged to meet the chairman of the Double-Cross Committee, and explained to him that the raid on Pangbourne was targeted at Lady Fitzgibbon because she was a close friend of Wing Commander Chadwick who led the raid on Göring. It was plain and simple revenge, and an amazing facet of the Reichsmarschall's character.

Viney suggested a follow-up to the deceptive message sent in reply to the Abwehr. Almost certainly Göring would initiate inquiries in Berne to find out who suggested the raid.

"Of course," Viney went on, "Göring will find nothing. But suppose we plant a lead in Berne for the German intelligence to find? For example, according to barrack-room rumors we overheard from Luftwaffe prisoners, Göring is rather fond of a woman who test-flies rockets at Peenemunde. If we plant her name and Göring arranges a retribution it would be rather fitting."

The chairman laughed. "You have a devious mind, Will. Run the idea past a few committee members this afternoon and show me a proposed message to our chaps in Berne."

Viney quickly corralled a few members of the committee and explained the real reason for the raid on Pangbourne. They grasped immediately that the reference to Berne required some amplification if Göring was to be misled.

"The problem, as you know, Will, is that our agents would never use the actual name of a contact. How do we finger this woman, Reitsch, without using her name?"

"She test-flies rockets, or something like that at Peenemunde. I think just mentioning Peenemunde would be enough. We must warn our man in Berne to expect some sniffing around by German intelligence. Then he needs a plausible way to feed the information, perhaps one of our chaps succumbing to a little bribery would work."

Another member of the committee spoke up. "Will, we're just trying to manipulate the Reichsmarschall. All jolly good fun but perhaps the whole question of what is happening at Peenemunde should be laid before the target planners?"

"Of course. You're right. A summary of what we heard from the Luftwaffe crew has already been sent to the group investigating other aspects of the activities at Peenemunde." A detailed message mentioning Peenemunde with specific suggestions was sent to the head of MI6 in Berne, Switzerland.

"Well, my face isn't much of a pretty picture at the moment, Allan. Ask the doctor about the rest." Her hand came up weakly and touched the bandages that covered her scalp and left cheek.

"I'm sure it will be as good as new in a few weeks," Allan said heartily.

"Oh, dear, dear Allan, you always were an optimist." After a pause, her hand moved down over her body. "I'm afraid it's worse down here. We always enjoyed the physical side, but, dear Allan—" she stopped and quietly wept.

"But what, my darling?" Chadwick cried.

"They had to cut off one of my breasts, I don't think you'll ever want to look at me again."

Chadwick was aghast, but before he could say anything the nurse returned. She saw that Melanie was weeping and said firmly to Chadwick, "I'm sorry sir, she's upset. You can visit tomorrow after ten." Chadwick found himself propelled back into the ward.

He asked to talk to the doctor looking after Melanie. The nurse looked at him sharply, "You're a close friend?"

"We were very close before the war, sister. Her son is fighting in North Africa. She has no other close relatives."

"Wait here, Sir. I'll find Dr. Finney." She gestured to a chair.

A few minutes later, a rotund man in a white jacket approached him. Chadwick rose to his feet, saying, "I'm an old friend of Lady Fitzgibbon, Doctor. I'm shocked by what has happened. What can you tell me?"

"She was injured by the collapse of the building she was in during the raid. The injuries are mostly to the left side—severe lacerations of the chest and her left arm. Several ribs were broken and penetrated the left lung. She's breathing with just the right lung at present. The humerus was broken in two places and the clavicle shattered. Unless infection creeps in, she should make a full recovery, but I suspect her arm will always be weak. The surgeon was forced to perform a left mas-tectomy, due to the severity of the injuries. She'll need care for quite some time, and for a woman of her age, the injuries to the thorax can induce psychological—ah, problems. Does she have a place to stay when she leaves this hospital?"

Chadwick replied. "Thank you, Doctor. I'm really shocked by what has happened. I'll look into the situation at Pang-bourne regarding a place for her to stay, and get back to you tomorrow."

Chadwick left the hospital, walked quickly to the station and caught the next train to Reading. From there he took a taxi to Clair Court Hall. He was horrified by what he found. The building was a ruin. He asked the driver to wait and started to look for someone in charge. Some soldiers directed him to a makeshift office in a partially wrecked Nissen hut. He found a harried major talking on a field telephone.

Chadwick introduced himself when the officer hung up the handset.

The major saluted. "Major Goodwin, Sir. How can I help?"

"I am tidying up a few loose ends for Lady Fitzgibbon."

Goodwin looked puzzled. "Lady Fitzgibbon?"

"Yes, she owns this house, lived above the stables when the Army moved in."

The major's face cleared. "Ah, I'm afraid I'm not much help, Just took over as temporary C.O. Colonel Weston was killed in the attack. The whole unit is moving to Aldershot. I'm here to get things tidied up. We should be completely gone by the end of the week. I have some squaddies sorting through the buildings, seeing what we can save and what we should scrap."

"Do you know what happened to the servants?"

"Servants?"

"Yes, Myrtle and Cedric."

"Sorry. But—I know, let's ask Sergeant Hills. He was stationed here for years." He turned to a private, who was sorting through some papers, and gave him a directive. "Hammond, please find Sergeant Hills and bring him here."

The pair returned in a few moments. Sergeant Hills was a stocky man with wide shoulders. His uniform was spattered with small pieces of debris. "Sergeant, Wing Commander Chadwick is making some inquiries on behalf of Lady Fitzgibbon, who resided here. Do you know what happened to the servants after the German bombing?"

"They was both all right, though Cedric was a bit shook up."

Chadwick asked, "Where are they now, Sergeant. Do you know?"

"Well, I helped them pack a few things from the wreckage of the house. They said they was going away with the estate manager."

"Thank you. That's very helpful, Sergeant."

Goodwin asked, "Is that all, Sir?"

"Yes, I think so. I'll chase the manager."

Goodwin turned to Hills.

"That's all, sergeant. Dismissed."

The sergeant saluted and left.

Chadwick said, "Thank you, Major. I'll take a look around while I'm here. I spent a lot of time here before the balloon went up."

"Very good, Sir. Take care, though. The wreckage is precarious. Some walls will have to be knocked down to make the site a bit safer."

Chadwick walked to what was left of the front door and stood on the familiar steps. A faint smell of decay rose from the ruins. He turned and walked to the stables. This was presumably where Melanie was hiding when she was injured. He was appalled at the sight. The roof had collapsed and an outer wall lay in an untidy heap of bricks on the ground. He could see the brightly colored wallpaper on the rest of a room still suspended in space. He carefully poked among the rubble at ground level, but there was no sign of Melanie's two cars.

The taxi was still waiting. Chadwick turned and took a took last look before driving back to Reading. He took a train to Oxford, arriving well after dark. He walked to a small inn at which he had a reservation. The young woman at the desk seemed unimpressed by his rank and brusquely demanded the ration card he had been given when he left North Weald. He was told he would have to share a room with another man, as accommodations in Oxford were overwhelmed.

He went up to the room, and found the other occupant was washing from a basin of lukewarm water. He greeted Chadwick with a cheery, "Good evening, buddy. Chester Gutterman, Associated Press. The bathroom is down the corridor, but there's a chamber pot under each bed."

Chadwick plonked his case on the other bed. "Allan Chadwick. Pleased to meet you." He put his greatcoat and hat in a large wardrobe. "I'm stepping downstairs to see if I'm in time for some supper."

"You'll regret it," Gutterman said, with a laugh.

But he was right. An unappetizing plate of boiled potatoes and cabbage, and a fatty piece of beef was placed before Chadwick, followed by tapioca pudding. He was given a pot of weak tea, with no sugar or milk. Back in his room he found Gutterman sitting on his bed, smoking.

"You were right about the meal," Chadwick said.

"There's a war on, they tell me," Gutterman replied.

Chadwick felt between the sheets. They were ice cold. He retrieved his coat from the wardrobe and spread it over the flimsy quilt. He found the bathroom was unoccupied. He did not want to use the chamber pot, something he hadn't done since he was a child.

When he returned, Gutterman was writing in a notebook under the dim light hanging from the ceiling. "Couldn't the Air Force find you something a bit better than this dump?" the American asked.

"Actually, Mr. Gutterman, I am on a couple of days leave. A friend of mine who lives nearby is in hospital, wounded in a raid. I'm helping out."

"Call me Chester, buddy. Sorry to hear that. Looks like you've seen a few scrapes yourself. Whaddya think about the Eighth? They just got clobbered—bombed a place called Sch-weinfurt. Rumor is they're stepping down operations for a spell."

Chadwick was intensely interested. He had not been keeping up with the war news. "Do you have any details, Chester?"

"Not really. I was just talking on the phone to our office in London. Eaker is trying to put a good face on it. They made three raids on the same target. Our reporter said if they did a couple more like that there would be no Eighth Air Force left."

Combined with his own personal anguish over Melanie, Chadwick felt a sense of real loss for the Americans he had come to admire, and resolved to call Colonel Butzke as soon as he got back to North Weald. The cold bedclothes did not dispel the air of despondency that he felt. *This bloody war is going to last forever*, he thought. *My dearest Melanie wounded, my American friends dying at twenty thousand feet, how will it end?* It took a long time for him to fall into a troubled sleep.

In the morning he shaved with tepid water in the basin in his room. Breakfast was watery boiled tomatoes with a shriveled sausage of dubious composition. Fortunately, there was some toast with margarine and artificial strawberry jam made from turnips, and the tea was again weak and without sugar or milk. Although the day was chilly, he walked slowly down the

High Street, admiring the colleges. He arrived at the hospital at ten, and was soon talking to Melanie.

"I went to Pangbourne after I left you yesterday, dear. The place is going to need a little work before you can move in. But, at least, the Army has decamped."

Melanie smiled wanly. "I don't know how we can ever pay to rebuild the old place."

"Surely the government has some way of recompensing for buildings destroyed by the war," Allan said.

"I don't know," Melanie replied hesitantly. "Our solicitor will deal with it anyway."

"That reminds me, I was asking after Myrtle and Cedric, and was told they had gone somewhere with the estate manager. I would like to talk to your solicitor."

"They're in Reading—Goggins and Goggins. Their office is just off Market Street."

"Do you mind if I pop in to see them, Melanie? I'll make sure Myrtle and Cedric are all right."

"Oh, they're being looked after. I'm sure the estate is still paying them. But yes, visit old Goggins. You would like that. The office is the same as when Queen Victoria was on the throne."

After a few minutes, the nurse came to shoo Chadwick away. He walked to the station and made the familiar ride back to Reading.

When Chadwick walked into the solicitor's office, he was expecting something that looked like a scene from a Dickens novel. However, although the furniture was heavy mahogany, the place was bright and modern. Bookshelves loaded with legal tomes lined the walls. Two middle-aged women sat at desks with typewriters. Chadwick offered his name and asked to see Mr. Goggins.

"You can put your hat and coat on this," one of the women said, indicating a wooden clothes stand. She knocked on a door, poked her head round, and then beckoned him through.

Goggins sat behind an old-fashioned desk. He was of advanced years with silver hair, a trim mustache, and gold-rimmed glasses.

"Mr. Goggins, I am Allan Chadwick, an old friend of Lady Fitzgibbon. I just visited her in hospital and she suggested I talk to you."

Goggins was silent for a few moments. He clearly recalled Chadwick as the recipient of small sums from the estate made before the war, which were actually payments made on behalf of the Isbell's Insiders. "How can I be of assistance, Mr. Chadwick?"

"I told Lady Fitzgibbon I would look into a few things."

Goggins made no reply.

"Do you know where the servants are?"

"I believe they're in the care of the estate manager, Mr. Llewellyn. He's employing them until her Ladyship is released from hospital."

"Yes, that's another thing. Clair Court Hall is totally demolished. Where will she stay?"

"I have informed an old family friend, Lord Lowestoft, of Lady Fitzgibbon's indisposition. He is looking into it."

Without expressing himself in words, Goggins managed to convey the feeling that the Fitzgibbons had many powerful friends, and she did not require help from casual acquaintances like Chadwick. But Allan persevered.

"Lady Fitzgibbon was unaware of any government insurance which would cover the cost of rebuilding after a bombing attack."

Goggins was again silent for a few moments. "That matter is one of national interest. Parliament is debating ways to ameliorate the financial damage caused by the war to private individuals. Naturally, we are following the matter closely. We will represent the estate when a decision is reached."

"I'm sure you will, Mr. Goggins. Thank you for your time."

Chadwick rose and walked into the outer office, donned his coat, and said, firmly, "Good day, ladies," as he put on his hat and stepped into the street.

He glanced at his watch. It was eleven thirty-five. He walked to the station and decided to get some lunch before riding back to Oxford. He was able to get a Welsh rarebit with a pint of bitter at the bar before boarding a train. At the hospital he was told Melanie had just eaten lunch and was sleeping. The nurse suggested he return at seven, when visiting hours lasted for an hour.

He went back into the street and decided to kill a few hours in a—hopefully, warm—cinema. He passed the Lido and noticed it was showing a war movie about the merchant marine. The poster outside described the film as based on a real event when the tanker *San Demetrio* was set on fire by a German battleship. After three days in a lifeboat, some of the crew chanced upon the ship, still floating, boarded her, put out the fires and sailed to Britain. Chadwick enjoyed seeing familiar actors of the British film industry in bit parts as the courageous crew. It was wartime propaganda but entertaining.

After sitting through the rest of the program Chadwick called the inn to let them know he would not be there for supper. He found a pub that was serving fish and chips, and smiled to himself. *That's my Lancashire upbringing coming out.* He arrived promptly at the hospital and was led into Melanie's room. She looked pale and tiny in the trim, tightly made-up hospital bed.

"Hello, dear, how are you feeling tonight?"

"If you want the truth, Allan, dear, I'm feeling ghastly tired."

"I'm sorry. You've been through a lot. I won't stay long. I saw Mr. Goggins. Myrtle and Cedric are being looked after. Freddie is looking for somewhere nice for you to convalesce when you get out of here."

"He's very kind," she said weakly.

"I went to the pictures this afternoon. Wartime nonsense. The Brits always win, the Germans are idiots." He gave a short laugh.

"Shame it's not really like that."

"Melanie, I have to leave early in the morning, so this is my last visit for a while. Don't worry about what has happened to you. You'll be as right as rain before long, just slightly more battle-scarred. Be a good story for your grandchildren. I love you and I will stay closely in touch." He bent down and kissed her right cheek lightly. "Bye-bye." He brushed a tear away from under his eyes and strode out of the hospital without looking back.

On the way back to the inn he stopped in a pub and moodily drank two pints of bitter. When he arrived at the inn they were clearing away the dinner plates. "You're a bit late for food, Allan," Gutterman called from the parlor.

"I've already eaten, Chester. Thanks."

"I say, your Raff chaps really clobbered the Krauts last night."

"What happened?"

"Bunch of Lancasters blew up a few dams with special bombs. The Ruhr Valley is full of water up to their armpits."

Chapter Twenty-Eight

Chadwick was granted seventy-two hours compassionate leave and caught a train from Paddington to Oxford. He was worried that there may be some bureaucratic obstacles to overcome when he visited Melanie at the hospital. If there were any objections to his visit, they melted away when the nurse greeted Chadwick in his uniform with the impressive battle ribbons.

"Lady Fitzgibbon was badly injured, Wing Commander. You must prepare yourself for some … disfigurement." Chadwick followed her into a small room and she pushed aside a screen. The smell of antiseptic was overwhelming. Melanie Fitzgibbon was lying in bed with her eyes closed. "You have a visitor, Lady Fitzgibbon," the nurse trilled.

Melanie opened her eyes. "My God, Allan. I was hoping you wouldn't see me like this."

The nurse turned toward Allan. "Please don't tire her," she said. "I'll be back in a few minutes."

Chadwick stood awkwardly by the bedside; his hand dropped to the sheet over Melanie's right arm. Her left arm lay on top of the bed covers, swathed in plaster of Paris up to her shoulder. "I'm so sorry, dear," he stammered.

"I know," Melanie replied. "It was always my fear that I would be visiting you in some hospital, and now our roles are reversed."

"Melanie, how bad is it? Do you have any serious injuries inside?"

Chadwick savored the news. Evidently Bomber Command had put together the precision raid Group Captain Hearne had mentioned earlier. "What were the losses? Do you know?"

"Sorry, don't know. It was just a short announcement on the BBC. There'll probably be more in the papers tomorrow."

Chadwick arrived at North Weald the next day by mid-afternoon. His squadron commanders had been busy. Bomber Command had ordered attacks on coastal shipping and the Mosquitos had been after German E-boats foolish enough to sail in the Channel without the cover of darkness. He called Colonel Butzke and arranged to meet him at High Wycombe as soon as he could get a few hours free.

They met two days later. The colonel was looking more careworn.

"Tell me about the last two months, Buzz."

"I think our original plan for strategic bombing in daylight with massed formations was initially viable. But the enemy adapted. They put up more fighters with well-honed tactics. Our losses went up. In defense of our original plans, I have to point out the economists now estimate that more than forty percent of German war production is for fighters and anti-aircraft guns. This means fewer tanks, submarines, bombers, you name it. So the strategic aims were met. But the Germans got smarter. Attacks from head-on, by multiple fighters, have resulted in heavier losses. This tendency culminated in the raid to Schweinfurt, to knock out ball-bearing production. We made three raids on the same targets, which was probably a mistake, and we took more than twenty percent losses, which is unsustainable, not to mention the effect on crew morale."

"My God, Buzz, I'm awfully sorry to hear this. What now?"

"As an interim measure, the Eighth will concentrate on attacks on coastal towns, where the planes can have protection by RAF Fighter Command. Fortunately, the plans for fighter escort we discussed nearly a year ago came to fruition. I strong-armed a lot of generals to get the P-51 with Merlin engines into production. They jawboned a lot of congressmen and funds were found. The Ninth Army Air Force, based in Britain, will be flying escort in a few months with P-51s and P-47s. Then the Eighth can go back to long-range bombing missions, with fighter escort all the way."

"We live and learn, and a lot of blood spilled on the way."

"Amen to that. What have you been up to, Allan?"

"At the moment I command a wing of high-speed fighter-bombers, the Mosquitos. Wonderful kite. We've made some precision raids, just a few planes, low level."

"Say, did you pull off that great stunt of bombing Göring while he was in the middle of a speech?"

"Yes, I was in on that."

"Fantastic, you guys! Stay for lunch, I'll introduce you to a few generals."

In the Officer's Club, Butzke suddenly said, "There's the big chief, General Eaker." Grabbing Chadwick's arm, he pulled him toward a knot of very senior officers. "General Eaker, I would like to introduce Wing Commander Chadwick, who's been providing liaison with RAF Bomber Command since we started operations."

Eaker swung round and grasped Chadwick's right hand in a firm grip. "Please to meetcha, Wing Commander. I guess Buzz has brought you up to date on the Schweinfurt show. Well, the Raff told us what would happen, but we had to find out for ourselves. What do you call that? Hubris?"

Before Chadwick could reply, Butzke hurriedly cut in, "Wing Commander Chadwick was very helpful in specifying the P-51 airplane for escort duties. They're arriving every day now. We should be back to long-range missions very soon. The wing commander was on the RAF strike that interrupted Göring's anniversary speech a few weeks ago."

"Great stuff, Wing Commander. Keep in touch." Eaker turned away to talk to others in his group.

Butzke dragged Chadwick away. "You did fine, Allan."

"Fine? I never opened my mouth."

"That's what I mean."

Chapter Twenty-Nine

Nearly two months after the attack on Berlin, four men met in an obscure office in the same city. They were senior officers responsible for day-to-day functioning of the Sicherheist Dienst—the SD, the intelligence arm of the SS. They were highly intelligent individuals, without a shred of moral scruples. Their underlings referred to them as the "Four Horsemen of the Apocalypse." Not openly, of course. Their wide knowledge of the foibles of the leaders of the Nazi Party left them with a deep skepticism about the competence of the men running the country. However, they had no choice but to make sure Germany won the war.

They discussed a request from the Reichsmarschall to investigate a tip that had originated with an Abwehr agent in Britain, who said the raid by low-flying RAF bombers which interrupted his speech to the nation was suggested by a source within Germany who had been in communication with British agents in Berne, Switzerland. There was an obscure mention of Peenemunde.

"Berne!" one of the men said with short laugh. "That backwater."

Although Berne was the diplomatic capital of Switzerland, the center of the banking institutions was in Zurich, which was where the agents of the belligerents were concentrated.

"What assets do we have in Berne?"

"There's a station chief. Keeps his ear open for Foreign Office gossip. The British and the Americans maintain the same level."

"This smells of British deception tactics. Can we ignore it?"

"The Reichsmarschall is very keen for some retaliation. The Luftwaffe has already bombed the base of the unit that carried out the raid. If there was some involvement on our side, we should dig a little deeper, without expending too much energy."

One of the men slapped his knee. "I have just the man to send to Berne. Originally joined us before the war, when we cranked up that group to support Himmler's obsession with the Aryan myths. He was a professor of Scandinavian history, and when we occupied Norway he worked there. His knowledge of Scandinavian languages was useful, but the leader up there tells me the fellow is a little squeamish about the methods we are sometimes forced to use. He is back in Berlin now. He recently complained to me he hasn't much to do. He's a trained agent we can easily spare."

One of the men spoke up. "If he fails, I suggest a transfer to the Waffen SS and a posting to the Russian Front."

"Brief him and let the station chief in Berne know he's coming. Now, let us turn to more important business."

Leutnant Carl Speidel arrived in Berne on an afternoon train and reported immediately to the SD station chief, who was expecting him. They sat in an office in the German Embassy. The chief looked at an open file on the desk in front of him.

"I have your file here, Leutnant. Five years of service, mostly in Sweden and Norway. Ph.D. in Scandinavian studies, fluent in Swedish, Danish, and Norwegian. German will get you by in this town, but many speak a bastardized version. How's your English?" Without waiting for a reply, he carried on. "You have been sent to track down a report from the Abwehr that mentioned Berne as the source of an unconfirmed rumor—that the raid on Berlin by the British on the thirteenth of January was at the suggestion of a German who made it to a British agent here. Frankly, I have no knowledge of it. It seems very unlikely.

"Let me tell you a little about intelligence work in Switzerland. The Swiss Security Service requires all agents of the belligerent countries to be registered with them. No violence is allowed, the Swiss do not want the corpses of mysterious foreigners found lying around. It is all very gentlemanly on the surface. Most of our intelligence activity is in Zurich. Very large sums of money and gold are processed there every day. Despite the war, the capitalistic principles are still followed. Believe it or not, some German automobile companies owned by the United States are returning earnings to the parent company for lorries manufactured for the Wehrmacht. This was done through shadow holding companies and Swiss banks. It's a complicated world we live in, Speidel. Any questions?"

"How am I to go about tracking down the source of this rumor?"

"It's difficult. Ingratiate yourself with the British diplomats. You are nominally a cultural affairs attaché—Professor Speidel, an expert on the Sagas, here temporarily to investigate the presence of the Vikings in central Europe a thousand years ago. It is well known that even the Fuhrer believes the present German stock can be traced to the Vikings. Some of the British diplomats were academics before the war. I will get you a list of possible acquaintances you may cultivate."

"It sounds like a long shot, Herr Obst, but I will follow whatever orders you give me. By the way, I read and write English quite well, but my speaking accent is noticeable."

"Even without violence there are ways, Speidel. Alcohol flows freely at the diplomatic functions, and we all use honeypots. I think the ladies report everything to the Swiss before their handlers get to hear it."

In London, Will Viney attended a meeting of the group keeping an eye on German activities at Peenemunde on the Baltic. They discussed new observations detected by RAF photo interpretation of several sites in northern France. Agents of the ground had first spotted the construction work and alerted MI6. Sweeps by photoreconnaissance Spitfires had followed. They discovered that the Germans were building what appeared to be steel ramps, angled slightly upwards and all pointing to England. The photographs were hard to interpret, as the work was camouflaged most of the time. The Group had been notified because similar ramps had been spotted at Peenemunde.

Viney was intrigued. It appeared the Germans were developing a new weapon, and a thousand questions had to be answered. Was it manned? What was the range? When would it be in service?

A few weeks later he read a report from the British Intelligence chief in Berne. As they had been warned, a German agent had appeared, posing as a professor, and had tried to buy information on the January 13th raid. Viney quickly reviewed the messages that flowed since the Double-Cross Committee had attempted to deceive the Abwehr. An early one mentioned Peenemunde. Would it be possible to deceive or turn this "professor" and get some new information on the developments at Peenemunde?

After a meeting of the Double-Cross Committee, specific orders were sent to MI6 in Berne. The German agent had to be turned, by whatever means possible. Then as part of his investigation of the Göring raid, he should request to be sent to Peenemunde. On return he would be spirited to England for debriefing, given financial rewards and a new identity.

When the station chief in Berne, Stanley Shipton, received these instructions he threw up his hands and appealed to the heavens. "What do they think we are, hypnotists?" Nevertheless, on reflection he conceded the plan made sense. Peenemunde had been mentioned in the original message to the

Abwehr, and if the agent in Berne made any progress he would naturally think of pursuing the lead to the Baltic. Shipton called a meeting with two of his most experienced agents, but when the chief first outlined the plan, they were skeptical.

"Nazi SD officers do not turn easily, if at all. They are usually zealots."

A dour Scotsman spoke up. "It won't work. We certainly cannot guarantee we could turn this fellow. But remember, he wants to succeed. I think one of our young ladies could be persuaded to make his acquaintance and give him enough hints so that a visit to Peenemunde would make sense to him. On his return we spring a honey-pot, a little blackmail with a well-made salacious film with sound track, and he would be happy to tell us what's going on up there. Let's keep an eye on the social functions coming up and arrange a little companionship for the lonely Professor Speidel."

Shipton thought it over, slowly and carefully. "We can't use any of our usual local ladies. For the information to be credible, the doxy has to be part of our staff. I don't think any of them would agree to bedding a lonely SD officer, but I'll go to Zurich. They have a much more flexible team there."

He made a long phone call, and two days later he took the one-hour train ride to Zurich. He outlined the situation to the station chief, Alistair Gould. He was familiar with the general plot and, after absorbing the details, he said they had an agent who would fit the bill—a Secret Service-trained female who was not unattractive, and she spoke fluent German and English.

Gould explained, "She had a German mother and an English father and grew up spending time in both countries. Her mother was also Jewish and perished in a concentration camp before the war. She has a loathing of the Nazis. Would you like to talk to her?"

"Yes, but before that let's get a few things straight. This woman has to pretend to fall under the influence of the professor to the point she can manipulate him to visit the site at

Peenemunde. If she has strong personal feelings that might be impossible."

"There is only one way to find out, Shipton. Let's give the lady a run-down and ask."

After a few minutes, an attractive woman of medium height entered the office. "Miss Jean Kershaw, I would like to introduce the station chief at Bern, Stanley Shipton."

Shipton offered his hand. "A pleasure, Miss Kershaw."

Gould went on, "Berne is handling a rather tricky problem that originated with the deception wizards in London. A female agent is needed, and Mr. Shipton would like to outline the situation and get your feelings about joining this shindig."

"In a nutshell," Shipton began, "a series of deceptive messages from London have convinced German intelligence that the Berne office of MI6 has been in contact with a disillusioned German who is involved with the secret work at Peenemunde, a research institution on the Baltic. Berlin has sent an agent to Berne to sniff out who this person is. The whole idea of the deception, from the British angle, is to get someone—someone who is above suspicion—to visit Peenemunde, find out what is under development there, come back to a confident in Berne, and spill the beans. It is the role of the confident we thought you might consider."

"You want me to seduce this Nazi lout, is that it?"

"You put it rather crudely, Miss Kershaw. We have identified the SD agent. Before the war he was a professor of Scandinavian studies and we suspect has been given this job as an unimportant matter needing a little attention. Seduction may not enter into it. You would have to play him like a fish, feeding snippets, in consultation with London, so that he rises to the bait of a trip to Peenemunde. Once he returns, we somehow have to find out what's happening there. London feels this is very important. Seduction may enter the picture at that stage, who knows? Our agent must possess great finesse to pull this off."

"I assume the potential confidante will meet this bewildered German agent at a social level first. Before going any further I will agree to that level of involvement. If he is not such a die-hard Nazi beast we can go from there." She firmly pressed her lips together.

"That's perfectly reasonable, Miss Kershaw. Come to Berne, and we'll work out a plausible way for you to meet and inspect him. You'll be operating under the name Sheila Aspinall."

When Chadwick returned to North Weald, he was overwhelmed with administrative work. Commanding three squadrons of active bombers resulted in demands for replacement planes and aircrew, spare parts and armaments, and participation in target selection. Only twice over a two-month period did he fly on operations himself.

One day Chadwick received a call from Colonel Butzke. The commander of a group in the Ninth had expressed a wish to meet Chadwick. Butzke had suggested that the American fly should fly to North Weald on a day when they were not too busy and he could try for himself the latest version of the P-51 Mustang.

Allan was delighted with the idea and greeted the young pilot, Major Eugene Wilcenski, enthusiastically when he landed at North Weald. They climbed aboard a Mosquito and Chadwick extolled its virtues.

"When my plane is refueled," the American said, "let's take it up and see if it can out-fly my P-51."

"Great idea," Allan replied. An hour later both planes took off together and climbed to 20,000 feet over Norfolk. They did not have a common VHF radio frequency but they had plotted their escapade before departing. They flew in close formation as Chadwick leveled off, and then he signaled by hand for a speed run. At 20,000, they were neck and neck, but as Chadwick climbed slowly to 30,000, the Mustang pulled ahead.

The navigator that Chadwick had chosen to fly with him watched the sleek fighter through the side of the canopy. "What a beautiful kite,'" he exclaimed excitedly.

"Not as pretty as a Spitfire," Chadwick retorted, defensive of his first love. Then he waved Wilcenski away and the Mustang flashed off to starboard and made a hard climbing turn.

"He's going to make a beam on attack, so we'll try to out-turn him. Keep an eye on him."

"He's coming in now, fast, slightly below us."

Chadwick flung the Mosquito into a hard right turn. The Mustang hung onto his tail.

The navigator twisted round on his seat. "I think he has us, Skip," he shouted, as he searched the space behind plane feverishly.

"Yeah, there he is."

The American plane zoomed over the Mosquito's canopy with a foot or two to spare. The bomber shuddered in the fighter's wake. Chadwick flung the Mosquito into a diving turn, and the airspeed rapidly shot up to 440 knots. "This will shake him off," he said to his navigator.

But minutes later, the Mustang popped up in close formation on the port side. Wilcenski gave a cheery wave. Chadwick pointed down and the Mustang followed the British bomber back to the distinctive triangular runways at North Weald.

Over lunch Chadwick congratulated the American for staying with him.

"Piece of cake," the American joked.

Chadwick walked back to the hard standing with the American major. "How about a short spin in your new shiny kite?"

"Sure, Wing Commander. You can use my helmet."

Chadwick lowered himself into the cockpit and Wilcenski stood on the wing, going over a few essentials about flying the plane that he thought Chadwick might not be familiar with.

Chadwick sniffed the characteristic smell of a new plane, a slight chemical odor. The aroma was quite different than an old Spitfire. Somehow the high octane fuel, hydraulic fluid, oxygen, burned cordite, and sweat combined to make a unique pong, once inhaled, never forgotten.

He energized the huge Merlin, taxied to the runway, ran up the engine, and then shut the canopy. With a green from the tower, he accelerated rapidly down the runway. The plane lifted off with barely any pressure on the stick. The wheels retracted with a satisfying thud and Chadwick climbed at maximum boost to 25,000 feet. He went through a series of maneuvers and found the plane was quick, but it was clearly a little heavier than the Spitfire. When he let down, Chadwick felt confident the Mustang could hold its own against the best the Germans had to offer—the Focke-Wulf 190.

"She's a beauty, Eugene, thanks for the ride."

Chapter Thirty

On many evenings when he had the time, Chadwick made a personal telephone call to the Oxford hospital. Over a period of ten days Melanie made considerable progress. She was walking and breathing better, and the doctor felt she could be released in a few days.

When Chadwick asked where she would be staying, he was told that Lord Lowestoft had made arrangements for her to convalesce at his country house near Stowmarket in Suffolk. Myrtle was also going to stay there and help her mistress. The house lay about sixty miles from his station at North Weald but there was no easy way to make a visit and Chadwick's duties as wing commander got more and more onerous, limiting his free time.

Although the demand from resistance leaders in occupied Europe remained high, the choice of Gestapo headquarters as precision targets began to fade. Most raids had resulted in civilian casualties because these targets were frequently located in dense urban areas. Also the German defenders began to get the measure of these types of raids and the losses of the Mosquito squadrons climbed. Chadwick had frequent consultations with the target planners and the commanders of the squadrons. As the summer nights shrank, the need for accurate target definition grew in importance and the planners suggested the Mosquito wing be converted to Oboe-equipped Pathfinder units.

Chadwick, of course, had participated in the very early experiments using Oboe, and so he agreed to have 613 Squadron re-equipped with the latest Mosquito version, the Mark

VI, which carried Oboe receivers. This variation was a potent bomber in its own right, and could carry two tons of bombs and flares for over two thousand miles. The navigators were sent on an intensive Oboe training course.

In Switzerland, Jean Kershaw was transferred to the Berne Embassy, and Shipton discussed with her the plans for attracting the German agent, Carl Speidel. "On the surface you're a replacement in the secretarial pool," she was told. "You must not appear to be too bright and a love of jewelry and nice clothes should suggest to Speidel his line of attack."

The professor had been under observation for several weeks and his daily routine was well-known. Most Saturday evenings he spent a few hours at a dance hall near the university, where Miss Kershaw was infiltrated. By the end of the evening, she had danced a quickstep with him and told him her name was Sheila. She agreed to meet him for lunch one day the following week.

When Speidel discovered that Kershaw was a secretary in the Embassy, he told her he was an Austrian professor with a deep interest in Scandinavian history and was researching the arrival of the Vikings in Central Europe a thousand years ago. They began to meet more frequently and Speidel asked her if there was any material in the embassy library which might touch on the Vikings. Of course, as a putative enemy subject, he could not visit the library himself.

London was kept in close touch and suggested an obscure British archaeological journal with an appropriate article which she copied for Speidel, saying she had typed it from the edition in the embassy library. On the surface, the professor was grateful for her help but in his role as a spy, he detected a means to find out more about the suspected German malcontent.

The SD station chief gave him the funds to buy a small ruby brooch, which he gave to Kershaw the next time they met, with fulsome thanks for her help. She "oohed and ahhed" at the gift, but said wistfully she didn't have nice frock to wear it on. This was clearly an invitation for more cooperation and within a few weeks Speidel was able to openly ask her to keep her eyes and ears open for communications from the Baltic region.

When he asked her how the Embassy communicated with London, her eyes opened wide. "Oh, there's a room that almost no one can enter. I was told they scramble all the messages there, whatever that means. Sounds like they're cooking eggs," she added with a laugh.

When Speidel heard that, he despaired of learning anything useful from Sheila. The next day he discussed his feelings with the station chief, who in turn spoke to his boss in Berlin. They decided there was one last chance to possibly rescue something from the investment made already—send Speidel to Peenemunde and see if anything there made a connection with Berne. The Reichsmarschall would expect nothing less.

Speidel was given his orders and after two days of travel, reported to the SD chief at the Peenemunde Army Research establishment. He traveled in civilian clothes until he could change into his uniform in Berlin.

The Peenemunde SD chief, Obst Fritz Gessner, listened to Speidel's tale. "Those assholes in Berlin are wasting manpower to find out if someone here hates the Fat Man? Believe me," he said, "we check all mail and telephone calls from here. Nobody could communicate with a Tommy in Switzerland." He shook his head and assigned a junior officer to give Speidel a tour of the facilities. The young man guided Speidel to a parked Kübelwagon, a utilitarian vehicle with canvas seats. He explained the two main projects at the institution were the development of two "Vengeance" weapons—the pilotless flying bomb known as the V-1, and the ballistic rocket, the V-2. Both carried nearly a ton of explosives. Hitler believed the bombardment of Britain by these new weapons would completely demoralize the enemy.

The Peenemunde site was huge, with many miles between the centers for development, testing, and production. His guide was extremely proud of the factory for V-2 production, as that was where he worked. Inside the huge building, thousands of men thronged the floor around dozens of rockets in various stages of completion.

"Compared to the V-1, which is quite simple and put together at the Fieseler aircraft factory, the V-2 is extremely sophisticated," he explained proudly. "But we are able to make them quickly and cheaply using prison workers."

Speidel then noticed that the assembly area was patrolled by SS men carrying rubber truncheons and whips. There was a commotion in a corner of the vast hangar and he saw two SS men beat a worker in striped rags to the ground. Blood flew as the batons fell on his bare skin.

"If a man makes a mistake we beat him in full view of the others," the guide explained. "You would be surprised to find out how few errors are made. The quality of the work is excellent. Unfortunately, the workers are not overly fed, and often die after a severe beating. But there are lots more where they came from. They are just Jewish pigs."

Speidel was secretly sickened by the violence, but two years with the SS in Norway had hardened him to the violent and even sadistic nature of the SD. He was amazed at the size of the production factory and expressed his admiration.

"This is nothing," his young guide said. "We are building a production line in a cavern in a mountain. We will soon have thousands of rockets."

The next day Speidel reported back to Berlin HQ, and confessed there was nothing he had learned that shed any light on the motivation behind the bombing of the Reichsmarschall's speech. A senior colonel listened and told Speidel to stop by the next office to deal with the travel paperwork. By chance, the communicating door to the office he had just left was slightly ajar, and Speidel had sensitive ears. To his dismay, he heard the colonel talking on the telephone about him—"No, nothing, waste of time. Speidel, yes? Transfer to Waffen." There was a pause when the voice was inaudible, then he heard him say, "Posting to the Eastern Front, that's rich."

Speidel left the building with his heart pounding and caught the train to Berne. The overheard conversation ran through his mind—*Transferred to the Waffen SS and sent to Russia.* That was a death sentence. SS men were never taken as prisoners in the Soviet Union, and if they were lucky they were shot.

He reported to his chief and then went to the lodging house he had used when posing as an Austrian professor. His mind was in a whirl. Through the window of a coffee shop he could see the front door of his lodging. Suddenly, two stocky men entered and five minutes later reappeared; they scanned the street and then marched off in the direction of the German Embassy. It was obvious to him that they were SS thugs, employed when a little muscle was needed, and he surmised they were looking for him.

Speidel realized he was facing a life or death situation. His life depended on quick, crucial decisions. After paying for the execrable "coffee," he scurried down the street, and entered the first cinema he encountered, grateful to find a seat in the dark auditorium. The film showing was French. *Am I overreacting?* he thought. *No, those heavies didn't show up by chance. The SD is looking for me.*

He hunched up and sat, depressed, watching the screen. His French was adequate enough for him to follow the film, and then to realize that it was based on a book he had read by Georges Simenon, about a porter who found a suitcase shipped from London containing a fortune in stolen money. London! That was the answer. But he needed professional help to get out of Berne, and he was fairly certain the British Secret Service would assist him.

Maybe Sheila is not such a dumb blonde as she appears? He looked at his watch. It was just after four. Sheila would still be at work. He had the telephone number of her hotel that he'd used when arranging a rendezvous with her. He resolved to call when he expected she would be there, but it would have to be from the cinema. He didn't dare risk walking the streets looking for a public phone.

At five-thirty he went into the lobby and asked the ticket collector if there was a telephone he could use. The man shook his head. "It's very important. I have to call at this time," Speidel implored.

"The manager may let you use his instrument, but you may have to pay." He nodded in the direction of the manager's office.

Speidel went to the door and tapped.

"Enter!"

"Good afternoon, Sir. I was watching the film when I suddenly remembered a pressing telephone call I have to make immediately. It's a local call. May I use your telephone? I will be happy to pay for the call."

"Well, that's unorthodox, but I have to check with box office about now. I'll step out for a few moments, so be quick, and no need to pay."

Speidel thanked him effusively and dialed the number as soon as the manager left. To his heartfelt relief, he was able to talk to Sheila without a long wait. "This is Carl," he said. "I have to talk quickly. The German police are looking for me and I need to hide. No. No. No questions. I'm in the Rivoli Cinema on Schönberg Strasse. Have your embassy park a car by the east side door. I will meet you in the foyer in thirty minutes. Don't fail me, it will be worth it to the British Secret Service."

Speidel heard her gasp as he put the telephone back in its cradle. He returned to the corridor, and the manager was not in sight. He glanced at his watch, carefully noticed the time, and went back to his seat.

Thirty minutes later he pushed aside the curtain and walked into the foyer. A handful of people stood at the box office window buying tickets, but there was no sign of Sheila. *Gott in Himmel!* he thought. *What now?* His heart was racing. He knew that his absence from the lodging would have been detected. He had backed himself into a corner. Then to his relief Sheila walked in from the street. She was alone.

"What's happening, Carl?"

"Sheila" he began, "I'm a member of the SD, part of the German contingent here in Berne. They plan to send me to Russia, and so I'm prepared to desert and come to the British side if your Secret Service people can get me out. I have just returned from a trip to Peenemunde, and the information I have is valuable."

Sheila—Jean Kershaw—knew he had been away because Speidel was under observation by British agents, but she did not know where. When she heard him mention Peenemunde her pulse quickened. This was the jackpot.

"Come with me. We have a car waiting in the side street."

Outside nobody approached them until they stopped at a nondescript Italian sedan. Suddenly, two men materialized and pushed Speidel into the car. Kershaw climbed in and told Speidel to kneel behind the front seat. They drove to the back of the Embassy and parked so that they could not be seen from the street. Inside, Kershaw led the German to meet the head of MI6. "Sir, Herr Speidel has just returned from a visit to Peenemunde."

"Has he? By God!"

"He claims he is willing to desert to our side."

Speidel broke in. " I happened to discover, by chance, that I was to be posted to the Russian Front, and for a man in my position that is almost certain death. I am prepared to swap my knowledge of the work at Peenemunde for a safe passage to England."

"Let's hear what we're buying," Shipton said. "Give me a brief outline."

When he heard that V-2 production would soon move into a mountainside cavern he realized that time was a vital factor, and Speidel must be thoroughly interrogated by the experts in England as soon as possible. An encoded message was sent to MI6 HQ in London, stressing the urgency of the situation. Shipton realized that Speidel's presence in the Embassy must be kept secret and later in the evening he was surreptitiously moved to a safe house.

He congratulated Jean Kershaw on the coup. "I know it didn't work out the way we planned but you were the essential lynchpin when Speidel decided to jump ship. I will stress your contribution to Zurich. However, his side knows who he was cultivating. They would probably like to talk to you. You must stay here tonight. I will send someone to the hotel for your belongings. In due course you can return to Zurich, Miss Kershaw."

London replied to Shipton's message within a few hours. When it was decoded, Shipton was staggered. Speidel would be flown to Gibraltar and then on to London by a specially-equipped Mosquito bomber that would land at an airfield near Lausanne. A secret squadron was operated by the RAF using modified Mosquitos to fly single VIP passengers to and from airfields in Europe. It was usually not possible to refuel the planes; the range had been extended by changes to the engines and fuel tanks. They carried no armaments. The passenger was carried in the bomb bay, wrapped in heated bedding and breathing oxygen.

The next day Speidel was smuggled to a little-used airfield and British agents met the Mosquito, which arrived exactly on time. It had left Gibraltar more than three hours before for the thousand-mile flight, and then crossed the Alps as dawn broke. Carrying Speidel, the Mosquito was airborne ten minutes later and landed at Gibraltar in time for lunch.

Carl Speidel was placed in an RAF transport which landed at Norholt by the late evening. For the next two days, professional interrogators gleaned every morsel of information they could from the German. They also used tricks to make sure Speidel was not an SD plant. Their report, which gave in detail the advanced state of development of pilotless planes and ballistic rockets, horrified the intelligence community. Churchill himself ordered an all-out bombing strike on Peenemunde.

Chapter Thirty-One

Oboe relay stations were set up in the North Sea in preparation for 613 Squadron Pathfinder Mosquitos to lead the way for the bomber stream. The same night that over 300 British bombers plastered the German Army Research and Development site at Peenemunde, an apparently elderly woman boarded a train from Berne to Zurich. It was Jean Kershaw, suitably disguised by padded clothing, a grey wig and glasses. She had done her part in countering the threat of the Nazi vengeance weapons.

Allan Chadwick led the Pathfinder planes to Peenemunde. The flight was made at almost full boost and low level. The Mosquitos raced over the Baltic sea at over 350 knots. Their mission was elaborate—three targets had to be identified by specific flares at the site: research laboratories, design offices, and the production factory. The Oboe receivers in the twelve planes were locked onto the signals relayed from ships in the North Sea. The various activities reported by Speidel, had been drawn on photos taken by high altitude Spitfires and converted to accurate grid coordinates, programmed into the Oboe receivers.

After Chadwick's plane had launched the flares, he flew in a tight circle to inspect the markers dropped by the other flights. All seemed satisfactory and the flak was quite light. The main stream of bombers was expected to arrive within a minute. As the Mosquito gained height, Chadwick saw the flashes of the falling bombs. Many of the captive workers were killed or injured in the destruction that rained down on the rocket assembly building. Senior scientists and engineers were killed by bombs on the laboratories.

British losses were light—two Lancasters went down due to flak over Peenemunde. Two Halifax heavy bombers were caught and shot down by fighters on the way back to England. An assessment by Bomber Command a few days after the raid pronounced the targeting had been very accurate and that the German "Vengeance" program had been dealt a severe blow.

As it turned out, however, this was optimistic. Certainly, the V-2 production had been impacted but V-1 flying bombs were assembled at many sites. They began to fly from northern France toward Britain within weeks.

After the raid on Peenemunde, 613 Squadron was stood down for a week. Chadwick was given five days leave and he arranged to visit Lady Fitzgibbon at Lord Lowestoft's place. It was a slow journey by stopping train to Stowmarket. And then a taxi ride to the Victorian house that Lord Lowestoft had inherited from his father. It had been built originally by a self-made tycoon who made his fortune from cotton spinning. He called it "Glossyplum," a pun on the Latin name for cotton. But the tycoon died without leaving an heir, and Lord Lowestoft's father had acquired it. Chadwick was greeted by Lord Lowestoft himself in the entrance hall.

"Let me take your coat, old chap. There's no butler nowadays."

As Chadwick shed his coat, Lowestoft looked at the ribbons on his tunic. "I say, looks like you have had a busy war, Allan."

Chadwick was not quite sure how to handle Lord Lowestoft, who had introduced him to the Isbell's Insiders before the war, a clique of upper class people who favored appeasement rather than war with Germany. Under the direction of MI5, Chadwick had written misleading reports on the effectiveness of radar, known then as RDR, and passed them on via Lowestoft. But to his knowledge, Lowestoft had never been accused of any unpatriotic act.

"I'm sure you want to see Melanie. She's resting in the solarium."

"Yes, thank you, Sir. It's weeks since I last saw her."

"Call me Freddy, old chap. Mustn't stand on ceremony. Besides you're a hero, too."

This was an oblique reference to the Victoria Cross, Britain's highest award for valor, awarded to Lord Lowestoft in the Great War.

Melanie was resting on a couch in a glass-enclosed solarium littered with small trees in tubs. She wore a tweed skirt with a cardigan, buttoned up to her neck. An afghan was draped across her feet. She had a dressing on her face and her left arm was in a cast, supported by a sling. Her skin was very pale.

"Allan, what a delight to see you! Come over here."

Chadwick grasped her outstretched hand and kissed her cheek lightly. "You are looking well, Melanie. How do you feel?"

"Getting better. Thank God I don't have to face that terrible hospital food."

Lowestoft chimed in, "Myrtle is helping my cook in the kitchen. She knows what Melanie likes. My goodness, I'm not being the proper host. Would you like some tea, Allan?"

"Yes sir. I still remember the wonderful tea and biscuits your secretary used to produce on my visits to the Foreign Office."

"Ah, sadly those days have past. The biscuits nowadays are homemade, but not bad." Lowestoft crossed to a bell-rope and then opened a door, and shouted to someone on the other side, "Tea for three, Mavis." Returning to Chadwick and Melanie he said, "We may as well be comfortable." He pulled over two white wicker chairs. "Sit," he instructed, and then asked, "Are you are staying the night, Allan?"

"That was my understanding, Sir."

"Top-hole, yes. I must let Mavis know you'll be here for dinner."

The conversation lagged, and then Melanie asked, "Is it any use asking what you are up to these days, Allan?"

"Not really. I'm still in Bomber Command, but I'm mostly pushing paper." Chadwick felt uncomfortable trying to explain to a civilian what it was like to be fighting in an air war. Somehow a sentence leapt into his mind that he had read somewhere. It was like trying to describe an elephant to someone who has never seen one.

Mavis arrived with the tea things on a trolley. "No sugar I'm afraid, but try the bickies," Lowestoft said. "They really are delicious. Mavis makes them with honey, which isn't rationed." He poured three cups and passed them out. "We don't change for dinner anymore, Allan."

"I brought a suit anyway, Freddy. It will be a nice change to get out of this uniform."

Melanie announced she was going for a rest before dinner. Lowestoft also begged to be excused, pleading paperwork that needed to be completed concerning the farm. He left Chadwick with the day's copy of *The Daily Telegraph* and asked Mavis to show Chadwick his room for the night.

After reading the war news, Chadwick went upstairs and dozed before donning his old suit. Melanie came down for dinner wearing a frock that fastened close to her chin. The conversation over the meal was desultory. Lowestoft was of the opinion that the war could go on for years. Chadwick pointed out that a landing had been made on Italian shores by British and American troops. Lowestoft did not think they would make much progress in Italy, and even if they did, the Alps formed an unsurmountable barrier.

"My friends in the F.O. told me Churchill wanted to invade the Balkans, but the American generals won the day."

Melanie protested that talking about the war was boring, and so they lapsed into a long silence while eating the meal, rabbit pie with potatoes and cauliflower.

Lowestoft said he had shot the rabbits on the estate and both vegetables were grown in the garden. "We're all doing our bit for the war effort," he said.

Chadwick smiled to himself. *Shooting rabbits was not quite the same as shooting Germans,* he thought to himself. *They didn't fire back.*

After breakfast they took their tea into the solarium, which was a little warmer than the rest of the house. Lowestoft said he had things to do, but he would be able to say goodbye after lunch when Chadwick left for London.

Melanie and Allan sat in silence for a while after Lord Lowestoft's departure.

"Freddy has asked me to marry him, Allan."

Chadwick was stunned. He said nothing at first and then blurted out, "He's very old, Melanie."

"No, he looks older than he is. He's just seven years older than I am."

"What are you going to do?"

"I will accept his proposal. It will be a platonic marriage. The injury has left me with horrible wounds. I am ugly. UGLY!" she almost shouted, her voice rising.

"No, no, Melanie dear. You're not ugly. They are honorable wounds, inflicted in a war."

"You haven't seen me," Melanie shot back sharply. "The damned surgeon, when he cut off my lovely breast, left hideous weals of bloody flesh. Nobody must ever see my body. I have made that quite clear to Freddy."

"I think a marriage without, er… physical love is going to be difficult."

"Before the war, you and I were young, Allan. Yes, we were lovers, but the war has changed everything in many ways. Freddy and I have discussed the future. Socially we are equals. I will make a perfectly acceptable Lady Lowestoft."

Chadwick's thoughts were whirling in his mind. "I had always hoped that, after the war, we could get to together … marry," he said lamely.

"Oh, Allan, you are a romantic—a dreamer."

Chadwick felt a rising anger. "Why not?" Then he said something he regretted and wished he could pull the words back. "Is it just because I am just a butcher's son from Liverpool? Is that why not?"

Melanie sighed. "You said that, not me. I'm truly sorry. We enjoyed a golden period together, but nothing stays the same, especially with men like Hitler around."

Chadwick rose abruptly. He felt if he stayed any longer he might really say something he would regret. "Please give Freddy my thanks for his hospitality. I'll catch an early train," he said coldly.

Chadwick could not remember the train ride to London. He still had three days of leave, but he decided to head for the only home he really had, the Royal Air Force. At North Weald the next morning on the way to his office, he passed a flight sergeant who saluted.

"Good morning, Sir. Back early? V for Victor is ready for a flight test if you would like to take her up."

"Good idea, Flight. I'll be down in thirty minutes."

All the air crew were on leave. The tradesmen had been kept to bring the twelve Mosquitos of 613 up to flying perfection. Chadwick flew without a navigator. Under wartime standing orders, aircraft with guns always flew full armed. Before he turned onto the runway he carefully ran up both engines, one at a time, and verified the magneto rpm drop, oil pressure, and coolant. With VHF clearance from the tower, he swung quickly to the center of the runway using the left engine, and then opened both engines to full power and accelerated rapidly.

At a hundred and ten knots the plane lifted smoothly off the ground and he selected gear up. He checked in with the sector radar control channel, and at ten thousand feet he throttled back and started a series of maneuvers to test the aerodynamic performance.

Chadwick was startled by a loud voice in his earphones calling him using the squadron call sign. "Bushmill two-three, this is sector control. We have some bogey traffic. Your position is the only one that yields an interception solution. Are you interested?"

"Affirmative. I am fully armed. Give me a vector."

"Steer two-two-five, angels six, full power."

"Roger." Chadwick turned quickly onto the heading and pushed the stick forward. With full power his airspeed shot up to 390 knots.

"Two-three, the Observer Corp report a single small bogey making very high speed."

Chadwick turned on the gyro gunsight and armed the twenty-millimeter cannon.

"Two-three, range four miles, ten o'clock on your left."

Chadwick scanned the sky ahead, and then he saw a small plane almost lost in the smog over London. It was like nothing he had ever seen before. The engine was mounted aft above the fuselage at the tail. It flew on a constant heading. He set the gunsight wingspan at fifty feet and steadily drew the illuminated dot ahead so that the target was in the center of the circle. His fingers tightened on the trigger. He was overtaking rapidly and opened up with all four cannons.

Pieces flew off the mystery plane and then it disintegrated with a tremendous explosion. The shock wave staggered the Mosquito which was flung onto its wingtips. The injured plane smashed through a dense cloud of debris, the right engine stopped with a shattering noise and the fire warning light came on. Chadwick was stunned by the explosion but instinctively leveled the plane and pulled up to gain height. As his head cleared he looked at the right engine which was pouring out clouds of black smoke with the flicker of flame just visible. Chadwick switched off the right magnetos, feathered the propeller and pushed the fire extinguisher button. He looked down, he was flying over central London. The gyroscopic direction indicator had clearly toppled, it showed him heading south but the watery sun in the east was on his right. Chadwick could just make out the Thames. As the old P-1 magnetic compass settled down, he found he was traveling roughly northeast.

He had full left rudder applied but the plane was turning right, caused by the drag of the shattered right engine. He glanced at the altimeter; 3,700 feet. Chadwick faced an unenviable choice. To regain directional control he had to increase speed by putting the nose down, this meant the ground was coming even faster. A quick glance at the vertical speed indicator showed him he was descending at over 1,200 feet a minute.

As the plane flashed over Tower Bridge, he searched desperately for some clear land. North of the bend in the river, through the smog, he could just make out an area that looked less dense than the thousands of crowded buildings that lay beneath him. The plane was down to 2,500 feet and descending precipitously. Large flames were now licking from the right engine. It was only a matter of time before the fuel tank blew up. He throttled back the left engine, mouthing a thanks it had kept running. As the plane skimmed the roof tops, he set some flap and aimed for a wide field.

Then he saw it was littered with anti-aircraft gun emplacements and lorries. He did not drop the undercarriage. He thought a belly landing would be slightly safer, but the plane was traveling far too fast. Chadwick put down the rest of the flaps and pulled on the stick as the machine flashed over the turf. For a second he saw gunners running for their lives and then the right wing struck a gun emplacement. The plane swung violently and plowed into the ground. The wing tore free of the fuselage and burst into flames. The fuselage continued to plow a path of destruction through tents and vehicles until it finally broke into pieces. Chadwick felt a blow to his head and left leg and as blackness descended he was spared any pain. He came to as men were placing him on a stretcher.

He was confused. "Where am I?" was all he could say.

"Why, you're at Stepney Green, mate. It was a lousy landing."

Chadwick's interception was the subject of an immediate meeting of the Air Intelligence Committee and also of an urgent meeting of the Air Defense Board the next day. It was clear the German V-1 offensive had started.

One attendee commented, "Well, it's obvious we can't afford to shoot these blighters down with our fighters. The explosion of the V-1 damaged the Mosquito so badly that it was a write-off after a crash landing. Our experts estimate a V-1 costs about a thousand pounds, including the warhead. The Mosquito cost twenty thousand pounds, an unacceptable ratio. However, the pilot deserves credit for downing the first V-1 to cross the British coast."

Another expert pointed out it was sheer chance that Chadwick had been in a position to pull off an interception. "The chap was just performing a routine flight test. Under normal circumstances the V-1 is too fast for a fighter to be scrambled in time."

Thousands of Londoners had witnessed the interception and seen the resulting explosion. The Ministry of Information, which controlled what newspapers were allowed to print, was bombarded with questions, which were passed on to Air Intelligence. No mention could be made of radar, which was secret, as was the system of radar interception. A bland statement was approved that appeared in all the papers together with as much additional nonsense as their reporters could contrive. It read:

An RAF fighter on routine patrol identified an experimental German plane over central London. It was believed to be a pilotless missile. After opening fire the German plane exploded and crashed to the ground. The defending fighter was also damaged by debris from the explosion.

As was normal practice, the type of fighter and the pilot's name were not given. British newspapers were routinely sent to Stockholm by the Swedish Embassy and the story of the interception was eagerly read by German intelligence. The Wehrmacht was keen to learn the fate of the first V-1 to be launched against England. The article confirmed that the navigation system of the V-1 was working properly and plans went ahead to launch as many as a hundred a day within the coming weeks.

The Air Defense Board's assessment that fighters were not the answers caused some head scratching. An Army artillery expert suggested that American radar-controlled guns firing shells with American proximity fuses were the answer. The chairman felt that Mr. Churchill should be apprised of their conclusions.

The group captain in charge of Air Intelligence was keen to have the pilot of the attacking Mosquito questioned as soon as possible. It was important to learn the distance separating the aircraft when the V-1 exploded. "Besides that," the group captain said, "I want to meet the chap who bought down the intruder with one pass while traveling nearly four hundred knots. If he missed he would not have had a second chance. Goodness knows where the bloody thing would have fallen. Possibly on Buck House, heaven forbid."

Two days later the doctors gave permission for the Air Force officers to question Chadwick. He was in a public hospital and would not be moved to an Air Force sick bay until he was stronger. A ward doctor guided them to his bed. "He was injured in the crash of his machine, but the wounds are not life-threatening. He had concussion and a number of facial injuries which required stitches. His leg is badly bruised, but not broken. Please be brief."

The group captain stepped forward and looked at the chart clipped to the bed rail, which read "Wing Commander Allan Chadwick."

"My God, Allan, I didn't recognize you. You have two beautiful shiners and the bandages are a pretty good disguise."

"Yes, Sir, we've met before at meetings of your committee."

"How astonishing it was you that nobbled the first V-1. I understand you were simply on a flight test."

"Yes, Sir. V for Victor had just received a new engine. I took it up for a spin." Chadwick spoke slowly and with some difficulty.

"Well, I'm afraid you're on non-flying status for a while. The chaps have a couple of questions, but we'll be quick."

Another officer spoke up. "How far from the missile were you when it exploded?"

"I would guess a hundred to two hundred yards. I was overtaking fairly rapidly. Wait a minute— the gunsight ring was set to fifty feet. It was full when I opened fire. The thing exploded a few seconds after that. That should give you the range."

"Was there any exhaust from the engine?"

"To be honest, I don't remember."

The group captain spoke, "That's enough. Allan. We'll have you moved as soon as the docs permit it. You did a wonderful job. I am going to recommend a bar to your DSO."

The next meeting of the Air Defense Board was gloomy. Only a couple of planes in the RAF inventory were fast enough to catch a V-1, but Chadwick's experience showed the range had to be over 400 to 500 yards, making the missile a difficult target due to its small size and high speed. A gunnery expert estimated the chances of shooting down a V-1 by anti-aircraft fire were almost zero, and would require many thousands of rounds. Again the suggestion was made that the latest American developments were almost tailor made for dealing with the V-1, but there were very few in Britain.

"What are the chances if the American guns and shells were used?" the chairman asked.

"I believe if enough guns were sited along the expected flight paths, the chance could approach fifty percent downed of those crossing the coast."

"How many guns and shells are we talking about?"

"Assuming MI6 is correct and we could expect about a hundred a day from various launching points. Let me see…" The expert was silent and then said, "We would need five thousand gun systems and a usage of about half a million rounds a day. Allowing for all the usual contingencies we would need a backlog of ten million rounds to be carried."

Someone whistled quietly. A voice said, "Christ." The conversation moved onto the possibility of bombing V-1 launching sites. An Air Force officer pointed out this was already a priority, but the sites were small and well-hidden.

After the meeting, the chairman briefed the Air Minister, who took him to meet the Prime Minister. The chairman was white-faced when he eventually emerged from the Prime Minister's office. The next day he spoke to several very senior Army and Air Force officers and to the Minister for Economic Warfare. Two days later he addressed a meeting of the Air Defense Board.

"The Prime Minister is desperate for a solution to this latest threat. The planning for the invasion of Europe has already started. In the coming months, Britain will be inundated by millions of soldiers from America and the Commonwealth. Thousands of tanks, planes, and other military equipment will be stored in areas vulnerable to these attacks. This will bring considerable pressure on the civilian population. Churchill feels that random bombings out of the sky could result in a catastrophic fall of morale. He calls it 'psychological warfare.' The actual damage to structures is tolerable. We drop far more explosives on Germany every night. He has been in touch with the ambassador in Washington and feels our concern must be brought to the attention of the highest levels of the American government and the U.S. military."

The Air Minister sent a summary in a memorandum to the Prime Minister, outlining the problem and the suggested steps to counter it. In the memo he mentioned that the very first V-1 had been downed by an RAF pilot, but analysis predicted that was not the best solution. He mentioned sending a delegation to the U.S. to prioritize the delivery of American guns and ammunition. Within a day he received a copy of his memo annotated by Churchill. The note on the delegation was circled in red ink with the comment, "Talked with FDR. Approved." He had drawn an arrow to the word "pilot" with the comment, "Send him."

Two days after the visit by the group captain Chadwick was posted back to North Weald, under the care of the doctors there. He was placed on non-flying status. Temporary appointments were made to cover the command of 613 Squadron and the Mosquito wing.

A day later Chadwick was ordered to report to the air officer commanding eleven Groups at RAF Uxbridge. A squadron pilot flew him there in a Harvard. Wearing his Best Blue uniform and still walking with a limp, he nervously entered Group Headquarters and was ushered in to meet Air Commodore Clifford Moore.

"Pleasure to meet you, Wing Commander. That was a wizard show you pulled, nailing that Nazi whatever-it-was. You're not too badly damaged yourself, then?"

"No, Sir. No bones broken."

"Jolly good. The group captain running Air Intelligence has recommended a bar to your DSO. Apparently the information gleaned from your attack was vital in setting the strategy to deal with these buggers. I heartily concur with the award. Please stay for lunch, I would like to hear more."

Two days later Chadwick was summoned to a meeting of the Air Defense Board in London. Attendees were told that Churchill had approved a delegation to fly to the U.S to expedite the delivery of radar-controlled guns and proximity fuses to Britain on an urgent basis. The Army was already preparing sites. Churchill was concerned about the impact of unguided missiles on civilian morale and on the possibility of disrupting preparations for an invasion of Europe, if not dealt with quickly.

There was a lot of discussion of the make-up of the team to visit the U.S. The Chairman of the Board, General Nicholas

Gage, said it was felt in the highest circles that the American military must be fully briefed on these new weapons. He then astounded Chadwick by saying, "Wing Commander Chadwick will take care of that aspect. He piloted the fighter which downed the V-I. I have already arranged for him to be briefed on technical matters concerning the V-1 by Air intelligence. It's felt that the Americans will appreciate briefings by a battle-hardened officer. After all, Chadwick has a closer acquaintance with a V-1 than anyone else in this country." There was prolonged laughter at this remark.

After the meeting, the general drew Chadwick aside. "You will be promoted to Group Captain and join the British Embassy in Washington as Assistant Air Attaché. I'm also told unofficially that there is a 'K' in this for a quick, successful outcome."

"A 'K,' sir?" Chadwick's mind raced. *Ah, a Knighthood! Sir Allan Chadwick.* He rather liked the sound of it.

And then another thought crossed his mind. *How about 'Lady Melanie Chadwick'? That has a certain ring to it.* Then he caught the unintended double entendre and laughed out loud, to the general's surprise. "Sorry, Sir," Chadwick said, struggling to stifle a smile. "I was just thinking of how proud my parents would be."

Epilogue

Melanie Fitzgibbon and Lord Lowestoft were married in a quiet ceremony in the early part of 1945. It was an unhappy union from the start. The social life she had anticipated did not occur; Lowestoft had been tainted by his friendship with Viscount Addenbury, who came close to being tried for treason at the start of the war.

Phil Donovan flew as Avro's chief test pilot throughout the war, but the odds finally caught up with him in 1951 when the plane he was flying collided in thick weather with a tower carrying the aerial for the new BBC TV service.

Colonel "Buzz" Butzke was promoted General in 1945 and played a major role introducing jet fighters into the U.S. Air Force. He was killed when flying an F-86 in Korea which crashed after running out of fuel. He was not flying a combat mission; he loved using the F-86 to inspect fighter bases.

The Prof was arrested by the Gestapo in early 1944 and died in Dachau six months later.

Mary Hancock took advantage of the adult education opportunities that opened up after the election of the Labour Party in 1945. She got a new position with the Department of Social Services of the London County Council, advising young women on career options.

Wilberforce Viney played a major role in deluding the Germans about the location of the invasion of France in 1944. After the war he was deemed too clever and too dangerous by the KGB, which engineered a scandal that forced Viney to resign.

Carl Speidel was sent to Canada on a freighter, his future was entrusted to the Royal Canadian Mounted Police when MI6 explained the circumstances of his arrival in Britain. He was given a phony background but kept his real name so that he could use his academic qualifications. He eventually became a professor with tenure at an American university.

Pierre Fournier was delighted when his daughter Madeleine announced she was pregnant. She gave birth to a healthy baby girl in the Fall of 1942. Charlotte married a Free French soldier who was part of the Allied Army which liberated Alsace-Lorraine in 1944. Charlotte eventually produced the heir Fournier wanted. Jean Fournier did not return from captivity in Germany.

Boadicea was honored by General de Gaulle after she persuaded the German general to surrender his troops and avoid a fight with the Allied Army. Later she was elected a Deputy in the French government. She never discovered what had happened to Chadwick after he disappeared from the farm at Talence.

Allan Chadwick was appointed Assistant Air Attaché to the British mission in the U.S. He was regarded with deep suspicion by the senior Air Attaché, who resented the way the visiting deputation bypassed the established team responsible for British arms purchases in the U.S. Colonel Butzke opened up many contacts for Chadwick at the Pentagon. Chadwick was very popular at social functions, especially with the wives of politicians.

Glossary

Equivalent Ranks

RAF	ARMY
Air Commodore	Brigadier General
Group Captain	Colonel
Wing Commander	Lieutenant Colonel
Squadron Leader	Major
Flight Lieutenant	Captain
Flying Officer	Lieutenant
Pilot Office	Second Lieutenant
Warrant Officer	Sergeant Major
Flight Sergeant	Staff Sergeant
Sergeant	Sergeant
Leading Aircraftsman	Corporal
Aircraftsman	Private

Common English, German and Technical Terms

Abwehr	The German military intelligence department
Accumulator	Lead-acid batteries made for early wireless receivers
Aerial	Radio Antenna
Ack-ack	Anti-aircraft gun fire
Albion	German term for the British
Andrew	Slang term for the Royal Navy, which flies the flag of St. Andrew
Angels	Height in thousands of feet
Artificer	Naval term for a sailor skilled in a trade

ATA	Civilian organization which delivered new planes from the factories; employed many female pilots
B-17	Four-engined bomber built by the Boeing corporation in America
Balloon went up	The start of something big
Bar award	Symbol that an award for gallantry has been given twice
Bawdsey	British establishment where radar was developed
BE-2	A WWI British biplane fighter
Bee in your bonnet	Overly concerned
Black out	Regulations to prevent building showing a light at night in war time
Blacked-out	A loss of vision or consciousness caused by high "G"
Blinker	A device used by pilots practicing instrument flying to restrict view of the horizon
Bobby	Slang term for a policeman
Boche	Derogatory slang for a German
Boffin	Scientist
Bogey	An enemy target
Bowser	Refueling lorry
Bradshaw	A book of train schedules in the British Isles
Bricky	Bricklayer
Brylcreem	A popular men's hair cream
Buck House	Slang for Buckingham Palace
Bunt	An aircraft maneuver which results in negative "G"
Butcher's bill	Casualty list
Button A&B	Used to deposit or retrieve coins on British public telephones
Chiaroscuro	Dramatic use of light and shadows in a picture

Claggy	Foggy, wet weather
Cossor	A commercial firm which manufactured electronic equipment
Crossley	Motor vehicle used by the British military
Datum	The reference point on a chart from which measurements are made
DFC	Distinguished Flying Cross; for single acts of heroism or extraordinary achievement while participating in aerial flight
Doxy	A lower class prostitute
DSO	Distinguished Service Order; awarded for meritorious or distinguished service by officers of the armed forces during wartime, typically in actual combat
Eaker	General who initially commanded the 8th U.S. Army Air Force in Britain
Eiderdown	A thick quilt filled with feathers
ETA	Estimated Time of Arrival
Finger Four	An aircraft formation positioned like the fingertips of one hand
Flak	Explosion of anti-aircraft shells at altitude
French Leave	Unauthorized absence
Freya	A type of Luftwaffe radar
g-force	Force due to gravity at earth's surface
G&T	Gin and Tonic
Gauleiter	A member of the Nazi Party appointed to govern a region
Gaumont	A British film and newsreel company
Gee	Navigational aid using radio transmissions
George	Nickname given to the automatic pilot by RAF crews
Gestapo	Geheime Staats Polizie, a branch of the SS

Glim Light	Very low intensity wing-tip light to assist formation flying at night
Gong	Slang for a medal
Green Machine	Chadwick's affectionate name for his 1928 Bentley
Grid	A common British term for a street drain
Gunnel	The uppermost part of the hull of a small boat
Guy Fawkes night	British annual celebration with bonfires and fireworks.
H.F.	High frequency radios operating on the short-wave bands
Honey-pot	Slang for using women to sexually exploit men to obtain information
HP	Houses of Parliament sauce, a spicy brown steak sauce
Hard standing	A paved area for parking aircraft
Harmonized	The aiming point for the forward-firing guns on a plane
Harvard	An American-made advanced flying trainer
Hovis	A propriety whole wheat loaf popular in Britain
IFF	A method of identifying friendly aircraft on radar
Isbell's Insiders	A clique of movers and shakers in Britain attempting to prevent war
Jamming	Radio signals transmitted to interfere with the enemies' radio signals
Jankers	Jail or confined to camp
Ju 88	A Luftwaffe twin-engined fighter/bomber
KammHuber Line	A defensive line along the German border to shoot down enemy aircraft
KGB	The Secret Service of the Soviet Union
Knickbeine	Luftwaffe radio system to achieve bombing accuracy

Knot	Speed in nautical miles per hour
Kraut	Derogatory term for a German
Kriegsmarine	The German navy
Mae West	RAF slang for a life-jacket
Malvern	British Telecommunications Research Establishment
Mancunian	A native of Manchester
Maquisard	French résistance worker
Merlin	A 12-cylinder aero engine built by Rolls Royce
MI5	Military intelligence responsible for domestic security
MI6	Military intelligence responsible for spying and espionage abroad
M.O.	Medical Officer
Mob	Slang term for the RAF by those serving in it
Nautical mile	Distance on a chart equal to a minute of latitude, 15 % longer than a statute mile
Nissen hut	Temporary building built mainly with corrugated, curved steel sheet
Oboe	A very precise navigational aid using radar signals
Observer Corps	Ground-based group, often civilians, reporting on aircraft overhead
Obst	German Army rank of Colonel
Off-license	A shop selling alcohol to be consumed off the premises
OTU	Operational Training Unit: a flying school teaching gunnery and battle formation
Pack Drill	A military punishment requiring an offender to march with full pack
Plaster	A cast to support a broken limb
Pongo	Slang term for Army personnel
Prang	RAF slang for an aircraft crash

Procuring	Promoting prostitution
Proximity Fuse	Fuse which detonates shell automatically within about 30 feet of target
Pundit	Airfield identification flashing light
QDM	An example of the radio "Q" code, requesting a bearing
Queen Mary	A specialized trailer to carry large aircraft parts
Quid	One pound currency
RDR	Early acronym for radar
Raff	Slang for "RAF," the Royal Air Force
Relay	An electrically operated switch
Scarper	Slang for one who "flees" or "escapes"
Scrag	A physical attack
Scramble	A massed take-off by a fighter squadron
Sleeper	A railway track tie, originally wood, later concrete
Slide rule	A hand operated analog calculator for multiplication and division
Smudge pot	Low intensity light using kerosene to mark runways
SD	Intelligence arm of the German SS
SNCF	Sociétié Nationale des Chemins de Fer, the French national railway system
SOB	American swear word, short for "Son of a Bitch"
Solarium	A room in a house with extensive areas of glass to admit sunlight
Sparks	Generic name for a wireless operator on a ship or plane
Special Branch	Unit of the London Metropolitan Police dealing with security
Spook	Slang term for a spy or intelligence officer

SS	Originally Hitler's bodyguard, evolved into the all-powerful State police
Stall	The condition in which an aircraft loses lift and descends uncontrollably
Tart	A part-time prostitute
Thermite	A metallic mixture that burns white-hot when ignited
Tinkle	A telephone call
Tommies	German slang term for British military personnel
Torch	Flashlight
Transponder	Device carried in an aircraft which emits a signal when properly triggered
TTFN	Ta Ta For Now—catch phrase used by a popular comedian
Twitch	Nervous tic caused by combat fatigue
Valve	British term for an electron tube
Very	A colored flare launched by a specialized pistol
Vis	Abbreviation for visibility
VIP	Very Important Person
WC	Water Closet, a toilet
WHSmith	A chain of newsagents found at many British train stations
Wallah	Indian term for a man in a trade
Wehrmacht	The German Army
Wimpy	Slang term for a Wellington bomber
Würzburg	A type of Luftwaffe radar
X-gerat	A Luftwaffe radio beam for bombing accuracy
Yoke	Cockpit control used in larger aircraft

Acknowledgments

Once again, I owe a debt of gratitude to Jody Freeman, who reviewed the first draft of Wings over Germany and gave me a concise critique mentioning style, clarification, and the possibility of confusion involving characters with similar names. My old friends Anne Flood and Lew Schatzer read an early draft and pointed out to me sections that may be confusing for average readers not familiar with military flying. Dr. Louise Hanson gave me the benefit of her wide interest in world history, and in particular her knowledge of German and German mannerisms. Jack Doyle, a naval flight officer who flew F-4 Phantoms and F-14 Tomcats, checked the draft for accuracy and authenticity. Peg Daisley was my tireless editor, who reviewed and corrected each chapter as I wrote them. Jay Pizer designed the striking covers, produced legible maps of Britain and Europe and managed the book lay-out.

Finally, I must acknowledge that I could not have written this novel without having had my experiences in the Royal Air Force. The adventures I had, flying what were at the time some of the most advanced fighters in the world, formed one of the most exciting periods of my life. I hope this has spilled over into authentic realism for the flying sequences. The men I flew with had experiences that dwarfed my own. Many flew in WWII. Their stories, which I still remember vividly, helped me write this novel. The Royal Air Force as I knew it in the 1950s has disappeared. It was a relic of the World War. In researching wartime RAF airfields for the novel I found most of them had been closed down and the manpower strength is a fraction of the number that served when I did. Perhaps my novel will serve to show the enormous difference in the skill level of both air and ground crews at the time I flew and those that fly and service the amazing aircraft of today.

Flying Officer Forsyth at the controls of a Meteor Mark 8, Britain's frontline fighter at the time.

Eric Forsyth was born in Bolton, England in 1932 and attended Bolton School. At Manchester University he joined the Air Squadron and following graduation with a Bachelor's in electrical engineering he completed pilot training in the Royal Air Force, flying the first jet fighters, Meteors and Vampires. He was posted to an Auxiliary Squadron, 613, and also worked at Avro Aircraft Company. He was involved in the design of a stand-off bomb for the Vulcan and occasionally flew as copilot in testing the Avro Shackleton. In 1956 he was awarded the City of Manchester flying trophy and he achieved a "Green" instrument rating.

Sadly, economic factors caused the British Government to close down the fighter wings of the Royal Auxiliary Air Force in 1957. Later that year, Eric emigrated to Canada where he obtained a commercial pilot's license for single and multi-engined land and sea planes. He married Edith, a physician, in 1958 but did not find a suitable flying opportunity. He worked for Canadian Applied Research Company on a variety of aviation electronic projects, including the autopilot design of the ill-fated Avro Arrow. Edith persuaded him to rejoin the academic field and he entered the Engineering Graduate School of Toronto University. He obtained a Master of Applied Science degree in electrical engineering and was hired by Brookhaven National Laboratory on Long Island, New York to work on particle accelerators. The laboratory also offered Edith a position in the Medical Research Department. Eric was very involved in building particle beams for the physics experimenters. Equipment he built provided neutrinos for a landmark experiment which yielded a Nobel Prize for the senior physicists.

For relaxation, Edith and Eric enthusiastically took up the popular local sport, sailing on the sheltered waters of the Great South

Bay. During a vacation in the Caribbean, they chanced upon a couple sailing to England via Long Island and in 1964 Edith and Eric joined them for a transatlantic crossing to Falmouth in a 46-foot home-made cutter. This trip ignited Eric's love of deep-water sailing and in 1965 Edith and Eric bought their first ocean-going sailboat, *Iona*, a 35-foot sloop built in Holland. Their son, Colin, was born the same year. In 1968 they sold their house and embarked on a fifteen-month cruise of the Caribbean, which was just opening up as a vacation paradise.

On their return Eric was offered a position on a project to design a new accelerator using superconducting material to achieve high magnetic fields. Edith worked for the Suffolk County Health Department in charge of children's and maternal health services. Their daughter, Brenda, was born in 1971 and Edith started her own medical practice a year later. In 1972 the Laboratory responded to a request by the federal government to apply some of the knowledge gained in designing superconducting particle accelerators to the improvement of conventional electrical apparatus such as alternators and power transmission lines. Eric was appointed project manager and built prototype power transmission cables which operated at the equivalent three-phase level of 1,000 MVA, 138 kV. Having demonstrated the technical feasibility of applying superconductors to power transmission cables over a four-year operating period, the project closed in 1986. For this work Eric was presented with the Herman Halperin Award, the highest annual recognition by the Institute of Electrical and Electronic Engineers for power transmission research. Eric was then appointed Chair of the Accelerator Development Department which was responsible for the pre-construction design of a superconducting heavy ion collider/accelerator, (RHIC).

Coincidentally, Eric bought the bare fiberglass hull of a 42-foot cutter and finished the construction himself on weekends and evenings. After eight years she was launched and named *Fiona*. In 1990 he stepped down from the Chairmanship and took a year's leave of absence with the intention of sailing *Fiona* through the Panama Canal to French Polynesia. Edith was able to join him there but when she returned to Long Island she was diagnosed as having ovarian cancer. Eric left the boat near Tahiti and flew home, but despite every attempt to find a cure, Edith passed away in 1991. Eric returned to the Pacific to retrieve *Fiona* and sailed round Cape Horn back to Long Island with a crew of two young men.

At the Laboratory he worked part-time designing aspects of the RIIC, and its construction was completed in 2000. It is now the most powerful nuclear physics research facility in the U.S. Eric retired in 1995 and sailed nearly full-time for the next twenty years with many different crew members. He made two circumnavigations of the globe, cruised the Antarctic and Arctic regions and traversed the Northwest Passage. He has now logged over 300,000 nautical miles. In recognition of his Antarctic cruise, he was awarded the prestigious Blue Water Medal by the Cruising Club of America, given annually to one amateur sailor worldwide. He published his first book, *An Inexplicable Attraction: My Fifty Years of Ocean Cruising* and it was named among the 100 Best Memoirs of 2018 by Kirkus Reviews.

Now in his nineties, Eric continues to sail and write historical fiction. He has published three novels depicting the adventurous life of an RAF pilot in the turbulent 1930s and '40s.